*Praise for* **The Killing**

'Turns television gold into literary gold'     *Daily Telegraph*

'For those who missed watching Sarah Lund and the Danish police in action, I believe they will get a great deal of pleasure from reading about them'     *The Times*

'A very fine novel, which is more of a re-imagining of the original story than a carbon copy – and with the bonus of a brand new twist to the ending'     *Daily Mail*

'David Hewson's literary translation . . . allows the characters more room to breathe . . . Hewson's greatest achievement is that it's compelling reading'     *Observer*

'Not just a novelization. Hewson is a highly regarded crime writer in his own right; he spent a lot of time with the creators of the original to ensure that he did not offend its spirit and mood, and he has provided his own, different solution to the central murder mystery'     Marcel Berlins, *The Times*

'A fast-paced crime novel that's five-star from start to finish'     *Irish Examiner*

'The book is an excellent read in which the author manages to dig deeper into the characters without having to rewrite their original television characterization. For those who haven't seen the series, this is a very cleverly constructed and beautifully written crime drama; for those who already know the ending, a new twist awaits'     *Irish Times*

# THE
# WRONG
# GIRL

## Also by David Hewson

The Killing

The Killing II

The Killing III

*Nic Costa series*

A Season for the Dead

The Villa of Mysteries

The Sacred Cut

The Lizard's Bite

The Seventh Sacrament

The Garden of Evil

Dante's Numbers

The Blue Demon

The Fallen Angel

Carnival for the Dead

*Other titles*

The House of Dolls

The Promised Land

The Cemetery of Secrets
(previously published as *Lucifer's Shadow*)

Death in Seville
(previously published as *Semana Santa*)

# DAVID HEWSON

# THE WRONG GIRL

MACMILLAN

First published 2015 by Macmillan
an imprint of Pan Macmillan, a division of Macmillan Publishers Limited
Pan Macmillan, 20 New Wharf Road, London N1 9RR
Basingstoke and Oxford
Associated companies throughout the world
www.panmacmillan.com

ISBN 978-1-4472-4618-3 HB
ISBN 978-1-4472-4620-6 TPB

Printed and bound by CPI Group (UK) Ltd, Croydon, CR0 4YY

Visit www.panmacmillan.com to read more about all our books
and to buy them. You will also find features, author interviews and
news of any author events, and you can sign up for e-newsletters
so that you're always first to hear about our new releases.

# THE
# WRONG
# GIRL

# 1

There was something new on the front deck of the houseboat. Standing tall amid the dead plants, rotting timber and scattered tools, she rose like a glittering beacon over the winter-grey waters of the Prinsengracht: a life-size silver plastic ballerina twirling on slender legs, twinkling coloured lights and tinsel round her neck.

Pieter Vos's little terrier Sam sat at the statue's feet wondering whether to growl or lick the thing. He had a string of multicoloured tinsel wound through his collar over the tight, tough fur. And didn't much like it.

The third Sunday of November. Christmas was around the corner, and Sinterklaas was on his way. He'd already finished the long journey from Spain and boarded his ceremonial barge up the Amstel river. It was two fifteen.

Vos, as a duty brigadier for the second shift of the day, would have familiar company for this welcome interlude in the calendar of the Amsterdam police. Two of his plain-clothes officers of different sometimes conflicting generations. Dirk Van der Berg, the easy-going, beer-loving detective, a Marnixstraat fixture in his mid-forties, was patting the little dog, cooing affectionate words. Laura Bakker, just turned twenty-five, a recent newcomer from Friesland, stood in a heavy winter coat, long red hair falling round her shoulders, glaring at the object in the bows. Vos glanced at his own clothes: the usual navy donkey jacket, fading jeans, ageing trainers. He'd meant to have his hair cut during the week but went to see a Danish movie instead. So the curly dark locks still hung loose over his collar and got him a filthy look from Frank de Groot, the station commissaris, from time to time.

It was seven months now since a curious murder case centred round a museum doll's house had dragged him out of a dreary, lost existence in his houseboat, back into the Amsterdam police. Some things had changed since then. A few hadn't.

'What in God's name's that?' Bakker asked.

'I *like* it!' Van der Berg declared before the argument could begin. 'Whatever it is . . .'

Bakker clumped down the gangplank in her heavy boots, pulled a white envelope out of the postbox without asking, then thrust the letter at Vos. It bore the stamp of the city council.

'I bet this is another warning about the state of this thing. They'll fine you if you don't fix it up properly.'

'I am fixing it up . . .'

She looked at the blackened, broken cabin, the windows held together by tape and shook her head.

'They were throwing her out from one of the shops round the corner,' Vos added, pointing at the ballerina. 'I thought she sort of fitted.'

'She does,' Van der Berg declared. He glanced hopefully across the road at the Drie Vaten cafe on the corner of Elands-gracht. Vos's local was the neighbourhood brown bar, black brick exterior, bare plank floor, rickety seats, open most of the day and busy already. The place the neighbourhood gravitated to when it needed good beer, a snack, a coffee and some idle conversation. A second home for plenty of locals, among them thirsty police officers from their Marnixstraat headquarters at the top of Elandsgracht. 'Is there time for . . . ?'

'We're on duty!' Bakker said, throwing up her long arms in despair.

Van der Berg was a heavyset man with a friendly, somewhat battered face. He looked offended.

'We don't go on duty for another fifteen minutes. I was about to say . . . is there time for a coffee?'

'Not really,' Vos said with a shake of his head.

A busy but agreeable day ahead. Sinterklaas, a beaming, friendly saint with a white beard, was set to mark his arrival in Amsterdam with a parade so celebrated it would be watched live on television throughout the Netherlands. Today the crowds would run into three hundred thousand or more, and the police presence would top four figures. The city centre was closed to all traffic as a golden barge bore Sinterklaas down the Amstel river, surrounded by a throng of private boats full of families trying to get close. Then he'd transfer to a white stallion for a procession through the city, ending at Leidseplein. There, welcomed by the mayor, he'd address the massed crowds from the balcony of the municipal theatre. Zwarte Pieten, Black Petes, companions to Saint Nicholas, would follow him everywhere, faces dark with make-up, curly black wigs, ruby lips, grinning in medieval costumes with ruff collars and feathered mob caps, handing out spicy sweets to every passing youngster they could find – and baffling foreign visitors who could scarcely believe their eyes.

After 5 December Sinterklaas gave way to Christmas. The *pepernoot* and chocolate letters were replaced with *kerststol* and *musketkrans* while the shop windows filled with pine boughs and fake snow.

There'd been a time when Vos was a part of all this. When he'd had a family of his own. A partner, Liesbeth, a daughter Anneliese. The doll's house case had stolen that from him completely.

Vos bent down and smiled at his little dog. The white and tan fox terrier looked up into his face.

'Can't take you to work, old chap. Even on a day like this.'

Sam detected something in the tone of his voice and narrowed his eyes, suspicious of what was to come.

The lead came out. Sam's head went down. Vos walked the dog to the cafe, handed him over along with a bag of dirty washing, another favour from the Drie Vaten's owner, Sofia Albers. He tugged on the lead, struggling to return to the canal.

Van der Berg and Laura Bakker watched in silence. Bakker was shaking her head again.

'Well!' Vos said when he was back at the boat. 'Let's go mingle. Tell you what . . . after the shift I'll treat you both to dinner. I know an all-night place.'

'You mean beer, crisps and free boiled eggs?' Bakker asked.

'No . . . real dinner. A restaurant.'

'Somewhere they have a proper toilet? You know such places? Honestly?'

'So long as it involves . . .' Van der Berg's hand made a glugging motion. 'That's fine with me. Oh dear . . .'

He pointed at the sleepy bar, its black brick frontage set at an angle where Elandsgracht met the canal. Gulls were scavenging the rubbish on the cobbles. A couple of afternoon drunks queued patiently to drop their empty bottles in the glass bin. Next to them Sam was digging in his heels, refusing to go inside, and glaring back at the canal with an expression of heartfelt canine resentment.

'Shame we can't take him with us,' Bakker suggested. 'I mean . . . it's Sinterklaas. It's not as if anything bad's going to happen.'

Vos stared at her, said nothing, went to the dog and led him inside by the collar.

Then came out and looked down the length of Prinsengracht.

'Don't you read the papers?' Van der Berg asked. 'They said there might be a protest about Zwarte Piet. People think it's racist or something. Disrespectful.'

One of them was marching up their side of Prinsengracht as he spoke. Tall, burly with a huge Afro wig, all exaggerated curls. Shiny scarlet costume, silly hat. Blackened face, ruby lips. Beaming, happy as a child, carrying a brown bag and a long-handled fishing net to reach the crowds.

'It is disrespectful,' Bakker complained. 'This is the twenty-first century for pity's sake.'

4

Van der Berg folded his arms and started on the lecture Vos had heard so many times. The other side of the argument.

'It's tradition,' he concluded.

'So was hanging. And bear-baiting.'

'Young lady . . .'

Vos closed his eyes, unable to think of a single phrase more calculated to infuriate the bright and awkward detective from Friesland.

Then the Black Pete heard the commotion, spotted her, scuttled across the cobbles, bowed graciously, said how pretty she looked, placed a handful of small biscuits in his fishing net and gingerly extended them towards her.

Bakker stopped mid-rant, grinned and took a few. Preened herself as the man in the bright costume paid her more compliments.

'Now you be a good girl,' he added as he wandered off down the street. 'Or Sinterklaas will know.'

'I love these things,' she said, stuffing a spicy *pepernoot* into her mouth with a half-guilty giggle.

'So do I,' Van der Berg told her, eyeing the two left in her hand.

Bakker ignored him.

'Where do you stand, then?' she asked turning her steady gaze on Vos. 'When it comes to grown men blacking up for Sinterklaas?' She nodded at Van der Berg. 'With him? Or me?'

Sam was at the window of the bar, one paw scratching at the pane, wagging his tail in forlorn hope.

'Out with it,' Bakker added.

'I think,' Vos answered, watching the Black Pete skip merrily up the canal, 'it's time we went to work.'


Another Black Pete, short this time and tubby. Ginger beard sticky with black make-up. The wig was on sideways, too shiny, brand new. Scared eyes looking everywhere as he listened to the growing racket of the crowd shuffling down the street.

The stuff was where they said they'd leave it, in the third rubbish skip from the back of a narrow dead-end alley. A blue one, just like they said.

Two handguns. Two knives. Three grenades. A length of rope. Some pieces of fabric that could double as gags or blindfolds. Five thousand euros in a bundle and a counterfeit Belgian passport with the photo taken in a booth at Centraal station two days before.

A single sheet of paper with lines of printed instructions. What to do. What to look out for. Where to go.

Born in the north of England. Radicalized after a spell in prison for a drunken burglary. When he came out he grew a scrappy beard, put on the long robe. Yelled at funeral processions for dead soldiers killed in Afghanistan. Went to the right preachers. Learned how to bellow slogans while he stabbed at a camera with his forefinger.

After he changed his name to Mujahied Bouali even his mother, a nurse, widowed when he was four years old, ceased to want to know him. Which was fine. He did what he was told, and finally the call came. Not Syria or Somalia as he expected. But Amsterdam, under the wing of a new master. A stern and autocratic man who drilled into him something he'd known for a while but never wanted to face.

They were all his enemies now. Every unbeliever. There was no middle ground. No such thing as a civilian. The decadent unthinking herds sat back and watched as the world fell to pieces.

There were the righteous and the damned. Nothing in between.

Alongside the money was a photo of a young girl in a pink jacket. A fresh page of instructions to be memorized then disposed of.

He read them carefully, took a good look at the picture. It

looked as if it had been snatched furtively in the street. He wondered for a moment what her name was. Then realized it didn't matter.

After that he placed the guns, the knives, the rope, the lengths of fabric and the grenades inside his red velvet bag alongside the sweets.

Christian sweets. But food knew no faith.

He picked one out, tasted it. Good, he thought. And that was probably down to the spices they stole from the east.

Bag slung round his shoulder he walked out into the street. The costume they'd given him was bright green, too loose, with a brown beret topped with a bright-pink feather.

Any other time he'd have felt a fool. Not now.


The Kuyper house was ten minutes by bike from Vos's houseboat, in a busier, more affluent quarter of the city beyond the Jordaan. Four centuries old, narrow, with four floors beneath a tiny crow-stepped gable, it stood on the street called the Herenmarkt to the side of the West-Indisch Huis, once headquarters to the Dutch West India Company. The location always amused Henk Kuyper. In the courtyard of the grand mansion was a statue of Peter Stuyvesant, seventeenth-century governor of the Dutch state called New Netherlands. The aristocrat who lost the colony to the British, handing over the tip of Manhattan he called New Amsterdam only to see it rechristened New York.

Between sessions on the computer and web chats with his many contacts across the world, Kuyper would sometimes walk down into the little square and take a coffee there, stare at the grim features of the man who gave away the New World's most important foothold and wonder what he'd make of the twenty-first century. Stuyvesant's early fortifications in America were now Wall Street; his canal became Broad Street and Broadway. The man they called 'Old Silver Leg' for his prosthetic limb lay buried in the vault of a church in Manhattan's Bowery – once his *bouwerij*, a farm – on the site of the former family chapel. Kuyper had wandered there during the Occupy Wall Street protests and camped nearby for a while. He'd stared at the plain stone plaque in the west wall that marked the old man's resting place, thinking about the distance from there to here.

Yet for most of the citizens of the twenty-first century Peter Stuyvesant was nothing more than a brand of cigarette. Such was history.

'Henk!' His wife's voice rose from the floor below, shrill and anxious. She always struggled with occasions. 'We're ready. Are you coming or not?'

'Not,' he whispered to the busy screen.

Sunday and the contacts never ended. There were seven emails in his inbox. Two from The Hague. Two from America. Three from the Middle East.

He heard her stomping up the stairs. Kuyper's office was in the building's gable roof beneath the crow steps. Tiny with a view out onto the cobbled street and the children's playground that occupied the open space behind the West-Indisch Huis. The pulley winch above the windows was principally decorative now, but it had probably sat there for three centuries at least. He liked this room. It was private, cut off from the rest of the house. A place he could think.

'Are . . . you . . . coming . . . ?'

She stood in the doorway wearing a too-short winter coat, hand on the lintel, Saskia by her side. Renata Kuyper was Belgian, from Bruges. They met when he was on a mission to Kosovo one scorching summer. She was a student on a research project, pretty with short brunette hair and an animated, nervy manner. It was a brief and passionate courtship conducted in hot hotel rooms that smelled of cedar wood and her scent. Outside the Balkan world was slowly rebuilding itself from the nightmare of civil war.

Henk Kuyper barely noticed. They were in love, desperately so. Then, in the middle of that frantic summer, her widowed father died suddenly. The news came in a phone call while they were in bed. After that she clung to Henk. Within the space of three months they were married. Another three months back in Amsterdam, Renata pregnant, trying to come to terms with the idea of being a wife and mother in a bustling, unfamiliar city where she had no friends.

'Are you coming, Daddy?' Saskia repeated.

Eight years old, nine in January. Pretty much the picture of her mother. Narrow pale face. High cheekbones. Blonde hair that would one day turn brunette like Renata's. Eyes as blue and sharp as sapphires. Didn't smile so much which was like her mother too. But that was the family now.

'Thing is, darling . . .' He got up from the desk and crouched in front of her, touched her carefully brushed hair. It was important to look your best when you met Sinterklaas and his little black imps. 'Daddy's got work to do.'

On paper Kuyper was a consultant in environmental affairs. His speciality was ground pollution issues, a subject he'd studied at university. Sometimes in person, he travelled to assignments mostly in Third World countries, a few of them perilous. But that was just a job. Words to put on a business card. He spent at least half his time anonymous on the Net, offering advice in activist forums on everything from fracking to biofuels and genetically modified crops. Attacking those in industry and on the right. Starting bush fires in some places. Putting them out in others. Always under the same anonymous online identity, one he'd picked deliberately: Stuyvesant. He even used a portrait of the old man as his avatar.

Saskia came up to him at the desk, a big pout on her face.

'Don't you want to see Sinterklaas at all?'

He just smiled.

She started to count on her gloved fingers.

'You missed him on the boat. You missed him when he was riding his horse . . .'

His wife was staring at him.

'You can stop saving the world, Henk. For one day. Be with your family.'

Kuyper pushed back his glasses and sighed. Then pointed at the computer.

'Besides . . . you know I'm not good with all those people around. Crowds . . .' He touched his daughter's cheek. 'Daddy doesn't like them.'

The little girl stamped her feet and wrapped her skinny arms around herself, tight against the bright-pink jacket he'd bought her the week before. My Little Pony. Her favourite from the books and the TV. He reached out and squeezed her elbow.

'Sinterklaas came early and brought you that, didn't he?'

'No.' The pout got bigger. 'You did.'

'Maybe I'm Black Pete. In disguise.' He gestured at the door. 'Go on. Tonight we can have pizza. I'll make it up. Promise.'

He listened as they made their way down the narrow staircase. One set of footsteps heavy, one light. Then he rolled his chair to the window and looked out into the street. His wife was pushing the expensive cargo trike he'd bought them. Orange. The colour of the Netherlands. She climbed on the saddle. Saskia parked herself in the cushioned kid's area at the front she called the 'bucket'.

His phone went. The call didn't take more than a minute.

Across the road he saw his first Black Pete. There'd be hundreds roaming the city, baffling every foreigner who stumbled upon them. Anyone could hire the costume, find some make-up and scarlet lipstick. Put on the stupid wig, the frilly jacket, the colourful trousers, the gold earrings. Then buy a bag of sweets from a local shop and hand them out to anyone they felt like.

Online some of his contacts had whined about them. How they were racist stereotypes. Kuyper had done what he liked to do on the web: put people right. Black Pete probably had nothing to do with Africa. The idea stemmed from an older, darker tradition rooted in something more mysterious than mere geography. One theory was they represented devils, enslaved by Saint Nicholas in the name of good.

He wasn't entirely sure any of this was accurate. But he liked to correct people all the same.

As he watched a second colourful figure emerged from the side of the Herenmarkt. It looked as if this one had been hiding behind the children's slides there. Waiting for someone.

Saskia waved and shouted something. He could hear her excited cry rise up from the cobbled street.

The new one wore dark green, a brown cap, pink feather in it. He didn't smile at all.

If he heard the girl Black Pete didn't show it. He pushed a rusty bike along the street then walked inside the ancient iron pissoir that stood at the end of Herenmarkt by the bridge that led over the Brouwersgracht into the city.

Kids don't always get what they ask for, Henk Kuyper told himself. And went back to his messages.


By the time they got to Leidseplein and the climax of the parade Bakker was very glad they hadn't brought Sam. She was a country girl from Dokkum, in Amsterdam only since the spring. Back home she'd watched the Sinterklaas parade on TV once or twice. Nothing prepared her for the reality.

The city had turned into a single, happy throng of humanity. From the waterfront to the centre the masses stretched, then out to the museums and the Canal Ring. Old and young with glitter and decorations in their hair. Fathers with toddlers perched on their shoulders. Mothers holding up tiny babies too young to understand what the noise and colour were all about. Everyone fighting for a glimpse of Sinterklaas himself, a red-robed figure astride a tall white horse moving down Rokin, waving to the crowds.

Vos and Van der Berg must have worked this day countless times. They knew where to stand, what to do. Listen to the radio mostly, stay at the edge of the multitude. Watch for pickpockets, drunks and doped-up pests. Then carefully weed them out of the equation.

One light-fingered Black Pete was already in custody, lifted by Van der Berg with extraordinary delicacy as the man tried to wriggle the wallet out of the back pocket of a man fool enough to wear nothing but a sweatshirt and jeans for the day. They'd been more generous towards the beer-filled fools who were making genial nuisances of themselves. A quick nod from Van der Berg, a backup word from Vos, a filthy glance from Bakker and the idiots were on their way.

Uniformed officers were handling the visible side of the police operation – guiding people into the allotted areas, keeping them back from the route the Sinterklaas parade was taking through the heart of Amsterdam. It was containment, not control. Three hundred thousand people . . . no police force in the world could hope to do more.

They'd now followed the parade on its last loop, to Leidseplein. It was twenty past three. In ten minutes Sinterklaas would be here, to be welcomed by the mayor. Then at four he'd address the children of the city from the theatre balcony and after that everyone would begin to go their own way, to the hot dog stands, the sweet stalls and the shops. Then finally, satisfied, to home.

Vos and Van der Berg were talking cheerily to a man in a clown costume who could barely stand, telling him to go home and lie down.

A meal with these two men. Usually they seemed to live off bar snacks and beer. She couldn't imagine what Vos meant by 'proper dinner'. Or what kind of restaurant he liked. It was seven months since they met during the doll's house case. She was now a full member of his plain-clothes team. They were close some-how. As much friends as colleagues. Vos did that to everyone. She felt sorry for him. In a way, she suspected, he felt sorry for her as a solitary young woman from outside town with few friends in Amsterdam.

Fewer than he knew. None, if she was honest.

She was starting to wonder where she'd spend Christmas – in Amsterdam or home in Dokkum – when she heard a rising angry voice behind and turned to look. A tall woman in an expensive-looking, fashionable coat was berating a uniformed female officer about something, her right hand clinging tightly to a bored-looking young girl in a bright-pink jacket with ponies on it.

Bakker ambled over, flashed her ID, smiled and offered to help.

'Why won't you listen to me?' the woman said, getting madder by the second. 'There's something wrong here.'


Oude Nieuwstraat was a five-minute walk from the Kuypers' house in Herenmarkt. A narrow, ancient lane behind the Singel canal. Hanna Bublik, just nine months in the city after fleeing Georgia, lived there with her eight-year-old daughter Natalya in the gable room on the top floor of a narrow terrace building near Lijnbaanssteeg. Their home was scarcely bigger than Henk Kuyper's office, two single beds, a bathroom and toilet shared with a young Filipina woman, Chantal Santos, who lived on the floor below.

At first glance during the day it seemed a pedestrian street much like any other in Amsterdam: locked-up bikes, a corner grocer, a couple of coffee shops, some adult stores. Around the corner in Spuistraat you could eat Thai, sign up for Scientol-ogy, catch a tram or walk to the city museum. But there were too many large, blank windows in Oude Nieuwstraat for it to be a normal part of the city. The authorities had designated this the Singelgebied, a second red-light district after the larger De Wallen. Cheaper, more often used by a few locals. Plenty of cabins for rent.

Hanna knew the afternoon was going to be taken up with Sinterklaas. So, eager to make what money she could, she'd left her daughter with the Santos girl that morning and chanced on a few hours in the nearest free unit she could find.

Two customers. One Danish, one from London. Quick, easy, casual business. After costs she was seventy euros in pocket. Enough to see Natalya through the afternoon.

This year, starting with Sinterklaas, she'd know a happy Christmas. That was a promise Hanna had made herself. Natalya was just a baby when the Russians and the Ossetians entered their home city of Gori during the brief South Ossetia war. Her husband, Natalya's father, died in the fighting. He was a baker from a village near the border. His relatives didn't want to know his Georgian wife and child when he was dead. Her own family, who'd never liked the idea she'd married an Ossetian, felt the same way. Poverty and desperation finally drove her west, hitching with her daughter across Europe. Finally doing what it took to keep them in food.

'Mum,' Natalya said, trying on her new jacket. 'Where'd you get this?'

Pink. My Little Pony patterns on the fabric. Natalya was growing. Asking questions. Starting to understand things. The Dutch authorities treated them with respect. She was going to a good school, quickly learning the language, English too. But still they lived in a tiny room on the top of a building in the middle of a red-light district while Hanna worked afternoons and nights, six days a week usually.

'I found it. Maybe some rich people didn't like it.' A smile. 'Do you?'

The little girl beamed back. Blonde hair. Pale, smart face. Children were shaped by the world they experienced. In her eight years Natalya Bublik had lost an adoring father, her home, been rejected by both sides of her family, seen her mother reduced to prostitution on the road.

She knew a lie when she heard it. Knew when to ignore it too.

Natalya hugged the jacket, the most expensive piece of clothing she'd ever had. In six months it would be too small for her. Her mother would be wondering how to earn the money to replace the thing.

There was an easier answer beckoning. Chantal Santos kept pushing it at her. Stop working the cabins alone, as a freelance. Sign up with the Turk who had connections throughout the area. Cem Yilmaz, a big, muscular hulk with a fancy apartment near Dam Square and a route into all the high-class escort services in town. Yilmaz controlled much of the top end of the sex trade. Through the Santos girl he'd promised he could double the amount she earned, for half the time on her back or on her knees.

'Let's go, Mum,' Natalya said and took her mother's hand.

First winter in Amsterdam. She was a good mother, had done her research. Natalya had to remember this forever. They'd walk out into the busy streets, watch Saint Nicholas ride through the city on horseback. Listen to him address the children from the balcony of the theatre in Leidseplein. Then eat chips and mayonnaise together, giggle like two little girls. And, finally, go back to the gable room in Oude Nieuwstraat where Hanna would tuck Natalya into the little bed then find a free cabin for the night, strip down to her bra and pants, sit on the stool at the window, wait for a customer. Answer the bell. Negotiate the fee. Open the door. Shut the curtains. Close her mind. Get the job done. Wait for the next one.

Chantal caught them on the stairs. Natalya's head went down at the sight of her. The two didn't get on. It was understandable. The Filipina kid didn't try to hide what she did. She was proud of her dark, alluring looks, boasted of the money they brought in.

Sometimes Hanna Bublik had no choice but to leave her daughter alone with this young woman.

'Wait in the hall,' she said and watched the pink jacket bob down the stairs.

'He's been on at me again,' the girl told her when Natalya was gone.

'Yilmaz?'

'Cem.'

She was wearing a skimpy T-shirt, what looked like a bikini underneath. Hanna wondered how this kid would feel the day she realized she was getting old.

'I don't want to work for anyone. I told you.'

'You work for someone every time you take off your pants. Don't you?'

Hanna reached out and touched the girl's shoulder, turned it. The badge of ownership was there in her skin, bright-blue, crudely done. Two letters in a fancy script, the initials of his name, 'CY'.

'I don't want any man's tattoo on my back. Tell him thanks but no thanks.'

'Didn't hurt so much,' Chantal grumbled.

'It's not about the pain,' she said and wondered if this kid had any idea of the things she'd seen in her twenty-eight years.

'Two thousand euros he gave me just for getting that.' She tapped the blue scrawl. It was only a couple of weeks old. The sardonic smile dropped for a moment. 'Gets worse if you hold out. And I don't have to sit in some stupid window any more.'

A voice rose from down the stairs.

'Mum? Are we going?'

Hanna Bublik forced herself to smile. She needed Chantal. Sometimes anyway.

'Thanks for looking after Natalya this morning.'

'Don't work mornings,' the girl said. 'Don't need to.'

'Are you coming to meet Sinterklaas?'

A grin. Quick and insincere.

'Got a sugar daddy of my own to see, thanks. Cem fixed it.'

There was something else she wanted to say.

'Nat told me she has nightmares. About monsters. Something big and black. Coming for you two. Up the stairs.'

'Natalya. Nightmares . . . ?'

'Monsters in broad daylight.' The Filipina girl laughed a little. 'Kids . . .'

'Have fun,' Hanna said then walked downstairs and took her daughter by her hand out into Oude Nieuwstraat.

She asked Natalya about the monsters. They'd turned up a year or two after Gori. She thought they'd left them behind in Georgia.

The answer when it came didn't amount to much. Chantal Santos, a dumb whore who was getting herself deep into something she didn't understand, probably got more.

'What did they look like?' Hanna asked even though she knew the answer. Could picture them herself.

Black demons full of smoke and thunder, fire in their guts, alongside sparks and tiny forks of lightning. The kind that had swarmed over Gori that bloody night the world collapsed around them.

'The way they always do,' her daughter replied in a small, sure voice and left it there.

Hanna pulled her cheap black nylon anorak around her. It was cold out on the street.

'There are no monsters,' she said. 'If there were I'd kill them.'


Arms folded, as sceptical as the uniform woman beside her, Laura Bakker listened to the story of the woman called Renata Kuyper. Smartly dressed with neat brown hair, a narrow, anxious face and a Belgian accent. She and her daughter had ridden to the square in a cargo trike from the Herenmarkt, parked in a side street, watched the parade. All the way from home to Leidseplein a Black Pete had followed them on a rusty bike. Watching, not coming close. Not offering sweets. Just stalking.

The uniform officer glanced at Bakker and rolled her eyes.

'Why would he do that?' Bakker asked as the band in front of the theatre struck up again with cheesy festive music.

'How would I know?'

There was a shrill and edgy air about her.

'It's Sinterklaas. We've got lots of Black Petes around,' Bakker said. 'Hundreds. Perhaps you saw more than one . . .'

'He was on a bike. Following us. Watching us. He was wearing green . . .'

'Lots of them wear green,' the uniform woman cut in.

'Look . . . look . . .'

'Perhaps you and your daughter should go home,' Bakker suggested. 'You seem upset.'

There was a roar from the square followed by frantic applause. Sinterklaas had appeared on his horse, surrounded by an army of Black Petes. Soon he'd be on the balcony and the crowd would go quiet for the ceremonial speeches.

'There,' the woman said. 'There he is . . .'

She was pointing at a green figure close by the entrance to one of the narrow side lanes, filled with tourist restaurants.

With a short sigh Bakker turned to look, closely, the way she'd learned through working with Vos. He didn't just see the world around him. The people in it. How they fitted into the narrow, sometimes chaotic streets of Amsterdam. He thought about them. Tried to imagine what brought these men and women here, and the story behind them.

When she did that Bakker found she was interested in what she saw. The Black Pete was of medium height, blacked up, a large curly wig, green satin costume, mob cap, baggy trousers. He had a red sack that ought to be full of sweets to hand out to the kids.

But he wasn't doing that. It was as if the sack scarcely existed. He was looking round. Watching for something.

This one didn't have a rusty bike but he was wrong somehow.

Vos and Van der Berg were still engaged with the drunk who looked ready to get punchy. Bakker told the woman and her daughter to stay with the uniform officer, then walked over to say hello.

So many of these odd characters were around at that moment. There were even a couple abseiling down one of the buildings. Anyone who felt like getting the costume, handing out some sweets and having fun could lose themselves in the disguise.

'There's a woman who thinks you're following her. I'm sure it's just a mistake.'

No response. Just two very white and angry eyes staring at her from beneath the shiny, curly wig.

'Perhaps if you could show me some ID.'

A grunt and then his gloved hands went beneath the loose elastic of the green trousers, fiddled around and came up with something she recognized straight away.

It was the card for Koeman, another plain-clothes agent in Vos's team.

She looked him up and down and stifled a giggle. He folded his green arms and tapped his right foot on the pavement.

'Is this work?' she asked. 'Or what you do off duty?'

He was a miserable bastard at the best of times. It seemed a worthwhile question.

'What do you think?'

'I don't know. That's why I asked.'

He closed his eyes for a moment.

'I'm street surveillance.'

She pointed to the woman who'd complained. Renata Kuyper was jabbing a finger at the uniformed officer again.

'Did you follow her all the way here from Herenmarkt?'

'No,' he said with a sarcastic whine. 'Why would I do that?'

'She says a Black Pete did. He was wearing green.'

Koeman reached into his bag and glumly offered her a spicy *kruidnoot.*

The cheesy music had stopped which meant they could hear Renata Kuyper yelling at the top of her voice alongside the rising clamour of the crowd. Bakker glanced up at the theatre balcony. Sinterklaas was there, along with the mayor, marching towards the microphone.

Something was missing.

The girl in the pink jacket.

Bakker strode quickly back. Koeman followed.

'Henk! Henk!' she was screaming into her phone. 'For God's sake where are you? Get down here, will you? Saskia just wandered off . . .'

She stopped, glared at Koeman.

'He's a duty police officer,' Bakker explained.

The female cop was getting irate.

'Like we said. It's Sinterklaas. Kids go missing. We'll find her for you. Jesus. You don't need to make such a fuss.'

The woman was still on the phone screaming at what Bakker could only assume was voicemail.

'We'll find her . . .' Bakker repeated.

The racket had attracted Pieter Vos's attention. He patted the drunk on the back and sent him off towards the exit then wandered over. Vos and Van der Berg seemed to recognize Koeman immediately. Perhaps he did this every year.

Bakker looked at them, radios in hand, alert, ready.

'We've got a missing girl. Pink jacket.' She turned to the woman. 'Name?'

Renata Kuyper gave up on the phone.

'Saskia Kuyper. She's only eight.'

Very like her mother, Bakker remembered. The same strained, narrow, pale face.

Vos nodded, introduced himself, was starting to explain how they had officers trained to deal with lost children throughout the square. Every year plenty went missing. They were always found.

Then Sinterklaas was at the microphone. Gruff, hearty tones booming throughout Leidseplein.

'Children of Amsterdam—'

The first explosion boomed through the square, deep, loud, painful. Alongside the noise came a blinding light that left those close enough to witness it reeling, stumbling to their knees.

A long, silent moment of shock followed. Then a frantic, high-pitched scream. The first of many.

That evening, when Marnixstraat had time to catch breath, they would establish the outrage was nothing like as threatening as it had seemed at the time. The explosions came from flash grenades, frightening but largely harmless. A duty policeman suffered minor burns when he tried to remove one close to a party of children near the theatre. Seven spectators were treated in hospital for shock, concussion from the stampede that followed, and a couple of broken limbs.

It could have been so much worse. But, like everyone else in Leidseplein that afternoon, Hanna Bublik and her young daughter Natalya knew none of this. All they saw was pandemonium. As Sinterklaas began to speak from the theatre balcony something streaked through the air, fell close to the front of the building, then exploded with a sudden flash and a roar of sound. Two more explosions followed and by then the square, packed with thousands of people, many of them young children, was beyond control.

She'd seen warfare first hand in Gori. Knew what a grenade sounded like, recognized the bright blinding light and the deafening racket that followed straight after. When the third missile crashed into the crowded square there was only a grim determination beneath the familiar panic.

*Flee.*

*Survive.*

*Hide.*

Without a word she grabbed Natalya's hand and dragged the girl close to her side, looked round. Saw a sea of terrified, puzzled faces. One moment Leidseplein was a placid mass of humanity. The next a howling mob. She barely knew this part of the city. Had no idea where to turn.

Gori haunted her for a multitude of reasons. There she'd been young, innocent, afraid. While her husband prowled outside their cottage, gun in hand, swearing to protect his wife and baby, she'd cowered with Natalya in an attic, wondering how the world had come to this.

All they wanted was security and a little money. The games the politicians played, setting cultures and languages against one another for their own private ends, meant nothing in the special, holy place called home. And here was the monster, tanks and soldiers, military vehicles, heavy weapons, circling the town, splitting it into two parties, victors and defeated joined by blood.

When she escaped – barely – with her life and the tiny child in her arms, glimpsing only the mangled corpse of her husband near the lane that led to their modest home, she'd sworn she'd never cower again. Next time if the blackness fell she'd fight, make sure no one came near the ones she loved.

In the mayhem of Leidseplein that meant one thing only: think of yourself and your child, no one else. Elbows jabbing, her left arm clutching Natalya's pink jacket, she launched herself into the fray. There was a narrow lane behind them. Not so many people. The rest seemed to be racing towards the broader streets.

Head down, cursing in a language none of them would understand, she made for the space away from the smoke and commotion in the square.

*You don't apologize. You don't make excuses.*

This was the world she knew, one that left her to survive on her own. And survive they would.

Fighting, screaming, punching, kicking, Natalya clutched tight to her, she forced her way to the periphery of the square. Were there more explosions? She didn't know. This wasn't Gori. There were no bodies on the ground. No blood. Just fear and dread. That was enough.

How long it took she'd no idea. Then the press of bodies around them eased. She found space to reach down and lift her daughter onto her chest, the way she did in Gori. A different child now. Natalya's strong arms gripped her neck. Hanna struggled with her weight, battering their way through the diminishing crowd.

Behind them sirens shrieked. People screamed. There were announcements over the PA system Sinterklaas himself had been using. Messages pleading for people to stay calm. To avoid trampling others. To wait for help to arrive.

No one said that back in Georgia. For the simple reason that it never came.

One last push and they were through. Breathless, head hurting, arms aching from the weight of her daughter, she got them free of the hubbub, carried Natalya to the little lane then stumbled into a blind, dark alley next to a kebab shop. Put her on the ground, touched her fair hair, wondered what to say.

There was a look in her daughter's eyes Hanna Bublik knew only too well. It wasn't just fear. It was an angry, uncomprehending bafflement too, one that carried with it a question that would never be answered . . . why?

'Mummy,' she said in a small, frightened voice as they waited in the shadows.

'We're fine, sweetheart,' Hanna said. 'It's over now. We stay here. Everything will be . . .'

For some reason she couldn't stop thinking of what Chantal Santos had said. They needed easy money. A better life than this. If it meant getting the name of a Turkish thug tattooed on her shoulder as a start maybe it was a small price to pay.

The sirens were diminishing behind her. Perhaps it was all a nasty, cruel prank. No one was hurt. Amsterdam was the safe if fallen city she'd come to know.

'Everything will be fine.'

'Mummy,' Natalya said again and the fear was still in her voice.

Her mother looked. The girl wasn't watching her. The arm of her strange pink jacket was extended behind, to somewhere Hanna couldn't see.

As she turned to look something green came into her vision. The pain followed. Then the blackness as the world revolved and she tumbled down to the hard, cold ground.


There was a procedure for events like this. A set of responses patiently planned and rehearsed over the years. The emergency services were already moving into place, uniformed officers trying to shepherd people away from the vicinity of the blasts.

Vos and Bakker had checked for injuries as best they could while Van der Berg, without a word, had taken off in the direction of the tram stop, the point from which the grenades seemed to originate.

The Kuyper woman was growing ever more frantic. Between yelling for her daughter she shrieked down the phone trying to get hold of her husband.

Bakker tried to console her. Vos said to leave it. Leidseplein was full of people who'd become separated from their family at that moment. They had other priorities: try to keep everyone safe.

Renata Kuyper yelled a flurry of curses and started to march off into the mass ahead, head turning frantically side to side, call-ing her daughter's name.

Vos took hold of her arm and stopped her.

'We'll find your daughter. It's best you stay here . . .'

Then her phone rang and she looked at the screen. Hope and fear and puzzlement on her face.


'You don't need that,' the Black Pete said and took the phone from Saskia Kuyper's fingers just as she pressed the shortcut for her mother.

She blinked and said nothing. This man was a grown-up. He was supposed to know things. All the same he seemed nervous. More than she was maybe.

'That's what sets bombs off,' he added. 'Phone calls.'

He put the handset in his pocket. His shiny green costume shone in the winter sun.

Shivering in her pink My Little Pony jacket she looked at him and didn't move. He'd found her beneath the theatre balcony, at the edge of the mayhem, staying clear.

She'd never heard the world this loud. Had no idea where her mother was any more. All she'd done was wander forward, trying to catch sight of Sinterklaas on the balcony. Just managing a glimpse of a man in a red suit with a long white beard before the earth shook beneath her feet.

'Your daddy wants to see you, Saskia. Your mummy too. I'll take you there.'

He had a brittle, foreign voice and spoke in English. The tone of it clashed with the black face, the ruby lips, the bright white teeth.

She didn't move. So he reached into his bag and held out a couple of sweets.

'Come on,' he said and she stared at the glittering objects in his white gloved hands.

Daddy hated sweets. He said they were bad for your teeth. They'd rot your guts. Make you smell like the other kids.

Saskia moved to take one. His fingers closed on hers. Not so tight she wanted to scream. Just enough so that she couldn't let go.

'I'll show you where they are,' he said and pointed towards the bridge over the canal.

Prinsengracht. Her father sometimes went to an office there. She'd gone with him once. Sat in a small room on her own for hours while he did business.

Perhaps . . .

'Come on,' he said again and tugged her hand.

She didn't move an inch. Dug the heels of her black patent-leather shoes hard into the pavement, leaned back to stop him. Then she stole into the jacket pocket of his green costume and snatched back the phone they'd given her for her eighth birthday. A cheap Samsung. Not the iPhone she'd asked for.

*Don't spoil her.*

Mummy said that a lot.

'I can call if I want,' she told him and put her finger on the screen, held it there again. Just heard the engaged tone before he snatched the handset from her, took hold of her shoulder, dragged her through a baying crowd lost in itself.

So much that no one noticed an eight-year-old girl shrieking and fighting as a figure in green pulled Saskia Kuyper out of the chaos of Leidseplein into the empty streets beyond.

Just across the square, frantic in the milling crowd, her mother was still looking at the screen of her phone. Reluctant to answer the familiar ring she'd set up for him.

But really she had no choice.

'Henk,' she said before he could speak. 'We're in Leidseplein. I need you here.'

A pause then. He'd blame her for this. She could see the sour judgemental stare already.

She had to say it anyway.

'Saskia's gone. I don't know where.'

Two minutes after the first explosion Frank de Groot, commissaris in Marnixstraat, called Vos and asked if he and his team were OK.

'As far I can see,' Vos told him. 'What about casualties?'

'Looks like they were fireworks,' De Groot said. 'From the monitors anyway. All the same . . .'

'You've been watching?'

There was a pause on the line then, 'What do you think?'

'Can you see who threw them?'

'Someone in a Black Pete outfit. He was wearing green. Near the tram stop.'

Exactly where Van der Berg had said.

'Dirk's on it,' Vos said. 'We'll catch up with him. We had a woman saying she was followed by someone like that from the Herenmarkt. You might want to check the cameras. And send me a few more people—'

'Wait, wait, wait,' De Groot cut in. 'This looks beyond us. Terrorism—'

'Do terrorists throw fireworks?' Vos wondered.

The Kuyper woman was still arguing on the phone. There were tears in her eyes. Bakker was with her. This wasn't the bomb outrage he first thought. No blood. Just lots of shocked and frightened people.

Before De Groot could answer Vos added, 'I've got parents here who can't find their kids. You need to fix an assembly point.'

'Yes, yes. But I don't want you chasing anyone. AIVD are on it.'

Vos wondered for a moment if he'd heard that correctly. AIVD were national intelligence and security. Not police. And the timing . . .

'Already?' he asked. 'We're three minutes in. Were they waiting or something?'

'You did read the bulletin before you went out?' De Groot asked. 'They upped the terrorism threat to substantial. It's all to do with that preacher they've got in custody. It said—'

'I was thinking about Sinterklaas,' Vos admitted. 'Not terrorists.'

'Yes. Well . . .' De Groot was rarely hesitant by nature.

'What do you want me to do, Frank?'

'AIVD have got a couple of their senior people in Leidseplein.'

'So they knew this might happen?' Vos asked again.

'One step at a time,' De Groot answered testily. 'The boss woman's called Mirjam Fransen. If . . .'

'What do you want me to do?'

A long pause. Then De Groot said, 'Whatever they ask. You really think we got lucky? No one's hurt?'

Vos looked round. The place was calming down. No more screaming. Just people trying to find their bearings. And their loved ones.

'Seems that way. We need to clear this entire area.' He remembered stories about past bomb blasts. Sometimes there was a false start to lure people somewhere more dangerous. 'Who knows what else there could be around?'

That long delay on the line again.

'I said that,' De Groot told him. 'The AIVD woman overruled me. They don't want a stampede. Everyone's to leave steadily. Then they can get their people in there.'

Vos nodded and found himself saying, almost to himself, 'Does that feel right to you?'

'Stay where you are. Do what you can. Wait to hear from me,' De Groot told him and was gone.

A tall man was walking towards them. Renata Kuyper stared at him, both grateful and wary. The two stood and looked at each other. He was thin in an expensive-looking winter coat. Business garb. Odd for Sunday. Early thirties, dark-rimmed glasses, dark hair, expressionless face.

Vos went over. Bakker was trying to help.

'Mr Kuyper?' she asked.

He nodded.

'We'll find your daughter,' she added.

He glanced sharply at his wife.

'You'd better.'

Van der Berg phoned from the far side of the square and said, 'I thought I had him, Pieter.'

'And?'

'We've got AIVD here.' There was an edge to his voice. No one much liked these people getting in the way. 'They seem to think this is theirs.'

Vos asked where exactly he was. Then got Bakker, told the Kuypers to stay with the uniform people. After that he thought for a second and called Van der Berg back.

'Don't start an argument without me,' he said. 'One minute and I'm there.'


Down the back lane Hanna Bublik came to, head hurting, and found herself scrambling in the dirt. Her arm brushed her forehead. Pain there but no blood.

She looked round anxiously. Nobody else in the little alley. No pink jacket. No quiet, worried young voice.

As she stumbled to her feet the winter light from the street vanished and a shadow fell on her. Shiny green and a face blacked up, large wig, red lips, no smile. She remembered going down as Natalya started screaming . . .

Got ready to fight.

But then his hands were up and she realized: this Black Pete seemed different somehow. Deferential. There was something in his fingers. A police ID card and a name on it: Koeman.

'Are you OK?' he asked. 'I'm a police officer.' Then he stepped back, let the light fall on her. 'What happened?'

'Natalya . . .'

She strode past him, walked into the square. Packed with people, more orderly than she remembered. The loudspeaker system Sinterklaas had used was urging everyone to leave the area slowly by whichever route looked easiest.

'Someone hit me. Someone took my girl.'

'Where are you from?' he asked.

It seemed a stupid, pointless question.

'Does that matter? Can you understand me?'

'Are . . . you . . . OK?'

'Yes!' she yelled, and added a few curses he'd never understand. 'Where's my daughter? Someone took her!'

'We've got a million parents looking for their kids,' the cop called Koeman snapped. 'Some idiot let off some smoke bombs or something. Give me a name for her.'

'Natalya.'

He wiped his cheek with the sleeve of his green costume. The make-up started to come off. She could see a pale face emerge from underneath. He seemed tired. Confused. Angry.

'Even better,' Koeman said, 'give me some ID.'

Reluctantly, knowing this was going from bad to worse, she reached into her bag and handed over her passport. He stared at it.

'Tourist?'

'I live here. My daughter's Natalya Bublik. She's eight. When are you going to start looking for her?'

He gave the passport back.

'Got a job?'

'Does that matter?'

He looked her up and down. She knew that expression.

'She's eight—'

'So you said,' he interrupted, then pulled a notepad out of his green trousers and scribbled something on it. 'I'll pass on the name.' He handed her the pad and pen. 'Stay on the edge of the square. Keep listening to the announcements. There'll be an assembly point for missing children . . .'

She lost it then.

'Some bastard hit me. Took my daughter.' She jabbed the green jacket. 'He was dressed like this. What are you . . . ?'

'Or maybe she ran,' the cop said. 'Got scared.' A shrug. 'Lots of scared people today. Thousands of them. We're dealing with it. Hanna . . .'

The way he said her name she got the message. This man had priorities. And a suspect Georgian woman who'd lost her daughter wasn't one of them.

So she threw a few curses in his direction and went to look for Natalya herself.


Van der Berg was by the tram stop getting angry. The crowds were dispersing. The medical teams were doing their job, which was a lot less than they'd expected.

When Vos and Bakker turned up he was arguing with a sharp-faced woman in her mid-thirties with jet-black hair and a smart raincoat. Her immobile face had a tan that must have come from a salon's lights.

'He went down there,' the detective insisted, jabbing a finger at Lijnbaansgracht, a narrow side street leading back towards the Melkweg arts centre.

'We know,' the woman said then held up a smart phone.

Vos came up, introduced himself and Bakker. It was the Fransen woman from AIVD, the one De Groot had talked about. Somehow she already possessed combined footage from the cameras in the square. They watched as a Black Pete figure in a green costume extended his arm above the crowd and threw the first grenade. A puff of smoke from somewhere. Then two more.

31

'Your job's to keep order here,' Mirjam Fransen told them. 'Get people out of the square safely. See if you can match up some of these missing kids with their parents.'

'If you need any help . . .' Vos said.

The giant phone rang. She took the call on an earpiece. It was short. Seemed to make her happy.

'We don't,' the woman told him then marched straight into the crowd behind them, on towards Lijnbaansgracht.


*Running.*

He was never good at that, even before he changed his name.

Sticky inside the green costume, aware his black make-up was starting to drip with sweat, he'd torn off the hot, uncomfortable wig then careered down the narrow street, back towards the place he'd picked up the hidden gear.

The money was in his pocket. More than he'd ever known. But he'd no idea how to use it. How to spend his way out of Amsterdam. The man said he'd fix that. The man said he'd be there where the stuff was left. Should have been too. Bouali had done everything he'd asked. Thrown the grenades, though they seemed more like playthings than anything else. Snatched the girl just as they asked. Took her to the place they'd ringed on the map. Dealt with her there, trying not to ask himself what he was doing.

But all there was in this grubby dark corner was rubbish and the odd rat. The hubbub from Leidseplein and the sporadic sound of a siren caterwauling around the square.

Two minutes he waited. Then he stripped off the rest of the Black Pete outfit. Underneath he wore a white sweatshirt and jeans. The only possession left was the red bag meant for sweets. The money was in there. Incriminating evidence too. He took out the cash, the gun, the shells, walked to the water and threw the rest into the canal.

For the last three nights they'd provided him with a room in a block for restaurant workers not far from Centraal station. Too dangerous to go back there now. He had his passport in the back of his jeans. His old English name. A photo from before.

*Maybe . . .*

The siren got closer. He couldn't think straight.

He put his head round the wall and looked back to Leidseplein.

Then turned and started running again. A man with a shiny black face, the make-up dripping down onto his white T-shirt. Arms flailing. A gun tucked into his jeans. He fled uncertainly towards the narrow tangle of streets and lanes and canals that was the Jordaan.


Henk Kuyper seemed content to do as the police asked. Stay near the theatre in Leidseplein watching the sullen, puzzled crowds disperse. Listen to the public address system calling for order. Promise his distraught wife everything would be fine. Everyone was safe.

The assembly point for meeting lost family members was close by. After fifteen minutes there was still no sign of their daughter.

His wife looked at him and said, 'This isn't my fault.'

'Whose is it then?' he wondered checking the square, eyes narrowed, scanning.

'Why do you always blame me?'

'I don't.'

'You could have come along, Henk. You could have been here. Maybe then . . .'

The cold, sad stare silenced her. He always managed that when he wanted.

She pulled out her phone. That morning, before she got worried about the Black Pete following them, she'd stopped the orange cargo trike on the canal near the open space by the Anne

Frank house on the Prinsengracht. There she'd taken a picture of Saskia in the bucket seat at the front.

Fair hair neatly combed. Eight years old in a pink jacket with ponies on it. Trying hard to smile against a crowd of bored tourists waiting to get into a museum dedicated to another lost child.

But this wasn't that dread world. Not an occupied Amsterdam, controlled by monsters. Thanks to Henk's family money they were comfortable. Protected from the worst of the wrecked economy. His work brought him into conflict with his staid, patrician father. But Lucas Kuyper never staunched the flow of money. He was always there, a quiet, grey presence, ready to help when needed.

The Kuyper name went back centuries, had its place in Amsterdam's lists of minor nobility. It looked after its own and kept them close.

'These things don't happen to us,' she told him, as if to convince herself.

Then left him at the assembly point, clutching her phone in her hand. The picture of Saskia was still there: a tiny figure in a cargo bike. The pink jacket was too big for her. It wasn't her style anyway. The only reason she wore it was because Henk came home with the thing saying it was a spur-of-the-moment purchase. A present for no good reason. He did that from time to time. He loved his daughter. More than he loved his wife.

Hand out, phone in it, picture uppermost, Renata stumbled through the diminishing crowd, asking, pleading for someone to look at Saskia's photo and tell her where her daughter might be.

An image rose in her memory. Didn't mothers around the world do this? In poorer places? The ones Henk thought he was helping? When a bomb exploded. Or snipers moved into nearby buildings.

A mother. A lost child. Was there any difference between an upper-class Amsterdam wife and a refugee torn from her son or daughter?

Henk would have something to say about that. A caustic comment that would tell her how stupid she was to think such a thing. Whatever she – they – believed society thought differently. The poor were poor. The rich were rich. And everyone in between seemed powerless to change a thing.

He stayed with the other nervous parents. Waiting for this strange day to right itself. As if they'd pick up the cargo trike, put Saskia in the front and go home. Have supper together, make small talk as he opened the inevitable bottle of wine. Then he'd return to his little office in the gable roof to lose himself in the computer and all those people he knew around the world. Strangers to her yet closer to him than his own flesh and blood.

She stumbled coming off the pavement into the square. A hand came out to steady her. She looked, recoiled. The Black Pete costume. Red this time. The same black face again.

Renata pulled herself away from him, showed the phone. A shake of the comic head.

Then she lurched on. Stopped everyone she could find. Aware that this was stupid. Irrational would be Henk's word. Unthinking. Unproductive. But what else was there to do?

After a couple of minutes she'd crossed the square. Looking back the crowds were working their way out in neat lines. The announcements over the loudspeakers seemed less frantic. Full of encouragement, words of comfort. Calling the lost to a single assembly point. Close to the place where Henk had stayed.

Hand out, mind blank. No sight of Saskia anywhere. Then a shadow fell across the phone and a hand reached out for it.

A woman about her age. Harder-faced. Lean in a cheap nylon jerkin and black jeans. A desperation in her eyes Renata thought she recognized.

'You've seen her?' she asked the woman.

A stream of words. Foreign. Incomprehensible. The hand went out for the phone again and Renata thought: wrong time, wrong place for a mugging. Amsterdam in chaos and all this foreign bitch wants to do is steal a phone with a photo of a young girl on the screen. Smiling in a pink jacket.

She jerked the handset away, stepped back, stared at her. As if she should have known.

*Not now. Not with a child missing.*

The woman grabbed her arm, the phone with it, put the screen close to her face, stared at the picture there.

Then let go, what sounded like a foreign curse on her breath, looked at her, shook her head and shuffled away into the crowd, shoulders bent, tears in her eyes.

The phone rang. Henk's number.

'I've got her,' he said, nothing more.


Vos was the first to see them. A group of masked men in black, hooded, armed, racing to the corner of the square, back towards the Melkweg. AIVD officers, he assumed.

He didn't care De Groot had told them to stay put. This was his city. His people. Men in masks had no place in it.

Koeman was wiping the last of the black make-up from his face, moaning as usual. About what a mess this whole thing was. How people – the police too – didn't know what to do.

'Dirk,' Vos told Van der Berg. 'You deal with things here.' He glanced at Bakker and Koeman, told them to follow him, then pushed through the line of families queuing to get out of the square, kept on until they were clear, looking down the narrow alley that led to the music venue. The men were past the place already, running by the grey buildings in Raamplein, chasing a distant figure who kept looking back as he stumbled across the bridge ahead.

A man in a white T-shirt and jeans. Black face like Koeman's.

Vos set up a jog. Best he could manage. Bakker was younger, fitter than the rest of them. As he watched she broke into a run, long legs, long arms pumping, red hair flying back behind her.

'They've got weapons,' Vos yelled, knowing it was pointless to tell her to keep back.

'Me too,' she cried, turning, patting her jacket. And then she was over the gentle rise of the bridge, heavy feet so loud on the cobbles the noise sent a small gaggle of coots on the water flying and flapping away in sudden fear.

Vos had left his weapon in his locker as usual. It was the Sinterklaas parade. Why would he need it?

Some four hundred metres ahead the fugitive figure dashed down a side street, black shapes closing in pursuit. Bakker was moving so quickly she was reducing the gap between them. Too far away for Vos to shout at her now. Even if it might work. Koeman was wheezing behind him.

The AIVD men turned the corner, Bakker close on their heels.


Back in Leidseplein Dirk Van der Berg waited, listening to the radio, watching the lines of people file patiently out of the square. He was forty-seven, unfit, liked his beer. He'd seen plenty of incidents in nearly thirty years with the Amsterdam police and something here didn't make sense.

Looking round at the odd Sinterklaas crowd he realized what it was.

Terrorists wouldn't lob flash grenades into an event like this. It wasn't their style. They were either cowards or heroes. Planted devices covertly, set them on a timer, then fled to safety. Or carried them proudly on their person. Explosive vests or weapons held out for all to see, waiting for the martyrdom they expected.

'This stinks,' he muttered and cast his eyes around the square.

The Kuyper woman was gone. So was her husband. He guessed they'd found their little girl. Why else would they leave the assembly point?

A gap emerged in the crowds. Van der Berg peered through it. Lots of kids in festive clothes. Grown-ups too.

There was a black delivery van parked in Leidsestraat, the street that led back to the centre, next to the Eichholtz delicatessen. Right on the tramlines, unused for once that day since all the public transport had been halted to make way for Sinterklaas.

As he watched a Black Pete came up to the back doors. The man was dressed in green. He held the hand of a young girl with blonde hair. And a pink jacket. Held it very tightly, then opened the back doors and half-pushed her inside.

People wanted to get their kids out of the way. That was understandable. Van der Berg thought. But civilian traffic was supposed to be barred from the city. He didn't see how anyone could get through easily.

Then the kid turned and he saw. She wasn't with this man, she was being taken away against her will.

The street was clear beyond the van. They could be gone in seconds.

A quick and random fear, the kind a police officer had sometimes as all the many unwanted possibilities began to run through his head.

Maybe this wasn't much about harmless fireworks tossed into a crowd. Not directly anyway. It was about spreading fear and confusion, seizing a young girl amid the chaos, knowing the scores of people who witnessed the deed would fail to see it for what it was.

He started to run, to yell. One of the grey secure people carriers the AIVD people used careered in front of him, windows covered in security screens, glass dark and opaque to the outside world. Two more followed.

Van der Berg leapt back, cursing.

By the time the way ahead was clear the black van had vanished.

———

It was a long journey from the back streets of Lancashire, growing up in poverty with a mother who barely had time for him, through crime, through jail, through the discovery of a kind of home in a foreign faith. He was christened Martin Bowers. The radical preacher in the mosque back home gave him a new name: Mujahied Bouali. Twenty-four years old, fleeing down a narrow canal in Amsterdam, sweat running through the black make-up on his face.

They'd never said what to do if you thought you might be caught. That was odd. The men who briefed him the day before, showed him the grenades he'd pick up later with the guns, told him everything else. What to do. How to do it. Where to run.

To a safe house back in the red-light district. But that was a long way from here. Too far.

He was on hard, rough cobbles now, struggling, money tumbling from his pockets as he fled. No time to look back. They were following. He tried to catch his breath, to run harder, faster.

But the booze and the fags back when he was Martin Bowers had taken their toll.

There was a narrow alley to the left. Shadows. Maybe somewhere to hide or lose them. He stumbled into it, caught his foot on a manhole cover, went down to the ground, whined as he grazed his knuckles trying to keep his face from hitting hard stone.

When he looked up he knew this was over. The place was nothing more than a blind passageway, a high brick wall at the end. No windows. No people. Just rubbish bins and a stray cat streaking out of the corner as if fearing what was to come.

'Bloody stupid,' he muttered and heard his old voice, bitter Lancashire grit, all the hope and little love it had once possessed thieved from him over the years.

*Think for yourself.*

He hadn't done that in a while. They did it for him.

Footsteps behind. A metallic sound he didn't want to think about.

A woman there, severe face, black hair. The boss. He could see that.

'Don't do anything stupid,' she ordered in English. 'We're taking you in.' She smiled. 'You're going to talk.'

'I don't know nothing,' he grumbled, half-hidden in the shadows, staring at her bland, hard face. 'Even if I did . . .'

The men around her had guns out.

'We'll see,' she said with a nod to a man by her, hooded, big, strong. He had a weapon in one hand. Cuffs in the other. 'Get him.'

'Take orders from a woman, do you?' Bouali yelled in his coarse, northern voice. 'That's what you call a man here?'

Her eyes were on him. Cold and unfeeling.

'Do as you're told, boy,' she said. 'You . . .'

Martin Bowers, Mujahied Bouali, scrabbled round on the ground, found the gun inside his belt, got his fingers round the grip. Sometimes things happened without him thinking. They just came into his head.

He was turning the gun on them before he even realized.


The phone in Vos's jacket pocket rang. Just past the Melkweg. He cursed and paused, out-of-breath, glanced at the screen.

Van der Berg. Not a man who wasted time or words.

'What?'

'There's something wrong here. I think I just saw a kid snatched. Pink jacket like they were talking about.'

'Where?'

'Off the square. A black van. It went back into the centre. I'd have got a number if it wasn't for all these damned spooks driving around like idiots.' A pause. 'Where are you? Where's Laura?'

Keeping up with the AIVD men. Out of sight.

'We'll be back in a minute. I think they've got the man.'

'What man?' Van der Berg yelled. 'I saw him here. Putting the kid in a van.' That gap again and they were both thinking the same thing. 'There's more than one of them, isn't there?'

'Sounds like it . . .'

The ducks and coots rose from the canal, filling the air with the sound of their wings and anxious, high-pitched cries. Then a staccato rattle of gunfire.


Saskia.

A pink jacket. A tall figure holding a young girl's hand. Renata ran and ran, down the long lane, past the Melkweg, out to the canal by Marnixstraat.

In the distance the grey modern building that was the police station. Fat use they'd been. It was Henk who'd found her. Bad Henk. Thoughtless Henk.

He'd throw that at her. She knew it. But right at that moment she didn't care.

She ran, bent down, held her daughter, hugged her. Looked at her pale, puzzled face and didn't dare to ask the obvious question . . . *Where the hell have you been?*

'She's fine,' Henk said in a flat, bored voice. 'She got lost. That's all. Let's go home.'

He ruffled Saskia's blonde hair.

'I'll buy ice cream. Whatever . . .'

A scream from somewhere. A sound like gunfire.

Three things then, simultaneous, no more than a few steps apart, separate yet connected.


Laura Bakker reached the blind alley where the AIVD team had raced in pursuit of Black Pete. A bloodied body lay bent on the floor. Next to it a hard-faced woman in a business suit chanting into a radio.

A wall of men formed ahead as soon as Bakker showed up. Her ID card meant nothing. They'd got machine pistols. Body armour. Balaclavas and riot gear. Pushed her back until she could see no more and left her fuming, cursing in the street. Stamping her big boots on the cobbles, all to no avail.

As the Kuypers placed their arms around their daughter like a shield a tall blonde-haired woman raced up to them, yelling something in a foreign tongue. Bent down, stared at the girl. Shook her head. Furious. Lost.

*You tried to steal my phone.*

A random thought. Unwanted in the circumstances. Renata barely noticed her husband slide away, turning his back, muttering he had to call someone. Then vanishing across the bridge.

Pieter Vos saw some of this, as did Laura Bakker retreating from the bloody scene in the alley, and Dirk Van der Berg walking from the square. Antennae tuned for trouble, the three detectives homed in on the odd little group.

There, by the side of the girl, her mother, the distraught woman, Bakker looked at Vos and said, still struggling to believe this herself, 'They shot him. Just like that.'

'Where's my girl?' Hanna Bublik yelled in broken Dutch as she clutched at the child in the pink jacket until Renata Kuyper snatched Saskia from her clawing fingers.

Van der Berg glanced at Vos. A nod. He seemed to know.

A sound. High-pitched. A jaunty childish tune, the kind set for a specific caller. Renata Kuyper took her phone from her pocket, checked the screen, turned to her daughter and asked, 'Saskia . . . ?'

The girl stayed silent, eyes on the canal and the returning wildfowl.

'It's from your phone,' said Renata.

Vos retrieved the handset from the mother's cold fingers. 'It's a video call,' he said, and tapped the screen.

There was a face on the little screen. Dark with make-up. Scarlet lips. White teeth.

'It's the mother I wish to talk to,' this new Black Pete said.

'My name's Pieter Vos. I'm a brigadier with the Amsterdam police.'

The face laughed then, the teeth perfect and even.

'Then you'll do.'

An ambulance tore round the corner, siren shrieking, down to the street where the men with guns were gathered.

'My brother Mujahied's a martyr, isn't he? We listen to your radios. We know your schemes. You murdered him.'

The speaker was turned to full so they could all hear and see. The voice was foreign. The accent hard to place.

'I don't know what happened. We're police. There's a girl . . .' Vos began.

'You're all the same. Dogs and criminals.'

'What do you want?'

'We have the Kuyper child,' Black Pete said. 'Granddaughter to your bloody soldier . . .'

'No,' Vos cut in.

The white eyes grew large with fury.

'Don't argue with me! Two decades on from Srebrenica, eight thousand dead there. So many more in Iraq and Afghanistan. Do you think we can't count? This murderer's offspring is with us now.'

Vos looked at the little girl, clutched to her mother's legs by caring arms. Then at the other woman. Foreign. A mark of desperate poverty about her.

*Pink jackets.*

'Saskia Kuyper's here with me. Safe with her mother. You've got the wrong kid. It's the same clothes but . . .'

Hanna Bublik seized the phone from him, glared at the face on the screen.

'She's eight years old. From Georgia. No father. No money. No . . .'

A wagging finger, a bossy hand, waved her into silence.

'I speak to the man now,' Black Pete said. 'Him only.'

One more time she tried and got the same. Vos looked at her, nodded, and she gave him back the phone.

'What she says is the truth,' he insisted. 'You've got the wrong girl. Let her go. Do this now. Make yourself scarce before we find you . . .'

The black face was laughing again. Then the picture changed. A brief view of what looked like a small room. Wooden walls. Something familiar about it for Vos.

Finally a shape in the corner.

Perhaps it was an easy mistake. She looked a little like the Kuyper kid. Prettier if anything, with long straight blonde hair and bright, anxious eyes.

There was red tape round her mouth, rope round her slender wrists, drawing them together on her lap. The pink jacket looked grubby and stained.

Hanna was snatching at the phone again, screaming like a banshee.

'Hurt her and I will kill you. I swear . . .'

A sudden move on the screen. A hand grabbed the little girl, dragged her to the camera, ripped the tape from her mouth.

When she cried it seemed more with fury than pain. Tough kid. Tough mother. But the woman was silent now.

'Name!' the Black Pete bellowed.

Nothing.

'Name!'

'Natalya Bublik,' the girl said in a firm, defiant voice.

Vos was looking at the walls. The timber planking. Not her. Trying to imagine where this place might be. Not far away. There wasn't time for that.

Black Pete stripped fresh tape around her mouth, pushed her back into the corner. Cushions there. Perhaps a makeshift bed.

'She's an innocent kid,' Vos pleaded. 'Let her go.'

'There were innocent children in Srebrenica. In Iraq. Afghanistan. Somalia. Men and women too. Do you beg for them, policeman?'

'What . . . do . . . you . . . want?'

'I want my brother Ismail freed and flown to a country that won't kill him.' A shrug. A glance in the corner. 'And some money too. I'd have preferred to hold your murderer Kuyper's offspring to ransom for his freedom. But a child's a child.'

The dark face peered into the camera and smiled.

'I'll keep this girl instead.' He laughed. 'Why test the mettle of a bastard like Kuyper? When I can try the conscience of you good and ordinary people?'

'Let her go now,' Vos begged. 'There's no justice in kidnapping a child . . .'

'Justice is what we make it. This kid will do. Tomorrow I return with instructions. This phone. No other.'

Gone then. Hanna Bublik cursed. The Kuyper girl held on to her mother's legs and closed her eyes.

The ducks and coots were returning to the water, bickering as if nothing had happened. Vos looked at Laura Bakker and Dirk Van der Berg.

'She's on a boat,' he said.


Four hours later in Marnixstraat Mirjam Fransen briefed them on Ismail Alamy, the Moroccan whose fate was now linked to that of Natalya Bublik. Fifty-one years old, an active recruiting agent for terrorist causes over the Internet. Resident in the Netherlands for six years. Suspected by AIVD of connections with a number of outlawed groups in the Horn of Africa, Al-Shabaab among them. Trained in Afghanistan, wanted in three Middle Eastern countries to face criminal charges for conspiracy, bomb plots and attempted murder.

Alamy was one of the few recognized members of an elusive terrorist cell led by a figure known as Il Barbone. Saudi by birth, but based in Italy for years. The nickname came from there, and the rumour he had a heavy beard. Fransen didn't want to talk about that much. Classified, she said. All they needed to know was that Barbone was behind something quite unlike the standard Islamist terrorist grouping: noisy, visible, relatively easy to track. Instead it was a well-organized operational unit dedicated to planning and funding, one that worked silently, often through conventional channels, to move money, people and intelligence around western Europe. Terrorism as a business process, everyday, difficult to detect.

For the last twenty-four months Alamy had been fighting a protracted battle against extradition. At that moment he was in a solitary secure cell in the detention centre at Schiphol airport awaiting one final appeal to the European Court of Human Rights. The moment that was lost – days away – Fransen predicted he'd be placed on a military plane and shipped out of the country to face trial in a friendly Middle Eastern nation.

'You can't do that until we've found the girl,' Vos said.

Bakker had joined them in De Groot's office. Fransen brought along her deputy, a taciturn, hefty man called Thom Geerts, grey raincoat and a crew-cut bullet head. Marnixstraat had almost sixty detectives working on the case already, going through CCTV and phone records, interviewing potential witnesses. The call to Saskia's phone was made through a Net connection. Untraceable. The black van had been found abandoned near Centraal station. They'd used a counterfeit security pass to allow them to take it close to Leidseplein.

These men were prepared.

'We don't base government policy on the actions of crimi-nals,' Geerts said with no emotion.

'You've been trying to ship this man out of the country for years,' De Groot told the pair from AIVD. 'A few more days won't hurt. He's not going anywhere. We need the time.'

Geerts was about to argue when Fransen put a hand to his arm, smiled without much warmth and said, 'That's fine. We can wait. A few days anyway.'

Laura Bakker sat silently fuming throughout the briefing. Fransen had admitted at the outset they'd received some prior warning of a possible attack during the Sinterklaas parade. Not details. Only chatter. She said it was insufficient to brief the police. They should have been aware the threat level was raised that morning. Standard practice in such circumstances.

'If we'd known . . .' Bakker said a second time.

Mirjam Fransen shrugged.

'What would you have done? We had teams of officers in place. That was enough. We couldn't cancel Sinterklaas.' A brief smile. 'Could we?'

Commissaris de Groot glared at her.

'I should have been better informed. We won't pursue that now.'

'No you won't.' She looked at her watch. 'I need to go back to the office. I want you to handle the practical matters. Deal with the family. This Georgian prostitute . . . does she have the right papers?'

Hanna Bublik was being interviewed downstairs by Dirk Van der Berg and a female officer. She didn't seem to have much to say.

'Her legal status isn't one of my priorities right now,' Vos said. 'The room where the girl was being held. It looked like a boat.'

Fransen frowned.

'You're sure of that?'

'I live on a boat. You get to know what they're like. Low walls. Timber planking . . .'

'There are a lot of boats in Amsterdam,' she said. 'Good luck . . .'

'Why did you shoot that man?' Bakker asked.

Fransen shrugged.

'You wouldn't have asked that if you were there.' She stared the young policewoman in the face. 'Bouali had a handgun. He looked ready to use it. We gave the standard warning.'

'I didn't hear any warning,' Bakker pointed out.

Mirjam Fransen waited a moment then asked, 'Do you think I'm lying?'

'I'm saying I didn't hear it.'

'And I'm telling you it was given. Bouali had a weapon. The idiot was turning it on us. I wanted him alive as much as you. Maybe he had things he could tell us.'

The dead man was a Briton by birth, had changed his name when he fell in with a radical preacher in the north of England. Vos's team had already talked to some of the people in the grubby tenement in the red-light district where he had a tiny room. His housemates were mainly foreign restaurant workers. He was a stranger, there for only a few days, had spent most of his time elsewhere and didn't talk much.

The AIVD woman turned to Vos and held out a hand.

'I need that phone now. We'll deal with the calls.'

He did nothing.

'The phone,' she repeated.

Frank de Groot got up and sat on the edge of his desk.

'Whoever this man is he insisted he'd only talk to Vos.'

'They don't make the conditions,' Geerts said.

'When they're holding an eight-year-old girl hostage they do,' De Groot replied. 'We keep the phone. Vos does the talking. We'll let you know what happens, naturally.' A pause. 'It would be nice if we got the same in return.'

Mirjam Fransen glared at him.

'Do you really want me to take this to the ministry?'

'No. I want you to work with us. So we bring Natalya Bublik home. This Alamy creature at the airport . . . that's up to you. We—'

'I can go over your head, De Groot.'

He nodded.

'Yes. You can. And I wonder how that will look. However this falls out we'll both be under scrutiny when it's over. Do you want it said we started with a turf war? When a young girl's life's at stake?'

They didn't like that. But they backed down and left for their own offices not long after.

'We should have been told,' Vos said when they were gone, and got a 'damned right' from Bakker straight away.

'We should,' De Groot agreed. 'But we weren't.'


The Kuypers were having dinner in their neat little terrace home by the Herenmarkt. A table by the window. Christmas lights, red and green and blue, blinking in a pattern against the glass.

Outside there were people dining in the West-Indisch Huis. A couple of drunks hanging around in the children's playground, messing about on the swings.

Saskia had gone to bed, exhausted, morose. As if she'd been cheated of something.

Henk Kuyper said little and drank a lot. He couldn't wait to get back to his computer.

Picking at the remains of a pizza she'd bought from the organic store round the corner she gently asked him about that afternoon.

'It was a mistake,' he said. 'We were lucky.'

He poured more red wine and gazed at her. A handsome man with long, flowing dark hair. Didn't smile much of late.

'Where were you?' she asked.

He groaned, glanced at his watch.

'Do we have to go through this again? I had work to do. I'm sorry.' He reached over and took her hand. This was the kind of look that softened her when they argued in the past. 'You've no need to blame yourself.'

'I wasn't.'

'Good.'

'I meant where were you when that woman turned up?'

His mood could change so swiftly. It was black and cold again.

'I told you. I had to make a call.'

'But—'

'No buts. I found Saskia. I went back into all that . . . damned mess and she was there. I saw that jacket I bought her. Then I got her out. What more . . . ?'

The doorbell saved them from an escalating argument. She went downstairs and answered. His father, Lucas, stood there, stiff and tall. More burly than his son. Just past sixty. Still the military officer, always smart, clean-shaven.

A decent man, his life had almost been destroyed by a single, flawed decision with terrible consequences. Henk and Lucas hadn't been on good terms for years. Not that it stopped his father bankrolling their lives.

'Will he speak to me?'

Henk came and stood behind her on the stairs and asked curtly, 'What do you want?'

The older man stepped inside without being asked. His son scowled down at him.

'I want to help. What do you think? You and Renata and Saskia . . . you need security. I can organize something.'

'Security? You? Really?'

What happened in Bosnia twenty years before would never leave either of these two men. She understood and accepted that. Henk had been a child at boarding school. He'd had to live with taunts as the papers went to town on his father. Lucas was a major with a NATO mission at the time, caught between two sides, charged with keeping the peace but lacking the authority and force to impose his will. A mistake had been made. Thousands of innocent people had died as a result. An official inquiry had cleared Lucas Kuyper of any blame. But that didn't stop the opprobrium and the hatred towards his family name.

'Not again, Henk,' the older man warned.

'Why? Because you don't want to hear it?'

'I don't. I'm happy to pay for some discreet security around the house . . .'

'No thanks.'

'Henk . . .'

He came all the way down the stairs and faced up to his father by the door.

'We don't need you. We're Kuypers. Amsterdam aristocracy. Not some poverty-stricken Bosnian Muslim you should have been helping years ago.'

Lucas Kuyper closed his eyes for a second, a look of pain on his lined, grey face.

'AIVD called. They told me what happened. And why.'

Henk folded his arms and grinned.

'Well there's a surprise. Those bastards never let you go, do they? Did they give you a file on me too?'

'What you do with your life's your own business. Saskia and Renata . . .'

Henk Kuyper walked up and held open the door.

'I can look after my own family.' He nodded at the dark street outside. 'Next time call ahead. I'd like some notice. Even better . . . don't bother.'

There was a brief flash of anger on Lucas Kuyper's stern face.

'Can't I even see my own granddaughter?'

'She's in bed. Tired.'

'Henk . . .' Renata intervened. 'We can always—'

'It's been a long day. For all of us.' He nodded at the street again. 'We'll cope.'

The stiff man in the long raincoat walked out into the drizzle. Widowed, he lived on his own in a mansion in the Canal Ring. Renata took Saskia to visit him regularly. He was lonely. Always pleased to see them. Henk never came.

'We'd be screwed if he cut off the money,' she said, and regretted immediately the mercenary tone of the remark. It wasn't how she meant it.

Henk shooed her back up the stairs.

'He'll never do that. Imagine the shame. A Kuyper on the breadline.'

She followed him back into the dining room, watched as he sat down and reached for the wine bottle.

'Saskia loves her grandfather. She doesn't understand why you don't.'

He nodded.

'One day, when she's older, I'll tell her. About Srebrenica. About power and war and what soldiers like him do. Then she'll understand.'

'You're too good for the rest of us,' she said as he poured himself more wine.

'You could drink with me,' he suggested. 'That might help.'

'Would it?' she asked.

'Maybe not.'

She still didn't understand why he'd found Saskia then made himself scarce.

'Don't open a second bottle,' she said then went to the living room and turned on the TV.

A few minutes later she heard his footsteps clumping up the stairs to his little gable office.

There was only one story on the news. The outrage in Leidseplein. No mention of a missing girl at all. Did Henk care? Did anyone?

She steeled herself and tiptoed up the stairs. The door to the tiny office was ajar. He was at the computer, the pallid light of the monitor flooding his stolid face.

'Can we talk?'

He sighed and got up from the desk.

'Not now,' he said and closed the door.


For thirty minutes De Groot listened to AIVD. Then another half hour was spent going through the logs. The commissaris set out what he wanted: an immediate review of the overnight investigation.

'Mirjam Fransen's right about one thing, Pieter. There are a lot of boats in Amsterdam. And we've nothing from this dead clown to point us in the right direction.'

Frank de Groot shook his head.

'I want you all wide awake tomorrow when this call comes in. Talk to the mother. Tell her we're doing everything we can. Check we're on course. After that go home and get some sleep.'

Bakker didn't move.

'I'd like to run over the CCTV we've got of Leidseplein.'

De Groot frowned.

'There are about forty different feeds. It'll take days, weeks to go through all of them.'

She wasn't happy with that. Any more than Vos. They had what seemed to be a version of events now, based on an initial interview with Saskia Kuyper and others in the square. Bouali had grabbed hold of the girl when she wandered off near the theatre then promised to find her parents. Saskia hadn't liked the way he was acting. So when he was distracted she gave him the slip.

After that they were left with guesswork. The assumption was that Bouali alerted one of his accomplices, dressed as a Black Pete too, who picked up Natalya Bublik by mistake. The two girls did look similar and they had an identical pink jacket with a very specific design.

'Timing,' Bakker said. 'It seems . . . confusing. And the Kuyper girl . . .'

'What?' Vos asked.

He'd sat in on that interview for a while. It seemed straightforward.

'She sounded really vague,' Bakker complained. 'That was all.'

'She's eight years old,' De Groot grumbled. 'What do you expect?'

'Just a touch more detail. It was almost as if she was telling a story.'

'Enough of this,' the commissaris insisted. 'Leidseplein had something like ten thousand people in it at the time. What looked like bombs going off. The kid had just been snatched. No big surprise she can't dictate a decent witness statement.'

'That's why I want to look at the video.'

De Groot glanced at Vos as if to say: this is your call.

'We need to look,' Vos agreed. 'But in the morning.'

He got up, brushed down his blue jeans and shabby donkey jacket. It still bore dust from the chaos in the square.

Downstairs they discovered Hanna Bublik had left the station already. Nothing Van der Berg could say would keep her there.

'I need to reconfirm the existence of beer on this planet,' the detective said mournfully.

Silence.

'Pieter?' he asked.

'Not tonight,' Vos said then wandered out without another word, strolled alone down Elandsgracht, picked up Sam from the Drie Vaten and led the dog across the gangplank onto the cold, dark boat.

———

The police had done their best to be friendly, especially the dishevelled, polite brigadier who seemed to be in charge. When they finally ran out of vague promises a friendly, bleary-eyed detective called Van der Berg took her to reception, gave her his card and one for the brigadier, Vos, then offered to find a lift home. While they were talking another man came up, miserable and guilty. He introduced himself as Koeman and said he was the officer dressed as Black Pete she'd first approached when Natalya went missing. The one who'd given her a hard time.

The moment he started a stuttering apology she just looked at him once then walked out.

November drizzle was putting a sheen on the broad street outside the police station. She didn't want their lift any more than she craved an apology. All she needed was Natalya back home.

They seemed to understand the price of that. The release of a man she'd never heard of. And money perhaps. How much they didn't know. Didn't seem to want to discuss it either. She was a foreigner. On tourist papers. No right to work, even as a whore. All she had to her name was three and half thousand euros kept in cash, stuffed in an envelope beneath Natalya's mattress, the pile steadily growing as she worked over the months.

As soon as it reached five she'd be able to put down a deposit on a place of her own. Try to find a real job. Hairdressing maybe. Or looking after little kids. She liked that idea. Felt she might be good at it. Perhaps overly protective but that would diminish with the years. One day they'd become normal, the way they used to be in Gori. One day she'd be able to walk down the street without feeling people were looking at her.

It took twenty minutes to get back to Oude Nieuwstraat. The red lights were on in the cabins running down from her house. Girls in the windows, sitting in their underwear, smiling, beckoning at the few men stumbling up and down the shiny cobblestones, hoods up, just looking mostly.

Chantal met her on the stairs. She looked shocked, worried. Younger than usual. No make-up either.

'The police were here,' the Filipina girl said. 'They said someone took Nat.'

She always shortened her daughter's name. It annoyed the hell out of her.

'What do they want, Hanna?'

'I don't know,' she replied and that was true.

'But . . .'

'Not now!'

She wasn't going to discuss this with the girl. And that wasn't because Marnixstraat told her not to talk to anyone about the case.

Chantal shifted on her bare feet. She was wearing girlish pyjamas with a flower pattern on them. No more work that day.

She glanced up the stairs in a way that meant something.

'What is it?'

The girl ran a nervous hand through her dark hair.

'I was out all afternoon. There was no one here. When I came back . . .' She nodded at the door. 'It was open. Someone's been in our rooms. They pinched some of my clothes. I didn't have . . .'

Hanna went up the narrow staircase, all the way to the little gable room at the top. The door was open. When she went in she could see straight away what had happened.

The few clothes they had were scattered around. Natalya's single bed had been turned over, the mattress spilled on the floor.

The padded brown envelope which contained all their money was ripped open and empty. They'd even taken the necklace her husband had given her when they were married all those years before. It was cheap, an amber pendant on a silver chain. But she'd kept it, let Natalya wear the thing from time to time. A reminder of when they'd been a family. Together. In love. Seemingly secure.

Chantal stood behind her in the door and said, 'I don't know how they got in.'

As if that mattered.

'They want the rent tomorrow,' the Filipina kid added. 'Will you be OK?'

'Not now. Can I borrow some?'

She said nothing.

Hanna turned on her.

'I've lent you money when you needed it. You know you'll get it back. What with Natalya . . . I might need money there too.'

Her round, brown eyes grew wide.

'What kind of money?'

'I . . . I don't know. They haven't said. I don't . . .'

No family. No friends. No one to turn to. That was the cost of coming all this way. Why it was so important nothing happened to them until she managed to find her feet.

She put Natalya's bed back the right way and returned the mattress, tucking in the sheets without thinking. They needed washing. So did some of her clothes.

The pink jacket.

A sudden wave of regret brought tears to her eyes. According to the sympathetic detective in Marnixstraat that was all that caused this mistake. The fact that her daughter and the kid of some wealthy Dutch family shared the same piece of clothing. A jacket Hanna would never have bought in the first place. It was too expensive. The thing had come to her as an odd gift. A tip from a customer who'd seen the two of them later on the street then found her again in a cabin not long after.

'You could always have a word with Cem,' Chantal said. 'Just do what he wants. You'll get the money. Maybe . . .' Her hand went to her hair. 'Maybe he can help with Natalya too. He knows people.'

'Like terrorists?'

That's what Marnixstraat said. They'd snatched her thinking

she was the granddaughter of a notorious Dutch soldier, one who'd been mixed up in a massacre a couple of decades before.

A black monster rolling up the stairs. An idle boast: *I'll kill it.* What kind of mother had she been?

'I don't know,' the girl whined. 'It was just a thought. You could call the police. About the money . . .'

'I didn't say they took money. Did I?'

'Why'd you want some from me, then?' Chantal snapped then walked back downstairs and slammed her door shut.

No choices now. None at all.

Hanna Bublik showered and got some work clothes. As she was about to go out her phone rang. It was the brigadier from Marnixstraat, Vos.

'Do you know anything?' she asked.

'We're working on some leads.' He sounded like a bad liar. 'I meant to ask. Do you know anyone with a boat?'

The question astonished her.

'A boat? Are you serious?'

He sighed. It was a patient sound. Not aimed at her.

'Yes. I'm serious. I think she's on a boat.'

'We don't really know anyone here. No one with a boat.'

He made sure she had his mobile number, said she was to call him any time, day or night.

'Is there anything I can do to help now?' he asked.

She looked at the little room and the ripped brown envelope.

'Nothing I can think of. Apart from the obvious.'

'I'll get Natalya back. We'll give them whatever they want.'

'Including money?'

'If it comes to that.'

There didn't seem anything left to say or ask. When he was gone she got her clothes, the cheap condoms, the gels, put them in the little plastic washbag that came with the beauty kit her husband bought her the last Christmas he was alive. Then she walked up Oude Nieuwstraat until she found a spare cabin, called the number for the rental guy, paid for three hours. That took half the money she had left.

The tiny booth was too hot from the electric fire. It smelled of damp and sweat from whoever had it before.

She stripped down to her cheap gold satin bra and knickers then perched on the high stool in the window. There to discover what she should have known. No one wanted a weeping whore, at any price.


Across the city Natalya Bublik sat where she was told, arms round herself in the pink jacket she'd hated from the outset. The only fixed points in her small life at that moment were sounds: the gentle lap of water against a wooden hull, the occasional screech of a bird, the rattle and hoots of trains pulling in and out of Centraal station.

Black Pete was still in the boat. Maybe two of them, beyond the locked wooden door. She'd do whatever they wanted, everything they said. Because somewhere, deep in the soft, formless depths of her memory, was an echo of this strange sequence of events. In a story her mother told her. Or a half-forgotten, deep-buried recollection hidden inside the nightmare that kept returning, that of a shadowy monster rolling up the stairs.

Real or imagined there was a message here, one she would not forget.

Do not move and do not speak.

Be nothing. Do nothing except wait and watch and think.

Then one day you will be invisible. And in that single precious moment slip free.

# 2

Hanna Bublik was waiting for Vos when he showed up at Marnixstraat the next morning. Sam trotted along beside him on a lead. Sofia Albers had to go out of town to see her sick mother. Someone in admin could look after the dog until she got back.

'What kind of policeman brings his pet to work?' she asked as the little terrier sat at her feet, bright eyes begging for attention.

'Sam's not a pet. He doesn't like being left on his own.'

The dog put a paw on her leg. Same clothes as the day before. Fake designer jacket, nylon masquerading as leather. Cheap jeans. No make-up on her thin, lined face. Poverty hung around this woman and she didn't like it.

'Down, boy,' he said gently and passed the lead over to the genial clerk from the back office who'd come out to greet them.

She watched the woman walk Sam away, chattering to him.

'I promised Natalya a dog. When we get our own place.'

'Then I'm sure she'll get one someday.'

He found some coffee. Bakker turned up. She'd started to dress less conspicuously now she was settling into Marnixstraat. No more home-made suits from her aunt back in Dokkum in Friesland. Today black trousers, a blue jacket, a plain jumper underneath. Her red hair tied back tightly behind her head. A look that said: *professional.* And . . . *I'm here to stay.*

The three of them went into an interview room together. The voice recorder stayed off.

'So you know nothing?' Hanna said when he had briefed her on the investigation.

'No,' Vos insisted. 'We know he took your girl by mistake. We know she's still in the city. We're looking for some associates of the man who was shot.'

'Nothing,' she repeated.

'Hanna,' Bakker said. 'This is the most important inquiry we have at the moment. We'll do everything we can to bring Natalya back.'

'And he'll call,' Vos added. 'He has to. They want something. As long as they do . . .'

The lost look on her face silenced him.

'Do you know anyone in Amsterdam?' Bakker asked her.

'Most of the people I meet don't give me a name. A real one anyway.'

Vos glanced at his watch without thinking. She glared at him for that.

'Am I wasting your time?'

'No. I was wondering when he might ring.'

'He said he wants money. How much?'

That had puzzled Vos. Still did.

'He was vague . . .'

'How can I pay him? The likes of me?'

A good question. One that worried him.

'Let's deal with that when it happens.'

'And this man he wants released? Who's he?'

Vos had thought he might not need to address that question. That the papers would offer all the answers that morning. They were full of the outrage in Leidseplein and the shooting of a young Briton who'd adopted a foreign name and thrown three flash grenades into the crowd. But there wasn't a single word about the kidnapping of a child. Given the time the press had to work on the story there could be only one explanation. Someone, De Groot or AIVD, had demanded and got a media blackout on the grounds that it might jeopardize the case.

He gave her the brief facts.

'I want to see this man Alamy,' Hanna Bublik said. 'I want to look into his face and ask him why my daughter's been stolen from me.'

'Why don't we find you somewhere to sit here?' Bakker suggested. 'We can keep you up to date during the day.'

'No!' Her voice wasn't shrill. Nowhere near hysterical. It was firm and controlled and when she spoke she looked only at Vos. 'What good am I doing like that?'

'If . . .'

'You wanted to go over the CCTV footage,' Vos cut in.

Bakker nodded.

'Then do it. We can talk to Alamy. If he can say something. Give us a message to pass on . . .'

Hanna looked at him, surprised. As if not many people took note of what she said.

'You'll do this?'

He got up, checked Renata Kuyper's phone. Lots of battery. A good signal.

'We need to go now. Laura, have a word with De Groot's office. Get us clearance into the secure unit at Schiphol. We'll keep it brief. Either Alamy plays along or he doesn't.'

Hanna finished her coffee, got up from the table. Looked grateful.

'What if the kidnapper calls?' Bakker asked.

He took out the phone.

'Everything coming into this line gets monitored whether I'm here or not. Control can listen in the moment I answer. He won't ring from a traceable phone. We know that . . .'

'But . . .'

He pointed to the door.

'Talk to Frank's office,' he said. 'We're leaving now.'


An awkward breakfast in the narrow house on the Herenmarkt. Saskia picked at her cereal, barely eating. Henk Kuyper ate steadily in silence, going over the details in the paper. He looked a little hung-over.

'Why's there no mention of what happened?' Renata asked when he wouldn't look up from the page. 'The girl . . .'

'They print what they're told,' he muttered and reached for another croissant. 'What do you expect?'

She blinked, fought to hold back the fury.

'This isn't a game. One of your crusades. It's about real people. That little kid's gone missing . . .'

Saskia brushed back her long fair hair and put her hands over her ears. Then shut her eyes tightly.

A nod at their daughter.

'Don't you think she's been through enough?'

'Jesus! It's nothing to what that poor woman's having to face. Are you serious?'

He reached out and touched Saskia's hair, then stroked her cheek. She opened her eyes and smiled at him. Renata couldn't read the look on her daughter's face. The girl was always closer to her father. Henk was never there to tell her what to do. He was in his study, working the computer, making quiet phone calls. Fixing the world. Drinking wine. She was the one who had to tell Saskia to tidy her room. To stay and do her homework however much she hated it.

'Go and get ready for school, sweetheart,' he said. 'Mummy and Daddy need to talk.'

Straight away the girl got up from the table and went into the bathroom, closed the door.

'She's not going to school,' Renata said. 'It's not safe.'

He laughed.

'There's nothing to worry about. If there was we wouldn't be able to move for police.'

'Your father . . .'

He leaned over the table and took her hands. The way he did when he wanted something.

'Do you think I'd let her out of the front door if I thought there was the slightest chance she'd come to harm?'

Put the onus on her. Always. She recognized this gambit so well.

'No. But if Lucas is willing to pay for some security . . .'

'I'm not taking any more from him than we need. He's the reason they targeted her in the first place.'

'All the same . . .'

'He said he'd hold the Georgian kid instead. You heard that, didn't you? You told me.'

That bugged her too.

'Where did you go? Why weren't you there?'

His face fell.

'I had to take a call. This is getting tedious.'

'From work? On a Sunday?'

'From work. It was international. Couldn't miss it.'

The police had taken the Georgian woman to Marnixstraat after her daughter was snatched while she and Saskia got interviewed in a van near the Melkweg. Henk had joined her there part way through.

'I needed you . . .'

His hand left her.

'I found Saskia. I walked that square until I spotted her jacket. She was alone, hiding near the stores. While you—'

'I didn't know what to do!' she shrieked.

'You're upset,' he said. 'It's understandable. I'll take her to school today. I'll talk to the teachers. Make sure they keep an eye on her.'

'Why can't we be normal?' she murmured.

'I don't know what you mean. How exactly have I failed you now?'

'I still don't understand how she got away from that man.'

He stared at her and shook his head.

'She told us. She ran away when he wasn't looking.'

'When he wasn't looking?' she echoed, voice high and cracked. 'Just like that?'

'You sound as if you wished she hadn't.'

She dashed her knife on the table. From somewhere a church bell sounded. Pigeons cooed out in the street. A car honked its horn. The city went about its business, unaware that somewhere tragedy was hiding in the shadows, waiting for its moment.

'Don't say that, Henk! Don't you dare say that.'

'I'll get her ready for school . . .'

'I want to take Saskia away for a few days.'

His head went to one side.

'Where?'

'Spain. Italy. Just for a week.'

'Who's going to book the tickets? Organize the hotel? How will you cope?'

'I can cope . . .'

He laughed off the idea. She watched him check his watch, pick up his tablet computer, flick through the messages there as if this strained conversation was of no consequence.

'You want me to leave, don't you?' she asked and waited for the sudden storm to break.

Yet that rarely happened. Even when he was arguing with his father.

'Not again,' he said with a sigh. 'You're upset. If you want to go away for a while. That's fine. On your own. Saskia stays here. We can manage.'

He tapped at the screen.

'Say where. I can book it. Rome? Might be warmer in Morocco.' He kept his eyes on her. 'If you meet someone I really don't mind.'

She closed her eyes and muttered an obscenity.

'Have we come to this?' Renata whispered.

When she opened them Saskia was back, ready for school. Henk had his arms round her.

'I really think Mummy should take a break,' he said looking down at their daughter. 'Don't you?'

Daddy's girl. Always.

'Yes,' Saskia said.

Renata rushed to the door and grabbed her coat. 'Time for school,' she said. 'Get your things.'

Saskia stayed at the table, head down. Pretty fair hair combed and straight and clean. Only came the third time her mother demanded.

He watched them go. Checked his watch. Made a call. Then went out himself.

De Groot cleared Vos's visit to the Schiphol detention centre straight away. Bakker went back to her office and found Van der Berg. He was hunched over a computer screen watching CCTV from the night before.

'I should have known something would happen,' he said. 'As soon as Pieter said we were going to have dinner.'

'Beer. A tosti. A boiled egg.' She pulled up a chair and sat next to him. 'I'm used to it by now.'

It was almost six months since De Groot took her on full time after the doll's house case. The brittle, naive young woman she'd been back then had matured a little. Marnixstraat had come to accept her. Laura Bakker had brought Vos back into the fold after his breakdown and fall from grace. No one else had managed that.

'Is Pieter OK?' Van der Berg asked.

He was a curious man. Heavyset, bumbling, almost feckless on the surface. Rarely went straight home to his wife. There was always a bar to visit along the way. But Vos had told her he was one of the most able detectives in the building. The best when it came to a murder investigation.

'He looks OK to me. I wish he'd fix up his boat. It's still a mess.'

'Agreed.' Van der Berg smiled pleasantly. 'But he's happy. He's got his little dog. That nice woman in the bar to do his washing . . .'

Was he fishing? She wasn't sure.

'He can't go on like that.'

'Why not?' Van der Berg asked.

'Because . . . at some point you have to grow up.'

He snorted then jabbed his finger directly on the computer screen the way some men did.

'There's footage from an awful lot of cameras here. We need to hand it over to forensic to sort out. Too much for us to deal with right now.'

'What else do we have?'

Koeman was trying to pick up more from the British man's associates. That was going nowhere.

'Have you seen a pink jacket?' she asked, pointing at the monitor.

'A couple.' He rolled through some footage and came on the frame. It had to be the Bublik girl after she was snatched. She was on the city side of the square, with a Black Pete figure in a green costume. Bakker looked at the time: just two minutes after the first grenade.

'That doesn't work,' she said.

He looked interested.

'Why?'

'Not enough time. Saskia told us she'd wandered away from her mother because she was arguing with the woman from uniform. She wanted to see Sinterklaas. As soon as the grenades went off Bouali . . . Bowers . . . whatever we call him grabbed her.'

'Correct,' he agreed.

Bakker pulled up a map of the area.

'Then he took her out of the square somewhere close to the casino. He got distracted. She ran away.'

Van der Berg nodded.

'That's got to take two minutes at least,' Bakker went on. 'Probably more.'

They had to assume there were at least two Black Petes in the abduction attempt. How else could Saskia's phone have changed hands? Then, in the confusion, the second went on to snatch Natalya by mistake when he saw the pink jacket, after Saskia had got free.

'Maybe the timer on the camera's wrong,' he suggested.

She didn't say anything, just looked at him.

'Unless you have another idea?' Van der Berg added.

Bakker pulled up a transcript of the witness statements taken from Renata Kuyper and her daughter the previous day.

'How did the first Black Pete know she was wearing a pink jacket?'

Van der Berg frowned.

'Because he followed her all the way from their house in the Herenmarkt. Not hard to work out Lucas Kuyper's granddaughter lived there. He saw what the girl was wearing and told his friend.'

She waited.

Van der Berg scanned the other pictures of the square.

'So you lose the kid you want,' he said. 'You meet your accomplice. Pass on the phone you took from her. And he picks up the nearest one with the same jacket by mistake. Could happen. Not sure why.'

'Timing,' Bakker said, pointing at the clock on the screen. 'From what we know it looks as if Black Pete Two's snatching Natalya just around when Saskia makes a break for it. Before maybe.'

Van der Berg screwed up his nose.

'We need to get that girl and her mother back in here.'

'And the father,' she added.

He went back to the screen.

'I can't see him anywhere. Where the hell did he get to? What . . . ?'

She went quiet. Koeman had turned up, dyed moustache more droopy than ever. Thom Geerts, the cheerless AIVD officer, was with him, looking inquisitive.

'Our spooky friends want to know if we've found anything,' Koeman told them.

'Still looking,' Van der Berg replied, eyeing the big, smartly dressed man. 'How are you doing this morning?'

Koeman grumbled something and walked off.

'I want a rundown on where you are,' Geerts said. 'Where's Vos?'

'He got called away,' Bakker told him. 'Not sure why.'

'You don't know where your investigating officer is?'

'I saw him with his dog,' Van der Berg said with a grin. 'Maybe Sam needed a walk.'

The AIVD man scowled at them.

'Isn't there a dress code round here? Give me an update by email. I've got things to do.'

'I'm sure you have,' Van der Berg murmured watching him leave, phone in hand.

Bakker rolled back her chair and whispered a mild curse. Van der Berg had turned up in his usual scruffy brown sports jacket and black trousers, tan shoes. With Vos forever in a donkey jacket, black sweater and old jeans they weren't a great sartorial advertisement for the force, knew it and didn't mind in the least.

'Are they always like that?' Bakker asked.

'Not always,' Van der Berg said.

'If he'd asked nicely we'd have told him. Wouldn't we?'

'Possibly,' he replied and nodded at her black suit. 'You look smart. Did your auntie make it?'

'C&A. They had a sale.'

He grinned. Pulled on the lapel of his brown jacket.

'Me too!'

She looked distracted. Bakker could do this sometimes. Drift off into a little reverie of her own.

'When?' she asked.

He let go of the jacket.

'A while back. A year or two . . .'

'No, Dirk. I meant . . . when's he going to call? The man who's got Natalya?'

A wan smile.

'When he feels like it. Nothing we can do is going to change that. You have to learn to wait.'

'But I hate waiting. And that nice man from AIVD isn't throwing anything our way.' A pause. 'What do we do?'

He pointed at the PC monitor and the CCTV footage.

'How about we try to make sense of that?'


Vos had clearance by the time they got to Schiphol. Two duty officers accompanied him and Hanna Bublik into the secure unit next to the sprawling airport terminal. Parts of it seemed relatively normal: holding areas for people detained at immigration, due for deportation. There was an outside space for exercise. Some men were lazily kicking a football around as they walked past. Then they went down a long passageway protected by high fencing and the mood changed. A body scanner, a pat down. More ID checks. The officers didn't like the look of Hanna Bublik at all and got quite short with her.

When they went away to check with Marnixstraat one last time Vos said, by way of apology, 'They don't know. If they did . . .'

She stared at him then asked why there was nothing in the papers. He told her about the blackout.

'And if this had been that other girl? The Dutch girl? With her rich parents?'

'It would have been exactly the same,' Vos said though he wasn't sure she believed him.

After a couple of minutes they were led through an electronic security door into a narrow, closed-off corridor. Grey metal floor, grey metal walls. Doors at regular intervals. Nothing on them except a small surveillance window with bars and a smart lock.

'Two people with you inside,' the guard said. 'Those are the rules.'

Vos had read the file the night before. Ismail Alamy styled himself a preacher. There was evidence to suggest he'd radical- ized a good number of young men, sent some of them to madrassas in Pakistan which had links with extremist groups, among them the network led by the shadowy figure Barbone. But he'd never been found with weapons or accused of violence himself.

'Fine,' he said and they walked into the cell. A single bed, neatly made. A tiny window looking out onto the recreational area. Seated cross-legged on the sheets was a small, unremark- able man in a bright orange boiler suit. In spite of the overlong beard he seemed younger than fifty-one, the age the reports gave, with a quick and mobile face and brown eyes that watched and judged them as they entered.

'Where's my lawyer?' Alamy asked in good English.

'You don't need one,' Vos said, showing his ID. There was a small TV set in the opposite wall. 'Do you know what happened yesterday? The attack? In the city?'

The Moroccan laughed and gestured at the cell.

'In case you didn't notice . . . I have an alibi.'

Hanna stared at him.

'Who is this woman?' Alamy asked. 'She doesn't look like one of you.'

'She isn't,' Vos said and started to tell him the story that wasn't on the TV.

Natalya Bublik had slept somehow. When she woke she could just make out daylight leaking through the cracks in the deck above her. The girl was no stranger to confined spaces. In Oude Nieuwstraat she'd shared the tiny gable room with her mother. Before that they'd moved around Georgia, never staying anywhere long. Skipping overnight sometimes. To avoid men who wanted money. She was old enough to understand that.

Tall for her age, smart, observant. There'd been a game she'd played for as long as she could remember. One that took her out of the world when it was bad.

Now seemed a good time to recover it. So she used the portable toilet in the corner of the tiny cabin, washed her hands and face in the bowl using the small lump of soap they'd left. Ate the bread she found on a plate, drank the orange juice. Then went back to the bed, lay on the hard mattress and closed her eyes.

*Imagine.*

Ducks. She could hear them quacking close by, bickering like the younger kids in the playground at the school her mother found for her. Sometimes she thought she even heard their tiny webbed feet strike against the hull.

Boats moving. Small engines, ripples through waves. The smell of diesel and dank water. This wasn't a busy place, she thought.

A railway line. Lots of trains moving to and fro. Not near but not so far she couldn't identify the sound. And in her head imagine the people on them, going to work, to school, into the city for all the reasons she knew too well and never mentioned. It wasn't just the black monster that followed them everywhere, lumbering through the night. Sometimes it was men. Embarrassed, awkward men shuffling up to the red-light windows along the street.

There was a connection there, one that left her mother both happy and sad.

It involved money. A present for her once. The pink jacket with the ponies. Expensive her mother said. All the more reason to sell it, Natalya thought. They needed the money and she hated pink, had no idea what use a pony might be.

The thing was the warmest clothing she had. And didn't much keep out the cold.

Outside she heard footsteps. A sudden angry flash of guilt hit her. All the time she'd been listening for things that might comfort her. The birds. The distant sounds of the city. Not taking note of the fact there was a man in the next room. Had been all along.

Just one at that moment. She felt sure of that. He spoke on the phone sometimes, too softly for her to hear. And once, she thought, he'd gone outside. There'd been the sound of steps on stairs, on a deck above, then a walkway. Then he came back.

Or another one did. She'd no idea and that was maddening.

Some time later he started moving things around.

Another one. That was what her imagination told her. They took turns. Like teachers at lessons. Or guards in a prison.

Natalya looked around and thought she had a good idea where she was. In the bow of a boat rocking lazily on the water. A space so small it might have been meant for storage, not to live in. Only a child could manage that. For how long?

As she watched the small, black painted door that must lead back to the main cabin opened with a creak. She sat on the bed and waited. As curious as she was scared. Would he still be in the odd green outfit? Curly wig? Black make-up? Red lips? White eyes and teeth?

A large shadow filled the door and then he walked in, so tall he had to crouch in the limited space.

A man in jeans, a black jacket, black balaclava.

She wanted to laugh, to throw an insult at him.

*You're scared of me? An eight-year-old girl? A foreigner whose mother has to deal with strangers just so we can eat?*

But she knew that wouldn't be wise.

'I want to go home,' she said instead.

There was a supermarket bag in his hands. Marqt. The organic place her mother wanted to shop but never could afford. He pulled out a packet of crisps, some tiny cheeses. Bread and bottles of soft drinks. A couple of toilet rolls. A toothbrush and toothpaste. A few packets of brightly coloured sweets. A box of crayons, a colouring book, and a cheap games console.

'I want a shower. I want to wash my hair.'

The balaclava nodded. He seemed surprised by that.

'You can't,' he said. 'Not yet.'

Then put the console on the table.

She stared at the pink plastic toy. That had a pony on it too.

'I don't play kiddy games,' Natalya said and stared at him.

A man too cowardly to show his face. Who hid behind a balaclava in front of a schoolkid. She hated the ones she knew her mother dealt with in the street. Even the man who left the present.

'Stay here. Do as we say. Be good. No harm will come to you, Natalya.'

He was Dutch. Sounded . . . like one of the teachers at her school. Clever. Sure of himself. Surprised she wouldn't cower in front of him.

*We,* she thought.

So she was right. He wasn't alone.

Outside a squabble between the ducks turned loud and aggressive. He picked up the little console, put it in his pocket, and got up.

She reached for the colouring book.

'This is for a baby,' she said. 'I want one with puzzles. Numbers.'

He sat down, took the book off her. Flicked through the pages, found something at the back and handed it over.

Sums. Addition. Subtraction. Multiply and divide.

They were easy. Natalya got the pen and flicked through them, line by line, scribbling the answers.

'This is for a baby too,' she moaned.

He got the book back, looked at it from behind the balaclava.

A teacher, she thought. They did that too.

'You got one sum wrong,' he said and jabbed his finger at the fourth question down the page.

Three times thirteen. She'd written in 'forty-one' for some reason. She scribbled over the answer and pencilled in a correction over the top. Then turned the page. The book went back to simple colouring games and 'spot the difference' pictures. She handed it to him and said nothing.

'I'll try and find you something harder,' he said and left, shutting the little door behind him.

A padlock, she thought. And a bolt on the other side.

She ripped open the sweets, got a couple out and started to chew.


Outside the city, in another cell, Ismail Alamy listened, nodding. When Vos was finished he opened his hands, frowned then asked, 'And . . . ?'

'An innocent child's been kidnapped to free you.'

'I have nothing to do with this,' the Moroccan insisted. 'No knowledge it was planned. No idea who these brothers might be. Do you have reason to believe otherwise?'

His hand rose, a practised gesture. An index finger and a long orange sleeve jabbed at them. Alamy was the preacher from the videos then.

'I'm as innocent as this child. And yet here I linger in captivity. Without charges. Without evidence. All so that you may send me back to a regime without the so-called democracy you worship. Where they torture men and women—'

'This isn't about you,' Hanna interrupted. 'It's about my daughter.'

'My hands are clean,' he said, pretending to wash them. 'Why waste your time? Besides . . .' A sudden grin. 'Soon there'll be news from the court in Strasbourg. They'll release me. I've no stain upon my record here. Nor my character. You've no reason to deprive me of my liberty.'

He'd arrived on a fake Libyan passport. Claimed political asylum from the then Gaddafi regime. Vos knew all this and was determined not to rise to the bait.

'All I want you to do is make a statement we can pass on to them,' he said. 'These people are your followers. If you ask them to release Natalya Bublik perhaps they will.'

The Moroccan scowled at them.

'I'm a man of God. I have no followers. Or any idea who these brothers might be.'

Hanna blinked, clutched her hands, bent forward, looked at him.

'She's my little girl. All I have. No father. He died in one more stupid war.'

'You think you're alone in this?' Alamy asked. 'You think I don't have a thousand . . . a hundred thousand tragedies . . . to set against yours?'

'If you say something and they ignore you . . . so what?' she asked, her strong voice close to breaking. 'Where's the harm? And if they listen . . .'

'A statement?' he asked curtly. 'That says what?'

'Let my little girl go,' she pleaded. 'Eight years old. She's no part in this.'

What amused geniality there was in his face vanished.

'We're all a part of this, woman. The world's divided. Between good and evil. Right and wrong. Those who believe and may be saved. Those who deny and will burn for it.'

Vos watched, hoping.

'One short statement,' she persisted. 'You say you don't want my daughter held on your account. No sides there. No complicated arguments.'

He was hesitating. Vos found this interesting on several fronts. Then the door burst open. Alamy looked up and all doubt fled from his face.

Mirjam Fransen was there. Furious.

'What's going on, Vos?' the AIVD woman demanded. 'Who gave you permission for this?'

Vos shook his head.

'You're following me?'

'Geerts went into Marnixstraat. They said you were out. It wasn't hard to find out where.'

Alamy hunched up on his single bed and scowled at the three of them.

'I've nothing more to add. This . . . discussion is ended.'

Hanna was on him straight away, clutching at the arm of his orange suit, begging, close to tears.

'Get this whore away from me,' he spat. 'Get—'

She broke then. Hands flying. Screaming. Tearing at his sleeves.

Vos strode over, took her arms. Led her to the door. Pushed past Fransen and the two detention officers until they were back in the corridor.

'How does he know who I am?' Hanna demanded. 'Who told him? You?'

'No one—'

'Do I wear a badge? Is it in my face?'

'Hanna. Hanna . . .'

Mirjam Fransen followed, watched, arms folded, interested but uninvolved.

'You touched him,' Vos said. 'That's all—'

'If I was that Kuyper woman . . .'

'He would have said the same thing.' Vos turned to Fransen. 'If we talk to Alamy again he may make that statement. One sentence. That's all. That he doesn't support this action. That may . . .'

She looked at the two guards.

'This prisoner is our responsibility. The police have no business here. You allow no one in to see him again without my permission. Do I make myself clear?'

They knew her. They nodded.

'Five minutes,' Vos pleaded. 'Why would you object to this?'

She pointed at the corridor and the electronic gate at the end.

'There are matters of national security here that don't concern you, Vos. Get back to Marnixstraat. Do your job. Stay away from ours.'

'Five minutes,' he begged.

'Not possible.' She beckoned to the guards. 'Get them out of here.'


Saskia's school was a short walk away from the Herenmarkt. A private place with a small playground. Renata Kuyper got herself a cappuccino from a nearby cafe and sat on a bench near the gates trying to think. The coffee got cold. She fetched another, closed her eyes, called home. No answer. Called his mobile. Got voicemail.

After a while it was break time and a noisy gaggle of kids, all well-dressed, the offspring of Amsterdam's middle and upper classes, tumbled out into the little square. She watched the children bouncing balls, chattering, playing on the slides, the swings and the single roundabout.

Couldn't force from her head the picture of another girl somewhere else in the city. Lost. Trapped. Not a word about it in the papers. AIVD had called Henk the previous night to tell them to keep quiet about what happened too. Publicity might endanger the child, they said.

Across the road, in the playground by the canal, Saskia was running around with her classmates still wearing the pink jacket Henk had bought her. In spite of everything that had happened she'd demanded it that morning and Henk, to Renata's disgust, had given in. She wasn't a smart child. That disappointed Henk, not that he let his daughter know.

Renata sipped at the new coffee. Then someone sat on the bench next to her. The suddenness of his appearance scared her a little.

Heavy winter coat. Sad, long pale face with chiselled cheeks, smooth from a careful razor. Lucas Kuyper wasn't elderly but he was getting there. The years and the pressure had worn him down.

He was gripping a paper cup of coffee too. Steam rising from the top. He touched her cup and smiled.

All the small words then, the easy pleasantries. Henk's father was so old-fashioned. Gentle of manner, quiet and thoughtful in conversation. It was hard to imagine him as a military man. Just as it was hard sometimes to imagine Henk as a hectic freelance activist, throwing himself into endless campaigns, usually over the web. About what she wasn't clear.

'You won't tell him I was here, will you?'

'Of course not, Lucas. Not if you don't want me to.'

'I think it might be best. After last night . . .'

It wasn't just last night. There always seemed a coldness between them. Sometimes it almost appeared deliberate.

'You're not going to hang around here all day, are you?' she said. 'Really . . . if the police thought there was any reason to worry about us they'd be here.'

He shrugged.

'I know. I'm sure you're right. It's just . . . I don't have a lot else to do to be honest. So I came out for a walk.'

He'd been widowed three years earlier. Henk had barely spoken to his father at the funeral. Now Lucas lived alone near the Nine Streets, wandering the shops there when he felt like it, buying presents Saskia didn't need, then going home to his grand and empty mansion, no company except for the cleaner who came twice a week.

What happened in Bosnia appeared to have destroyed his life. His relationship with his son. Both were irrecoverable, and now it seemed it almost cost them Saskia.

'Why do you blame yourself about Srebrenica?' she asked. 'They decided what happened wasn't your fault.'

'Henk doesn't think so.'

'No. But Henk doesn't see much good in anyone.'

'It can't have been easy for him either,' Lucas Kuyper said. 'All the hatred. Some of it came his way.'

'If they decided it wasn't your fault who are you to argue?'

That didn't seem to please him.

'Because I was there and they weren't. We'd no idea those people were headed for a massacre. Even if we had . . .' He closed his eyes and there was such a look of pain on his lined face she wanted him to stop. 'The truth is . . . even then we couldn't have stopped it. We were a peacekeeping force. Not an army. Not fit or set for combat. If I'd had the weapons and the clearance . . .'

'Then you'd have died too.'

He nodded.

'Possibly. But if that had happened there would have been a reaction. Perhaps those eight thousand innocents would be alive. Or free to suffer another day.'

The Kuypers were a military family. Lucas followed a long line of army officers going back more than a century and a half. That ended with Henk.

'You did your duty,' she insisted.

'Did I?' he replied with an uncharacteristic edge in his voice. 'Henk was at boarding school when the publicity started. He had a terrible time. Me . . . I could cope. In a way I welcomed it. All that venom towards me . . . it was deserved.'

She put a hand on his arm.

'You mustn't think that.'

There was a moody expression on his face.

'Really? Someone tried to abduct your daughter yesterday. Because of what I did . . . or didn't do . . . nearly two decades ago. You think I can simply forget?'

There were no words she could think of then.

'And Henk seems to hate me more with every passing day,' he added.

Across the road the children were filing back into school. More lessons. Saskia would be safe in the comfy, private world Lucas's money bought for them.

He stared at her and there was a steely determination in his eyes that must have been there when he was in uniform.

'Are you happy?'

'No,' she replied without thinking. 'Are many people?'

'You have every right to be,' he said, and sounded almost cross. 'We were. At Henk's age I was a career officer. We had one enemy. The Russians. No one but a fool thought it would come to war. Then the Berlin Wall fell and everyone was cheering.'

She smiled and patted his knee.

'This is history, Lucas. The past. You should let it go.'

'A friend of mine was there when the Wall collapsed. He told me everyone was delirious in Berlin. And then he said it would all get worse from now on. There's no balance left to keep us in our place. We had sides back then. We knew where we stood. A decade later we were trying to stop ordinary men murdering their neighbours in the Balkans. Had Henk followed me into the army he'd have gone to Iraq, Afghanistan . . . God knows where.'

He finished his coffee and crumpled the cup in his fist.

'It wasn't just me that failed. It was all of us. And every year we fall apart a little more.' Lucas Kuyper's face became stern and hard. 'Terrorists in Amsterdam. Stealing children off the street.'

'All the more reason not to blame yourself,' she interrupted.

'But Henk blames me. He hates me.'

'Me too, I think.'

'He's no reason to hate you, Renata. I don't believe that for a moment.'

'Perhaps he doesn't need one.'

He sat back on the seat, closed his eyes, trying to find the words.

'You're thinking of leaving him?'

'Is it that obvious?' she asked.

He nodded and said, 'It is.'

'Where would I go?' she asked and both of them understood she was fishing for an invitation. His house was big and empty. She could imagine living there.

'I don't know,' he answered. 'We all make sacrifices. The price of a little joy is often a little pain. You've a beautiful daughter . . .'

She found herself blinking back tears and wondered what he'd make of them.

'All I want is my family. A normal family. A loving family. All I ever wanted . . .'

The playground was deserted. It seemed desolate that way.

'Besides, Saskia would never come,' she said and knew that was true. 'There's a closeness between them. As if they share some . . . secret. I don't understand it. All I know is I can't get inside that. I never will.'

'This is not a time for rash decisions.'

'Rash?' she asked. 'Do you think this only happened yesterday? We've been struggling for years. Didn't you notice?'

She waited and waited. The only answer was an unfamiliar

ringtone from her bag. Henk had given her a spare phone of his that morning. The police had kept hers for the call about the Georgian girl.

'Where are you?' he asked.

'I went for a walk.'

She could hear him sigh. Traffic behind his voice. He was out in the street somewhere too. She thought she heard the rattle of a train.

'That doesn't tell me where you are.'

'I'm near the school. OK?'

'Those idiots at Marnixstraat called. They want to see us. Saskia too. Something about inconsistencies in the statements.'

Lucas shuffled away on the bench as if he didn't want to hear. The chaos of the previous day came back to her in an instant.

'What inconsistencies?'

'I don't know. Get Saskia out of school. There's a cafe in Elandsgracht, the Prinsen end, near the bridge.'

'I can be there in fifteen minutes . . .'

'Well I can't. Busy. Eleven thirty I'll see you in the cafe. Then we go in together.'

Without another word he hung up. Lucas was clutching his hat, ready to leave too.

'I'm glad we talked,' he said, getting to his feet. She joined him. 'As for Srebrenica . . .'

'What?'

'It's not a subject I care to return to.'

'Maybe you should. Maybe you and Henk . . .'

'One small step at a time,' he said. 'A family must always try to stay together. Once those bonds are fractured it's difficult to put the pieces back together again. Henk loves you. Saskia as well. We all do.'

She didn't know what to say. He tipped his hat and left.

———

Vos drove Hanna Bublik back into the centre, Renata Kuyper's phone in his coat pocket, silent. Accusing somehow.

As they fell into heavy traffic she looked at him and asked, nervously, 'What am I supposed to do if they ask for money?'

'The important thing is to start the dialogue. After that we can deal with what they want.'

She hugged herself in the cheap black jacket though it wasn't cold in the car.

'You can stay in my office as long as you like,' Vos suggested. 'The moment he calls I'll let you know what's happening.'

She stared out of the window as they pulled into the long straight stretch of Marnixstraat that led to the police station.

'You mean you're going to sit around all day waiting for the phone to ring?'

'I hope not,' Vos said.

'Then what's the point in having me around?'

'I'm trying to help.'

'I've only got one thing to give anyone and it's not something these people want.'

'I can get a woman officer to be with you. We can try and get some help—'

'I need my daughter back. That's all. I don't want anything else from you.'

He rarely lost his temper but she was getting to him. Vos pulled into the side of the street by the secure entrance to the station.

'We're doing all we can, Hanna. We'll find your daughter.'

She glared at him.

'You say that so easily.'

'I mean it. Either we track down where this man's keeping her. Or we negotiate some way out of it.'

'She's a whore's kid. Illegal. What's there to negotiate with?'

Sometimes sympathy was ineffective.

'What else do you want of me?' he asked. 'Say it so I know.'

She struggled with that.

'I get the message, Vos. You care. The thing is . . .' She almost looked guilty at that moment. 'A woman like me always worries when someone seems to care. It doesn't work out well. Sorry. My problem. Not yours.'

She got her bag, checked the money inside. Vos could see it wasn't much. He reached for his wallet and she put a hand on his arm.

'I'm getting out now. There's someone I need to see. Call when you've news.'

He watched her walk straight through the busy traffic, holding up a hand to stop an irate taxi when she felt like it. She wasn't beautiful but she was striking. Tall, straight-backed in her fake leather jacket and jeans. He could imagine she'd stop people in her cabin window, seated on a stool beneath the scarlet lamp. Just half a smile would do.

She was headed back towards the centre. In a minute she'd be in the middle of the Nine Streets, the shopping area where middle-class Amsterdam bought its luxuries. The red-light district wasn't far away after that.

Laura Bakker probably thought they could fix someone like this. Prostitution wasn't a career move. It was a solution, perhaps the only one available at the time. But Bakker was new to the city and still had the optimism of the young. Vos had worked vice for a while, dealt with so many of the criminals who ran the sex rings, usually with a hard, sometimes brutal, discipline. Most women working the cabins gave up through age and a lack of business. Nothing else.

There was the sound of a different ringtone. He took out Renata Kuyper's phone and looked at the screen. Number withheld. He waited a couple of seconds knowing that Marnixstraat would be hooking on to the call, trying to start a trace. Doubtless finding it was a Net connection that might, at best, provide a general city location, nothing so precise as a mobile mast.

On the fourth ring he answered.

Vos was so occupied by the phone call that he never saw the short and odd encounter across the road. The Kuypers heading into Marnixstraat, Saskia holding her father's hand.

And Hanna Bublik staring at them, curious. As if the sight of them meant something.

'Don't look for me,' the man said. 'Do what I say or you'll make the child suffer.'

Vos checked his watch. Forty-three minutes past eleven.

'What do you want?' he asked.

'I want my brother free.'

The voice was Dutch, educated, calm, with an inflection he couldn't place. Possibly forced. The man spoke slowly, surely, as if he had no concern about being traced.

'I need to know the girl's safe and well.'

There was a pause. Then a high, young female voice said with no audible fear, 'My name's Natalya. Who are you?'

'A policeman. Pieter Vos. Your mother was here a moment ago, Natalya. I'm sorry you missed her. Are you—?'

A sound, an angry squawk that might have been pain. Then he was back on.

'Enough,' the man said.

'Did you hit her?'

'Not yet.' He sounded offended by the question. 'She's a . . . handful. I guess it's in the genes.'

'What do you know about the mother?'

'The kid told me. What is this? An interview?'

Vos tried to imagine an eight-year-old girl telling a stranger, a hostile one at that, her mother was a prostitute. It was hard.

'I want you to organize a plane for Alamy, out of Schiphol. We'll give you the destination. I want safe passage guaranteed at the other end. And . . .' He was thinking on the fly. 'A hundred thousand euros.'

'You don't want much.'

'You're the government,' the man said. 'Fix it.'

'Give me time. A day.'

'A day?' He sounded outraged. 'Do you want this kid alive or not?'

'This isn't simple. We need political approval for any money. To fix the plane. Do you think I can click my fingers and make that happen in an instant?'

'A day then,' the man said. 'Play no games.'

That was quick. And easy.

'So you told me. I want to talk to Natalya again.'

A long sigh. Then she came on the line.

'Your mother loves you,' Vos said. 'Tomorrow we'll have you home. I promise.'

There was a pause on the line. A sound in the background he couldn't place.

'Thank you,' Natalya Bublik told him very slowly, very politely.

The line went dead. He called Bakker straight away.

'Did you get that?'

She was in the main office with Van der Berg, Koeman and the rest of the team, sitting in front of the computer, going through the logs coming in from the tracking software.

'It was Skype,' she said.

'Did you record the call?'

'Of course we did!'

'Good. I'm coming in. There's something behind the voices. That last time when Natalya talks really slowly. I think she did that deliberately. See if you can work out what it is.'

The moment he was off the line his phone rang again. It was Mirjam Fransen. The call had been patched through to the AIVD office in the centre of the city too.

He told her he was going into Marnixstraat. If she wanted a meeting it had to be there.

'Too busy, Vos,' she said. 'Just one thing to remember.'

'Which is?' he asked when she didn't go on.

'I understand you have to lead him on and think we'll give him what he wants.'

'Good.'

'Don't think for one moment he's going to get it. The Dutch government doesn't submit to ransoms. For money or kidnapped children. Ismail Alamy's going nowhere.'

He started the car and looked for a gap in the traffic.

'Do you want to tell her mother?'

'We've got better things to do. I'll leave it to you.'

She was gone after that. Vos phoned Hanna Bublik and got voicemail. Then walked into the station. Bakker and Van der Berg already had technicians going over the recording of the phone call. The Kuyper family were sitting in an interview room.

'Why . . . ?' he asked.

'Something doesn't add up,' Bakker said. 'The technical people want twenty minutes to try to enhance the quality of the phone call. Can we talk to them in the meantime?'

'Have AIVD got anything?'

'If they have they're not telling us,' Van der Berg said with a grimace. 'We need to get yesterday straight, Pieter. They ought to be able to help.'

He called Hanna Bublik again. Still no answer. Vos watched the three figures in the interview room. All well-dressed, the girl seated closer to her father than her mother. They had the look of money about them. Not that it seemed to bring much in the way of happiness with it.

'Fine,' he said.

———

She got the address from Chantal Santos. An old building on Spooksteeg, a pedestrian alley between Zeedijk and Oudezijds Voorburgwal. Graffiti on the walls. There was a high iron security gate topped with spikes, closed at night to keep out the riff-raff. The place was in the heart of the red-light district but ring-fenced from the trade that was the lifeblood of this part of the city.

Cem Yilmaz lived off that stream. He was thirty-seven, from Ankara via Hamburg. A hulking, muscular man. There were exercise machines in the penthouse, by the window so everyone could see. Yilmaz owned the entire building, countless rows of cabins through the city, four sex clubs, a pizza restaurant and a shop that sold novelty condoms. Most of his business was legal. Only the way he treated his girls when he judged they'd stepped out of line threatened to bring him to the attention of the police. But even then the women were always too scared to complain.

Hanna knew what he was. Knew a little of his background too. When she rang his bell and pleaded with him through the door intercom she was already working out in her head what she might do if he let her in. Then the door buzzed. She walked into a modern atrium behind the old facade, found the lift open and ready and went to the top floor.

The lift opened straight into the living room. Yilmaz was alone on a vast bright-red sofa. An unsmiling man with skin the colour of pale leather and bulbous, restless eyes. He reminded her of some of the criminals her husband had briefly encountered back in Gori. Thugs who'd come round demanding protection money. For security against themselves usually.

The Turk wore a lurid blue tracksuit bottom. His barrel chest was shiny with sweat. The place smelled of exercise. He told her to sit down then rolled over the sofa, found a box on a coffee table, took out a cigar and lit it. The bright room started to fill with noxious smoke. Hanna had seen him once before, driving round the district in his Maserati. Yilmaz liked to display his wealth.

'Four times I have asked you here, Mrs Bublik. And on each occasion you deny me.' He had a deep baritone voice and spoke in a tone that never wavered. 'Why now?'

She wondered how much to say. The police had been adamant. The fewer people who knew of Natalya's kidnap the better. But they were struggling in the dark.

So she told him. About the chaos in Leidseplein the day before. He knew of that, of course. Sat and listened to the story of Natalya's disappearance without blinking. Hanna left out the Kuypers. They seemed irrelevant.

He listened, nodding, then made himself a coffee, Turkish-style, one for her too. She sipped the strong, black liquid. The grounds were like mud at the bottom. When she was finished he sat down again, shrugged his huge shoulders, got a towel to start wiping down the sweat on his chest and biceps.

'And?' he asked.

'I thought you might be able to help.'

'How?'

This was awkward. It had to be said.

'I heard you were Muslim too.'

The big eyes narrowed.

'Do you think every Muslim's a terrorist?'

'No.'

But she'd heard rumours. Some money went from the gangs into the brotherhoods. That was one way they managed to get girls smuggled into the city, especially from the countries of the Caucasus that had fallen out of the old Soviet Union. Sometimes they'd be trafficked through Georgia. Everyone knew that.

'I just thought I'd ask. In case you hear something. You could tell me. As a favour.'

He finished his coffee and put the little cup on the table in front of him.

'What am I? A charity? How many people do Cem Yilmaz favours?' He looked her up and down. 'How many favours have you done me?'

For some reason he kept a blazing fire in the room. Logs crackling beneath a large, old chimney. It made the place too hot. Exaggerated the smell of him.

'I've never done anything to get in the way of your girls. I never would.'

'Nothing is nothing, Mrs Bublik. You want my help. Why should I offer it?'

Not now, she thought. Not with Natalya missing. Taking his money was, she understood, a one-way trip. There would be no turning back. Not in safety.

'I just want to get my daughter back. When that's over . . . we can talk.'

The look again. Up and down. Like a butcher scanning a carcass.

'You're a decent-looking woman. I could do business for us both. More than you could ever imagine on your own behind a window. They say they want money? How much?'

'I don't know.'

'How much do you have?'

'Not a lot. Perhaps . . . perhaps the police will help.'

He laughed.

'Why would they help you? You're not Dutch. You're just a piece of meat to them.'

'And to you I'd be different?'

The words just slipped out and she regretted them immediately. Yet he didn't seem offended. If anything he looked impressed.

'The offer was made in good faith,' Yilmaz insisted. 'I'm a businessman, nothing else. We trade. We both prosper. If you wish to come to work with me perhaps I can assist. Ask questions of people who may answer them. Perhaps . . .' He shrugged.

'I guarantee nothing. Except that if I ask no questions there'll be no answers.'

'I can't work with this going on.'

He shook his big, crew-cut head.

'Yet last night you were sitting in a cabin window looking for customers. Or trying to.'

She stared at him.

'I own those cabins, Mrs Bublik. I'm a good landlord and an excellent employer. All I ask in return is loyalty.'

'I'm begging,' she murmured.

'I can hear it.'

Yilmaz beckoned her to a desk by the long window over the narrow canal. There he pulled open a drawer and let her see the contents. It was stuffed with money. Euros. Sterling. US dollars. Notes in currencies she didn't recognize. Lots of it.

'Money comes. Money goes.' He picked up a wad of euros and held them out. 'All I require is your agreement to join my little family of ladies. No more freezing in cold cabins. You meet better gentlemen. They pay more. You work less.'

*And I am your slave.*

He knew that was what she was thinking. It was written in his face.

'She's eight years old,' she pleaded. 'All I've got.'

'I'd like to help. But for a man like me there must always be a price.' He laughed. 'What's the problem? It's one you're paying already.'

She said she wanted to think about it and asked for a phone number. He frowned, wrote one out, asked for hers, then put the bundle of notes back in the drawer.

'I'll ask around in any case,' he added. 'I'm not a heartless man. Just a practical one.'

He opened another drawer, pulled out a vial of oil and took off the top. It smelled strong yet fragrant, almost feminine.

Yilmaz held out the bottle and said, 'You can do me a favour now and rub it in if you want.'

She got out her phone and typed in his number. The voicemail icon was flashing. Nervous, with shaking fingers, she found the one message there.

It was Vos, asking her to come into Marnixstraat. They had something.

'I have to leave,' she said. 'The police want me.'

He watched her go without a word.

Outside, in the graffiti-stained alley of Spooksteeg she wondered about the Turk. Did he really know people? Or just want her as part of his tame circus of willing whores?

There was no way of knowing. So she called Vos, got his voicemail then, and left a message that she was on her way.

Henk Kuyper was adamant: they were interviewed together or not at all.

Van der Berg listened to his whining and shook his head. Vos sat at a desk wondering when forensic might have a finished version of the phone recording. They were late. Bakker kept crossing and uncrossing her long legs, punctuating the performance with awkward, tetchy sighs.

'We're not accusing you of anything,' Van der Berg told the tall, unsmiling man across the table.

'I don't want Saskia left on her own. You can't interview an eight-year-old as if she was a criminal.'

'No one was suggesting anything of the sort,' Vos broke in. 'We're just . . .' He'd had a quick chat with Bakker before the interview began and checked through her notes. 'We want to make sure we understand what you think you saw yesterday.'

Kuyper sat back in his chair. His wife was at the end of the table. The girl stayed between them, close to her father.

'I'm not a fan of the police,' he grumbled. 'I don't like the way you're partial.'

Van der Berg blinked.

'Partial? We're trying to find a kidnapped girl. It might have been your daughter.'

'But it wasn't. Maybe if you'd been doing your job none of this—'

'Ask your questions,' Renata interrupted. 'Ask anything you like.'

A cold, bleak moment between the two of them. The girl took out a shiny new phone and started to play a game on it. Bakker placed a laptop on the table and took them through the CCTV. If the timings were right – and there was no reason to think they weren't – she had spotted something. Natalya Bublik was snatched just moments after Saskia vanished. It wasn't impossible this was a mistake on the part of whoever kidnapped her. Two people looking for a pink jacket. But something still seemed odd.

Renata followed everything carefully, listening to the timeline Bakker set out.

'I don't know what you want me to say?' she told them. 'Saskia wandered off while I was in the square. She wanted to see Sinterklaas. Then we heard the explosions. Henk turned up. He went into the crowd and found her.'

'Where?' Vos asked, looking straight at him.

'Around the back of the theatre,' Kuyper said. 'It seemed the obvious place to look.' A sly, caustic glance at his wife. 'At least it seemed obvious to me. If you were a frightened child, running away from a stranger and all that panic in the square, you'd try to hide, wouldn't you? Saskia?'

The girl looked up from her phone and said in a bored, petulant tone, 'I was trying to hide. Then Daddy found me.'

Bakker looked at the phone.

'You've got a new one, Saskia?'

'I keep spares,' her father snapped. 'Don't most people?'

The girl went back to her game.

'How did you get away from Black Pete?' Bakker asked.

'Ran.'

That was it.

'Wasn't he holding you?'

'Not when I ran. He let go.' She looked at her father. 'That was the right thing, wasn't it?'

'The right thing,' he said and patted her hand. 'Then I found her. And brought her back.'

Saskia was still in the pink jacket.

'Given the circumstances,' Bakker said, 'I'm surprised she's still wearing that thing.'

'Not my choice,' Renata snapped. 'I asked her to wear something else. Ignored as usual.'

Kuyper glanced at her, briefly furious.

'Why shouldn't she wear it? She likes it. We were lucky. That's all it was. I don't know about your . . .' He waved a finger at the laptop. 'Timings. Why you're asking us. Wouldn't you be better helping that woman? Finding her child?' He hesitated then said it anyway. 'You could let Alamy out of jail too. He's no reason to be there.'

'You know about the case?' Vos asked.

'Enough. You don't have a shred of evidence he's committed a crime here. Just because he says things you don't like you want him extradited to a country that doesn't even pretend to care about justice. Or democracy. Or freedom. What . . .'

His wife cast him a vicious look.

'Wrong time for a lecture, Henk,' she said quietly.

'Is it? If Alamy wasn't in jail for no good reason would we even be here?'

There was an urgent knock on the door. Bakker went to answer it. Koeman was there. She listened and looked at Vos. He got the message and went outside.

'We got something off that call,' the detective said. 'There was the sound of ducks. And trains. When they got it as loud as they could they think there's an announcement.' He paused. 'It's got to be near a station. We're guessing Centraal.'

'A boat,' Vos said. 'I knew it was a boat.'

'You did,' Koeman agreed. 'That probably means somewhere around Westerdok. Closest place I can think of. I've got uniform down there asking questions.'

'I want to see,' Vos said, and glanced at Bakker. 'Get us a car.'

'What about this lot?' she asked looking back at the interview room.

Van der Berg had joined them.

'Sadly,' he said, 'it's not illegal to be a complete jerk. I think that stuck-up bastard likes to wind us up. Best we don't give him the pleasure.'

'They've nothing for us,' Vos added. 'You saw what it was like in Leidseplein. If there were two, three, more Black Petes looking for a kid in a pink jacket it's hardly surprising they got confused . . .'

'The timing!'

'Westerdok,' he said. 'A car.' A nod at Van der Berg. 'Three of us.'

'Also,' Koeman added, 'that nice lady from AIVD has been on the line asking how we're doing. And the mother's in an interview room wanting to see you. She says it's important.'

'Tell Mirjam Fransen we're still looking. I don't have time for the mother right now. Keep her happy.'

The detective grimaced.

'She's still pissed off with me for giving her a hard time yesterday. Every reason to be.'

'Buy her a coffee,' Vos added, patting his shoulder. 'Make amends. Say you're sorry. See if she'll accept some help. She's a decent woman. No fool.'

Then he returned to the interview room. Kuyper got to his feet. His daughter did the same.

'Thank you for your time,' Vos told them. 'We appreciate it. You can leave now.'

'I know,' Henk Kuyper said and led his family out into the corridor, down towards reception and the street outside.

Footsteps in the cabin outside again. Natalya closed her eyes and listened intently. Through the cracks in the timber planking she could see it was starting to get dark. Trains somewhere. People going out, going home.

A few hours earlier he'd come back with more food: a sandwich of strong Dutch cheese, a packet of crisps, a fizzy drink. She'd told the black balaclava she didn't like fizzy drinks. He'd said nothing, just gone out and got a glass of water from somewhere. Left her little cabin and took a phone call she could just about hear. This was the man who'd given her the book. She felt sure of that. Not the one from the night before.

Bored, more than a little angry, she waited, watching the cabin door. He came in. Same clothes, same black mask to hide his features. But he didn't put the balaclava on until he was just inside.

She saw something. Saw him.

And maybe he noticed too.

Trying to look stupid she stared at the food as he cleared away the wrappers from the sandwich.

'I did the sums you gave me.' She pulled out the colouring book and went to the page she'd done that morning. 'Don't you want to check?'

He grunted something about being busy. This one had an accent. Much like the one from the night before. The Black Pete who'd snatched her.

Only two of them, she thought. They took turns, leaving her alone for hours, locked in the tiny bows of a boat somewhere near the station.

'Are you frightened of me?' Natalya asked.

He stopped, hands full of rubbish like one of the hunched men she saw on the street, clearing out the bins.

'Be silent, girl,' this Black Pete told her. 'Know your place.'

She cocked her head to one side and looked at him.

'What place is that?'

He raised his hand. She didn't flinch. This one was very different.

'Eight years old, Natalya Bublik. Shut up and be grateful you're alive.'

The other man had never mentioned her name. Nor asked it. And yet they knew.

She put her head down, picked up the colouring book and a crayon. Drew something on the page.

He didn't look. Then his phone rang again and he left her, bolting the door behind him.

Natalya found the blank page behind the cover. Drew and drew. And wrote.

First though she remembered the brief conversation she'd heard and thought about what she saw.

Then she turned to the back of the colouring book and in careful writing, in Dutch so someone else would easily understand, set down two lines.

> One of them is called Carleed or something.
> I think he's a kind of boss.

> He's got dark skin, a big beard, all black and shiny,
> like a pirate.

Then, her hand shaking at the thought . . .

> I think he knows I've seen him.

———

In a small and stuffy interview room in Marnixstraat Hanna Bublik sat with a miserable, embarrassed Koeman. Not saying what she wanted to tell Vos because that was for his ears only. This man was the fool who'd let them down the day before. Eyed her suspiciously as a questionable foreigner when he should have been helping, listening to her pleas.

She ignored the coffee and listened to him trying to justify what he'd done.

'Can I get you something to eat?' he asked eventually.

'I'm not destitute.'

'I was trying to be polite.'

She scowled and looked at her watch.

'When will Vos be back?'

'I don't know. I can call you when we know something.'

She looked into his sad, bleary eyes.

'Will they find my Natalya?'

'Yes,' he said without conviction.

'Then I'll wait.'

There was a commotion outside in the corridor. Through the door she could see the hard-faced woman who wasn't quite a cop marching purposefully past. She was with the big man who'd been with her the day before in Leidseplein. Hanna understood these people were intelligence or something. They didn't like the police much. The feeling was reciprocated.

Koeman saw too, and heard. Then muttered a curse under his breath.

In a loud and uncompromising voice Mirjam Fransen was demanding to see Frank de Groot. She didn't sound happy.


Westerdok ran out from the railway lines into the stretch of water called the IJ. Once a run-down port area it was now in the midst of redevelopment. On the station side stood new hotels, cafes and a modern courthouse to replace the old building on the

Prinsengracht, not far from Vos's home. The adjoining islands housed apartment blocks, industrial buildings, dead warehouses . . . and lines and lines of houseboats along the grey canals.

By the time Vos, Bakker and Van der Berg got there uniform had twenty officers out in the street, knocking on doors, asking questions. Van der Berg parked the car not far from the sparkling new courthouse, looking at the long line of boats that stretched alongside the straight road running north. Fifty or more of them. Uniformed officers were a third of the way along already.

'Can't be here,' Bakker said. 'It's too obvious.'

'True,' Vos agreed.

This area wasn't made for cars. The streets were narrow. Sometimes roads ended in nothing more than a pedestrian alley or bridge.

He got out, talked to a crew of uniform and relieved them of two bikes.

Van der Berg looked worried. He wasn't a cycle man. Vos told him to stay near the car, work the radio, keep them up to date. Then he passed a bike to Bakker and the two of them rode to the adjoining islands, working their way into the centre of the quiet, half-residential, half-industrial streets there, just a stone's throw from the busy city.

After a few minutes they were on the opposite stretch of water to the courthouse, looking at the boats, Vos frowning. There was money coming into Westerdok. This was more a marina than a community made for living. Fancy speedboats, cruisers that could cope with the sea if necessary. Real houseboats never moved. They were wired into the mains, plugged into the phone system, connected to water and drainage. Permanent homes on the water.

'What are we looking for?' Bakker asked as they came to a halt next to a fancy yacht with a couple seated by a gas fire in the stern, sipping wine, watching them suspiciously.

'Something old,' he said. 'Like a klipper barge. It never moves.'

He got off the bike and went to the yacht. The man in the back stood up. He was smoking a cigar. Looked fat and comfortable. Didn't react when Vos showed him his police ID and asked about strangers and barges.

'We don't get all that poor shit around here,' the man said. 'You need to go . . .' He gestured to the area east of them. 'Few of them around there.'

'Lived in?' Vos asked.

His big shoulders heaved.

'I guess. If you want to make money you sell them to the speculators. Rent them out to dumb tourists for fifteen hundred euros a week. Let them bang their head on the roof and deal with all that damp.'

Vos said thanks.

Bakker followed him back to the bikes.

'If you were going to kidnap someone would you take them home?' he asked.

'No. I'd rent a place somewhere.'

'Quite.'

He called Van der Berg and asked him to get someone in Marnixstraat looking at the web rental sites for any houseboats in the Westerdok area. Then they cycled over the Bickersgracht bridge, into Galgenstraat and started poking around. There were more uniforms working the canal. But the man on the yacht was wrong. Hardly any old houseboats here. And every one of them had checked out.

Ten minutes more fruitless searching. Night had fallen, cloudy and dark. They were pedalling down narrow, ill-lit streets getting nowhere when Van der Berg called back with news. There were seven boats out for short-term rental on the web. Four of them were empty. Two others had been checked already and cleared. The last was in Realengracht to the north.

'I'll send someone round,' Van der Berg said.

'Don't bother,' Vos told him. 'We're nearly there.'

Fransen and Thom Geerts had to wait outside De Groot's office until he was clear of a management meeting elsewhere. That didn't help their mood. The moment he returned they followed him into the room squawking all the while.

Koeman had accompanied De Groot up from reception, warning him along the way. Updating him on what little they knew of the situation in Westerdok too.

De Groot liked his office. There was a view of the canal from the window and the broad thoroughfare of Elandsgracht down to Vos's houseboat. It was a place he could think. But not with two intelligence monkeys whining in his ear.

He listened to Fransen's moans, glanced at Koeman and said, 'What is this? We're chasing a lead. That's all. We don't have anything of substance. No address. No—'

'We've got a phone call with ducks, trains and a station announcement, for God's sake,' Koeman told him. 'We're guessing it's Westerdok. We could be completely wrong. The bastard might have taken the kid out of the city for all we know.'

Fransen sat down. Geerts did the same. He looked as if he mirrored her every move.

'You need to keep us in the picture,' she said. 'This is the second time today Vos has marched off without telling anyone.'

'What?' Koeman squealed. 'We don't have time to call you every time someone farts around here. What about this Alamy guy? The ransom? What do we do when this bastard calls back tomorrow and gives us a deadline?'

'There'll be no ransom,' Geerts insisted. 'We told you that already. The Dutch government doesn't give in to blackmail.'

De Groot waited. That was it.

'So what do we do?' he asked.

'Stall,' Fransen said. 'Spin it out for another day. We're expecting a final court ruling on his appeal tomorrow. Maybe that will change things.'

Koeman scratched his head and asked, 'How?'

'Tell him there are problems arranging the plane,' Geerts suggested, ignoring the question. 'Get one more day out of him. Then another if we need it.'

'And in the meantime find him,' Fransen added. 'How about that?'

Koeman rolled back his head and said, 'We're trying.'

'Whereabouts are you looking in Westerdok?' Fransen asked.

'All over,' De Groot said. 'Nothing to report yet. If there is . . .' He looked at the door. 'I'll pass it on.'

'Do you have anything to tell us?' Koeman asked them. 'Any little thing that might help?'

'If we did you'd know it,' Fransen told him. She didn't look ready to move. 'Where's Vos? Where *exactly*?'

Koeman kept quiet. So did the commissaris.

'Enough,' Fransen said. She nodded at the detective. 'Out of here. I need to talk to De Groot alone.'


The narrow old house in the Herenmarkt felt cold. Winter was coming on the night wind, brought in from the chilly waters of the IJ and the sea that fed it.

They ate the food she put on the table: spaghetti carbonara, bought from Marqt around the corner, made with the sauce they provided. Everything in the place came from somewhere, she thought. None of it was made. Was hers.

The pregnancy was an unwanted surprise but when the child turned out to be a daughter she was hopeful. Together they'd be a joint buffer against his forceful, demanding personality. But then Henk stepped in somehow, not long after Saskia was born. Before she could forge a bond between them he was there.

Pushing the pram, talking to her, singing to her. Keeping her for his own. Another possession to be put in place for the moment she'd be needed.

He liked everything in order. Filed away. Predictable. So she went down to the organic supermarket with orders about what to buy: the right kind of food, nothing from China, nothing mass-produced. Though it all tasted the same in the end. That pickiness on his part was just another facet of his need to control her.

And criticize. That was important too. Already he'd informed her the Parmesan tasted a little stale. She'd grated it carefully two days before, the last time they ate like this. Kept it in an airtight container. But Henk, with his fine, discerning palate, could taste something old and dry, not that she noticed. So in future she'd have to grate it afresh on every occasion and get the quantities wrong as usual, which meant he could scold her when he found her trying to empty out the unused dregs into the food recycling box without his noticing.

She watched him curl the pasta round his fork and spoon so carefully, with a precision and neatness she could never emulate. Saw that Saskia did the same now. Copied him, always.

Her mind wandered to the Georgian woman again. Hanna Bublik. She'd asked the name at the police station and for some reason the young woman detective Bakker had told her.

What kind of life had she led with her daughter? How did poverty feel? What measure of desperation would drive a woman to sit in one of those glass cabins of a night, trying to entice a stranger to her hard single bed, to service him like a living machine? All for no more euros than she might spend in a single shopping expedition down Marqt making sure Henk got the wine he liked, the cheese he preferred, the right kind of pasta, meat from a guaranteed organic farm and salad leaves so odd and exotic that she'd no idea what they truly were.

The woman and her child must have lived in a kind of hell. But there were other sorts too.

She looked at Henk and said, 'How did you find Saskia in Leidseplein? I still don't understand.'

The girl sighed, looked at her plate of food. Put her knife and fork on the pasta that remained and got up muttering something about going to read in her room.

'You know,' he said lazily when she'd left, 'I long ago accepted I'd never get any thanks for what I do. But ingratitude seems a touch boorish in the circumstances.'

'There's a little girl missing. If we can help . . .'

'It's called observation,' he broke in. 'You should try it.'

'That's not fair,' she muttered. 'I do my best.'

His hand came out and patted hers.

'I appreciate that.'

He grabbed the bottle of wine. An organic Amarone. Too heavy for her and he knew it. The glass he filled very precisely, swirling it under his nose before taking a sip.

'I take it you no longer want to get away,' he said. 'If you do the offer's still open.'

It struck her then: he desired this. Wanted her out of the house. Perhaps never to come back. That way he'd have Saskia forever. The battle would be won for good.

'I changed my mind. I'll stay and see this through.'

'Good,' he said with no conviction.

'I saw your father this morning. He's a kind man, Henk. He doesn't deserve your hatred. He—'

'Kind?'

'That's what I said.'

His eyes were on her. She could see the drink in them.

'You always think you know people,' he said, with a half a slur. 'You never really do.'

'Is that me you're talking about? Or are you just speaking for humanity in general?'

More of the blood-red wine went down.

'Why do you hate me?'

'I don't have the energy for hatred,' he said with a sudden savage glance. 'That's for children. I really think after all this time you might have realized. But . . .'

His phone buzzed. The thing seemed a part of him. It was out in a flash, his fingers racing over the screen as if they knew every millimetre.

'Work?' she asked lightly.

'I have to go out for a while.'

This was new.

'Out? You mean . . . in the real world?'

He grinned then winked at her.

'Good one that. You're sure you don't want to take a break somewhere for a week or two? We can cope. I'll look after Saskia. She'll look after me.'

'I'm fine here,' Renata said.

He picked up the Amarone. Two thirds full. Placed it in front of her.

'Leave me half a glass for when I get back.'

She pushed it back over the table.

'All yours,' she said. 'Just for a change.'


The boat was a klipper. Not that different to Vos's own but smarter, a little less old, a lot tidier. It sat near the junction of two channels of water beneath a line of trees shedding their leaves into the winter wind. There was a light on in the main cabin. Behind closed curtains they could make out a figure moving to and fro inside. Then a second, smaller shape came into view. Words they couldn't hear were exchanged. The diminutive silhouette vanished as if ordered somewhere.

Vos parked his bike against the house opposite. Bakker did the same.

'Maybe there are things we could put on the walls?' she said. 'Microphones? And listen in.'

'I imagine,' he agreed and set off for the waterfront.

'Pieter!' she said and put a hand to his arm.

He turned and smiled.

'I live on a boat, Laura. I know what it's like. Not a house. It sits below everything else. You don't look out. You can't easily. That's one reason I liked it in the first place. It's like a . . . a cocoon.'

The long road looked empty. No one observing them.

'They're not looking out for us. Besides . . . it's probably a waste of time.'

He walked on. Bakker joined him. A few steps from the gangplank she went ahead. Before Vos could stop her she was taking out a forensic glove, putting it on her right hand, dragging something out of a smouldering brazier near the steps to the houseboat.

Vos pulled out his torch. It was the burned remnants of a Black Pete costume. Green fabric, smoke-stained and charred. A ruff. A black hat.

'We'll bring in a team . . .' Vos started to say. Then froze. There was a sound from the boat. Lights there. A voice. Male. Commanding.

Bakker had her handgun out already. Fresh from firearms training a couple of weeks before. She was more at home with the things than he'd ever be.

The door opened. The shape of a man there, barking orders. A big man.

Vos turned, told her to wait.

But she was young and keen and quick, soon dashing over the gangplank, weapon out. No stopping her.


Koeman closed the door behind him. The two AIVD officers stared at De Groot. The commissaris leaned back in his chair and rubbed his black walrus moustache.

A smart, intelligent man. Easy with his own people. Hated

dealing with anyone outside the service. Especially faceless agents who'd never worn a uniform, never quite said who was pulling their strings.

'Well?' he asked.

'In a couple of minutes you'll be getting an email from The Hague. The minister's taking a personal interest in this case. She requires a happy outcome.'

'Don't we all?' De Groot asked.

'The minister wants the lines to be clear,' Geerts cut in.

These two worked like a double act. It was hard to see daylight between the two of them.

'The lines are clear, aren't they? You deal with national security. We pursue criminal investigations. Kidnapping's a crime. Finding that young girl's our job. I want your help. If there's something you know that can assist us I want to hear it. But . . .'

'Not as simple as that,' Fransen said with a sigh. 'This is about Ismail Alamy. He's in play. Between us. Between the people in the Middle East who want him.' She paused for effect. 'The Americans would like a chat too.'

'Then let the Americans talk to him in that cell in Schiphol.'

'This man could take us to Barbone if he wanted,' Geerts said. 'That's about as precious a prize as we could get right now. Vos should never have been out there this morning. Did you know he was in Schiphol?'

A weak point. He wasn't going to give them an answer.

'Thought not,' the AIVD man said. 'You're out of your depth here, De Groot. It's best you know it.'

'Careers die at times like this,' the woman added. 'It's a kind of suicide usually.'

De Groot looked at them, shook his head and laughed.

'Are you really saying you don't want us to find this girl?'

'There's more at stake than the life of an illegal hooker's daughter,' Fransen answered. 'More than you could begin to imagine.'

'Do you have children?' he asked.

'That's irrelevant,' Fransen snapped. 'I've got a job to do.'

'So the answer to my question is . . . yes. You want us to stop looking.'

They glanced at one another. Then Fransen said, 'I want to know where you go. I want to hear what you find. I want to be told what you plan to do. Before you do it. And if I say you do nothing. Then nothing's what you do.'

The commissaris folded his arms and kept silent.

'Where's Vos?' she asked.

'Pieter?' De Groot said brightly. 'Most talented man I've got. And the most infuriating. Very difficult to manage. Goes off on his own. Doesn't say where. Doesn't answer his phone. And then . . . when you're about to bite his head off . . . he comes back with everything you want, neatly wrapped and tied. Sometimes anyway. So you just want to give him a big hug instead.'

He released a long and measured sigh.

'And that's the truth of it. Nothing's going to change. With either of us.'

Mirjam Fransen glared at him.

'I'll take his neck along with yours.'

'You can try,' De Groot replied. 'But you keep forgetting. This media blackout on the kidnapping won't last forever. At some stage it comes to an end. There'll be publicity. An internal inquiry. Perhaps a judicial one too if we really screw up. Who knows?'

There was a flicker of concern on their faces then and he knew he'd won. For now anyway.

'When the public realize you've been playing games with the life of an eight-year-old girl . . . Georgian, illegal, whatever, I don't care . . . what do you think? Will they see your bigger picture? Or something a little simpler?'

She didn't answer.

'Just a thought,' he added and looked at the door. 'When I hear anything of substance I'll let you know.'

After they left he phoned Vos. Got voicemail. Then went through to control. They could track him through his handset.

Westerdok, the desk said. Something was happening. Backup was on the way.


A tall and hefty figure, reaching for something. Bakker pushed ahead in spite of Vos's cries, yelling at the man to get down, flat on the damp planks of the houseboat.

From somewhere nearby came the sound of cars. Headlights. Voices. Running feet.

Vos raced over the gangplank, wished she'd do as he asked for once. Caught the man's face as Bakker dealt with him. Moustache. Fifties maybe. Scared in the dark.

From his fingers something slipped and fell into the black water. A couple of ducks squawked angrily.

He wasn't sure but to Vos it looked like a phone.

Pushing past he got to the door of the boat and strode inside. The lights were on. The place looked tidy. To the right was a small door to what must have been a cabin in the bows. There was a heavy padlock on it, unlatched. The fixture looked new.

In the stern of the boat stood a diminutive Asian woman in a pink cleaner's jacket. She held a vacuum cleaner and a duster and was staring at him, more than a little outraged.

'Is there a girl here?' he asked, already knowing the answer.

'No girl,' she said, baffled. 'Who you? What you do? Pushing in like this. Mr Smits . . . he gonna be dead mad with you.'

Vos looked round the place. She must have been busy cleaning for a while. It was spotless. He couldn't help but wonder what had vanished under her polish and duster. He showed her his badge and asked her to get outside then followed her. The big man with the moustache was seated on the deck moaning out loud. Van der Berg was there with a couple of uniform officers.

They got Smits off the boat and sat him in a squad car. He was a flabby individual with a beer gut and a grumpy demeanour. The story seemed straight enough. He was the owner of the klipper barge and lived round the corner. An hour earlier he'd walked past the boat and noticed it was empty. When he went inside it looked as if the holiday tenants had cleared out. The place had been booked three days earlier. The agency people had let them in. He'd never seen who was there. But it seemed obvious they'd gone.

'Sometimes people leave early,' Smits said. 'They don't like the area or the boat or something. I saw it was empty. So I called in the cleaner. Maybe we can get a last-minute booking in the morning.'

He gestured at Bakker.

'Next thing I know this crazy cow's pointing a gun in my face.'

'You're the owner,' Bakker threw back at him. 'You're supposed to keep details of people who rent. Copies of their passport for one thing. What do you have?'

He shrugged.

'I was busy. It was just for a week. They didn't ask for a receipt or anything.'

'Give us a description,' Bakker demanded.

'Ask the agency. I told you. They let them in. I never even saw the people.'

Vos told Van der Berg to cordon off the area and start door-to-door checks to see if anyone had seen who'd been using the boat. Then bring in forensic to go over whatever might have been left behind.

After that he went inside again. Bakker followed. Forensic gloves on they opened the door to the little cabin at the front and looked inside.

Black timber planking. The same as they'd seen on the phone.

'This was the place,' she said. 'Why did they leave?'

'Maybe they planned it all along.' Vos was trying to think the way they did. Some steps seemed obvious. 'They know this could take days. They'd have places all over the city.' He looked at her. 'Wouldn't you?'

A thought.

'They can only move at night. Too risky during the day. Get onto Marnixstraat and see what they can pull out of the traffic CCTV.'

She was barely listening. Bakker was looking at something in the tiny cabin. A scrawl in the condensation on the tiny porthole window.

Ducking down to avoid the low doorway she walked in and looked more closely. The place smelled of disinfectant from the portable toilet in the corner, of stagnant water and diesel from outside.

Vos joined her. Just four words in the drops of water against the glass, 'Mum. I love you.'

Bakker swore and stomped back out into the main cabin, heavy feet hard on the planking.

Half an hour they waited watching the teams assemble. Vos told Van der Berg to go home and get some sleep. Had to say it twice to Bakker before she listened.

Then he sat on the bonnet of one of the squad cars watching the team go to work. It could take days to get any DNA out of the place. The burned Black Pete costume might never reveal a thing. There was nothing coming from the rental agency either. All they had was a reservation made using an untraceable temporary email.

If they'd located the boat sooner they might have found her. He called De Groot and briefed him. The commissaris seemed subdued, as if there was something he wanted to tell him but couldn't.

'We need to tread carefully, Pieter,' De Groot said in the end. 'This Alamy character complicates things. AIVD are pulling strings behind my back. There are people keeping an eye on us.'

'Is an eight-year-old girl important to them?' Vos asked.

'That preacher is. Maybe there's more to it than we know about. Go home. Get some sleep. Let's talk in the morning and see where we stand. And keep me posted. I need to know what's going on.'

Vos agreed and ended the call. Then handed back the bike he'd borrowed and started on the long walk home, past the Kuypers' house in the Herenmarkt, on to the Jordaan.

He was passing through the Noordermarkt, beside the squat shape of the church there, when Renata Kuyper's phone rang. The restaurants were busy. A couple of lovers were walking arm in arm on the cobbled pavement by the canal. The city was over the previous day's nightmare, in ignorance of the legacy it left behind.

Vos sat down on a bench beneath an ornate street light to take the call.

'Yes,' he said.

'I told you. No games. So why are you in Westerdok?'

Control would be on the call by now, recording it, looking for clues behind the voice. But Vos could hear nothing at all. Perhaps they were getting more careful.

'The girl's missing. We're police. Do you expect us to sit on our hands all day?'

'I expect you to free my brother. And give me my money.'

'When?' Vos asked and wondered: how did he know we were there? How did he find out so quickly? Was it possible they guessed the police were on the way?

'When I tell you.'

'Is she safe?' he asked. 'Is she well? Can I talk to her?'

'The kid doesn't know you from Adam. What good would that do?'

'I could tell her mother. You know who she is. Just another immigrant. No papers. No money. And you've taken—'

'Please don't make me cry, Vos,' the man cut in with a laugh. 'I can, you know.'

'Tomorrow . . .'

'Tomorrow I'll call you. On this number. The afternoon. We'll make arrangements. If you try to pursue us again all bets, all promises are off. She's an OK kid. Be a real shame if you let her down.'

The phone went dead. The pair of lovers were kissing, arms entwined around one another, shadows falling on the sparkling surface of the canal. A winter wind was starting to work its chilly breath around Amsterdam. Somewhere, Vos knew, a small, determined child was trapped, listening, thinking, wondering.

And there wasn't a damned thing he could do to help her.

Twenty minutes later he arrived at the Drie Vaten. Someone from Marnixstraat had taken Sam to the bar. The little dog greeted him. Waggy tail. Bright eyes even though it was gone eleven. Not a moment's thought for Sofia Albers who'd fed him, walked him, looked after him again.

Much like his owner, Vos thought. He smiled, said thanks, bought a beer and a toasted sandwich, then took a table by the window and looked out on the canal. No lights in his houseboat. Still there were memories of what happened earlier that year, when his daughter emerged from the darkness eventually and so, in a sense, did he. In the end Vos had saved her. Now she was on the other side of the world with her mother, enjoying the Caribbean sun, reluctant to return to the scene of the nightmare that had torn their family apart. The relief he felt at finding her was real but tempered always by an aching sense of loss.

'You want me to look after him tomorrow?' Sofia said as she came over with the sandwich.

'If you can. How's your mother?'

A shrug.

'Getting old, Pieter. Aren't we all?' She looked out of the

window at the slumbering city. 'I know I can't ask. But . . . this business in Leidseplein. Is it finished with?'

He smiled and kept quiet.

'I suppose that's an answer anyway,' she said with a shrug. 'Can I join . . .?'

A shape at the door. Vos looked. Hanna Bublik was there. She'd been to the scene of the houseboat on Westerdok. One of the uniform men had told her where to find him. It wasn't a secret.

'I'll leave you,' Sofia said after the Georgian woman ordered a coffee and sat down opposite him.

She was angry. Deserved to be, he thought. So he let her fury expend itself on him, listened, nodded, did what he could to explain. There were explanations too. This was an abduction that was planned. The Black Petes may have snatched the wrong girl but they knew what they wanted and how they would go about it. Some aspects of the case continued to bother him. The demand for money seemed wrong somehow.

But Natalya's mother neither knew nor cared about any of this. All she saw was failure. The police had located where her daughter was being held and arrived there too late. When they did they sealed off the boat and refused to let her on board to see the conditions Natalya had been kept in. To her this seemed unnecessary and cruel.

'We have to search the place,' he said when he had the chance. 'It's possible we can pick up some prints, DNA . . . some other material that will help us find her. It's a scientific process. Even I can't walk around when that's going on. But . . .'

He took out his phone to bring up the photo of the words Natalya had written in the porthole window.

'They probably plan to move her frequently until we get a handover. At night always I guess. Natalya left us this.'

She peered at the picture, moved by the careful writing in the condensation of the glass.

This woman didn't cry much, he thought. But at that moment she was close.

'Your daughter must be a bright girl. She's thinking about you. Probably wondering how she can escape.'

'She would.'

The heat had come out of the conversation. She drank her coffee, said yes when Vos asked her if she'd like something to eat. Two more toasted sandwiches appeared. He wished there was something more he could offer.

'Why do you care?' she asked.

'Because it's my job.'

'There's more to it than that. A woman at the police station told me. About your own girl. How you live here now. On the water. On your own.'

He looked outside towards the boat. Above the line of the pavement there was little to see except the deck with its pots of dying flowers, feeble vegetables and the upright figure of the plastic ballerina. Vos told her how his daughter Anneliese went missing and was found, almost three years later. Alive but damaged. So much so she was still living with her mother in the distant Caribbean. And probably wouldn't return. Not soon anyway.

As he recounted the story the little dog put his paws on Vos's feet then leaned against his right leg, the way he did when he sensed something was wrong.

Sofia came over with a plate of liver sausage for them and Sam sniffed the meat, leapt out from under the table, jerked it with his lead, barked once, a high-pitched yelp for attention.

Hanna Bublik looked briefly amused. That only made the dog bark again.

'Sam!' Vos chided him. 'Remember your manners.'

Another yap.

'He wants some food,' she pointed out.

Sam barked as if in agreement. Vos handed him a piece. The

dog took it very delicately, ate the morsel, thought about barking for another, then changed his mind and curled up at their feet.

'Is he all you've got now?' she asked. 'If your daughter's on the other side of the world?'

'No. I've got my work. My friends.' A nod at the window. 'Home.'

Sam started to snore.

'But you learn things from a dog,' he added.

'Like what?'

'Like . . .' He'd never thought about this much before. 'Like . . . Sam never looks back. Sometimes, on the boat, there are . . . accidents. When they happen he hangs his head. He's ashamed. I get a bit cross on occasion. And then, five minutes later, it's done. All that matters is now and what's to come.'

'Must be easy if you're a dog,' she said.

'He never knows his size,' Vos continued. 'There's a Great Dane down the street. A massive thing. He's terrified of Sam. Every time we meet he goes for him. He doesn't mind the creature's three times his size. In Sam's head he's top dog. The boss. That's all that counts.'

'Like you?' Hanna asked.

'Sometimes. When I need to be.' There was one other thing too. 'You know the biggest lesson I learned from him? He's a terrier. You saw it. When he wants something he doesn't give up. He barks. He hangs on. He keeps going until he gets what he wants. Doesn't matter how hard . . . how hopeless it looks. That's Sam.'

He reached down, patted the sleeping dog's head and got a growl in return.

'Clever little animal,' she said.

'Not really. He's just bright at the things he needs to be bright at.'

'That's clever, isn't it?'

She pulled out her bag, ready to pay. Her fingers fumbled.

Coins fell on the floor. He could see very clearly there was nothing in her purse but a single twenty euro note.

'This is mine,' he said.

'I pay my way.'

'Hanna!' Her stubbornness could get infuriating. 'I'll get this.'

He pulled out four fifty euro notes and placed them on her purse. She closed her eyes for a moment than glared at him.

'I've money of my own.'

'Just take it will you? I don't want you working while this goes on. I may need you at short notice.'

She didn't remove the notes.

'Jesus,' she murmured. 'I must be getting old and stupid. There was something I wanted to tell you. That man I saw today. Outside the police station. With the posh woman and her stuck-up kid.'

'Renata Kuyper?'

'Who is he?'

'Her husband. Why?'

She grimaced.

'All I was thinking about was Natalya. That maybe you'd find her.'

'What is it?'

She sighed.

'I could be wrong.'

'You know him?'

'We did business. A week or two ago. The usual twenty minutes.'

Vos rocked back on his rickety chair.

'Let me get this straight. You slept with Henk Kuyper?'

'If that's his name. Came back for more four or five days later. He was the whiny type. I just listen. Don't take much notice. He said he'd seen me in the street with my kid. He liked the fact I had a family. His own was a bit of a mess.'

She reached over and grabbed his glass of beer, took a sip.

'You'd be amazed how many men tell me their wives as good as sent them.'

'Do you remember anything else?'

'I remember he seemed sorry for himself. Guilty. As if he didn't want to be there at all. That's not unusual. Truly. The thing is . . .'

She screwed her eyes tight shut for a moment as if this memory hurt.

'That second time he left something. He said he'd bought it for his own little girl but realized he'd got the wrong size. I could have it if I wanted.'

Vos shifted on his seat. The dog got himself upright and stared at the pair of them.

'The jacket,' he said.

'You don't think I could afford something like that, do you? I went back to Marnixstraat to tell you. They said you'd gone out. Then all that stuff with the boat happened. It didn't seem important.'

'I need a positive ID. We can bring in Kuyper tomorrow.'

She cocked her head.

'If you like. Do you think I take much notice of their faces? I think it was him. I just glimpsed the man today.'

She took the notes from her purse and threw them on the table.

'And I don't need this.'

He put his hand on hers and stopped her. Close up her face lost its hardness. She looked exhausted. But not defeated.

'Men usually want something when they give me money.'

'I got something, didn't I?' he said. 'A reason to talk to the Kuypers again.'

She brushed the money into his lap.

'Find my daughter, Vos. That's all I want of you.'

'And when I do. What then?'

Her face was hard again.

'Then I go back to trying to stay alive. What else?'

'As a sex worker?'

'Don't call me that. I'm a whore.'

'There are ways out.'

'It's Natalya who needs saving. Not me.' She put the purse with its pittance of money in her bag. 'Call tomorrow whenever you like.'

She left then, a solitary figure stepping through the cold night back towards her tiny home in Oude Nieuwstraat. Sofia Albers came over, cleared the table and told him it was time to go.

Pieter Vos took Sam outside and called the night team. Rijnder was running the show. A good man. He'd check out Henk Kuyper. As they talked the little dog sniffed the air and tugged on his lead, always hunting something. Always curious.

*Never look back. Never think yourself so small or insignificant nothing matters. More than anything . . . never give up.*

Three good lessons he'd learnt without realizing it.

'Come on, Sam.' He reached down to stroke the dog's wiry fur as they walked the gangplank onto the ramshackle houseboat with its peeling paint, dying plants and a silver ballerina glinting under the moonlight. 'Time for bed.'

In the postbox there was another letter from the council telling him the boat needed to be cleaned up or he'd face legal action.

'Not now,' Vos muttered and threw the thing in the water.

# 3

Hanna Bublik slept throughout the night, not waking once. Which meant the guilt hurt even more when a hard winter sun flooded through the flimsy curtains of the gable window and brought the bleak world with it.

Exhaustion, physical and nervous, had taken its toll. The intriguing but evasive police officer Vos baffled her. Did he know or suspect more than he was saying? Or were the men and women in Marnixstraat just as much in the dark as she?

With a low curse she rolled out of bed, checked her phone straight away. The message light was flashing. Even the ring hadn't roused her. She fetched the voicemail: Vos, sounding friendly, determined and vague. They'd heard nothing more from the kidnapper. A team of forensic officers was still trawling through the boat in Westerdok. He wanted her to think about Henk Kuyper and whether he really was the man who'd visited her. They needed to make sure before approaching him.

Could she offer them that certainty? Going through the daily motions that seemed so strange without Natalya, washing, dressing, the same black jeans, shirt and jumper, she wondered. There was only one way to survive in the solitary, unattached life she'd chosen. That was to forge an absolute divide between the two parts of her existence: the woman in the cabin, the loving mother at home. The first was an automaton, unfeeling, unresponsive. The second as caring a parent as it was possible to be. For that to work she had to divide herself too. The prostitute, taking off her fake satin bra and pants, lying down, turning over, kneeling, doing whatever they wanted, never met the woman free of make-up walking round the city, dealing with school and the doctor, trying to make sure Natalya enjoyed the best childhood Hanna could provide.

She hadn't been entirely frank with Vos when she said she never looked at their faces. Things were never as simple as they seemed. When she was working her mind fled mostly, leaving her body to muscle memory, habits, tricks, old routines. All that mattered was to make this slow procession of men happy. Because that meant more money. Enough to go home early if she was lucky. The woman in the cabin focused on the physical alone. Skin to be touched, positions to be taken. Grunts and squeals to be uttered on cue, like an actress fallen on hard times.

And then the man came. As quickly as she could manage without risking his wrath. Which wasn't always easy.

She watched their faces because that told her the moment their time would soon be up. Nothing more. What she didn't see was a person there. An identity to be recalled. The hint of a relationship to be developed.

The man she'd seen the day before with the posh mother of the Dutch girl was familiar. The one who'd visited her twice and left, on that second occasion, a pink jacket that would, through a set of circumstances no one seemed to understand, rob her of her daughter.

And that only added to her burden. Barely a minute went by without her wondering about the possibilities.

What if Natalya had worn something different? Or they'd seen Sinterklaas earlier in the city then gone for pizza somewhere? This entire sequence of black events seemed to hang on coincidences and chances gone wrong, all of them within her ultimate control. Because she was a parent. The parent. The only one. It was her responsibility to make the right choices. Her fault when they went so badly awry.

She wasn't a forgiving woman. History had made her that way. But when the blame fell she knew where it was properly directed. At herself. In the end when Natalya needed her she'd turned to be the thing she feared most: a bad mother. The worst.

With that bitter thought poisoning her mind she went downstairs, ready to retrace her steps to Marnixstraat again.

Chantal was in the hallway, looking stupid as usual in flimsy clothes, ready for whatever job the Turk had found for her.

Guilty too, a flash of uncertainty in her dark and darting eyes.

'Did you hear anything about Natty?'

'Her name's Natalya,' Hanna snapped without thinking.

Chantal glared at her.

'Sorry.'

'No. I haven't heard anything.'

'Maybe Cem can help.'

'So you said.'

There was still something going on.

'What is it?' Hanna asked.

'I saw Jerry last night. He's putting up the rent.'

Jerry was the front for a foreign owner for the building. She was sure of that. The man had the worried look of someone who was always watching his back.

'How much?'

'For you six hundred.'

'I only pay four fifty! He promised it'd stay that way for a year.'

The teenage shrug again.

'Talk to Jerry. Not me. I said I'd tell you.'

'And what about you?'

Cornered, Chantal glanced at the door.

'Same for me.' Her room was twice the size, with a bigger window. 'He says it's backdated. He wants the extra this week.'

'Shame he can't stop people breaking into my room and stealing all my money.'

The girl shifted awkwardly on the spot.

'Same for me,' she said again.

'You can pay him. I can't.'

'Talk to Cem! I told you!'

Hanna walked right up to her and smiled. Not nicely.

'You know what we do to thieves? Back where I come from?'

Nothing.

She picked up Chantal's delicate, olive-skinned right hand.

'We chop off their fingers. One by one.'

'Trying to help you, Hanna. Why the fuck I bother?'

'Because someone's told you? Did Cem take my money? Does he own this place too?'

Fear. That was always there, however hard this stupid little kid tried to hide it.

So she did what little kids liked to do when caught. She started to cry.

There's the answer, Hanna thought. No need for anything else.

Cem Yilmaz wanted her name on his list and wasn't in the mood to be disappointed.

'Tell him he'll get his money,' she said. 'As soon as I can earn it.'

'There's always a man that owns you!' Chantal yelled at her, sobbing. 'You no different to me.'

Hanna slapped her round the face. Hard. Regretted it immediately.

Then went outside, blinking against the bright daylight. That brought the start of tears to her own eyes. She wiped them away and set off down the narrow cobbled street, past the cabins, looking for the best, preparing herself to smile at the passing men, do a come-on wave with her finger. Morning customers were scarce and always argued about the price. But it was money all the same.

The one she wanted was empty. So was the street. Outside the door she called Vos. It was a brief conversation.

'Are you sure?' Vos asked.

'I told you. He was different. Sad. As if he felt guilty about the whole thing. They don't normally leave a gift for your kid either. Something else I remembered . . .'

He waited.

'When he left me the jacket he asked me something about Sunday and Sinterklaas. What we'd be doing.'

'And?'

'I think I said we'd be there like everyone else. In Leidseplein. I think . . .'

He hesitated then asked, 'Did you tell him Natalya would be wearing that jacket?'

Hanna thought for a moment.

'Maybe. I don't remember. Pretty obvious she would be, isn't it? Nicest thing she's got. I really wasn't taking much notice to be honest. We were done. I wanted him out of there.'

'Thanks,' Vos said. 'It's enough. I'll call the moment I hear anything. Where will you be?'

She looked at the long window. The red glass. The stool and the single bed in the corner next to the tiny shower, sink and toilet. If she'd taken Vos's cash the night before maybe she could avoid this. But not now. Not with Jerry demanding money she didn't have. And besides there was something tempting about being in that place. Losing herself behind the glass. It was a selfish escape from her sense of impotence outside.

'Around,' she said and left it there.


Vos had got out of bed just after six, talked to Marnixstraat, gone through everything the night team had. It didn't take long. Then he checked what information they'd found on Henk Kuyper and made two calls: one to the missing girl's mother, the second to Laura Bakker, asking her to join him for breakfast in the Drie Vaten.

He was with Sam at their usual table in the raised section at the back when she arrived. Bakker's dress sense had regressed.

She wore green tartan trousers and a brown jacket with heavy black boots. She marched in, feet clattering, glanced around and said, 'You always look as if you live here.'

The little terrier ran up, tail wagging, and put his paws on her knees. She never told him to get down so Vos didn't any more.

Coffee and croissants came without a word.

'Is this really necessary?' she asked when they were alone.

'How long is it since you joined Marnixstraat?'

She shook her head, pulled back the red hair when it annoyed her, wrapped an elastic band to hold it in place in a loose, untidy ponytail.

'Eight. Nine months.'

'And you've taken no leave.'

Croissant crumbs went everywhere as she spluttered at this.

'Seriously, Laura. It's not good to work all that time without a break. Why don't you go back to Dokkum for a week? I'm sure your aunt can—'

'Right now?' she cut in. 'This very instant?'

He nodded and said, 'I think that would be a good idea. This is a stressful case. I've noticed you're getting worn down by it.'

'What?'

Sam heard the beginnings of an argument, got up and trotted back to the bar.

'I'm just saying . . .'

'What have I done wrong? Tell me. I'd like to know.'

'Nothing specific . . .'

'Something unspecific then? You don't want me here, do you?'

He took a long swig of coffee.

'You can call in sick today. I'll fix a holiday from tomorrow . . .'

'Pieter! What is this?'

'Nothing,' he insisted. 'I just—'

'I'm not calling in sick. I'm not taking holiday. The only way you can get me off the team is to take me off yourself.' She raised the cup in a toast. 'That's your prerogative but I'll want to hear a reason.'

'You're young,' he said. 'You've got a career ahead of you. Cases like this can damage them.'

'You want me to walk away from this girl's kidnapping because it might hurt my prospects?'

'Pretty much.'

'No. Tell me, please.'

Too smart for her own good sometimes. Too judgemental and inflexible. He'd been like that once. Experience changed him, nothing else.

So he told her.

She listened carefully then said, 'AIVD. That means deep water?'

'Fathomless,' Vos agreed.

'And we're bringing Kuyper into Marnixstraat? Am I allowed to be there?'

The young always thought in straight lines. That was one reason they found trouble so easily.

The dog was happy with Sofia Albers, trying to beg cheese from one of the locals who'd just walked in. The outrage in Leidseplein two days before wasn't forgotten. It still rumbled on in the papers. People talked about the shock and the outrage. But it lay in the past. An event the city had put behind it. AIVD's blackout was still in place. No one knew a young girl was being kept captive somewhere, her freedom depending on one of three things: the investigative skills of the police, the release of a suspected terrorist from imprisonment, and the payment of an unspecified ransom.

If they did there'd already be a public collection to raise the money for the last – one that would meet its target in a couple of hours. Amsterdammers were like that.

'Please,' Bakker said meekly. 'I need you to tell me what I'm supposed to do.'

'I told you that and you said no.'

She folded her arms and gazed at him. Waiting.

'You get your bike. We ride to see the Kuypers.'

'Ride?'

'Location matters, Laura. If we drag Henk Kuyper into Marnixstraat he'll be on his guard immediately. Prepared. Knowing what he wants to say.'

'So we surprise him at home instead,' she said with a nod and got up. 'Are you going to tell that woman from AIVD? If he was one of theirs once . . .'

'Seems a touch premature, don't you think? Later . . . They're still mad about last night.'

She laughed.

'Why care about my career? You clearly don't give a damn about yours.'

He walked to the counter and paid. Stroked the dog. Didn't need to ask Sofia to look after him.

Outside in the bright sun, eyeing the battered houseboat with the dead plants, the windows held together by tape, the dog toys and the silver ballerina on the deck, Vos said, 'I can always go back to what I was. I wouldn't mind.' A shrug. 'Maybe I'd prefer it.'

'No you wouldn't.'

'And you?' he asked brightly. 'What would you do?'

Her long pale face fell into a familiar, half-amused scowl. Then she climbed on her bike. The smart new one she'd bought herself when Marnixstraat took her on full-time. A black Dutch-made Batavus, old-fashioned with a looped frame and high handlebars that made her sit upright, head in the air.

'Whatever I felt like,' Laura Bakker said and pedalled off down the canal.

––––––

Just before ten the AIVD team turned up unannounced at Frank de Groot's office. He let them in and listened to Mirjam Fransen rattle off a list of questions about the investigation. None of which had easy answers.

Then she asked, 'Where's Vos? Where's that mouthy girl who follows him around like a tame puppy?'

De Groot was an easy-going man, aware they were all treading water in dangerous seas. All the same he'd come to develop a marked antipathy towards this woman. She wanted everything he had and was unwilling to give much at all in return.

'Brigadier Vos is out on a call,' he said.

'You heard the question,' Thom Geerts grunted. 'Where?'

So they had friends in government quarters in The Hague. This was Amsterdam. His city.

'I'm not answerable to AIVD for my officers' movements. Nor do I follow them every minute of the day.'

'Find out,' Fransen ordered. 'We don't want any more screw-ups like yesterday.'

De Groot pushed back his chair and stared at them. An unsmiling woman who looked as if she belonged in an office. Geerts was ex-military. He had the stance, the build, the grim and unforgiving demeanour of a certain type of army man.

'I'm not aware of any screw-ups yesterday. Vos had every right to talk to the man in custody at Schiphol. He tracked down that boat in Westerdok. The pity is the bird had flown. If . . .'

A sudden rap at the door. Van der Berg barged in without waiting.

'I think,' he said, nodding at the TV set, 'you need to turn on the news.'

He looked agitated and that was out of character. De Groot reached for the remote and got the channel.

The lead item had already started but there was a text summary running underneath the announcer. The appeal court ruling on Ismail Alamy's expulsion order was due in a few hours.

The news channel claimed to have a leak ahead of its announcement. According to their sources the preacher was about to win his case. The judges would demand his release before the day was out. The government had no more avenues of appeal. Alamy was going to be a free man. The outstanding arrest warrants for him in the Middle East would lie on the table on two grounds: that the so-called evidence behind him had been obtained through illicit means, and he might face torture if he was returned to face trial in any of the countries that wanted him.

'A greater embarrassment for the government is hard to imagine,' said the channel's legal correspondent. 'Our understanding is that Alamy will now be able to press for compensation for his imprisonment over the last eighteen months. It could run to hundreds of thousands of euros. In the meantime he could be back in his public housing property, living once again on state benefits, by tomorrow. Or leave the country for a friendly destination. A hero to those who've been supporting his case, some of them here in the Netherlands.'

Geerts reached over, grabbed the remote and turned off the TV.

He didn't blink. Neither did Mirjam Fransen.

'You knew this was on the cards,' Van der Berg butted in. 'You knew the bloody case was going to get thrown out and you never told us.'

'It hasn't happened yet,' Fransen replied. 'And if it does you can arrest him over the immigrant kid's abduction.'

'How?' the detective yelled from the door. 'He's been in solitary for more than a year. You listen to every conversation he has. God . . . you couldn't invent a better alibi.'

'Enough,' De Groot announced and waved him out.

When Van der Berg was gone he looked at the two AIVD officers and asked, 'Did you know?'

'All our legal advice suggested he didn't have a leg to stand on,'

Fransen said without a moment's hesitation. 'I'd no reason to think otherwise. We knew a decision was imminent . . .' She glanced at her watch. 'I'll talk to the lawyers. Find some way we can stall. Rearrest him on something else. There has to be—'

'What about the girl?' De Groot cut in. 'Natalya Bublik. Remember her?'

'She's your concern,' Fransen replied, a little puzzled. 'Not ours.'

He shook his head, as if this might help him think this through. If Alamy was released would the kidnappers do the same for the girl? They'd asked for money, which seemed odd to begin with, as Vos had pointed out. But if Alamy was free why continue to hold her and risk being caught?

'Either they'll dump her at a bus station or somewhere,' Geerts suggested. 'Or if they think she can identify them in some way . . .' He shrugged. 'She's dead.'

Mirjam Fransen got up, phone in hand.

'Go nowhere near Schiphol,' she said. 'I'll brief you when I've got something to say.'

De Groot watched them leave then called Vos and told him what was going on. He could hear the outside world behind the call. People on bikes. Just another day in Amsterdam.

Geerts was right. Maybe they would just let the girl go. It was a big assumption though.

Vos had stopped with Bakker when the call had come. They were in the Herenmarkt, by the playground. Saskia Kuyper was there sitting sullenly on a swing. Her mother was watching. She hadn't noticed there were visitors. Eyes only for her daughter. There was something dark and unlovely between these two.

'If we're lucky we get a miracle,' De Groot said, with the tiniest note of hope in his voice.

'We've got to find her,' Vos said straight away.

'You can try.'

'We have to,' Vos insisted. 'If Alamy goes free they've lost control just as much as us. We've got nothing they want. And they've got Natalya Bublik who's worthless to them unless they want to go through the risk of a ransom handover.'

Silence on the line. De Groot was a decent, kindly man. Trapped in an organized, logical frame of mind.

'You really think Henk Kuyper's involved?' he asked.

'I don't know. But you read the logs. Henk Kuyper worked for AIVD until they threw him out five years ago for leaking material to the left-wing press. It seems he had sex with Natalya's mother twice and left her that pink jacket. She thinks he may have asked whether the girl would be wearing that jacket in Leidseplein.'

'She doesn't know for sure?' De Groot asked.

'It wasn't a date, Frank. I don't imagine she paid much attention.' Vos couldn't take his eyes off Laura Bakker. She was watching the children in the playground, her long, plain-pretty face full of fear and melancholy. 'Keep Van der Berg looking for someone who knew that dead Brit. And I'd prefer it if AIVD stayed in the dark about where I am. For now.'

Silence again.

'Agreed?' he asked.

'Agreed,' De Groot said eventually.

Vos walked over and caught Bakker's attention. Renata Kuyper still hadn't seen them. She was staring at her daughter. Saskia sat on the swing barely moving, looking ahead, at nothing at all.

'I loved my mum,' Bakker said, her voice cracked and uncertain for once. 'I still miss her.'

'Mine lives outside Utrecht,' Vos said. 'I go to see her once a month. We've been getting on since I went back to work.'

She nodded at the Kuyper woman and her daughter.

'It shouldn't be like that. Should it?'

'No,' he said then pushed his bike to the door of the narrow terraced house with the crow-stepped gable, put his finger on the bell, kept it there until he could hear footsteps coming down the stairs.


Natalya was in another boat, listening to squabbling ducks and the waves lapping against the hull.

She was starting to feel grubby. At home she changed clothes every other day, sometimes helped her mother take the dirty washing to the launderette, watched the sheets and shirts and underclothes go round and round.

Here, in this strange and unreal life, it was as if time had stopped altogether. There was nothing but a new cell, this time lit by two opaque glass portholes. A bathroom with a toilet and a small tub. A little dressing table and a mirror.

She could get in the bath, take a shower if she wanted. Feel clean. Feel different. And perhaps she would. But not now. He was there. Or one of them. She'd logged at least three in her head now. One with a quiet, refined Dutch accent. The kind one, she thought. The other two foreign. Grumpy. Scary. Scared too.

This was a frightened one. She could sense the fear in his sudden, nervous movements, hear it through the angry grunts of an alien language that came muffled through the bathroom door.

Scared people are weak. Or so her mum always said. Scared people could be dangerous too. Because the way they tried to hide their feebleness was through a cowardly show of strength.

But you had to push them. If you didn't you never knew where you stood.

Birds beyond the window. A church bell not so far away, chiming every fifteen minutes with a longer, more musical set of notes on the hour. That extended set of sounds was a while ago. Had she still possessed her cheap little watch – the first man took it from her in the van – it would have read, she guessed, half past ten.

And still they hadn't fed her. The flight from that initial boat had been hasty and unexpected. As if someone had warned them to snatch her away. A blindfold. A van. A short trip through winding streets. Then bundled again across a gangplank into somewhere new.

The Dutch one hadn't turned up at all since then. Perhaps he was scared as well. It was as if she'd become an object. A piece of furniture to be moved around the city without a second thought.

That idea made her mad. And they had to be tested. Her mum said so.

Natalya walked to the flimsy wooden door of the bathroom and banged on it with her little fist. She didn't shout or scream. They'd said they'd gag her if she did that. But they didn't mention anything else.

Three times she hammered on the door. Then she waited and listened. He was on the phone. She heard a snatch of something, made a mental note of it.

Silence. She banged again, twice and the door was thrown open. A tall man there. Black balaclava, beard peeking out of the bottom, bright-blue jeans, a brown leather bomber jacket. He towered over her and asked in a harsh foreign voice, 'What do you want?'

'You didn't give me any food.'

He stood there stiff, embarrassed maybe. They didn't want to hurt her. None of them. Or so it seemed.

'I'll get you something, child. Don't bang on the door like that.'

Outside she heard the sound of a small boat chugging down the canal and loud, happy voices. American, she thought. Tourists probably.

'Wouldn't if you fed me,' Natalya said, trying to give her voice the scolding tone of a teacher dealing with a naughty child. 'And a book. Some crayons. The other man did.'

'He's not here.'

She didn't move.

'Wait,' he said and walked away from the door.

She could see a little of the space beyond. It looked like a low, narrow living room. A television set, a computer on a desk. Chairs and a sofa. In the corner a small kitchen hob and a tiny fridge. The windows were bigger here and clear. Through them she could see the walls of the canal and just make out the bare trunks of trees above the black brickwork.

And a set of steps rising to what had to be an open door, judging by the flood of light pouring down to the timber planks of the boat.

She looked.

He looked.

A big man. Between her and the world outside. Natalya was quick and lithe and smart. But she couldn't get past him, not at that moment. And both knew it.

A supermarket bag stood by the little gas hob. Not Marqt any more. The man bent over the shopping, roughly hunting for something. There was a mirror on the wall. Through that she could watch him closely even though his back was turned. Bad-tempered, worried. He was going through the things someone had bought. The balaclava didn't fit well. He couldn't see. Still with his back to her he pulled up the front of the balaclava to peer at the groceries.

One moment then, so short she didn't know herself how much either of them saw.

A face in the glass. Dark-skinned. Unusual. Black eyes glaring back towards her. Beard like a pirate.

Natalya retreated into the bathroom and waited out of sight behind the door.

A few moments later he came back, the balaclava pulled down. In his hands a pot of yoghurt, a croissant, a carton of orange juice.

She took them and said, 'I told you. The Dutch man promised me a book.'

Which was a lie. A little white lie. Perhaps he'd know. But grown-ups lied all the time. How else did children learn to copy them?

He handed her the food. She placed it on the closed toilet lid. Then he went back to the bag, rifled through it again. This time he kept the balaclava on.

When he returned he had a new colouring book and a fresh set of crayons. She looked at the cover. *My Little Pony*. Like the jacket she'd got. Too girly. Too young for her. But she took it anyway, watched as the man closed the door and seemed to bolt it.

That must have been new, she thought. No one locked a toilet from the outside.

Natalya Bublik wondered what that meant and whether it was any use to her. Then she waited a few minutes, ate the yoghurt, then the croissant, drank the orange juice. Took out the new book and the crayons. Couldn't think of a thing to write.


Koeman got called to reception in Marnixstraat to deal with the visitor causing trouble there. He took one look and thought: *Why is it always me?*

The man was wearing a suit that must have been smart once upon a time: dark blue with grey pinstripes. A pipe stuck out of his right-hand pocket and a bulge that must have been a tobacco tin. He smelled like an eighty-year-old who lived in an ashtray.

As he started to talk he offered two ID cards. One standard EU issue. The second an old soldier's card showing he'd been discharged three years earlier, not long after the Royal Netherlands Army pulled out of Afghanistan. Sergeant with the Regiment Johan Willem Friso.

His name was Ferdi Pijpers and he'd just seen the TV news.

Koeman did a double take on the ID. Pijpers was thirty-nine but looked a good ten years older. His leathery face was lined and tanned, either from dirt or pipe smoke. There was a tic in his right eye and an anxious timbre to his deep voice. War debris, Koeman thought. He knew this type. How they came out of the forces and never managed to make their way back into civilian life.

He listened as best he could then said, 'Ferdi, Ferdi . . . calm down. Please.'

'I am calm,' Pijpers said. 'Got a coffee?'

The incident with the Bublik woman still bothered Koeman. He didn't like to appear rude or unhelpful. It was just that the job brought it on sometimes.

So he went to the downstairs machine by reception and paid for a cup then watched Ferdi Pijpers take it with shaking fingers.

'There are service charities, you know. People who can help.'

'Who says I want help?' Pijpers snapped, stung by the remark. 'You're the people who need it. Not me.'

'Why's that?'

'Because those fools in Strasbourg are going to let that bastard Alamy back out onto the streets. And then we get even more crap like we had in Leidseplein all over again.'

The detective tried to think this through. The papers had run plenty of pieces about the attack the previous Sunday. Most had extensive profiles of Martin Bowers, the young Englishman who'd changed his name to Mujahied Bouali, fallen into extremist circles then travelled to Amsterdam to die in a back alley not far away from Marnixstraat. But that was it. Thanks to AIVD's blackout Ismail Alamy wasn't part of the story. Not for the public.

'Ismail Alamy's been in custody for eighteen months. He can't have had anything to do with what happened in Leidseplein. We're looking into that. I can't elaborate. You wouldn't expect me to. Unless you've reason to believe he had some connection—'

'I shed blood for this country,' Pijpers cut in, tapping at his chest, coffee spilling all over the table. 'I saw what these animals are like when you let them loose. All the same. They'll kill you as soon as draw breath. Fucking ragheads—'

'Whoa, whoa, whoa,' Koeman interrupted. 'You can't go around talking like that. We've got sensitivities these days. And besides . . .' This was true and worth saying. 'Most of the bad men I've met think they're good Christians. Or Muslims. Or whatever. People like Alamy . . . like that kid AIVD shot on Sunday . . . they're just the lunatic fringe.'

'You're a fool,' Pijpers told him. 'All of you. Clueless. No idea what's round the corner.'

Koeman glanced at his watch then back at the stairs to his office. There was real work still to be done.

'Which is what?'

'Sharia courts. Treating our women like scum. Telling us what to do in our own country.' He tapped his forehead. 'I've seen it. I know what it looks like.'

Koeman sighed and briefly closed his eyes.

'We're really busy right now. Chasing the very things you think we should be looking at. Bad people. Ours. Theirs. Sometimes a little of both.'

'Idiots,' Pijpers added.

'Reception called me down because you told them you had something useful to tell us. I would be really grateful if you could pass that on. Then go back to talking to Mr Heineken and his friends. Because frankly they're probably better listeners than me right now.'

There, he thought. The nice-guy act didn't last.

'You can't let that bastard Alamy back out on the street. I know these people. Better than you ever will. I'm done listening to monkeys. I want to talk to your boss.'

'About what?'

Pijpers brushed down his old, battered suit as if getting ready for a job interview.

'That's for him to hear.'

He took the ancient and smelly pipe out of his pocket, sucked on the end, then pulled out a can of tobacco.

'I'm waiting,' Pijpers said.

'You're not actually. And you're not lighting that stinking thing in here either. If you've got something to say you can say it to me.'

The man glared at him. Then he muttered a curse and got to his feet.

'I should have known I was wasting my breath on you morons,' he muttered with the pipe still stuck between his teeth.

Koeman tried to smile.

'I really recommend you try one of the charities. If you like I can find you some names. A number.'

'I don't need your pity. You know what I did in the army?'

'I can guess.'

'No, you can't. I was military intelligence. I did your job. Only better.'

Koeman stood up, took out a twenty note and waved it in front of Pijpers's unwashed, surly face.

'Promise it goes on food. Not booze or something worse.'

The man just stared at the money.

'Cretins. Shit for brains.'

'Well I tried,' Koeman sighed and watched him go.


Henk Kuyper took them to the first-floor dining room. Through the long windows they could see the playground across the street. His wife sitting glumly on her own. Saskia barely talking to the other kids.

'You want me to fetch them?' he asked. 'I have to say I'm getting really sick of this. Shouldn't you be looking for that child?'

'We are,' Bakker said and sat down.

Vos glanced at her, a look that said, 'Mind the tone.'

Then took the chair opposite Kuyper and asked him what he

did. The answer didn't add up to much. Environmental consul-tancy. Liaison. On the side he offered voluntary political advice for anyone who needed it. He made it clear that money wasn't his first concern. He came from a 'good' family. Finances weren't a problem.

'You volunteer for radical causes?' Bakker butted in. 'People like Ismail Alamy?'

'I support people the rest of you ignore. I don't pick and choose on the basis of religion. Or skin colour.'

'Didn't answer the question,' she pointed out.

He frowned.

'I've never worked on Alamy's case. A few similar. But not that one.' He stared straight at her. 'But if his lawyers had come to me I'd have done what I could. From what I've read we've no reason to hold him. Or to hand him over to people whose idea of justice comes nowhere close to our own. If they were our enemies we'd never dream of it. So why change when they're supposedly our allies?'

Neither answered. He smiled a sarcastic smile and said, 'It's OK. I wasn't expecting a response on that one. You do your job. I know. That's all that matters.'

'As best we can,' Vos answered. 'The thing is you weren't always on the side of the oppressed were you, Henk?'

The tall man in front of them wasn't smiling any more.

'In fact you were, in their terms, an oppressor. You worked for AIVD as one of their agents.' Vos paused, watched him closely. 'What happened?'

'I'm a Kuyper. We're a military family. Going back genera-tions. I was pushed into that job. Wasn't even asked about it.'

'And then you leaked something to the papers and they kicked you out?' Bakker added.

He thought about his answer, shrugged and said, 'There are things the public have a right to know. AIVD came to accept that.

I was never prosecuted. Never named in public.' He gazed at them both. 'You shouldn't be aware of this. It's classified.'

'There's a missing girl out there,' Laura Bakker told him. 'We're turning over every stone to find her.'

'No stones here,' he said easily. 'I worked for AIVD for two years. My father got me the job. I didn't have much choice. What I saw there . . .' He stopped, frowned. 'Do we really have time for philosophical discussions?'

'So what you saw in AIVD turned you?' she asked. 'Radicalized you? Just like that British kid your former colleagues shot two days ago?'

'Not quite like that,' he answered with an edge. 'But I saw things . . . learnt things . . . that altered my view of the world. We fool ourselves we're a liberal democracy. It's a lie. The richer get richer. The poor get poorer. And all the time we turn our backs on those who need us. If—'

'We don't need the lecture, Henk,' Bakker interrupted. 'We're looking for a missing girl. The daughter of a Georgian sex worker. We're not turning our backs. Where were you when Saskia went missing?'

'I was on my way to Leidseplein,' he said. 'Renata was pissed off with me because I didn't have time to see the parade earlier. I thought I'd try to make it up. I was just getting there when she called and said she'd lost her.'

'And then?' Vos asked.

'Then I looked around and found her. I was fortunate I guess. So was Saskia.'

'Good fortune,' Bakker murmured.

'Exactly,' he agreed.

'Was it good fortune that made you give Hanna Bublik that pink jacket?' Vos added, watching him, following every move, every tic. 'After you'd paid her for sex? A second time?'

A long moment. Henk Kuyper looked at him, at Bakker, then returned to Vos. And laughed. Just for a second.

'She saw me, didn't she? Going into Marnixstraat yesterday? I should have guessed.'

He got up, glanced outside at the playground. Saskia was playing finally, with a little boy. Bossing him around it looked like. Her mother sat and watched, clutching a paper cup.

'Coffee,' he said and went into the kitchen.


One customer. A surly American kid who didn't know what he wanted and haggled over everything. Hanna Bublik saw him off in twenty-five minutes, waited another quarter of an hour. No one passed her window except a street cleaner picking up stray beer cans from the night before.

She was prevaricating and knew it. So she wrote off the remaining three hours she had on the cabin, got dressed and walked outside.

A beautiful early winter day in Amsterdam. The remorse hit her straight away. She'd have taken Natalya down to the canal and fed the ducks. Watched her play in the park. Bought chips and sauce in little paper cornets, eaten them in the street.

Instead she walked across town to the main red-light district, cast a professional eye on the girls working there. More business in this part of the city. A higher price to seek trade here too. Different people to negotiate with. At least in Oude Nieuwstraat she knew mostly where she stood.

Spooksteeg was quiet at this time of the morning. She rang the bell on Yilmaz's building and waited for an answer. It took a while. Then she was buzzed in and took the lift to the top floor, wasn't surprised this time when it opened directly into his living room.

The Turk was half-naked in baggy trousers, his barrel chest covered in what looked like oil. He wasn't alone. There was a muscular blond man in the same room. Younger. Covered in sweat and oil too. Both of them breathless.

She stared. The younger man had the most extraordinary tattoos all over his torso. A pair of eyes on his stomach either side of his navel. A skull in a basket on his right shoulder. A bleeding heart inside a triangle on his back.

'We're not finished,' Yilmaz said when she started to speak. 'You can wait.' He grinned. 'You can watch.'

There was a mat on the floor in front of the roaring fire. The Turk went back and gripped the younger man by the neck, fat, strong arms round his sinews. Then the two of them started to wrestle.

She'd seen things like this in Georgia too. Big, strong men trying to prove themselves. Was it sexual? She didn't know. Or watch much. It went on for a while, grunting, one on top of the other, elbows, fists, fingers grabbing for purchase on slippery skin. Then Yilmaz twisted the other one round and threw him hard to the mat. The young man's hands went up in surrender. The Turk laughed, got to his feet, slapped his big tanned belly.

'Dmitri, Dmitri,' he complained. 'You make it too easy for me.'

The blond said something in what sounded like Russian. A language that always sent a shiver down Hanna's spine. Then he got up and smiled like a young boy waiting for a present, picked up a towel and rubbed himself down. Some of the sweat and oil disappeared. He glanced towards what looked like a bathroom.

'Shower in your own time,' Yilmaz ordered then glanced at Hanna. 'We've got business.'

He walked to the desk and opened the drawer stuffed with money. Some notes came out and he handed them over to Dmitri.

'Half price,' the Turk said. 'You gave in too easily. You let me win.' A grin. 'And the rest I get for free.'

The Russian's smile vanished but he didn't argue. Then Dmitri found some clothes and left. Yilmaz disappeared into the bathroom and came out wearing a white fluffy robe, two cans of health drink in his hand. He told her to sit down and gave her one. Something with pomegranate.

'Any news?' he asked from the leather sofa.

'No. I was wondering if . . . if you'd heard something.'

The big shoulders shrugged.

'I told you, Mrs Bublik. I'm willing to help but I need you in my family. A man doesn't protect strangers. We need some give and take here.'

'You said you'd ask. My daughter's been kidnapped!'

He sighed.

'Yesterday you say the same thing. Yet this morning you're working again. Trying to take a few euros from some passing fools in Oude Nieuwstraat. Really—'

'Are you spying on me?'

'I own those buildings. I keep an eye on my investment.'

She thought of the way someone had broken into their bedroom. Chantal's guilty look that morning, and the news that Jerry was looking for more rent.

'Is the dump I live in yours too?' She wondered whether to say it. 'Can you come and go as you please?'

He waved a dismissive hand.

'I've lots of interests. More than you can imagine. This is irrelevant. You need your daughter home. I can appreciate that.' He swigged at the can and leaned back on the shiny sofa. 'I've asked questions. Even though you've offered me nothing.'

She waited.

'There are evil men in this city. They call themselves devout. They're not.'

'What did you hear?'

'Only gossip. Nothing worthwhile. If you want me to help you know what you need to do.'

A phone trilled on the desk. He went to answer it. Glanced at her, put his hand over the mouthpiece and said, 'I need to deal with this. Stay here.'

Yilmaz walked through the door at the end of the room. She heard his big feet padding down what sounded like a long corridor. Gone. For a while anyway.

Stealing was bad. It was something she'd never done. But now . . .

She got up and walked to the desk. He displayed this money to everyone, she thought. It was his way of saying, 'I'm king here. I live to my own rules.'

The door to the corridor was half open. She could hear his voice. Almost distant. He was speaking Turkish or something. Loud and commanding.

She opened the drawer and stared at the money. Did he know how much was there? Would he even miss a thousand?

Hanna picked up a few fifty euro notes and felt odd and dirty. Money was to be earned, always. However that was done.

But she snatched at some anyway and stuffed them in her pocket. The stacks of notes moved. At the back there were other things there. Watches. Phones. Wallets.

And something silver glinting, an amber pendant attached to the chain. Cheap but beautiful. To her anyway.

The necklace her husband had given her that night they were married in distant Gori. She touched the chain, the glassy brown and yellow stone.

Stolen when someone broke into the gable room she'd shared with Natalya.

There was a gun beyond it and a pack of ammunition, right at the back, like an afterthought. Dusty as if the weapon was there for an emergency and hadn't been needed in years. Cem Yilmaz ruled this world. He had others to protect him.

Footsteps down the corridor. The sound of a phone conversation coming to an end.

She let go of the necklace, reached out and snatched the weapon and the pack of shells, fumbled them into her pocket, closed the drawer, walked quickly back to the centre of the room and took the chair.

Yilmaz marched in and stared at her.

'A good man would help me,' she said, just to get out some words.

'A good man will. When you're ready.'

He glanced at the desk. The drawer was shut. Was it like that before? She didn't feel sure. Perhaps he was in the same position.

'Are you, Mrs Bublik?'

He broke into their room when she was out dealing with the police. Stole everything she had to force her into his clutches. She'd never fired a gun in her life. Would have to go to an Internet cafe to learn how to use one. But she knew this was not the time. Cem Yilmaz was a big-time gangster in the city. He surely heard things that never reached the police.

'Not yet,' she said and got up, aware, and a little frightened, that this clearly left him furious.

There was a street cleaner working in Spooksteeg. Sweeping up rubbish, putting down disinfectant. The place stank. Hand shaking, with trembling fingers, she turned to face the wall and placed the gun and the cardboard box of ammunition deep inside her bag. Then took out her phone.

No messages.


Three cups of macchiato on the table. Bakker didn't touch hers. Vos pushed his to one side. The sun was bright outside. They could just hear children's voices rising from the playground.

'What do you want me to say?' Kuyper asked finally.

'The truth would be nice,' Bakker suggested.

He looked at her and laughed. Then turned to Vos.

'Is she always this . . . rough at the edges?'

'Seems a reasonable enough request to me,' Vos told him. 'If you like I can arrest you and we can carry on this conversation in Marnixstraat.'

'Arrest me for what?'

'You've got extremist sympathies,' Bakker cut in. 'You used to work for AIVD. You slept with Natalya Bublik's mother then gave her the jacket that got her kidnapped. You checked out she was going to be in Leidseplein. Don't you think that's enough?'

'What do you mean I checked out where she'd be?'

'That's what she said,' Vos replied.

'Don't be ridiculous,' he said and casually sipped at the coffee. 'Maybe I asked what she was doing with her kid that Sunday. That's all. And my opinions are entirely legal by the way. What I did in the past's irrelevant. It's not illegal to have sex with a prostitute. If it was your jails would be full.'

'And the jacket?' Bakker asked.

He put down the cup and stared at her.

'How old are you?'

'Is that relevant?'

'To me it is.'

'Twenty-five.'

'I've got ten years on you. Long years. Things change.' He closed his eyes for a moment and looked briefly fragile. 'The news said Alamy's going free. The court's going to let him walk. Is that true?'

'Possibly,' Vos answered. 'Until the ruling's released we don't know.'

'He'll let her go then, won't he?' he said, a note of hope in his voice. 'I mean . . . why would he keep her?'

'We don't know.' Bakker was getting cross and that always worried Vos. 'We can't stop searching for her, can we?'

Vos looked round the room.

'You've got such a nice life, Henk. Money. A fine home. A family. Why wander into the red-light district and poke your nose in one of those cabins? I'm interested. It won't go any further.'

Nothing.

'Was it a habit?' Bakker demanded. 'Couple of times a week. You'd say you were going for a walk. Did Renata know . . .?'

'She didn't know. And it wasn't a habit either. Just twice. With that woman.' He pushed the coffee to one side and sighed. 'Believe it or not. Either way I don't care.'

Vos waited a while then asked again . . . why?

'Because things are bad here,' he said with a scowl. 'Renata thinks she wants to leave me but can't pluck up the courage. I don't have the heart either. Saskia and her mum don't get along. She still needs a mother. I'm not . . . enough.'

'So you skip along the road and throw fifty euros on a quick roll with an East European hooker?' Bakker said.

'This one really doesn't do subtlety, does she?' he said to Vos.

'Sometimes subtlety's wasted,' Vos replied. 'I still don't understand why.'

'To spite her. We haven't made love in months. I tried one night. Been drinking. It didn't happen. So the next night . . . I'd had a few. I was walking back from the centre, down Oude Nieuwstraat and saw this woman sitting in a window. She looked . . . interesting. Intelligent. Maybe . . . different.'

'Then a couple of days later you went back and gave her a pink jacket for her daughter,' Bakker went on. 'You said it was the wrong size, Henk. It wasn't, was it?'

'No.'

He leaned back in the chair and shut his eyes again.

'Shit. This is such a mess.'

Vos checked his phone for messages. Nothing.

'We need to know, Henk. We need . . .'

'I saw her in the street. OK? With the kid. A pretty kid. Like Saskia. You could see they didn't have a cent to their name. And here I am . . .' His hand swept the room. 'Pretending I make a difference and living off my old man. A bit later I went shopping.

I bought that jacket for Saskia. Really. Then I walked down the street again. And she was back there in the window.'

He frowned.

'I didn't want to have sex but it was like . . . she expected it or something. As if it was a contract. A business deal. I paid. She delivered. Then I got her talking about the kid. She came alive then. She wasn't just a hunk of meat on show. She couldn't stop talking about how much her girl wanted to see Sinterklaas turning up on Sunday.' He looked round the room. 'Didn't get that kind of enthusiasm here. So I made up some story. The jacket was the wrong size. She could have it.'

Kuyper caught Vos's eye.

'It wasn't easy. I don't think that woman likes the idea of charity. But she said the girl might like some new clothes for Sinterklaas. So I left it there. Then I told myself I'd never go back. Never do that again.'

Bakker said, 'And then you went out and bought another pink jacket for your daughter.'

He glared at her.

'Yes. I wanted to give her a present. Is that OK?'

'I don't know,' Bakker answered. 'Is it?'

That infuriated him.

'Listen! I would have given that woman more. Not just a stupid jacket. Money. A couple of hundred euros or something. But the stupid bitch wouldn't take it. Some kind of pride or something. Perhaps she thought she wasn't really a whore.'

'Perhaps in her head she isn't,' Bakker noted.

'Are you serious? If you sit under that red light in your underwear and let men do what they want for pocket money . . . what else are you?'

'A mother?' Vos suggested.

'Only outside that place,' he insisted. 'And I saw that. In the street. It's why I went back.'

Bakker unfolded her legs and stared at him.

'You're lying, Henk. Sticks out a mile.'

'No I'm not. You're just young and ignorant.' He nodded at Vos. 'Ask your boss. He knows.'

'Don't start that . . .'

Her temper was fraying. Vos held out a hand and got her to calm down a little.

'What else do you want?' Kuyper asked. 'I know this looks bad. It is bad. Bad between me and my wife. Nothing to do with you. Or that poor kid. If I knew anything that might help you get her back I'd tell you. That's the truth.'

Vos got to his feet and couldn't stop himself glancing out of the window, down to the playground and the two uncommunicative figures there. Then Saskia got up and went off with the other kids. Back to school he guessed.

'I hope so,' he said. 'If I find any part of this tale doesn't stack up I'll bring you down to Marnixstraat myself. And then this is formal.'

'Fair enough.'

'I don't see any reason why your wife needs to know what we've talked about,' he added. 'Not at the moment.'

Bakker sucked in a long breath and glared at the man opposite her. But she kept quiet.

Kuyper got up and went to the door.

'You're wrong there. She does need to know,' he said. 'From me. It's time . . .' They watched him. For a few seconds he seemed a man in agony. 'It's time we sorted this out one way or another.' He gazed at them both. 'I should be grateful to you for bringing that to a head. Maybe one day I will be. Miracles do happen they say.'

Outside they passed the playground. Renata sat alone and miserable on a bench seat, oblivious to them. Then her phone rang.

———

In this dream she was at the top of the stairs. The monster at the bottom, thinking she couldn't see him, grinning, leering, happy. Hungry.

And then he started to come for her. Step by step. Slowly. Deliberately.

Outside was the deafening racket of a world in chaos. Bombs and chattering weapons. Men yelling. Women screaming. The smell of something sharp and hot. The walls of the building, old and dusty, kept moving in and out, like a great animal made of brick, breathing its last.

Blood came into it somewhere. It was on the face and the chest of a man she thought must be her father. But he was dead. Long dead. All she'd seen was the single picture her mother had brought with them all the way from Georgia to Amsterdam. A handsome, beaming man in a baker's apron, standing in the countryside somewhere in summer, his arm around a young and happy woman wearing a garland of flowers in her hair.

The wounded, dying apparition she saw in her dreams wasn't quite like this. But dreams lied. And so did pictures.

This nightmare had been rumbling around her head as long as she could remember. She'd first woken screaming, sweating, terrified from its grip in a rickety cot that smelled of pee and worse somewhere in the dead, lost land they'd travelled through on the way from an uncertain past to a fragile present.

But in Amsterdam, in that little gable room she'd come to like, love even, it hadn't visited much of late. It was only a week ago that the night terrors returned. Worse than ever. Noisier. Bloodier. And a monster who kept getting closer with each passing night.

Still invisible now but so near she could smell him. Something rank and rotten on his hot and steaming breath.

This dream girl backed against the wall. Looked down and saw something moving in the dark. Just three steps left now and then he had her.

'Mummy,' she whispered.

'Mummy's not here,' the creature said in a deep, strange voice, amused.

'Mummy!' she shouted.

One more step on the stairs. Her little arm swept the darkness in front of them.

Swept the dream away too. Memories returned. The knowledge that she was still in the second place, the little cabin where the Black Pete had taken her, rattling around in the back of an old and rusty van.

'Mummy's not here.'

Natalya Bublik looked up, fearful but curious too because a Bublik woman always was. Her mother told her that.

It was just a man, dark-skinned, clean-shaven. Khaki jacket like a soldier, black jeans. Heavy boots. Something in his hand. She looked. A mobile phone and a set of keys.

No balaclava, she realized, and knew this was bad somehow.

'Who are you?' Natalya Bublik asked straight out, looking into his dark and unfeeling eyes, trying to see something there.

He didn't answer. Someone behind spoke, though, words she couldn't begin to understand. Then he came too. Bigger than the first one. A rough brown sack in his hands. Some words on the side. Like the name of a company.

He shook out the sack. It was bigger than she was.

'Get in there,' the man said in gruff and guttural Dutch.

She stood up, ready. Before she could step inside the sack they dragged the thick hessian over her.

This was what happened when you fell asleep in the daytime. Monsters coming for you. Strange men treating you as if you belonged to them. Like a thing.

Their arms lifted her, not roughly, not gently either. And then, with a warning to keep quiet, she was taken out of the little bathroom, rushed into fresh cold air and the city.

———

In Noordermarkt, a few minutes from the Kuyper house, Vos suddenly stopped and got off his bike. There was a new cheese shop he'd heard of. A pretty little place on the square by the church. Bakker followed him in, clucking all the time. Then watched as he bought two cheese croissants and took them to a bench outside.

Every Saturday the square was packed for the weekly farmers' market. But this was Tuesday, in winter. The place was empty.

Vos gave her a croissant and asked her opinion.

'I still think he's lying,' she said.

'I meant about the croissant.' He looked very sage. 'Good way of judging a cheese shop. I mean . . . it's not just about cheese.'

She took a bite and said it was lovely. He tried his and nodded.

'Not as good as my local in Elandsgracht.'

'Should we really be discussing the merits of cheese croissants right now?'

'I'm thinking too.'

'Thinking what?'

'Thinking I wish you'd called in sick as I suggested.'

She grimaced and cast him a filthy glance.

'Not going to happen.'

'I know,' he said. He took another bite. Crumbs tumbled down his scruffy winter jacket. 'Doesn't stop me wishing.'

'Because . . . ?'

'Because there's something wrong here. Something we haven't seen. And maybe our friends in AIVD have. They knew there was going to be trouble in Leidseplein.'

'And they shot that British idiot damned quickly,' Bakker added. 'Doesn't change the fact Henk Kuyper's lying, does it? We should bring him in.'

Vos finished the croissant, balled the paper bag and threw it into a nearby bin. She tried the same and missed.

'He's lying. But not about everything. Didn't you see when he talked about his marriage? That's real enough. He feels guilty.

Dirty. Perhaps he doesn't know why he did it. Or if he does he's not letting on.'

Bakker half smiled and for once looked reluctant to say something. Vos pressed her.

'Don't men just do things like that? If they've had a few beers and . . . feel like it?'

'Well I don't . . .' he objected.

'I didn't mean you! You're not normal.'

'Thanks!'

'Not like that anyway. Kuyper's ex-security services. He must know about operations and guns and stuff. He's shifty as hell and we're sure he's not telling the truth. We should pull him in.'

He wasn't in a rush to answer. Then his phone rang. De Groot with confirmation of Alamy's release. The man would be freed from detention at Schiphol that afternoon then handed over to his lawyers. Much to AIVD's fury there was nothing anyone could do to stop his release. If he wanted he could simply cross the road, go into the airport terminal and fly out of the country.

'Is it on the news?' Vos asked.

'If it isn't it will be any minute. Have we got anything on the girl?'

'No.'

'Not a word on that woman's phone? Nothing from this interview with Kuyper?'

'Not really.'

A long pause.

'I want to be at Schiphol when they let Alamy out,' Vos said. 'Maybe I can get a statement out of him. Something we can relay to the kidnappers, asking for her to be set free somewhere.'

'Fine,' De Groot said.

'And I want Henk Kuyper's mobile and landline tapped. There's something funny there.'

De Groot sighed.

'I'll have to ask AIVD to do that. He used to be one of theirs. I can't just ride roughshod over them. Are you sure?'

The question surprised Vos.

'Of course I'm sure. I wouldn't ask otherwise. He saw Hanna Bublik twice. He talked about being in Leidseplein. He gave her that jacket. Out of guilt and sympathy he says. Maybe he's right. Maybe not.'

'I'll talk to her,' De Groot said with a sigh and then was gone.

Side by side mostly, except when the odd wandering pedestrian got in the way, the two of them cycled back along the canal. Just before Elandsgracht, not far from the Drie Vaten, Renata Kuyper's phone rang in the pocket of Vos's worn navy jacket.

He'd been thinking about this conversation ever since he heard Alamy might soon be released. It was important to be prepared. A step ahead if that were possible. Four if he was lucky.

'I've seen the news. You've lost,' the caller said calmly. 'Now you know how it feels.'

Same man. Foreign. Confident.

'How's Natalya?' he asked. 'Can I talk to her?'

There was the noise of traffic. Of people. He was outside, somewhere busy and anonymous. No second chance of finding him through a stray sound. Perhaps, Vos thought, he knew this was how they'd discovered Westerdok.

The message tone beeped and a new photo came through. Natalya still in the pink jacket, seated on a tiny bed. In her hands a tablet with the TV news on it. Lead item: confirmation of Ismail Alamy's release.

'There's nothing for you to bargain for any more,' Vos said with real conviction. 'She's an eight-year-old kid. A little girl. Let her go. Just leave her somewhere and tell her to walk into a cafe and call us. You can be long gone by the time we start looking.' He had to say it. Not least because it was halfway true. 'It's Natalya I'm interested in right now. Not Ismail Alamy. Not you. She should be back with her mother.'

There was laughter on the phone.

'What is this, Vos? Are you a detective? Or a social worker?'

'I want her freed.'

'Really? Then why are you all so reticent?'

This was new. Unexpected.

'Reticent?' Vos asked.

'A child's kidnapped. And you never tell your citizens. What kind of country is this? Where a little girl can disappear and no one cares?'

'When a kidnap's live publicity doesn't help,' Vos said.

'Doesn't help you.'

His voice was cultured, light, amused.

'Tell me what you want,' Vos said.

'Money.'

'Hanna Bublik's just a poor immigrant. She's got nothing. She—'

'I know who the mother is. I know what she does.'

'How?'

'Never mind. You must pay a price to see this child again. I don't care how you find it. From your rich citizens, perhaps. The Kuypers for a start. Tomorrow we'll call again and discuss details.'

'We can discuss them now,' Vos interrupted. 'How much?'

'Tomorrow,' the man insisted. 'Then this . . . adventure is over. One way or another. Good day.'

The line went dead. Vos leaned against the wall.

Bakker came to him and said, 'I gather that didn't go well.'

'Why the hell wouldn't he name a price?'

'I can't imagine.'

'Can't you?' he grumbled and to her annoyance said nothing more.

Vos called control straight away to see if they had anything on the number. He wasn't in the least surprised when they said no.

One minute later the email and the attached images and

videos started to hit their targets. All the city newspapers. International and local news channels. News blogs. Amateur radical websites that had never been party to the blackout AIVD had engineered among the traditional media.

By the time they got back to Marnixstraat the story was breaking everywhere but Holland. The local media were bound to follow suit before long, however much the authorities begged them to stay silent.

This was the modern world. Some things would never remain secret. Soon Natalya Bublik's photo would be on Dutch TV just as it was on CNN and the BBC at that moment, the same picture Vos had seen earlier, and others too.

'I need to call the mother,' Vos said. But all he got was voice-mail.

In the dining room overlooking the park, Saskia back in school, Renata Kuyper listened to her husband say what he wanted.

He spoke with little outward emotion, as if this were a business conversation. A transaction to be concluded. A relationship in the course of amendment.

Then, when he was done, he looked into her eyes and asked if there were any questions.

A million.

'Why?' was the only one that came out.

'Because I was bored,' he said. 'And curious. Resentful for the way you used to sneak into the spare room as soon as you thought Saskia was asleep. I thought you didn't want me any more. I wanted . . .' For a moment the words seemed to elude him. That was rare. 'I wanted to know what it was like to be detached. From emotion. From love. If there was still any meaning left.'

'Was there?'

'Not that I noticed.'

She nodded.

'So you went down the red-light district and banged the first hooker you found out of intellectual inquisitiveness? Not because we sleep in separate beds and you felt like it?'

He was barely listening.

'I gave her a jacket I bought for Saskia. I thought maybe that would ease the pain. Mine. Not hers. I felt guilty. Ashamed. And all it did was make things worse.'

'But you had the peace of mind to go out and buy another in its place?' she asked. 'To bring it here? Because that evened things out?'

No answer. She got up and went to the coat rack, took down her daughter's pony jacket, pushed it into the bin.

'Did that help?' he wondered.

'What do you want me to do? What am I supposed to say?'

'That we'll work on this,' he answered with a shrug. 'Saskia needs a mother and a father. She's confused. Frightened. I can't bring her up on my own. I know I made a mistake. I admit it. Won't happen again. I will . . .'

He turned to the window where the Christmas lights sat dead and dull, wouldn't look at her when he said this.

'I'll make more time for you. I'll do what it takes. Counselling . . .'

'You'd never have told me, would you?' she said. 'Not if you hadn't been caught. If that whore hadn't seen you in Marnixstraat . . .'

'There's a saying in Italian, Renata. Better a beautiful lie than an ugly truth.'

'You don't base a marriage on lies!'

'We're not children. Please.'

The slightest tremor of fear ran through her.

'What do you mean?'

He shook his head and closed his eyes for a second.

'Do you know what I'm thinking? Can I see in your head? No. And I don't want to. We get by through acquiescence and ignorance. You. Me.' His hand went to the window. 'The world out there.'

'Henk—'

'I didn't tell you because I was scared. And ashamed. And I'm vain enough not to want to appear stupid. But most of all because there was nothing to gain. It's what you know that kills you. Not your ignorance.'

She got to her feet.

'You loathsome shit. I . . .'

'Fine,' he said with a nod. 'I deserve that. Throw whatever you like my way. I guess I deserve it. The fact you slunk out of our bed—'

'I didn't! I just . . .' It had happened without a conversation, even a second thought. 'I just realized I didn't recognize you. Stuck up there in your office for hours on end.'

'Then I'll change that. For Saskia's sake. For yours.' He tried to catch her eye. 'For mine too. We're a family. We need to stay that way.'

He joined her, took her hands, came close. She wondered if she saw the man she'd married then, in a rush after her father's sudden death. Someone who'd been lost to her for years. Since Saskia's birth somehow, as if that was what had come between them. The arrival of a child. The thing that was supposed to bring joy.

'I need you. Saskia needs you. Whatever you want . . . I'll try to make it happen.'

'What if it's too late?' she asked, as much of herself as him.

He didn't answer that. Just said something about how he'd go out for a while and give her some time to think.

Then his phone beeped and he was grabbing it off the table. He turned on the TV. The news programme was out at Schiphol, a live report from the gates of the detention centre.

Renata listened to the excited tones of the reporter and asked, 'What does that mean? For the little girl?'

He seemed lost in his own thoughts. Deeply miserable again. 'Henk?'

'I don't know,' he grumbled, back to his recent self in an instant.

She left him there staring at the screen, went out into the street, looked at the playground and the school.

Fear kept them together, on both their parts. As always there was a logical, cold, indisputable side to his argument. But there was something else too: a picture in her head. One she couldn't lose. The man she'd married, behind the curtain of a red-light cabin. Grunting over a woman who'd take . . . how many men a day? Ten? Twenty?

The city changed with every step. Soon the bourgeois trappings of the Herenmarkt were gone. The streets were grubbier. The people too. Grubbier and more mean.

She walked down Oude Nieuwstraat with fingers crossed. Hoping, hoping. Wondering what the woman would look like when she was trying to hook men for the morning.

It was mid-afternoon. A few of the curtains were closed, busy. Most of the women were out on show, for sale. Half-naked figures behind a pane of glass, bold beneath the red light. All kinds. Big and small. White and black and in between. They all met her searching eyes with puzzlement.

Then, in the last but one cabin, she saw one who shrank back a little in puzzlement. She was thin, long blonde hair, ruby lipstick. Cream satin bra and knickers. Stretch marks on her stomach as she sat on the narrow stool in the window. Though perhaps the men never noticed that.

Renata Kuyper put her finger on the intercom and waited.

From the office window Vos and Bakker watched the AIVD pair leave Marnixstraat by the front entrance, getting into a long black Mercedes saloon that was waiting for them.

'Let me guess,' Bakker said. 'Schiphol.'

'Going to be a circus,' Van der Berg told them. 'The media are waiting outside. We've got protesters too. People who think he should be strung up from the nearest lamp post. A few who feel that should happen to us.'

He briefed them on the hunt for Natalya Bublik. There were prints in the klipper barge in Westerdok. Nothing on the system. Some DNA samples. Clearly the girl's. The rest couldn't be identified but they indicated that three different individuals had been in the boat, excluding the rental man and the cleaner. A resident in a local house had seen someone going in early the previous morning. He didn't have much to say except that he was white and in his thirties.

Vos got to his desk and turned up the volume on the TV. Bakker called up the *Telegraaf* website. Alamy's release was the lead item, along with news of the kidnapping. The Dutch media had made a collective decision to break the embargo requested by the authorities after the story broke internationally.

'Are AIVD bugging Kuyper's phone?' Vos asked.

Van der Berg frowned.

'The lovely Mirjam didn't seem too interested when I put it to her. Bigger things on her mind.' He tugged at his chin. 'They really want to keep their hands on Alamy. Something about this Barbone figure they're chasing. She's desperate.'

'If we had the evidence I'd turn the key on the cell myself,' Vos said, scanning the *Telegraaf* story. 'Do we?'

'Not a thing I've seen,' Van der Berg replied. He hesitated then asked, 'What happens with the girl? If Alamy goes free? I don't get it.'

Vos waited. Bakker said, 'Get what?'

'These people have put the story out there. They sent it everywhere. Photos. Details. Names. All the usual propaganda crap. But . . .' He looked round the office. 'They haven't set a price. Why would you do that?'

Bakker nodded at Vos and said, 'He knows. At least he thinks he does.'

'Do we get in on the secret?' Van der Berg asked.

Vos closed the web page. He didn't want to see any more.

According to the internal bulletin on Schiphol Alamy was due to be released at five thirty. They were expecting big crowds.

Plenty of time.

'Get us a car,' he said then, as Bakker went about it, called Hanna Bublik again.

Still voicemail.

'Vos,' he said. 'Call me please. When you can.'


'I don't do women,' said the tinny voice coming through the intercom.

Renata Kuyper pulled out her purse and with shaking fingers removed some notes.

'What does it cost?' she asked, trying not to look at the slim blonde woman in her underwear behind the glass.

'I . . . don't . . . do . . . women.'

'For God's sake I need to talk. My husband . . .'

'Talk to him.'

'What did he pay you? Here.' She waved a couple of hundred notes in the cold winter air. 'Have more if you want.'

A long pause and then the lock buzzed on the door.

The tiny room was hot and smelled of sweat and cheap shower gel. Hanna Bublik drew the thin red curtain to hide them from the street then sat on the bed and watched as Renata Kuyper took the stool by the window.

'If you want an apology you should ask him. Not me.'

Renata put the notes on the table. Then added another fifty.

'I'm not looking for an apology,' she said quickly. 'I'm just trying to understand.'

Hanna found a flimsy dressing gown on a hook behind the

bed, threw it round herself, got a can of Coke, opened it, offered some, swigged at it when Renata said no.

'Understand what?'

'Why he did it.'

'Ask him.'

'I'm asking you. What did he say?'

'The usual. Life's not so good at home. Their wives won't do the things they want. They're bored. They're lonely. They need to feel . . . wanted.'

It seemed so pathetic. And quite unlike Henk.

'Fifty euros buys them that?'

'No. It buys them the pretence. And a little relief. Then they put on their clothes, go out into the street. Walk home. Go to their offices or a bar. I don't know.'

Questions. She didn't know where to begin.

'Did he enjoy it?'

'I don't think so. I thought maybe I wasn't going to get paid. That second time I couldn't even make him come.'

She winced. The woman watched her, amused.

'I'm sorry. Did that offend you? I thought you wanted to know. Otherwise . . . why?' She wrinkled her nose. 'Why are you here?'

Renata got up.

'This was a mistake.'

The woman rose and put a hand to her arm.

'You asked . . .'

'Why are you working? If you can call it that? Your daughter's missing—'

'Do you think I forgot?'

There was a phone at the back of the cabin by the wall, plugged into a socket. It looked dead.

'Why aren't you doing something?'

There was a look on Hanna Bublik's face. Unpleasant. Daunting. It was a cruel remark and Renata knew it.

'I'm doing what I can. I'm not . . . like you. Didn't you notice?'

She picked up the money and held it out.

'I don't want this. I didn't earn it.'

'Why did he give you that jacket?'

The question seemed to interest her.

'I don't know. I thought perhaps he felt guilty. He said he saw us in the street. Natalya reminded him of his own kid. Only a lot worse off.' She shrugged. Got her clothes out of a tiny cupboard at the back. 'I've had enough of this.'

'If he hadn't given her that thing . . .'

The woman picked up a pair of black jeans, a black sweater.

'If it means anything I don't think his heart was in it. You can tell the ones who do it all the time. They know what they want. What it costs. What to ask for. He hadn't a clue. I couldn't believe it when he was back a second time. Like I said—'

'He didn't come,' she broke in. 'I got that message. Thanks.'

'Funny. They usually manage it in the end. You get problems if they don't. That's why they're here. But . . .' She dragged the jumper over her head, pulled back her hair, put it in a tie, then climbed into the jeans. 'He was just bored and curious. That's all.'

She picked up her mobile. Started to swear at the cable. Renata came and looked. There was nothing on the screen. The power point must have been dead.

'Even the phone hates me,' Hanna Bublik whispered and looked ready to fling the thing onto the floor.

Renata stopped her. Pulled out her own.

Then told her what she'd heard. The story on the news about Alamy being released.

'I thought you knew. I'm sorry. That's why I said what I did.'

Hers was a new smartphone. All the stories on there. Video too.

Just about every reporter in Amsterdam seemed to be camped outside the detention centre at Schiphol, waiting for the preacher to walk free.

While Hanna raged Renata keyed in Vos's number and got straight through. Then passed over the call without a word.

A marked police saloon on the way to the airport. Down dark streets, blue light on to cut through the traffic. Bakker sat next to him on the passenger seat, making calls as they went. He got her to shut up.

'I've been trying to reach you,' Vos said, hoping it didn't sound like criticism. 'Things are happening.'

In the hot cabin, watched by Renata Kuyper, the air full of cheap scent, she said, 'They're letting that man out. Those bastards don't need Natalya any more. They can let her go.' A long, pained pause. 'Can't they?'

'I don't think it's as simple as that. They still want money.'

She shrieked. So loud the sound was painful in the tiny cabin.

'Who do they think I am?'

'Forget about that,' he said. 'We'll find an answer. They called. Tomorrow they'll come back to me.'

'Tomorrow . . .'

'I know, I know. We're going to try to talk to Ismail Alamy again. See if he'll ask for her release without any conditions. If he'll listen . . .'

'Why should he listen? He didn't yesterday.'

Silence then. For some reason she felt bad for yelling at him.

'Please,' Vos said eventually. 'Go to Marnixstraat. Wait for me there. I'll fill you in. If we make any progress with Alamy at Schiphol I'll call you straight away.'

The line went quiet. Then he disappeared and didn't come back.

Renata was staring at her. She felt bad for the way she'd treated this woman too.

'What did he say?'

'What they always say. Sit and wait. They know best.'

She stared at the woman. Her clothes were casual but expensive. Just like the bob haircut and the careful make-up.

'Yes,' she agreed. 'They do always say that.'

'I want to go to Schiphol. I want to be there when they let that man go. If I can plead for my daughter . . .'

Renata looked at her watch.

'I'll take you,' she said and didn't wait for an answer.


The mob was building by the time the unmarked police car pulled into the entrance to the secure detention area. Lines of TV cameramen and reporters held back behind a makeshift fence erected by hordes of busy uniform officers. They knew Vos. Started yelling questions the moment he and Bakker got out of the car.

He said nothing then looked around. Uniform seemed to be in control. On one side of the media pack was a bunch of right-wing protesters carrying the usual anti-Islam slogans, yelling abuse that stopped just short of arrest. On the other, separated by both the press and a line of officers on each side, was a second group, this time waving banners complaining about illegal detention, racial and religious discrimination, and a few anti-war slogans citing Iraq, Syria, Somalia and Afghanistan.

'No one ever mentions Libya,' Bakker grumbled, eyeing them. 'Were we right or wrong there?'

'Who knows?' Vos answered with a shrug. They went to the secure entrance he'd visited the day before with Hanna Bublik, showed ID and got led into an anteroom.

No sign of Alamy. Or anyone who looked like his defence team. Just Mirjam Fransen, her sidekick Geerts and three lawyers, two men and one woman, all of them whispering anxiously down their phones.

'Still trying?' Bakker asked.

The lawyers wore the wearily detached air of defeat that seemed the privilege of the legal profession when it found itself on the losing side.

'We need your help, Vos,' Fransen pleaded. 'You've got to

have something we can hold him for. I don't care what it is. If we let him out of here we can't stop him crossing that road, walking straight into Schiphol and out of the country. God knows where . . .'

Bakker shook her head.

'I thought you wanted rid of him.'

Fransen told the lawyers to get out of the room. Just the four of them. Two police. Two security service officers.

Vos wasn't sure if it was a trick or not. But Mirjam Fransen looked genuinely lost at that moment.

She caught Geerts's eye. He took a deep breath and nodded.

'I could lose my job for this,' Fransen told them. 'You don't say a word to anyone. You don't—'

'Then don't tell us,' Vos cut in and headed for the door.

Geerts got there first, put his big body in the way.

'De Groot knows,' he said. 'No one else in Marnixstraat. Three of you now. Keep it that way.'

The big intelligence officer wasn't moving. Vos shook his head and returned to Bakker. She was listening intently with all the enthusiasm of the young.

'Ismail Alamy's bigger than you know,' Fransen said in a flat and jaded tone. 'As far as we can work out he's the liaison man for Barbone. His fixer. He's dealt with money, recruiting. Operational planning.' She leaned forward and said, half to herself. 'If we could turn him. Christ, if we could get him to point us towards Barbone himself . . .'

Bakker nodded.

'You're saying he's behind actual attacks?'

'Planning, yes,' Geerts agreed.

'But you can't prove it?'

They turned awkward again.

'Not without jeopardizing our own,' Fransen went on. 'These are muddy waters. We can't hand him over to the Americans for rendition. The courts have blocked that. We can't prosecute him for anything meaningful. So the policy's been one of containment. Keep him here. Keep putting him through the courts.'

She pulled up a chair, sat down.

'If Alamy gets out he can take a plane to a neutral destination. Then he's gone. For good. If he's faced with going back to a Middle Eastern country that's on our side I've got leverage. He can have a choice. If he helps us find Barbone he's a free man.'

Bakker kept quiet, waiting on Vos.

'What did De Groot say?' he asked.

Fransen sighed.

'He said your lawyers gave him the same advice as ours. There's nothing to hold him.' She touched Vos's arm. 'So find me a reason. Make it up. I don't care. Just give me a couple of days and then we can come up with a real charge to hold him. If—'

'And Natalya Bublik?' Bakker cried. 'What happens to her if we cook up some fake accusation to keep him in jail? Have you thought about that?'

Geerts shrugged his big shoulders.

'This isn't about protecting one individual. Alamy's had a hand in bombings, hijackings, assassinations. If we let him out he'll be gone from Amsterdam for good. Causing us no end of shit from somewhere we can't even touch him.'

'And the girl?' Bakker demanded once more. 'Do you have anything to offer us?'

'I told you before,' Fransen said straight away. 'If we did you'd know it. The chances are she was as good as dead the moment they took her.' She nodded at Vos. 'He understands even if you don't.'

Silence.

Vos looked at Bakker then took out his phone. Pressed a button and started to play back the conversation they'd just had.

'Give me that now,' Geerts ordered.

'I don't have time for this,' Vos said, pocketing the handset.

'Nor do you. Asking a police officer to fabricate evidence is a criminal offence. Consider yourself warned.'

Geerts was blocking the door. Bakker walked up and told him to get out of the way. She was almost as tall as he was. An imposing figure when she wanted to be.

'They'll never let you charge us with a damned thing, Vos,' Fransen called after them as they walked outside. 'Get real. This is our world now. Not yours.'

Down the long corridor, Vos behind Bakker to make sure Geerts didn't attempt anything.

Then they were outside, listening to the two opposing mobs get ever more vocal.

'What if they're right?' Bakker asked as they stood by the security gate. 'What if . . . they've got a point?'

He stopped in his tracks.

'Are you really asking that?'

She wasn't listening. Bakker was pointing to the crowd. Two women there, pushing their way to the front, arguing with a couple of uniform officers along the way.

'Isn't that . . . ?'


A different van. Different men. Three of them. They didn't bother to hide their faces any more.

Foreign. Dark. They'd carried her in the hessian sack, told her to stay quiet as they lugged it inside.

Then a short journey to a new place. One that was worse. Worn, slippery steps down to a cellar. The light came on, a single bulb. Walls dripping with moisture. The place was cold even with a three-bar fire burning orange beneath a barred window with black plastic taped to the outside.

'Here,' the big one said and put a cold, greasy kebab on the red plastic table by the mattress on the floor.

He pulled a bottle of water out of a plastic bag. The name on the side was Chinese, with oriental lettering and a roaring dragon spouting flames above it.

Then they left her. No pens or drawing books any more. Probably no point in asking for them. These men weren't the same at all.

She looked around.

The place must have been old. The floor was nothing but worn brickwork, like the walls. A storeroom. A cellar. The city centre. Where the shops were. Where her mother had said they might live one day. Not soon. Not ever maybe. They didn't belong here. Natalya knew it then and, for the first time since she'd been taken, felt tears sting her eyes.

There was a hurt in their lives that she could only guess at because it happened before she could know. Her father's death was a part of the monster. But there was more and it lay in what followed as they travelled from place to place, never finding money or friendship, never staying long.

Something abandoned them along the way and that loss scared her mother. Made her wonder if their old life, a happy one Natalya thought, would ever return.

She'd seen that when she'd caught her mother behind that glass window, wearing almost nothing. Couldn't help it sometimes when she was walking back from school. Though she always made sure she stayed out of sight, in the shadows, behind some other kids. They told her what her mother was. Not that they teased her. Much anyway. This was the city. Bad things happened alongside the good. Sometimes it was hard to tell the difference.

Tears formed in her small, sharp eyes then rolled down her cheeks as she stood in the chilly cellar, aware it would only get colder as the night wore on.

*You don't cry. You do something.*

That was what her mother said when things turned bad in the past. Natalya wiped her face. There was silence from the place above. She stood on the mattress and managed to reach the bottom of the barred window. If she struggled she could just reach the edge of the black plastic set behind the iron frame to block out the world beyond.

On tiptoes she lifted the sheet a fraction then edged close to the damp brickwork and tried to peek out.

A bright scarlet neon dragon just visible on a building on the other side of a narrow street. And a sign, flashing red, yellow and green. It said, 'Golden Paradise Restaurant, Best of Szechuan Cooking'. Beneath the lettering was a glittering bowl with electric steam coming off noodles.

She felt hungry, glanced at the cold kebab, couldn't face it.

*You do something.*

She couldn't raise the plastic any further so she got down from the mattress and walked around the cellar. It was bigger than their gable room in Oude Nieuwstraat. At the top of the stairs was a door, solid metal, locked from the outside. Next to the lintel was what looked like a light switch, taped over with black plastic so she couldn't get at it easily. She gave up on that and went back down the steps. In the corner furthest from the door, next to the bucket she guessed was supposed to be her toilet, was a small cabinet on the wall just a short way up from the floor.

It was metal. Grey and old. A tiny, rusty handle on the front that wouldn't budge. But there was nothing else in the room and the fact the thing was locked seemed infuriating.

Two days she'd been a captive, barely spoken to. And now a piece of stupid metal defied her too.

So she kicked it and yelled when it didn't budge.

No sound from upstairs. They weren't there. Something told her the place was empty. Just her and a stupid locked cabinet.

She kicked it again. And again. Getting more violent, louder with every blow.

Finally the hinge broke. She was able to get her fingers round the edge, avoiding the rust and the fresh sharp metal, then wrap her grubby pink jacket around her hand and prise it open.

The lone bulb cast a weak yellow light inside. Tools. Chisels and screwdrivers. A small handsaw. A couple of retractable utility knives. Behind that a set of fuses and switches and the whirling wheel of an electricity meter.

She thought about these things and wondered what her mother might do with them.

Then, after she sat on the mattress for a while, listening for a sound from upstairs, still hearing nothing, she went back to the box on the wall and looked at the electricity panel and the little metal wheel going round and round.

Natalya reached forward and tried the first switch. Nothing happened. Then the second. Nothing. Two more left. She tried the fourth and thought she saw the turning wheel slow a little.

Then the third. The lone bulb in the room went off. She sat in the cold darkness, thinking.

Guessing. That was all it was. She got herself comfy by the wall, put her finger on the third switch, started to flick it up and down in a steady, tedious rhythm. The solitary light flashed on and off.

She'd no idea if anyone would see it. Or whether they'd think it was anything other than a faulty bulb if they did.

After a few minutes she heard voices. Men. Angry. Puzzled.

Then footsteps above the stone stairs. She left the switch on, did her best to push the cabinet closed, crawled to the mattress and tried to look asleep.


Things were moving in Schiphol. Every last option had gone.

Mirjam Fransen told Geerts to see Alamy all the way to his coterie of camp followers and then stick with him.

The stocky AIVD man nodded, not happy about this.

'What is it?' she asked.

'How about immigration?' he said. 'If he tries to leave the country they can stop him.'

'I wish . . .'

She showed him the message on her phone from The Hague. Alamy had been offered visas for transit to three different countries. All 'non-aligned'. He could wait for a direct flight – or find a private one – and leave. Nothing they could do to stop him.

'The Americans have got a warrant,' Geerts said. 'They can track his airspace. Someone can force down the plane.'

She scowled.

'Like they tried with Snowden? Get real. It's not going to happen. We're the bad guys now, remember? We can't pull those stunts.'

There was a sound from down the corridor. A group of people approaching.

'I'm going to nag Vos again,' she announced. Then nodded at the coming crowd. 'You deal with it.'

He grunted something she didn't hear then wandered over to Alamy's people. A couple of lawyers he half-recognized. One of their civil rights people who was always on the TV. Two heavies who looked like hired bodyguards.

The slight preacher was in a dark suit, beard freshly combed, beaming, happy. He had a small case with him. A man going somewhere.

'Who are you?' one of the bodyguards asked.

'AIVD.' Geerts opened his jacket, flashed the badge. Let them see the handgun in its leather holster. 'It's noisy out there and we've got some people who don't think Mr Alamy's such a hero. I plan to stick with you until you're clear of the crowd.'

'You're not wanted,' the civil rights woman told him.

'I rarely am,' Geerts said cheerfully. 'But I'm here. Get used to it.'

They kept quiet.

'Do you want me to call a cab?' he asked.

'We've an appointment,' the woman said. 'After we make a statement to the media.'

'I wouldn't advise that,' Geerts answered. 'Like I said. It's noisy out there.'

They pushed past. Alamy didn't look at him. He wasn't wearing a raincoat and it was cold and wet outside.

Geerts let them go a few steps ahead then called Mirjam Fransen and told her. It was obvious. He was going inside the terminal. On his way from Holland.


A key in the lock. The metal door was thrown open. The big one marched down and stared at her. Then the light bulb.

He said nothing. Walked to the cabinet. Saw the broken door. Came and sat down next to her on the bed. Put his strong arm on her leg and squeezed.

'Do that again and I'll hurt you.' He pointed to the cabinet. 'Don't touch it. I will know.'

She thought of the Chinese restaurant. He was there. Must have seen.

Natalya pointed to the kebab.

'That's cold. Disgusting. I want hot food.'

He looked at her and laughed.

'They said you had spirit.'

'Hot food,' she repeated.

'Such as?'

The girl thought about this and said, 'Noodles.'

He nodded.

'And if I get you noodles . . .' A glance at the cabinet. 'No more games? You stay here. Be quiet. A good girl. Then soon you get to see your mum.'

''Kay,' she said and wondered if he thought she meant it.

Five minutes later he came back with a plastic tray of food and a bottle of water. She began to wolf down the meal as he watched in silence. Then he took the bucket, went upstairs, emptied it somewhere, came back and placed it in the corner.

While she was eating he took out his phone and snapped a picture. Natalya blinked at the sudden bright flash, plastic fork in hand, food to her mouth.

'Give me the jacket,' he said.

'Why?'

'Because bad girls can freeze here in the dark. Give me it.'

His fist came out, demanding. She shuffled it off. Looked at the pink fabric and the ponies. The jacket was getting filthy.

'Learn your lesson,' he ordered and left her there.

A noise from outside. The single bulb went out and she knew there was no way to turn it back on.

It wasn't so cold, she thought. She could huddle under the blankets.

There was the tiniest leak of coloured neon through a gap in the blacked-out window.

Just enough to let her take out the tools she'd stolen from the cabinet before she played with the switches. The knives. The saw. The chisels and the screwdrivers. Hidden under the little bed.


Big occasion. Lots of people. A few neo-Nazis on one side. The media in the middle. Alamy's supporters and enemies kept apart. Just.

No moon. Growing clouds had seen to that. Rain was starting to spit from the black sky.

*Decisions.*

In the army they were made for you. Soldiers like him, men in the ranks, weren't there for their opinions. They existed to obey without question. He'd done that most of his life. And got what in return? Nightmares and an overreaching sense of guilt.

Ferdi Pijpers looked at the two opposing sides in front of him and wondered which to join. The ones who hated the preacher. The ones who adored him.

There was no middle. That was the place the police wanted to be and it was cold and lonely and full of pain.

So he went with the preacher's people. They didn't ask questions as he wandered up, mingled among them, joined in their mindless, repetitive chant. They were much like the neo-Nazis on the other side. Same dumb rhythm. Just different dumb words.

There were crowds like this in Afghanistan sometimes. Always for a lynching.


Hanna Bublik wasn't made for begging but she did it anyway and the Kuyper woman echoed her every plea.

'Just get me to see him, Vos. To talk to him.'

Bakker had carved out some space for the four of them beyond the camera crews. Renata listened carefully by Hanna's side.

'I can't,' he told them. 'Ismail Alamy's been freed by the court. We've no legal control over his movements. No right to demand anything of him . . .'

'What does this mean for my daughter?'

He didn't answer. Bakker looked at her boots.

'I need to know . . .'

'It means we carry on looking,' he said. 'And tomorrow they come back with a demand. More money I guess. A different . . . strategy.'

'Alamy's going to make a statement,' Bakker added. 'I've talked to some of the reporters. They're going to push him about Natalya. See if he'll say something useful. It's better coming from them than the police. Really.'

'Do you think it'll work?' Renata Kuyper asked.

Vos couldn't understand why she was there. How these two had got together.

'I think it's worth a try. I think . . .'

His words were drowned by the noise of the media mob spotting their prey.

Across the grey courtyard the high security gates opened. Alamy's followers cheered wildly. The protesters on the other side howled with fury. Camera flashes seared the black night like brief snatches of lightning.

Shouted questions.

Mirjam Fransen came over, grabbed Vos's arm, tugged him away from the rest of them.

'This is our last chance,' she begged. 'I'm out of options. If you can't think of a way to stop him we could lose years of work. There's got to be . . .'

He broke in with something feeble, about the law and due process. Then ran out of words.

The reporters surged forward with such force part of the fence broke. A couple came through. Uniform men and women struggled to keep them back.

Ismail Alamy strode forward, a victory smile on his face. Smart suit, more businessman than preacher, ready to depart the country and lose himself in a distant hotbed of jihad, probably in the Horn of Africa.

The lawyers assembled behind as he pulled a prepared statement out of his pocket and began to read.

Bakker grimaced. Hanna tried to push through the mob. Alamy's voice rang out, accented English, loud and defiant.

'What about the girl?' interrupted a woman reporter at the front, thrusting a microphone at Alamy's face. 'Natalya? What about her, Alamy?'

The broadest of grins. He opened his arms wide. Thom Geerts shuffled behind him, scanning the crowd.

'I know nothing of this child. I'm a man of peace and justice. That is why they seek to imprison me. To stop the truth being known. To prevent—'

'She's my daughter!'

Hanna's voice rang out as she fought to claw through the crowd.

An odd silence then. Even the hacks looked lost for a moment.

'My daughter,' she repeated, almost at the fractured fence, hands out, clutching for him.

The microphones and cameras hovered between the two: a woman in a cheap black jacket; a man in a smart grey suit, almost amused by the spectacle.

Alamy smiled. Shrugged. Then said, 'I must leave this damaged country to its own sad devices. Goodbye.'

Geerts came up by his side. Vos watched the big AIVD man. Tried to work out what was going through his mind. Mirjam Fransen had vanished again. It wasn't beyond the intelligence service to pull some last-minute trick at this stage of the game.

The crowd of Alamy's supporters rushed forward to embrace him.

Then came the first shot.

Vos heard it and found his right hand patting his jacket for the handgun. Just like it used to.

Thom Geerts staggered back from the tall man in the grey suit, blood on his neck, spurting like a fountain.

*Second shot.*

Alamy was down. A shambling shape came and stood over him, screaming obscenities, free of the crowd for a brief moment.

The media crews hovered, cameras running, flashes sparking, scared but unable to turn away.

*Third shot.*

The wounded preacher's body shook with another impact.

Uniform got there. Weapons out. Semicircle round the figure with the gun, calling on him to get on the ground, hands out. All the usual.

In the Drie Vaten later, watching the short and bloody drama replay itself on the TV, Vos came to accept that none of this mattered. Events sometimes possessed a momentum all of their own. Nothing would stop them. However hard one tried.

Ferdi Pijpers never meant to drop the weapon. This was the end of a long journey, one that started on the far side of the world, across a bleak, dry landscape he'd come to hate.

One more shot into the preacher on the ground. Then the uniforms opened fire and Pijpers was down, twitching, dying too.

Three corpses. Ismail Alamy. Thom Geerts. A lost military intelligence officer, breathing his last on the Schiphol asphalt.

Mirjam Fransen coming out of nowhere, shrieking for help. And Laura Bakker looking at the slaughter. Perhaps seeing for the first time a horror that would come to haunt her.

Sirens started. The cameras, the floodlights, the reporters with their mikes and notebooks recorded every moment.

Vos watched and thought.

*Never look back. Never think yourself so small or insignificant nothing matters. More than anything ... never give up.*

He didn't bother with the dead. Instead he found Hanna and Renata Kuyper and led them away from the carnage. Took them to the edge of the nightmare and tried to think of something to say.

The words weren't there. Instead it was Natalya's mother who found them.

'What will they do now?' she asked, face pale, hands shaking.

For the life of him Pieter Vos couldn't think of any good answer.

# 4

The next morning Vos was woken just before six thirty. A damp nose on his cheek. A busy tongue licking at his ear. He put his arm round Sam, sighed, stroked his fur and said something about not getting up on the bed. Again.

The dog had that wet fur smell about him. He must have been out on the deck in the rain.

Vos got up, dragged on fresh jeans, fresh grey shirt and black sweater. Looked much as he did the day before when he peered through the ragged curtains. A damp morning. Drizzle and a gloomy sky.

Sam followed him everywhere as he made coffee and toast, checked his messages, turned on the TV, watched the running newscast about the previous night.

'What is it?' Vos asked as the little terrier pestered him even more than usual.

A small saucer of milk lapped up noisily. One corner of toast eaten at Vos's feet. A dog's breakfast. And still the flustered terrier kept whimpering and running around Vos's ankles as he got ready to go to work.

One hand went down to pat him from time to time. The other dodged between coffee cup, toast and his phone. Renata Kuyper's handset sat attached to a charger by the porthole. Nothing on it overnight. His inbox was full of messages. From De Groot. And Rijnder working through the small hours.

Nothing from Hanna Bublik. She'd stayed around with Renata Kuyper until it became obvious the mess at Schiphol was going nowhere. AIVD were running things by then, closing down the area, marshalling the media, uniform, passing spectators out into the terminal. Their night teams came in and handled the dead.

Around nine she'd finally agreed to let Bakker drive her and Renata back into the city. Vos wondered what happened then. No family. No friends as far as he knew. She needed money. Something to fill the hours. She wasn't going to hang around Marnixstraat like a distraught victim. That wasn't in her nature.

He passed another piece of toast to Sam hoping it would shut him up then called Marnixstraat. AIVD had retreated into its own shell of secrecy. The police night team had done a good job of chasing down background on Ferdi Pijpers, the man who'd come out of the crowd and shot Alamy and Thom Geerts. Former military intelligence officer. Discharged with post-traumatic stress two years before. To Vos's dismay he'd come into the station the previous day and spoken to Koeman, making vague accusations about Alamy. Koeman had dismissed him as a nutcase. Probably with good reason. That didn't mean the detective wouldn't feel guilty.

'Have you got an address for Pijpers?' Vos asked the duty officer.

A bedsit in the Oud-West. The man had an estranged wife who'd moved to Turkey. No other family they could trace.

He told them to keep him up to date. De Groot had just texted in. An eight o'clock meeting with AIVD in his office.

Not one of the messages spoke about Natalya Bublik. It wasn't that they didn't care. The case had simply spiralled beyond them.

By the time Vos went through all his mail and tidied away breakfast it was close to seven. Sofia Albers would be up and ready to take Sam in for the day. There might just be time to walk him along the canal before that happened.

Bakker was waiting for him in the Drie Vaten, picking at a croissant, an empty coffee cup in front of her. She'd turned up in her old clothes, the ones her aunt made back in Dokkum. A pale-green suit, ill-fitting and ugly. It was as if she'd wanted to wrap something familiar and comforting around herself.

'How are you?' he asked.

'Pissed off.' She hesitated. 'Puzzled.'

'About what?'

'About why we didn't stop that lunatic for starters.'

'It's hard enough to stop the things we can predict, Laura. Something out of the blue . . .'

Silence. This wasn't it.

'What's really bothering you?'

'I don't get it. They're terrorists. They thought they were kidnapping the daughter of a minor Amsterdam aristocrat. A military man. A kid they could hold to ransom.'

'That's the way it looks,' Vos agreed.

'But they screwed up. They got the wrong girl. And when they knew Alamy was coming out they didn't let Natalya go. They asked for money.'

'You have to try to think the way they do,' he suggested.

'I told Van der Berg that last night. He gave me a nasty look and said he'd rather not.'

'That's Dirk. You're you. What would you do?'

'I'd get some money quick.' There was a low curse over the coffee. 'The mother gets bought and sold, doesn't she? Why not her daughter?'

Vos looked out of the window then got his donkey jacket, the dog lead and a plastic bag. There was time for a walk. He needed it and so did Sam still fussing around his feet. He thought he knew why the dog was being so frantically affectionate now. He'd sensed something in the atmosphere. The depression, almost despair, that was starting to hang around the dilapidated houseboat that was their home on the Prinsengracht.

Maybe he feared where that might lead. Vos did if he thought about it too much.

'Am I getting close?' Bakker asked.

'Quite. If you were smart you'd pass her on to someone in the extortion business in return for a cut. Selling things involves negotiation and a different kind of risk. They don't have time or the talent for that.'

'That must mean they've moved her again.'

'Probably,' Vos thought.

'Or killed her. They gave me some kidnapping cases to study at college. Sometimes they're haggling for money when the people they've taken are dead.'

'Sometimes,' he agreed.

'Can I hold Sam's lead?'

Bakker was stretching out her hand. She looked like a teenager at that moment. A hurt one.

'No time for that. I've a meeting in Marnixstraat. I want you to join up with Dirk round the soldier's place. Ferdi Pijpers. Call when you find something.'

The long pause then, a silence he had come to recognize.

'You don't want me there?'

'I want you in Oud-West. Like I said.'

'You never talk to people, Vos! It's like we're all supposed to stay in the dark until you're ready.'

He groaned, found the dog, put on his lead and walked outside. The day smelled of coming winter: cold, damp, unforgiving.

She followed, wouldn't leave this.

'You still make me feel I'm still an outsider.'

'Sorry. I don't mean to.'

She walked to her bike and pedalled off into the grey morning, stiff and upright on the sturdy Batavus.

'I'm coming, I'm coming,' he grumbled as the manic bundle of fur started to yap. Sofia Albers was returning from the bakers, her arms full of loaves for that day's customers. She smiled, waved. This corner of the Jordaan always seemed so normal, so mundane, whatever else was going on in the city.

Sam tugged so much the lead fell from Vos's fingers. The little

terrier raced to the prow of the boat. To the silver statue he usually ignored.

'What is it now?' Vos sighed.

Then looked and knew.

They'd had a visitor some time that morning. A plain white
plastic bag dangled from the mannequin's arm.

Vos walked over, took out a pair of latex gloves, unhooked it
then looked inside.

One sheet of paper. Letters cut from something like a colour
magazine then stuck to the page to make a message. And an
ancient Samsung handset, fully charged.

This was the old way of doing things. The method of someone
who didn't want the risk of traceable mobile phones.

The paper said, 'Two hundred thousand euros. Don't make us
shoot her.'

Beneath the snipped letters was an inkjet printout of a poor
quality photo: Natalya on a low bed in the pink pony jacket, about
to tuck into some food.

The Samsung rang.

He jumped. Looked around. They knew who he was. They
had to be watching.

'How do I know she's alive?' he asked straight away.

Laughter. Deep and confident.

'You find two hundred thousand euros. I hope you have an
intelligent question for me too.'

The voice had a practised cruelty to it.

'How long do I have?'

'Four o'clock this afternoon I'll call on this phone. Not one
minute before. Not one minute after. You answer. Have the
money ready then. We do this tonight.'

He sat down hard on the damp, broken wooden seat on the
deck.

'You're giving me eight hours to put together a small fortune?
The mother's got nothing.'

'Eight hours is all you have. Four o'clock precisely.'

'For God's sake give us a chance. You want your money. I want Natalya. Make it possible.'

A low, unfeeling sigh.

'It's possible if you want it to be.'

'Listen—'

'No. There's nothing else to say. Except . . .'

A brief silence. Vos tried to imagine what he was thinking.

'Except what?'

'Trust is everything. If I feel you betray that at any point . . . that your intentions are anything less than serious then the deal's off. You'll hear from me no more. You understand what I'm saying?'

'Of course.'

The dry, mirthless laughter again.

'I don't think so. What I'm saying is . . . if this kid winds up dead it's down to you.'

An electronic click and then the line went silent. Vos stared at the photo of Natalya Bublik, alone with a plastic container of food. Cowed but not scared. Her mother's child. He could see that in her eyes.

Vos led Sam over to the Drie Vaten and said, 'Sorry, boy. Not today.'

Sofia would walk him. Not the first time. Nor the last.

Eight hours and not a word about the shooting of Ismail Alamy.

It couldn't be done. And he wondered if they knew that.

When he'd left the dog he called her. Hanna Bublik was wide awake already.

'I need you in Marnixstraat,' he said.


Lucas Kuyper took breakfast in the same place every morning: a smart cafe in the Nine Streets on the corner of Wolvenstraat and Herengracht. Good coffee and fresh orange juice. This morning *Wentelteefjes*, fried bread dipped in egg, sprinkled with sugar and cinnamon, served with home-made apricot jam.

A copy of *De Telegraaf*, not that he felt much like reading it. The European edition of the *Financial Times* was more to his taste. And a couple of pages of emails he'd printed out that morning, planning to deal with them at his usual quiet and solitary table in the corner.

The streets were getting ready for Christmas. Decorations strung from wall to wall across the narrow lanes. Posters in the windows. Images of Sinterklaas and his Black Petes beaming at shoppers and schoolchildren everywhere.

When he lived in France, working at a small and secretive NATO base, Kuyper had grown to love the French version of the dish before him. *Pain perdu*, lost bread, soaked in cognac before the slices went into the pan. On this cold morning, one full of bleak thoughts, he missed that added slug of spirit. The cafe knew him. Maybe they would have added in a shot of Dutch Vieux if he'd asked. But then his mouth would taste of spirit for the rest of the morning. And perhaps he'd meet someone . . .

He turned to the *FT*. The death of Alamy, an AIVD officer and a vengeful former military intelligence officer made three paragraphs on the front page. He felt outraged it was there at all. This was not why he read the paper.

There was only one other customer in the place, a middle-aged woman wrapped up as if the weather was about to turn arctic. She sat in the window. He watched her carefully. Professionally. She grabbed some kind of tablet out of her bag and started to play a game.

Bored. Like him. He pulled out the sheets he'd printed that morning and began to go through them. Then he heard a familiar voice at the door and quickly stuffed the pages in his pocket.

Renata Kuyper ordered a coffee and sat down.

'I thought I'd find you here.'

'It's where I eat breakfast,' he said. 'Where else?'

'I phoned you. Left messages. You never called back.'

A small TV was droning away up on the wall in the corner. The news was on. There seemed to be nothing to talk about in Amsterdam but the shooting of Ismail Alamy in the presence of a woman whose daughter had been kidnapped in order to secure his release. Not that they had an interview with Hanna Bublik, barely even a photograph. She'd refused to speak to the media.

'I watched the early morning news,' he said. 'You were there. At Schiphol.' A brief scowl and then he folded away the pink paper. 'I thought I must have been dreaming.'

'Of course I was there. This is our fault. Henk gave her the jacket he bought for Saskia. If it wasn't for us . . .'

He reached forward and took her hand. She fell silent.

'You and Henk are responsible for nothing. The men who kidnapped that child bear the blame. Just as this deranged soldier must for what happened at the airport.' Another scowl. 'Though at least he's paid for it.'

The coffee came. She waited for the waitress to leave and said, 'You know, don't you? About Henk? About what he did?'

Kuyper liked this woman but appreciated the burden his son sometimes had to carry.

'He phoned me last night. He was worried. He didn't know where you'd gone. Then he saw the pictures from Schiphol.' He picked at the sweet, spicy toast. His appetite had vanished. 'You didn't even phone him. What do you expect?'

'I don't expect my husband to go screwing street women behind my back.'

He looked at his food and kept quiet.

Her head went to one side. She seemed permanently tense and angry these days. But at times the strained anxiety left her and he could see a shadow of the young woman his son had married. Though even then there'd been difficulties. It was an odd match. A rash one, based on passion rather than logic.

187

'Is that unreasonable of me, Lucas?'

'Marriages are always tested one way or another. Life's not a bed of roses. Only children believe that.'

'Do you think Natalya Bublik's life's a bed of roses now? Or her mother's?'

Her voice had risen. The waitress behind the counter was starting to look worried.

'That's the girl's name?'

'Don't you read the papers?'

'Not for that kind of news. There's enough of it in the world already. It doesn't need me to make it real.'

He drained his coffee and said, 'When I had to face all that nonsense over Kosovo Ruth left me. Henk never told you, I imagine.'

The look of surprise on her face said everything.

'My husband doesn't tell me much, does he?'

'Perhaps he thinks that's for the best.'

'I thought you and Ruth were the happiest couple in the world. Until she fell ill.'

He frowned.

'Some of the time we were. Not when the press were at the front door wanting to know whether I was some kind of mass murderer. Or a coward. Or . . . God knows what. She left me. When I needed her most.'

He wanted her to know the memory was still distasteful and that this was a conversation he resented.

'I'm sorry, Lucas.'

'Well there you are. Had she not fallen sick she'd never have come back.' He leaned forward to emphasize the point. 'Nor would I have accepted her. That's how bad matters had become. But when she returned . . .' He picked at a piece of the sugary bread in any case and placed a piece in his mouth. 'After a while we realized that happiness doesn't arrive of its own accord. Sometimes you have to build it. On occasion from nothing. Or ruins. And one happy day in a year of misery is sometimes the best you can hope for.'

'I didn't come here for a lecture.'

'Why then?'

'Hanna Bublik's going to need money.'

He shook his head.

'You think paying criminals solves problems? What about the next child who's kidnapped by these scum? Would that lie on your conscience? It should. You don't put out a fire by throwing petrol on it.'

She hesitated at that. An intelligent woman. Kuyper was sure she understood the dilemma.

'That's an intellectual argument. Mine's an emotional one. I've met her. She doesn't deserve this any more than her daughter does.'

He sighed and before he could speak she broke in, 'If it was Saskia they'd snatched would you feel the same way? Would you let her die for these . . . principles? Can you call them that?'

A grunt of impatience.

'Of course I'd feel differently. But it's not Saskia, is it? There's nothing wrong with speaking from your heart. Sometimes you have to listen to the head too.'

'So the life of the child of an East European whore is worth less than that of your granddaughter?'

'I'm not a wealthy man. Whatever people say. The army never paid well. The family name's just that. A name.'

There was the briefest of smiles. She was thin, still pretty and there was a strength inside this fragile facade. He'd seen that from the outset.

'I'm leaving Henk,' she said. 'We need somewhere to live. Saskia and me. I don't have anyone else to turn to. You've all that room.'

He shook his head.

'You want me to help you abandon my son?'

'Lucas! I can't stay in that house with him! Not after this.'

'Henk loves you. He loves Saskia. I won't be a party to breaking up my own family.'

'If he loves me why does he go and have sex with prostitutes behind a curtain in the street?'

He waved her away.

'Enough. Forgiveness takes time. It's important to work on it. You know my opinion.'

He got up and paid the bill for both of them. She followed him to the door and grabbed his arm.

'Lucas . . .'

'If I may drag you away from your battered pride for a moment and ask a question,' he cut in sourly. 'Can't you see Henk needs you? Now more than ever? Or do you believe you're the only one in the world capable of feeling a little pain?'

'A little pain?' she echoed, then swore at him and that was a first. 'Do I get some money from you or not?'

'In return for what?' he demanded. 'Nothing comes for free.'

She squinted at him in disbelief.

'What do you want?'

'I want you to give Henk a second chance. If I pay up for this insane pipe dream will you do that for me?'

She stared at him.

'Is that meant to include sleeping with him too? Because if it does . . .'

'You're man and wife! That comes with duties and responsibilities. To one another. To Saskia.'

'Jesus . . . I don't believe . . .'

'If I match your money will you at least give him the opportunity to put things right? And get off his back for a while?'

'Do I have a choice?'

'You can say no. Lose your marriage. Your daughter. Your home. This madcap scheme to help some prostitute you don't even know . . . There's your choice.'

She thought for a moment.

'Very well. I'll do it. I think we can raise thirty thousand on our own. I expect you can double that, can't you?'

'Tell me when you need it.'

Kuyper watched her stamp off down the street in her expensive winter coat.

*Who paid for that?* he wondered. *Did she ever even ask herself?*

When she was gone he strode to the edge of the canal and found a quiet spot. Called, got through on the second ring.

'What the hell are we going to do about this bloody mess?' he demanded. And waited for an answer.


Ferdi Pijpers's home was a spotless, bare studio in the basement of a run-down block in one of Oud-West's less salubrious streets. Social housing for the impoverished. The place had a single bed, a table, two chairs, a few pots, pans and plates, not much else.

The night team had been scouring the room. Two forensic officers were still tramping around in bunny suits. Van der Berg was with them looking faintly ridiculous inside the white plastic.

One of the forensics glanced at Bakker when she turned up and said she didn't need to join them in the protective clothing.

'We're just about done here,' the woman added. 'Not a lot to see.'

They'd found one more weapon, an old handgun, and some ammunition. Probably stolen from the army.

Van der Berg climbed out of his suit and asked if she wanted to go and get four coffees from the place round the corner.

'Not really,' she said.

He looked her up and down.

'I'll get them then,' Van der Berg replied and walked out of the room.

The two scene of crime officers shuffled on their plasticized feet. Bakker asked what they'd found. Not much. The neighbours barely knew Pijpers who'd been placed in the flat by a military charity. From the contents of the kitchen it appeared he lived off ham, eggs and beer.

She pulled on a pair of disposable gloves, went to the sideboard by the bed and opened the top drawer.

'We've done that already,' the woman officer said.

'Good,' Bakker noted and rifled through the old clothes, underpants, socks, sweatshirts, found nothing.

The next drawer down had much of the same. And the third.

'The most interesting thing we've got is this,' the woman added.

She went to a police storage box and pulled out a small photo in a frame, now enclosed in a plastic evidence bag. Bakker took it out and found herself staring at a picture of a young boy in scruffy clothes, perhaps seven or eight. He had olive skin and a gap-toothed smile. Behind him was desert with a big khaki military vehicle manoeuvring in the half-distance, throwing up dust.

Van der Berg came back with the coffee and placed four cardboard cups on the table. She didn't touch hers.

'Afghanistan,' he said. 'Rijnder got the story out of the army overnight. The boy was an orphan that the camp kind of adopted. He lived with them. Used to run errands. They were teaching him Dutch and English.'

He swigged at his coffee.

'Pijpers looked after the kid apparently. He wanted to get permission to bring him here. He said it wasn't safe to leave him behind. Not after he'd lived in the camp and learned the language. The bosses said no.'

She knew what was coming.

'And?'

'One afternoon he wandered out of the compound and never came back. They found him a couple of kilometres away two days later. You don't want the details.' More coffee. It looked as if he needed it. 'Ferdi Pijpers went crazy. Accused the commanding officer of abandoning the lad. Next thing he's out of the army and back here trying to live on a pathetic pension.'

Van der Berg took the photo and put it back in the evidence bag. He didn't bother to pull on gloves. Perhaps there was no point. It was obvious what had happened here. A sick ex-soldier had come back full of hate. Seen what was happening with Alamy. Decided to take it out on the preacher. And perhaps Holland too.

'The fool didn't do that Georgian kid any favours,' the forensic woman grumbled.

'Ferdi Pijpers was crazy,' Van der Berg remarked. 'Don't look at someone like that for logic. And we made him that way.' He stabbed his chest with a forefinger. 'Us.'

Silence then. A little embarrassed by his outburst Van der Berg asked if there was any news from Marnixstraat.

'Not that I know,' Bakker replied. 'But then I only know what I'm told. Which isn't much.'

'Laura . . . we could all just buy badges, print "I apologize" on the front and stick them on our chests if you like. Would that help?'

She laughed. Bakker liked this funny, decent man.

'It might. Sorry. I just feel . . . out of things somehow. Am I a pain?'

'On occasion.'

The two socos were packing up.

'Is that it?' she asked. 'A photo of a dead boy? Is that all we know?'

The woman went to the box and pulled out a bigger evidence bag. Inside was an old and heavy laptop.

'It's got a password. We need to hand it over to technical. Maybe they can get inside.'

'Can I see?'

The forensic officer muttered something but put the computer on the table anyway. With her gloved fingers Bakker took it out of the bag and turned it upside down. The battery was missing. There was a power cable still plugged into the wall socket by the table. Ignoring the groans from the soco she attached it and hit the power key.

The log-on screen came up after a long wait and lots of whirring.

'Like we said,' the other forensic officer announced, 'it's got a password on it. We hand these things over to technical. They can deal with it.'

Bakker clicked on the button marked 'Password hint'.

'Oh for God's sake,' the man moaned.

They all looked at what came up next. A very long reminder. One line that said, 'Unless you change and become like little children you will never enter the kingdom of heaven.'

Bakker thought of her Sunday school classes. The quote was from Matthew if she remembered correctly. Ferdi Pijpers must have had a religious upbringing too.

'What was the boy called?' she asked. 'The Afghan kid?'

Van der Berg checked his notes.

'Farshad. We checked with one of the translators. Apparently it means happy.'

She typed in the name.

*Farshad.*

Nothing.

'This is ludicrous,' the forensic woman murmured. 'I want that thing now. It's going to people who know what they're doing.'

*FARSHAD.*

One last try.

*farshad*

The screen cleared.

The desktop came up.

Her fingers flew across the keyboard.

'We're in,' Bakker said.

———

De Groot's office. The commissaris, Vos and Mirjam Fransen sat uneasily, aware Hanna Bublik was on her way. Coffee and biscuits on the table. No one touching them.

Vos checked his watch. Just over seven hours now before the old Samsung in his pocket rang again. This was going to be delicate. He'd discussed the approach with De Groot. Fransen would have to OK any ransom bid. They had to wait until she'd got through what she wanted to say.

She'd turned up pink-eyed and pale. Much of the night had been spent dealing with Thom Geerts's family. He was separated from his wife. They had two kids, ten and twelve. The wife hated the service, blaming it for the failure of her marriage. Geerts's murder was one more thing to lay at AIVD's door.

'We're all shocked,' De Groot said. 'If there's anything we can do . . .'

'Such as what?' she cut in sharply.

'Such as anything,' De Groot added and caught Vos's eye with a look that said: *I had to offer.*

They went through the file on Ferdi Pijpers. He was, as he'd told Koeman, ex-military intelligence. At one time he'd been a liaison officer with AIVD. But the contact was minimal and came to an end when he got bounced out of the service.

'There's no reason we should have had him under surveillance,' Fransen added.

'None at all that I can see,' Vos agreed.

She stared at him.

'He was in here yesterday. He spoke to one of your officers.'

De Groot took care of that. Koeman had acted properly, he insisted. The man had made vague racist comments, the kind of thing officers got all the time on the street. There'd been no reason to take him seriously.

Mirjam Fransen nodded and stayed quiet.

'We haven't heard anything about wiretaps on Henk Kuyper,' Vos said. 'I asked for that yesterday. We're still unhappy about his movements in Leidseplein. His radical sympathies. This business with the kid's jacket . . .'

'I've got a colleague to bury,' Fransen interjected. 'A bereaved family to deal with. An internal investigation of my own. This bastard Barbone on the loose. I don't have time to piss around bugging people like him. His father was a senior officer in the army for God's sake. It was his kid who nearly got snatched . . .'

'Nearly,' Vos repeated. 'A phone tap can rule him out. I'll fix it.'

She shook her head.

'Not in something like this. It has to come through us. We were chasing big fish here. Now I've got nothing except a dead officer.'

He waited. That was it.

'Barbone . . . whoever he is . . . he's your business,' Vos went on. 'The rest's a straight criminal case. One solved murder. One kidnapped kid.'

She shot him a vicious look.

'Don't be naive. We're talking terrorism. I've got the ministry and all manner of people in The Hague on my back right now. When I get a break I'll see what I can do.'

There was a knock on the door. One of the uniform women officers came in and said Hanna Bublik had arrived.

Fransen glared at them both in turn.

'You're not offering any ransom. I won't allow it.'

'Fine,' De Groot said. 'Let's see you tell her that to her face.'


The one who brought her food this time was new. Skinny, short, dim, she thought. Barely spoke Dutch. He looked scared and muttered to himself in a language Natalya couldn't identify.

He had a pack of orange juice, a pastry and a carton of milk. And the grubby pink pony jacket. He watched her put that on then emptied the bucket and fetched a bowl with hot water, soap and a towel.

She looked more closely at him then. He was like one of the older brothers who came to pick up the little kids at school. In his teens, no more. Dark eyes, clean smooth skin. She was starting to feel detached from the world beyond the blacked-out window. It felt important that she try to work to stay close to the idea she'd rejoin it before long. One way was wondering about her mother. Worrying what she'd think. Trying to imagine what she'd be doing.

She had no friends. At least Natalya had a couple at school. Little Ollie, the funny kid whose mother was on her own, working the night life too. Tom, the serious one, who always told her off if she didn't eat the muck they handed out to the poor kids for free at lunchtime.

Boys. She always preferred them. The girls seemed weak, frightened or just plain silly. They liked to gossip about clothes and other kids in school. To form alliances and start vendettas. To scuttle round the playground whispering about the latest girl they hated.

Her, sometimes.

That was how it went. She was foreign. They had no money, no nice clothes. Her mother did some kind of job Natalya dimly understood. It involved things, secret things, that were both necessary and wrong. Accepted by the city. Welcomed by a few of the men she'd seen come round, knock on the front door, whisper words that always seemed to be accompanied by a flash of money. And then her mother would say sorry, leave for half an hour or so. Come back looking happy and sad at the same time.

This life set them apart. Even serious Tom, whose mum was a teacher at the school, on her own, kind, a little severe sometimes, seemed to go home to a different world to the one she knew. But that was the way it had always been. They'd been alone for as long as she knew, travelling, fleeing, rushing out penniless into the night. Life wasn't going to change. Not quickly.

On top of which she was getting bored.

Natalya looked at the skinny kid watching her eat breakfast and asked, 'What's your name?'

Just the sound of her voice seemed to affect him.

'What's that got to do with you?' he asked in a gruff, odd voice.

'Being friendly.'

'You don't need my name. You're in jail here. People in jail don't ask things.'

They'd double-taped the box on the wall so she couldn't mess with the light switch any more.

'You only go to jail if you've done something wrong,' Natalya told him. She pointed a tiny finger across the room. 'That's you. Not me.'

Scared. She could see it.

'Can I get a book?' she asked. 'Some crayons. I want to draw something.'

'Draw what?'

He wasn't going anywhere either.

'I could draw you. Even if you won't tell me your name.'

He laughed then. Big teeth, a little yellow, gap at the front. She felt her head was a camera sometimes. It memorized everything she saw.

'Little girl can draw?'

'Can if I have the stuff.'

He got up and climbed the stairs. Five minutes later he was back with a plastic bag. Red dragon on the side. A sketchbook and a pack of cheap crayons.

'Make me look good,' he said.

She took out a black crayon and a red one. Quickly drew something on the first page and showed him.

It was a crude animal. A big dog. A wolf maybe. Red eyes, red claws, red teeth in a big leering grin.

He laughed and something about the way he did that made her smile too.

'Knew you were rubbish,' he said. 'Little girls.'

'Where are you from?'

'Long way away. Place called Anadolu.'

'Never heard of it.'

'Here they call it Anatolia. The Dutch get everything wrong.'

She drew something else too. Something he didn't see.

'You?' he asked.

'Nowhere,' Natalya Bublik said.

He didn't like that answer.

'Everyone comes from somewhere.'

She didn't answer. Didn't take any notice. Her head was over the book, crayons out, four in the crevices of her fingers of her left hand. Busy.

He soon got bored watching her.

'Girls,' he said and left her on her own in the semi-dark of the damp, chill cellar.

Natalya looked at what she'd scribbled. It was a Black Pete. Not bad either. And underneath the word 'Anatolia' in clear, careful letters.

Her mother liked to watch her mess with crayons. She said that was a talent she'd got from her father. Not from her. She had a joke. One thing she could draw, she said. A black cat at night. And then she'd scribble out a square in black pen. Nothing but ink. And they'd laugh.

Tears then. She wiped them away quickly, hating herself for the way they'd crept up without warning.

Then she looked under the bed and found the things she'd hidden the night before.

The knives. The saw. The chisels and the screwdrivers.

If the big man saw this it would be trouble again. He was

strong, brutal. She recognized that look. He could do worse than take away the stupid pink jacket.

But a little kid from Anatolia . . .

She picked up the biggest knife of all and gingerly ran her finger along the edge.

The tiniest line of blood appeared and she had to stifle a whimper.

*Sharp.*


Vos ran through where they were with the search for Natalya, leaving that morning's message till the last. Hanna Bublik listened carefully. Sceptically. When he was finished she said, 'They know where you live, Vos?'

'Seems so.'

'How's that?'

He shrugged.

'It's no big secret. A brigadier with a boat on the Prinsen. Also . . . I was running organized crime investigations here for a while. There were a couple of cases that got me into the papers. Anyone could find out if they wanted.'

On the desk was a photo of the note left in the bag on his silver statue. Hanna picked it up and examined it.

'They called me when I got it,' he said. 'He was foreign. Good Dutch. I'd guess he's lived here some time.'

'Can't you find him?'

He sighed.

'We keep looking. Have you thought of anything since last night?'

'Such as?'

'Anything.'

'You must be desperate,' she said, putting down the picture. 'If you're looking to me for answers.'

'We're exploring every avenue,' De Groot cut in.

That annoyed her.

'Do they teach you these words? In police college?'

The commissaris apologized.

She looked a little regretful then said, 'Two days ago they're calling you. Using Renata Kuyper's phone. Now they leave notes and you've a different phone altogether. Their preacher's dead. I thought this was about him. Why keep my girl? Do they need this money?'

Vos wasn't surprised she'd worked this out already. He wondered what else she might be thinking.

'It's possible Natalya's changed hands,' he said. 'The men who first took her may have passed her on to people who are more used to dealing with extortion.'

'What kind of people?' she wanted to know.

'If we had to guess we'd say a local crime gang,' De Groot suggested. 'They've got experience. Plenty. Terrorist organizations use them from time to time to launder money. Get weapons. False documents. They have links.'

The way she took that news made Vos wish they'd kept quiet.

She looked at Mirjam Fransen and said, 'You don't have much to say.'

'We're doing everything we can,' she answered. 'Natalya's release is a high priority.'

Hanna pointed at De Groot.

'Did you go to the same lessons as him?'

No answer. She gazed at each of them in turn, finishing with Vos.

'Renata Kuyper says she can help me raise some money. I don't know if it's as much as they want but maybe they'll take less. We could go public. Make an appeal. People here are kind. She says it won't matter we're foreigners. If we can—'

'Not going to happen,' Fransen broke in.

'Why?' was all Hanna Bublik could think of.

'Because there are rules,' Fransen went on. 'The government

doesn't sanction the payment of ransoms for two simple reasons. It rewards illegality. And it encourages more kidnappings.'

'It's not your money,' Bublik protested. 'Or your daughter.'

'Doesn't matter. It would be a criminal act to pay these people. The police . . .' She pointed to De Groot, then Vos. 'They can tell you that. If you—'

'We're not threatening anyone here,' De Groot barked.

'Fine!' Fransen replied. 'You tell her then. Are you going to authorize paying a ransom?'

Vos intervened.

'We'll go along with what they want, Hanna,' he said. 'We'll be in contact every inch of the way. They want the money. That's all. This is good. Maybe easier than before. If we keep talking to them . . . arrange a handover . . . While they think a transaction's going on we'll find Natalya.'

Hanna Bublik closed her eyes for a moment.

'And if you don't? If you screw up again?'

'We won't,' De Groot insisted.

'If you fail you won't pay them, Vos.' Her keen and burning gaze never left him. 'Will you?'

'I hope it won't come to that,' De Groot said.

'Is this what my daughter's life depends on? Your . . . hopes?'

She got to her feet, grabbed her bag and the black jacket.

'Hanna,' Vos tried to persuade her to sit down again. 'Listen to me . . .'

'Why?' she cried. 'To hear you plead you're doing everything you can? Was this for my benefit? Or yours?'

There was a rush of curses in a language they didn't understand. Then she stormed out slamming the door behind her.

No one spoke until Vos said, 'For ours mainly.'

His phone rang.

In a car coming from the apartment in Oud-West Laura Bakker said, almost shouted, 'Jesus Christ, will you answer when I call? You don't even have voicemail turned on.'

He'd turned the handset to silent the moment the meeting began, suspecting it might turn difficult.

'Sorry.'

'Was there a camera on Ferdi Pijpers when he got shot?'

'I don't know. Why?'

'I'll tell you when I get back. Can someone check his belongings in the morgue? This matters. OK?'

'What was that?' Fransen asked when he came off the call.

'Nothing.' He checked his watch. 'I have to go.'

She got up and stopped him at the door. Looked back at De Groot.

'I need you both to understand this. When they call this afternoon you agree to the ransom. You go through all the motions and try and pick up these bastards when they come to collect. But that woman doesn't have the money. Even if she did I'd stop you using it.'

'Mirjam . . .' he began.

'No. Don't try and get friendly now. We don't know who these people are. If they're criminals or the men who snatched her in the first place. Either way they're in bed with one another. You put together a dummy ransom and grab them before they find out.'

'One phone call,' De Groot said bitterly. 'If they see it's fake that's all it takes. One call and that kid's dead.'

'Then make sure you get it right this time,' she said then checked her watch, her messages, and left.


Hanna Bublik was halfway along the Prinsengracht when her phone rang. Renata Kuyper. She sounded both daunted and determined.

'Can we meet?' she asked.

'What's the point? The police won't let me pay the ransom anyway.'

'You don't do what men always tell you. Do you?'

Her voice was odd. Dutch but with an accent to it. She'd said something about growing up in Belgium. Not far away but different. As if she was a kind of stranger in Amsterdam too. Just one with money.

Ten minutes later they were in a tiny, deserted place overlooking the empty space of the Noordermarkt. Steady breeze. Sheets of newspapers and rubbish rolling across the damp cobblestones. Some council workmen were putting up Christmas lights. A giant Sinterklaas picked out in red and green and white, two shorter, happy Black Petes next to him. December the 5th, the feast of Sinterklaas, was fast approaching. Natalya's school had organized an evening for the poorer kids. A treasure hunt. Sacks of presents. She'd so wanted her to be there.

Renata wore a long tweed coat. Expensive. Her brown hair was perfect. Her face made up, composed as she stirred her cup of Earl Grey tea, picking at a tiny chocolate ginger nut.

'Why do you keep talking to me?' Hanna asked. 'I screwed your husband. For money. You should hate me.'

'I want to help.'

'Why?'

She shook her head.

'Do I have to explain? Henk gave you that jacket. If he hadn't . . .'

'You feel guilty. Now I get it.'

'Does it matter? Help's help. Who cares where it comes from?'

No answer.

'What did the police tell you?'

Hanna took a biscuit off the table and nibbled at it. She'd barely been eating much of late. Food was something she shared with Natalya, always had. Now it was just a cruel reminder she was alone.

'They think they've handed her over to criminals. They're the ones demanding the ransom now. They want two hundred thousand euros. Vos said they'd call at four o'clock on the dot to tell him how to deliver it. Otherwise . . .'

The coffee was bitter and strong. Like punishment.

'We can go to the media. Forget about politicians. About police. Ordinary people are kind. They'll understand. I can find someone . . .'

She decided to say it.

'Really? You didn't even know your husband was hanging round the red-light district.'

Renata's face fell, turned sour.

'He said you were the only one. He'd been drinking. It was a mistake.'

'They always say that. Two mistakes by the way.'

'Do you want me to help or not?'

'Two hundred thousand euros? Even if the police let me pay it . . . how would I find that kind of money?'

'They're bargaining. They don't expect that much. We'll meet them part way. We can find something.'

Hanna stared at the coffee cup and the wrapper for the Christmas biscuit.

'Unless you have some other suggestion?' Renata added. 'If you want to go back and hide yourself in that little cell . . . wait for some other man to come along and pay you to open your legs?'

Chastened, she mumbled, 'I told you. They won't let us hand it over. Unless . . .' She couldn't stop thinking of Cem Yilmaz. Wondering what he was really like. Who he knew. 'Unless I can find a way round them.'

The woman patted her hand.

'That's more like it.'

'Maybe,' she murmured, and just that admission made her feel guilty. 'But not in public.'

She was thinking this through as they spoke.

'The last thing Natalya needs is me plastered all over the papers.'

'Fine,' Renata said. 'I can put together some people you can talk to in private . . .'

'There isn't time! They're calling Vos at four this afternoon. They want their money by tonight.'

A truck turned up outside the window. A group of men started to unload scaffolding and more street decorations.

'Then best you don't talk to Marnixstraat,' Renata said. 'We do what we can ourselves.'

She got up from the table. Hanna didn't move.

'That woman from the security services. She hates me. She'll stop us.'

Renata shook her head.

'They said they could stop Ismail Alamy getting out of jail too.'

'Someone did, didn't they?' she replied without a second thought.

Silence for a moment.

'Don't give up hope.'

'You sound like the police.'

'Forget the police. If you can get a message through . . .'

Hanna didn't speak.

'Can you?'

'I can try,' she said and went to the door then looked out at the lights, the Sinterklaas figure, the images of Black Pete everywhere.

Renata scribbled a mobile number on a napkin.

'I'll find some cash,' she said. 'You work on the rest.'


When they got back to Marnixstraat Van der Berg and Bakker sat down with Vos and Aisha Refai, the young technician in forensic, to look at the laptop.

'Wow. I was probably at little school when that thing was made.' She was twenty-five but looked nineteen, bright, pretty and outspoken in a headscarf, red ski sweater and jeans. 'Can we sell it to the Rijksmuseum once we're done with it?'

Bakker plugged in the lead and turned the thing on. When the login finally came up she typed in the password.

'How'd you get that?' Aisha asked, not waiting for an answer to her first question.

Bakker told her, adding, 'It was a guess.'

'Good one. Though to be honest . . .' Her fingers tapped lightly on the keyboard as she worked her way around the system. 'I could have got inside this piece of junk in about thirty seconds flat. Password or not.'

'It belonged to Ferdi Pijpers,' Bakker explained. 'He was ex-military. Some intelligence experience. Old habits die hard I guess. If you look at the pictures . . .'

'Wait, wait, wait,' Aisha said, almost slapping her hand when it went to the keyboard. 'There are procedures here. That's what I do.'

Vos cleared his throat then looked at his watch. Not that it made much difference.

'OK,' she said when she was finished. 'Your man got this laptop fifteen days ago. It was wiped before that. The thing's deeply dysfunctional. I hope he didn't pay much for it. There's no Wi-Fi, no sign it's ever been used for a web connection. So naturally no email. Nothing but—'

'Nothing but a picture folder,' Bakker interrupted.

'Quite.'

Aisha pulled it up. Sixteen images taken the previous Thursday. The same two people in every shot.

'That,' Bakker said, 'is Martin Bowers. Or Mujahied Bouali if you prefer. Either way he's dead thanks to AIVD.'

Vos leaned forward and peered at the laptop screen. It looked like the young tubby Englishman with a ginger beard in the file photos they had. He was in a black anorak talking to a man of Asian appearance. Middle-aged. Smartly dressed. With a full beard, neat hair and a ready smile. If the date stamp on them was correct they were taken around midday. The background was familiar, a tall, medieval building, circular, surrounded by tourists.

'Munt Tower,' Van der Berg said. 'Good place to bump into someone by accident. Or pretend to.'

'Ferdi was following someone,' Bakker said. 'Bowers. The other man. He must have had a reason.'

The technician dumped the photos onto a flash drive and handed them to an assistant.

'Get them to intelligence, community liaison officers and AIVD,' Vos said. 'Let's see if we can pick up a name for the second man.'

Van der Berg ran a finger across the screen.

'I guess Ferdi had nothing else to do except work on his obsession. If he lost that boy in Afghanistan no wonder he went wild when the Bublik girl got snatched. We should have listened to him when he came in here.'

'We should,' Vos agreed. 'Aisha?'

She was back to fiddling with the photos, looking at metadata on the files.

'He didn't exactly have a decent camera, did he?' Bakker grumbled.

'He didn't have a camera at all,' Aisha said. 'He was using a phone. A Nokia N96. Fancy when it was new. Not exactly impressive now. The trouble is . . .'

She was doing things to the machine Vos couldn't begin to understand. Suddenly a whole new set of photos came onto the screen. Nine. Every one of them half the size of a postage stamp.

'Either your man didn't know how to sync pictures to an old laptop. Or his software was screwed.' She gestured at the screen. 'This was Saturday. The day before Leidseplein.'

'Great,' Van der Berg cut in. 'Just make it bigger, will you?'

He got a sarcastic smile in return.

'That never occurred to me,' Aisha said brightly.

Flying fingers again. The postage size images did get larger. But they were so pixellated it was impossible to see any detail.

They were taken outside judging by the wan daylight, against a wall in what might have been an alley. There were three figures in every shot. One around the size and appearance of Bowers. The second too tall for the unidentified man in the earlier shot. The third just as tall but slimmer perhaps. The same man. Someone else. It was impossible to tell.

'Make it better,' Vos pleaded.

She shook her head.

'I can't. The original files never got downloaded. All I have here are the thumbnails. I can blow them up as much as I like but they're a hundred by fifty pixels or so. That's five thousand dots. We've got software that can try to interpolate things but really . . .' She frowned at the laptop. 'There's just not enough data there. Sorry.'

'Shit,' Bakker said.

'There is another way,' Aisha suggested. 'You could get me that Nokia.'

Van der Berg called down to the morgue, asking for the inventory of items taken from Pijpers's corpse when he came in.

'It's there,' he said and went straight downstairs to fetch the thing. Puffing and panting he returned with an evidence bag in his hands, a hefty old Nokia inside it. There was a bloodstain on the case.

'This looks interesting,' Aisha said as she took it out with gloved fingers. 'Let's see if it needs charging.' She seemed to know the right button to press by instinct. 'Nope!'

The screen lit up and her face fell.

'Is this a joke, Dirk? I asked for his phone. Not one from the charity shop.'

Van der Berg bristled.

'That is his phone. AIVD took him to hospital. We picked him up when he was declared dead. The morgue did the inventory. That's what came with him.'

She turned the phone away from her and showed them. The screen said: *Start setup wizard?*

'It's been reset. Wiped clean. No pictures. No call logs.' She opened the back and poked around inside. 'Dammit. There's not even a SIM here. What gives?'

Bakker stared at Vos. So did Van der Berg.

'You're a genius, Aisha,' Vos said. 'You can do something.' She didn't look flattered. 'Can't you?'

'I don't know. I need to ask around. It's one thing getting stuff off a hard drive.' She waved around the back of the phone. 'This is more complicated. Especially if someone's hit reset.'

'Why's it wiped?' Bakker demanded. 'Can you do that by accident? Did it happen here? Or Schiphol? Or . . .'

Vos's phone rang. He waved at her to be quiet. When he came off he said, 'We'll ask those questions later. Intelligence have got a name for Bouali's friend.'


The street cleaners were finishing up in the red-light district. Washing down the narrow cobbled lane ready for another night of heavy trade. Hanna Bublik walked into Spooksteeg from the Oudezijds Voorburgwal end and stood outside the door of Yilmaz's block, hesitant, thinking.

Then a big, muscular figure appeared by her side so quickly it made her jump. She found herself looking into the Turk's beaming face.

Yilmaz was wearing a black leather overcoat that fell all the way down to his shins. In his right hand he had a carrier bag from one of the nearby oriental supermarkets.

'Do you like Thai food, Mrs Bublik?'

'Not hungry.'

'Better than Chinese. Healthier.'

She folded her arms and leaned against the wall.

'Do we have something to discuss?' he asked.

'You tell me. Have you heard anything?'

The laugh again.

'How many times must we go through this? There's business to transact before I can become involved.' He pulled an apple out of the bag and took a big bite. 'Otherwise you're wasting your time and mine. And yours is even more precious I imagine.'

Yilmaz reached out and keyed a code for the door. She watched. Carefully.

'Well?'

'OK,' she said. 'I'm yours.'

He grinned.

'Good. Finally you've seen the light. You won't regret it.'

'You've got some news?'

He pushed open the door.

'There are formalities we must go through first. Come inside please.'

She hesitated. Not scared. Never that.

'Please,' Yilmaz said again and took her arm, pushing her into the lift, keyed in another code as she watched. 'It's cold out here. I have a log fire. You must make yourself at home.'


Back in the office Vos got the details. The man talking to Martin Bowers in the pictures on Ferdi Pijpers's missing phone was Saif Khaled. There was a file on him in intelligence. They suspected AIVD might have more but Mirjam Fransen wasn't taking calls. Her assistant said she was back dealing with the family of Thom Geerts and no one else was much minded to help Marnixstraat at that moment.

He got the impression they blamed the police for the shooting at Schiphol the previous night, not that they dared say. There didn't seem much point in pressing for more information about a wiretap on Henk Kuyper either. The intelligence agency had done nothing about that as far as he could see.

Khaled was forty-seven, born in Egypt, active in Palestine and Syria before seeking political asylum in the Netherlands ten years before. Like Henk Kuyper he called himself an 'activist'. Just as with Kuyper it was unclear what that meant. The intelligence Vos could find indicated he was a sympathizer who'd offered vocal support for a number of extremist groups over the years. But there was no indication of illegal activity, of fundraising, or any public statements that might result in prosecution. He'd been vocal in the press too, speaking out at public meetings. According to one of Ferdi Pijpers's neighbours that was how the former soldier came to be following him and the people he met in the first place. It had become something of an obsession.

His home was a narrow terraced house on the edge of Chinatown. The property was owned by a shell company based in Yemen. From time to time men stayed with him. Never for long. That was it.

'Well?' Bakker asked when they got to the end of the skimpy details on the PC.

Vos turned to Van der Berg and asked if intelligence had come back with any link between Khaled and the local crime gangs. Or some gossip about one of the mobs having a new candidate for extortion.

'All they hear out there are Christmas bells,' the detective replied with a sigh. He put a fat finger on the photo of Khaled on the screen. 'Like it or not he's all we've got.'

'True,' Vos agreed. 'You stay here and see if you can dig up any more.' He got up, nodded at Bakker. 'Put some discreet surveillance around Khaled's place. Get them asking questions. We'll take the bikes.'

It was almost twelve.

'What if your man rings early?' Bakker asked.

Vos took the old Samsung out of his pocket and showed her. The battery was nearly full.

De Groot walked in with a couple of men from operations. They were carrying a small red suitcase. The commissaris asked them to place it on the desk and unzip the thing.

The top layer was fifty euro notes. Just enough to look convincing. Under a thousand in real money.

'I take it this is inked?' Vos asked.

'Every last piece,' one of the operations men agreed. 'Ultra-violet. We can trace it back.'

He pulled on a latex glove and gently moved aside a few of the genuine notes. Underneath lay plain pieces of paper cut to the same size.

'It only needs to fool them long enough for us to get in there,' De Groot said, a touch of regret in his voice. 'That's all. When we know where the handover is we'll have teams in place.'

Silence. Then a protracted sigh from Bakker.

'Unless you have other ideas,' the commissaris added.

'We're still chasing leads,' Vos replied. 'I'd rather track her down if we can. Laura?'

'Where . . .?' De Groot began.

'Dirk,' Vos said, heading for the door. 'Fill him in.'


Renata Kuyper didn't go into her husband's office much. He didn't like it. Said he needed space and room to think on his own. Except when she came up the stairs with coffee. That was OK.

So she brought him a cup, put it on the desk by the window and pulled up the spare chair. The top room of the house, right beneath the crow steps. Tiny. He seemed to love being locked in this place looking out over the Herenmarkt, the kid's playground, the trees and the ancient pissoir.

His eyes stayed locked on the computer. He'd been unusually

quiet that morning. Maybe there was a nagging conscience there, one he'd buried. Which would only make it hurt more, though being a man he probably never understood that.

'Henk . . .'

'I don't have the energy for another argument. Sorry.'

She reached out and touched his arm for a moment. Smiled at him in a way that tried to say sorry for both of them.

The room was always cold in winter. He seemed to like it that way. There was something solitary, almost monastic about the way he hid himself away here.

'I don't want an argument. We need to talk.'

He closed whatever he was working on – a short email, not that she saw the contents – then pushed his chair back from the little desk.

'If you want me to nag my dad about letting you live with him just say. You shouldn't be forced to stay here. Not if you don't want.'

She might have guessed Lucas would call him. They were father and son. And there was still a kind of closeness between them, in spite of all the differences. She felt sure Lucas would tell him about the conditions behind the ransom money. There was no way out of this. Nor, in a sense, did she want one. His father was probably right. It was worth one more try.

'I really don't have any secrets, do I?' she said. 'Anyone here I can confide in?'

'He's worried about us. What do you expect?'

She picked up some papers from the desk. Boring environmental reports. The stuff he always kept around. For show probably.

'What are you working on?'

'Another damned logging case in Sumatra. There's an orangutan charity asking for help.' A grimace. 'They can't afford to pay, of course.'

He went to Borneo not long after they married. Or so he said.

She never really knew where he vanished to when he was travelling. The things he brought back, presents for her and Saskia, were just the usual airport crap. He might have picked them up at Schiphol.

'I wish we could retrace the way we got here. Don't you?'

He folded his arms.

'Find the place we took the wrong turning,' she added. 'Go the other way instead.'

He sighed, stared at his hands.

'I can't undo what's done.'

Everything was so literal for him.

'We could work at putting it behind us. For Saskia's sake. Ours too.'

Henk Kuyper nodded.

'Is that possible?'

'Lucas thinks we should try. He seems very certain of that.'

He laughed, was briefly young again.

'My dad's never troubled by doubts. About anything. Is he?'

She didn't let her eyes leave him.

'I want to raise money for this girl. Lucas says he'll help. I want us to hand over what we can too.'

To her surprise he didn't break into a scowl. Or tell her she was stupid.

'We don't have much in the bank, love. Without my dad . . .'

*Love.*

When did he last say that? How hurt would he be if she laughed in his face?

Instead she said, 'I've checked the statements. We could free up thirty thousand. It'll hurt. We'll survive.'

He didn't shriek.

'Have you mentioned this to the police? Do you really think it can do any good? Dad seems to think the authorities won't allow it.'

'Maybe it's not their choice. I've talked to Hanna. The woman.'

A caustic observation so nearly slipped into her speech. 'She's got no one else.'

He leaned forward and took her hands.

'They won't let you pay it. They're the police. The state. They run things here.'

'They don't run me,' she said firmly. 'Or you. Do they?'

Again he didn't slap her down.

'You mean you'll pay it without telling them?'

'Maybe.'

'How?' he asked.

'She moves in those circles. She thinks she can come up with a way. We have to try. I can't just sit here knowing her daughter's out there . . . and it should have been Saskia. I won't.'

There was a sound. A new email on the computer. He didn't even look at it.

'What do you want me to do?'

'Go down the bank. Take out what you can. Bring it back here. I can talk to people. Your father. See what we can do.'

He seemed amused.

'There's nothing funny about any of this,' she said.

'Isn't there? Here we are. The king and queen of lost causes. Me trying to save a few endangered animals in the rainforest. And you . . .' He retreated, took his fingers away. 'Trying to help . . . someone . . . who . . .'

His hand went to his forehead. She wondered if she'd ever seen him in such obvious pain. And whether she was enjoying it too.

'Just run down to the bank and do it, Henk.'

'Yes,' he said and got up straight away, kissed her shyly on the cheek, then set off down the narrow stairs.

The front door closed with a slam. The walls of the old house trembled with the shock as always. She went to the window, watched him walk down the Herenmarkt, saw him look back and wave.

So she did too. Nothing special or obvious. That wouldn't have been right.

There was a sound on the computer again. Another email coming in. Normally he was so careful. He always logged off, never left his phone without a number lock in it.

Not now.

She shuffled over and took his chair at the desk. Worn, creaky, overused. So many hours spent here working. For places he never talked about. Seeing people she never met.

Renata moved the mouse and brought the window alive. Then memorized the position of everything on the screen. It was important he didn't think she was snooping. This side of him, 'the work', was his alone.

Slowly, carefully, she went through his files. There wasn't much apart from the emails and a few documents. Some photos of Saskia. A couple of her on honeymoon by a courtyard in the Alhambra in Granada. One shot that tugged at her heart: the two of them on a Spanish beach, his arm around her shoulders. He looked young, handsome and fit, bare-chested in skimpy trunks. She wore a bikini. One of her favourites though she'd left it behind. It wouldn't fit her now anyway.

Long before he came back she withdrew from the computer, went downstairs, started to make coffee again.

To think about what she'd seen too.

Nothing about Sumatra or orang-utans anywhere.

She wondered whether that should be a surprise.


Vos stopped at Kaashuis Tromp and bought a couple of cheese croissants. Then the two of them rode past the Drie Vaten, over the gentle hump of the Berenstraat bridge, into the centre of the city, spilling flaky crumbs along the way. A few metres short of Spui he finished his, kept riding, balled the paper bag, aimed it straight into the nearest bin without even breaking speed. Bakker tried the same, missed, got off her bike cursing, padded over and picked it up then tidied it away.

Feet on the ground he watched.

'I'll never get the hang of that,' she moaned.

'Yes, you will. It takes practice. Like everything.'

She didn't move. There was something that needed to be dealt with here.

'Where's the mother?' Bakker asked.

'I don't know,' Vos answered honestly. 'I wish I did. I wish we could just reel her in and keep her safe with some uniforms around her. But we can't. She's not like that. Can't make her either. Too smart for that.'

She stayed silent. That was unusual.

'What would you do in her position?' Vos asked.

'Anything I could. Not sit around waiting for us to get on with it. I mean . . .' She swept back her hair and gathered it with a band. 'We haven't done much so far, have we? Except get it all wrong.'

Laura Bakker so wanted the world to see her as a confident, capable young police officer. Which she was for the most part. But there was still an insecurity about her. It was there from the beginning, when she thought she was about to be thrown out of Marnixstraat as unsuitable for the job. He'd yet to find a way to deal with that.

'This isn't an exact science. We're not filling in a spreadsheet. Sometimes things don't add up. At least not in the way they should.'

'And then?'

'And then we go back to the beginning and try again. If there's another way of doing this I'm too stupid to know.'

Still she didn't move.

'I can't bear the idea we won't find that little girl, Pieter. I don't know what . . .'

'We will find her.'

'And if we don't?'

'How can I answer that question?' he demanded. 'What do you expect me to say?'

She didn't move. Might have been a teenager at that moment.

'Does it get easier? Do you just get . . . hardened to all this shit? I mean—'

'No,' he broke in, checked his watch. 'You don't. Stop scaring me. In three hours I'm supposed to find out how we deliver a ransom that's not a ransom and save a young girl's life. I'd much rather we didn't have to face that. Can we go, please?'

She bristled.

'You were the one who stopped for a cheese croissant. Not me.'

For once Vos swore, quite mildly and under his breath. Then before she could ask another question he couldn't possibly answer, he pedalled on.


Cem Yilmaz's living room was too hot. She could smell the logs on the fire. Taste the dense smoke they were putting out. In the bottom of her bag the stolen gun sat whispering to her. She knew how to use it now. Had looked that up on a PC in a cafe not far from home.

It was obvious he wanted something. An act. Proof of her devotion. Pimps all did and Yilmaz was one of the busiest, most powerful, in the city. Not like the rest, or so he thought. A 'businessman'. Legitimate. There to give other men what they wanted.

She sat down and drank his too-strong coffee. Listened as he outlined what he was going to do. Put out feelers to his contacts offering to pay the ransom direct, without any police intervention. None of them, Yilmaz emphasized, were part of the criminal community. But they knew people. Heard things.

If she was lucky one of them would come back with a link into whoever was holding Natalya. And then they could try to set up a handover.

She told him what Vos had said about the new demand. Not once did he question Vos's assumption that the original kidnappers had passed Natalya over to criminals more versed in the complexities of extortion. Either he knew something or wasn't saying. Or it really was as obvious as Vos seemed to think.

'I've a little sister back home,' Yilmaz said when she finished. 'I know about family. What else is there?'

'I just want her back.'

He nodded.

'Of course. I'll do what I can.'

'The money . . .'

'This sum they ask for's ridiculous and they surely know it.'

'They'll want something. Now that preacher's dead.'

He smiled. Big teeth. Round face. A muscular, commanding man.

'Everyone wants something. That's what makes the world work. Let me see if we can establish a line of contact. Get them to talk to you direct. Then . . .' He turned his dark, intelligent eyes on her. 'You'll have to come up with something?'

'I'll try. Can you help?'

'You want a gift?'

'No. A loan.'

Yilmaz looked her up and down.

'You're an attractive woman. All the more if you could learn to smile. You've four, five, maybe seven years of work left in you. For my purposes anyway. How much do you think you could earn in all that time?'

She wanted to fly at him.

'No idea.'

The searching eyes again, as if she were a business proposition being examined.

'You might net me ten thousand a year in pure profit. If I give you a living allowance would you turn over every cent to me? To save your child?'

'Every cent,' she said without a moment's hesitation.

'And work as a waitress in the evening if I ask? You don't make private calls. That I won't allow.'

'If that's what it takes.'

'Good.' He thought to himself. 'Seventy thousand euros is a lot of money.'

'Not enough,' she mumbled.

'Then find some more. And I negotiate.'

Yilmaz got up and stood in front of the fire, warming his backside. She knew that look.

'I need to know what I'm paying for,' he said with a wry shrug. 'I'm sure you understand.'

She took off the black jacket and said, 'What do you want?'

He pointed to a low leather chaise longue set back in an alcove, out of sight of the window.

'Take off your clothes. Lie there. On your front.' He reached up to the mantelpiece and retrieved what looked like a jar of cream, examined it in his fingers then replaced it on the wooden shelf. 'I'll be quick.'

In a little cabin she had a measure of control. It was her place, for an hour or two. She could choose, say no if she wanted.

Not here.

The sweater came off. The boots and socks and jeans. Soon she was looking at her naked limbs. Seeing all the imperfections, the blotches, the stretch marks, the odd scar. Skin and hair. Touched and mauled time and time again, not that she thought about that much any more.

You never knew what they wanted. In different circumstances she'd always ask and say, 'Do this, don't do that.'

But she recalled Yilmaz wrestling with the hefty young blade here the day before. No way of guessing what he'd desire by way of proof, of entry fee. No point in wondering.

The chaise longue looked expensive and cheap at the same time. The leather shiny but soft with frequent polish. She lay down, put her arms under her chin, kept her head up, didn't even try to look back. Opened her bare legs just a little.

She hoped he wasn't lying when he said it wouldn't last long.

A sound she couldn't quite place. As if the logs in the fire were shifting position, trying to get a better look. Then footsteps. She sensed him over her, heard the soft, rhythmic sound of his wheezing breath.

'A man must leave his mark,' Cem Yilmaz said and his big knee rammed down hard on her back, pushing her face sideways, right cheek hard into the leather.

Then came an agony so intense, so unexpected she started to shriek and wail, squirming, fighting as something hot and excruciating seared and scorched her.

There was a smell it took a second to recognize amid the agony. Then it came. Burning flesh and skin.

Not long, he said. Just a few agonizing seconds. He let go, stood up, short breath coming in snatches.

She turned to her left side. It hurt the least.

He went back to the mantelpiece and placed a long iron rod in the blazing grate. It looked like a thin sword with an emblem on the end, just fading red. He picked up the jar of cream again and pulled what looked like a surgical pad out of a wooden box above the fireplace.

Then a vanity mirror. The kind upper-class women used in British movies.

'Sit up,' he ordered and she did, half-choking with anger and hate.

The burning smell wouldn't go away. It was her.

Yilmaz walked round with the mirror and told her to look backwards.

One glance towards the window and she knew what she'd see in the oval glass. Seared into the skin by her right shoulder blade was an ornate figure, the source of all that stinging agony. It looked like the letters 'CY' in a curious script. Bloody and brown ridges in the flesh where he'd branded her.

She should have guessed. Not that it mattered. She still would have allowed him to brand her anyway. Knowing would only have made the anticipation worse.

'Here,' he said and threw her the cream and the dressing. 'There are some painkillers in the bathroom.'

Her head wasn't working right. She couldn't even think of Natalya at that moment. Just how small and frail and damaged this man had made her feel.

'Put your clothes on. Go take those pills like I ordered. You're one of my girls now. Like all the others. They'll know you. So will the men I send.'

Shivering, mouth open, bent over, shoulder shrieking with pain, she clutched at the cheap jacket as if it offered some kind of protection.

'Get out of here!' he cried. 'I don't want to look at you like this.'

Yilmaz reached into his pocket and took out a fifty euro note.

'You won't work until Friday. This can keep you. Someone will call and tell you what to do, who to meet.' His finger jabbed towards the livid mark on her back. 'If a man sees that and he didn't come through me I'll know. Remember. Now move.'

She scooped up the money and ran into the bathroom. The wound was too tender, too fresh for the cream. So she attached the dressing very lightly, washed down her face, got rid of the tears. Sat on the toilet.

*Sobbing.*

*Fearing.*

*Hating.*

And finally . . . *thinking.*

She had her bag with her. Took out a ballpoint pen. Scribbled the codes for the front door and the lift on the inside of her left wrist.

He didn't look at her as she walked out fifteen minutes later, went down to Spooksteeg, tottered along the cobbles on unsteady feet.

Then did something she'd never tried before even though so many men had offered her the opportunity. Walked into the nearest coffee shop, one owned by Yilmaz for all she knew, and asked for some dope. Ready-rolled.

She didn't know how to handle it or what she was paying for. How strong it was. How quickly it might call up an oblivion she craved.

They didn't allow you to light up inside any more. She didn't even smoke. Hanna Bublik walked out and sat in the cold, damp winter air, next to a couple of stoned idiots on chairs in the street. Got one of them to pull out a lighter, drew the thick, heavy smoke inside her.

Closed her eyes. Found herself looking into a black empty place inside. One that seemed to go on forever.


Saif Khaled lived in a narrow pedestrian street not far from Zeedijk. Chinese shops and supermarkets. The exotic fragrance of a nearby restaurant filled the air.

Bakker parked her bike by the grubby brick front wall and pressed the bell. Vos stood back and looked the place up and down. Four floors and a cellar with a blacked-out window and a separate door at the foot of some stairs.

It took a minute then someone answered. Khaled looked much as he did in the pictures Ferdi Pijpers had taken. Full black beard, wavy shiny hair. Late forties, calm. He grunted when Bakker showed her ID and then, on her tablet, the photos from the previous weekend.

'I'm amazed it took you so long,' he said and showed them in.

A neat house. Clean floors. Clean rooms. The smell of disinfectant mixed with incense. He led them to a front room, went to the kitchen and came back with three glasses of mint tea.

Vos sipped his, struggling with the too-hot glass. Bakker pointed out Bowers in the shots.

'Bouali,' he corrected her when she spoke his name. 'That's what he called himself.'

The story came out. Pat and straightforward. Khaled occasionally took in Muslims in trouble. Broke, lost, looking for help. Temporary accommodation to get them back on their feet. No questions asked usually. None stayed for more than a week. That was a strict, unbreakable rule.

'Who pays for this?' Bakker wondered.

'I've got relatives who can afford it. Many times over.' He raised his glass in a kind of toast. 'Charity doesn't cost much. He said he needed somewhere to stay. He wasn't asking for money. Just a bed.'

Khaled looked at the images on Bakker's tablet again.

'Who took these? Your people?'

'A deranged soldier,' Vos said. 'The man who shot dead Ismail Alamy last night.'

He looked at them again.

'Was he following me? Or Bouali?'

'We don't know.'

He didn't believe that.

'Really? This Englishman got my name from somewhere. He called and asked to see me. I wouldn't let him in here. So we met in the street. I listened. I said no.'

'Why?' Vos wondered.

'He wasn't being honest with me. I don't ask many questions. But when I do I expect good answers. He wasn't long in the faith. Wouldn't say what brought him here . . .'

'So why were you expecting us?' Bakker asked.

The pleasant facade vanished.

'I do read the papers. I saw what happened to him.'

'You could have come forward,' Bakker suggested.

'And say what? I met this man for ten, maybe fifteen minutes. Once. All I knew was he wanted somewhere to live. Someone to talk to maybe.'

'You should have told us,' Vos said.

That got to him.

'Why? Out of some misplaced duty? This lunatic was taking photos of me. Am I truly supposed to believe you didn't know? Just because I'm Muslim. Then you shoot Ismail Alamy—'

'We didn't shoot him,' Vos cut in. 'I told you. It was a disaffected soldier. We think he picked up your name through the newspaper. If Alamy had accepted our offer of protection it would never have happened.'

'Protection?' Khaled scowled at both of them. 'Are you serious?'

'Very,' Vos said. 'Did you know Ismail Alamy too?'

The veneer of friendliness had disappeared altogether.

'I knew of him. We never met. I wish we had. But then you people threw him in jail. For no good reason, as the courts said in the end.'

'We'd like to look around,' Bakker said.

'Do you have the authority to do that?' He laughed. 'No. If you did you wouldn't be asking, would you?'

'If there's nothing to hide . . .' Bakker began.

'The basis of your law, as far as I understand it, is that you must show my guilt. Not that I must prove my innocence. It didn't happen for Ismail Alamy, of course. But why stop trying?'

He got up and took their glasses.

'Where were you on Sunday?' Bakker said, watching him.

Khaled thought for a moment.

'I don't have any guests at the moment. I went down to the canal and watched a little of the nonsense. A man in a white beard. Little blacked-up elves running round doing his bidding. The things that amuse you people . . .'

'And then?'

'Then I came home and read. On my own. I didn't bother with Leidseplein if that's what you mean. There's only so much pantomime a man can take.'

'On your own?' she repeated.

He put their glasses on a tray.

'I've answered your questions. I met Bouali for a few minutes. I've never spoken or communicated with Alamy at all. And now they're both dead.' He stared at her. 'Are you happy?'

'There's a young girl missing,' Bakker snapped. 'Kidnapped by people associated with them. Don't you even care?'

A shrug.

'There's so much to care about in the world. I try to focus on matters that are close to me. Things I can affect in some way. There's nothing I can do for that child. I'm sorry.'

He gestured at the door.

'Perhaps you'll have better luck elsewhere?'

Outside Bakker was fuming. Vos looked at the house again. A big place for one man. In front of the nearby restaurant a couple of Chinese waiters were starting to argue with a customer. Someone who'd rushed outside without paying. Not a good idea in this part of the city. He was going through his pockets for money, trying to stay out of sight.

'What do you think?' Vos asked.

Bakker took the lock off her bike.

'I think he probably enjoyed wasting our time. We don't have enough for a warrant. Do we?'

He shook his head, walked over and looked at the menus. The fleeing diner threw some money at the waiters then scuttled off down the street.

'Do you like Chinese food?'

'This isn't the time, Vos.'

'No,' he agreed. 'It isn't.'

He turned and looked at the house again.

'Did I miss something?' she asked.

'Probably not. Let's get back to Marnixstraat.'

Halfway there his phone rang. Vos pulled in to the side of the road to take it.

They were in the Nine Streets. Vos found himself staring at a shop window full of seasonal kid's clothes. Snowflakes and reindeer. Thick wool caps. Expensive children's toys.

Bright jackets. A pink one there with a pony on it.

Mirjam Fransen, furious as usual.

'What in God's name do you think you're doing, Vos? Saif Khaled's on our watch list. You're not supposed to go near him without our permission.'

He wondered if he ought to buy Bakker something for Christmas.

'I never checked your watch list. I'm looking for a little girl.' He told her about the photo of Khaled and Bowers on Pijpers's phone. 'We have to follow these things up.'

'Did you find anything?'

The pony jacket cost seventy-five euros. Probably as much as a woman like Hanna Bublik could net in an hour or two.

'I found out your surveillance people have a habit of leaving Chinese restaurants without paying the bill. Why did you have people there?'

Silence then.

'Is there something I should know?' he asked.

'About what?'

'About Saif Khaled? Martin Bowers? That phone tap I asked for on Henk Kuyper?'

'Enough of this shit, Vos. You're making things worse.'

'Is that possible?'

'It is.'

'We need to offer a full ransom when they call.' He was trying to sound reasonable. Hoped it worked. 'Not this fake one De Groot's put together. You can come up with the money. Mark the notes. Put GPS in the bag. Do stuff I don't even know about . . .'

'Not going to happen.'

Vos had a pretty clear picture of how the handover might take place. Plenty of examples of extortion and kidnapping in the past. A minion, sometimes an innocent one, would be sent for the pickup. He'd check the money was there then take it to a more senior party. A stack of paper wouldn't fool them for more than a few minutes. Then the link man would be on the phone.

He walked away so that Bakker couldn't hear him.

'If we don't go through with this the way they want . . .'

'This is your case, Vos,' she said and didn't try to hide her disdain. 'You said so. Deal with it. But you're not giving criminals government money.'

Bakker ambled over. Vos called Hanna Bublik. Still voicemail.

'Jesus, Hanna,' Vos whispered. 'Where are you?'

Then left one more message.


The Nokia phone found in the pocket of the dead Ferdi Pijpers now lay dissected on a plastic tray. Aisha Refai was poking through the pieces with a pair of tweezers, messing with the sixteen gig flash memory, when Thijs the freelance phone geek walked in. Twenty-three, tall and earnest. He worked as a consultant for telecoms firms in the city. She only called him when she was stuck. He knew that too.

Thijs stared at the dismantled phone on the desk and said, 'What in God's name are you doing? An N96? That's like a work of art.'

'It's a phone,' she said. 'A phone.'

'A phone in bits now.'

She told him what had happened. How the Nokia was found in a shot man's pockets. Already wiped.

'Hard or soft reset?' he demanded.

'Hard?' she said uncertainly.

He sat down, pulled on a pair of latex gloves and started to reassemble the thing.

'So you turned it on and found nothing?'

'Correct,' she said, trying to sound patient. 'Why do you think I called you?'

'Because you need a genius.' He grinned. Thijs looked nice when he did that. 'Coffee helps kick off the genius cells by the way.' He nodded at the new machine. 'Double espresso.'

She grunted something and went and made him one. When she returned the phone was back together again. He was sliding out the keyboard from under the body. It looked neat. Small screen, early smartphone, made in 2008 from what she'd read. But a museum piece.

Thijs put in the power cable and hit the on button.

'There are two ways to reset an N96. Hard and soft. You type . . .' He scratched his head, as if trying to recall something. 'Asterisk hash 8780 hash for hard. Three zero for soft.'

'You can't imagine how much that knowledge has enriched my life.'

He grabbed the coffee cup, raised it in a cheery toast and took a sip.

'UDP.'

Nothing more.

'Pardon?'

'UDP. User Data Protection. Clever little thing Nokia came up with to make sure you wouldn't lose your stuff. Even if the phone crashed. So long as the flash memory's intact you're covered. So . . .' He watched the screen come alive. 'It's still there. You just need to know where to look.'

She folded her arms, kicked her stool back from the desk and watched him.

The supercilious grin on his face didn't last long as he clicked through the buttons.

'Any luck?' she asked as he started to run out of options.

He put the phone down, took a deep breath and asked where the SIM was.

'There wasn't a SIM in it.'

'Really? And this is how you found it? In the morgue? Wiped?'

'At the risk of repeating myself . . . yes.'

'It doesn't work like that. This thing's been completely erased. The data area. The system area. Completely blank. You can't do that from the phone itself. The only codes that work are the ones I told you.'

This was interesting.

'But you could do it, couldn't you?'

He waved his arm.

'Naturally. But not from the phone. You have to plug it into a laptop. Go deep. If you know what you're doing it's a minute's work. But you need your gear.'

She tried to think this through.

'He could have done this himself. At home. Before he went out.'

'Then why take the phone with you?'

'To make calls?' she said wearily.

'You're not listening, sweetheart.'

'Don't call me . . .'

'It's blank. Not even set up. My theory . . .'

He liked to think of himself as a detective from time to time. Which drove her nuts.

'Someone got the phone after he was shot. Either on the way from the airport or here they plugged it into a laptop and knew what they were doing.'

'So there's nothing there at all?'

'Devoid of data. Not a bit or byte in sight.' He turned the phone over in his hands. Almost affectionately. 'Cool piece of kit in its day. Five megapixel camera. GPS. Carl Zeiss optics. Wi-Fi. HSDPA. DVB-H, not that *that* was much use . . .'

'Enough. Enough.'

He got paid by the hour and liked to lengthen things with gobbledegook if he could.

'Sorry,' Thijs said putting the Nokia back on the tray. 'I take it you didn't find the micro SD card.'

'What?'

He checked his watch. She scowled at seeing that.

'Who was he?'

She told him, with a little background.

'So he was a secret squirrel?' Thijs asked.

'Used to be military police. Intelligence possibly.'

He turned the phone in his hand.

'Good kit for the job. You realize that if he took photos he'd have a GPS fix on them? The exact location. This little beast has A-GPS too. Probably accurate down to five metres or so if you're lucky.'

'Clearly I'm not lucky.'

He found a tiny slot on the side. Then picked up a magnifying glass and took a good look at it.

'If I was a spooky person I wouldn't store my important stuff on the flash. I'd keep it on a little SD card and take it out until I needed it. Those things are smaller than a baby's fingernail. No one ever looks. See?'

He passed over the magnifying glass and pointed to the open card slot on the phone.

Scratches there. Clean and recent from the look of it.

'So someone removed the memory card too,' he said.

'And wiped the phone?' she asked. 'Why do both?'

'To be careful?'

'A careful spook would hide the card, wouldn't he?' She got to her feet and said, 'Come.'

'Where are we going?' he asked a little nervously.

'To the morgue. To hunt through a dead man's clothes.'

Thijs turned pale.

'No, no, no. I do phones. Corpses are so not my scene.'

'You're getting paid and you're getting free coffee,' she said then slapped him on the shoulder. Hard. 'If I find something down there I want you to look at it.'

'But . . .'

Hands on hips she glared at him until there was silence.

'Don't touch anything nasty,' she added. 'That's my job.'


One drag and Hanna Bublik knew this was the first and last time she'd try dope. The message light was flashing on her phone. Vos demanding she go to Marnixstraat at three thirty. Important, he said. The call was coming in at four. The man was insistent on that. If she could talk to him perhaps . . .

She thought about calling him back and asking if the security people might change their mind about putting together a real ransom. Then decided against it. There was a choice here. Between Cem Yilmaz, a man who'd just branded her as one of his own, the hurt still burning through her shoulder. And Pieter Vos, a decent police officer trapped in a system he seemed to know was flawed. Powerless to do what he thought right.

Not much of a choice at all.

So she left the dope cafe and walked along the little cobbled street, trying to dodge the stag-party Brits clutching beer cans and joints, the kind who'd ring her cabin bell out of bravado.

Somewhere along the way her phone rang. She heard Renata Kuyper's firm, clear voice in her ear.

'We have to meet.'

'Why's that?'

A long pause then, 'Are you OK?'

'What do you think?'

'Where are you?'

She looked around. Spuistraat.

A pause. The Kuyper woman was using a computer.

'There's a cafe two streets down towards us. Florian. I'll see you there in ten minutes.'

The place was smart with twee furniture and paintings of Venice on the wall. The woman behind the counter gave her an odd look as Hanna came through the door, asked for a coffee and took a seat.

The cannabis stink was probably on her. Just from that one deep drag she could taste it thick on her tongue. Feel it in her head, mingling with the pain of the Turk's fiery iron brand.

From the very beginning, that strange, cruel Sunday in Leidseplein, she'd been racking her head with a single, simple question: what to do? And there'd never been an answer. She was a stranger in this place. Alone. Illegal. Suspected. Hated by some. On Sunday the police told her to be patient and wait. To watch. To trust them. Yet it was Wednesday and they seemed no closer to knowing who'd taken Natalya. Or who might be holding her now the reason for her abduction, getting Ismail Alamy freed, had vanished.

Cem Yilmaz might be her only option, however much she loathed the idea. And his seventy thousand wasn't enough. She needed Renata Kuyper. There was nowhere else to turn.

Then she turned up, immaculately casual as usual. Paid for the coffees, sat down, took her hand.

Hanna withdrew her fingers.

'What in God's name have you done?' Renata asked. 'You look awful. You stink of something.'

She shrugged, took a bite of the pastry Renata bought for her. The shoulder hurt like hell. She needed the toilet.

A dash, a lurching race. Then she was inside and heard the door open and close behind her.

She threw up in the basin. Breathless, gasping, she washed

out her mouth and stood in front of the mirror, removed her jacket, and the sweater, the cheap shirt beneath.

'Jesus,' Renata whispered looking at her back. 'What's that?'

'Price of entry,' she said when she got her breath. 'It gets me some money for Natalya. Someone I know. Seventy thousand if he's telling the truth.'

She found the cream. Renata took it and smoothed on the ointment while she winced, nearly cried from the hurt. Then came the dressing. She put it on loosely, said they'd stop at a chemists and buy some more. It was important to change the thing frequently and avoid the risk of infection.

'Infection?' Hanna asked. 'What does that matter? I need money.'

'Henk took out what he could. Thirty. His father's promised to match it. That gives us sixty. A hundred and thirty. That's more than half what they're asking. Still a lot.'

She put her clothes back on.

'We still need a way to get it to them, Hanna. Have you got any ideas there? Because I haven't.'

A middle-class woman from the Herenmarkt didn't mix with criminals. But an illegal hooker from Georgia . . .

'I'm trying,' she said and left it at that.

A long, well-manicured finger pointed at her shoulder.

'And that was part of the price?'

Some things were beyond tears. Beyond feeling.

'Why do you care?' This still puzzled her. 'I'm just a whore from a place you couldn't find on a map. You don't owe me any-thing.'

Renata got off the toilet, looked at her, nodded.

'True.'

'Then why?'

'For God's sake, does it matter?' The sudden anger silenced her. Took Hanna by surprise. 'Maybe I'm being selfish. Is that OK? Looking for something to do. Something that . . . makes me feel good about myself.' She leaned against the mirror. 'Not a lot does if I'm honest. Happy?'

'And that's it?'

Renata paused, didn't look at her then.

'If you'd rather I wasn't here . . .'

Hanna put on her black jacket, walked out through the cafe and called Vos. He asked the usual questions. Where was she? Was there anything he could do?

'You could tell me you're getting somewhere,' she said straight out. Her head felt clear now. The pain from Cem Yilmaz's brand helped in a way.

'I need you here in Marnixstraat,' said the patient, thoughtful voice on the other end of the line. 'I want you to talk to him when he calls. To talk to Natalya too.'

Compassion. That was the word. He had it, and so, in a brittle, difficult way, did the red-haired young woman who worked with him. But was that worth anything? What was the point of kindness in a world that didn't value it?

'You think they've got a conscience, Vos?'

A long pause on the line. Then he said, 'I think we have to chase every option. We can go through with this handover—'

'With what? Toy money?' she shrieked. Renata was outside now, watching, listening. 'What happens when they find out?'

'Please,' Vos begged, his voice riddled with embarrassment. 'Just come into the station. I need you here.'

He suspects, she thought. A clever man, he understood she might be pursuing other options.

'I'll be there,' she said meekly then put the handset in her pocket.

Renata walked over.

'I've got our thirty thousand,' she said. 'Henk's father promised to match it. He should have the money within an hour or so. Just call me and tell me what to do.'

Silence.

'Hanna?'

'Yes,' she said. 'I will.'


At three fifteen, while Vos was in De Groot's office, engaged in one more phone plea to Mirjam Fransen for real money, Koeman got called to the station front desk. There was a small, frail Asian woman there. Old clothes. A supermarket carrier bag on her lap. A face that spoke of years of hard work, eyes that didn't want to look straight at him.

She wanted to talk to someone about the kidnapping. Koeman took a deep breath, determined to hear out this visitor.

The woman was a cleaner for Smits, owner of the rented houseboat in Westerdok where Natalya had been kept the night she was seized. When Vos came on them, thinking the girl was still inside, she was close to finishing her work there.

'You won't tell Mr Smits I'm here, will you?' she asked in a faint, scared voice.

'I don't see why I should,' Koeman replied. 'Would that be a problem?'

She didn't exactly explain why it might be. But Koeman got the drift. Smits ran the boat rental on the side of his main business, a travel agency. The money he got from it all came in cash and probably didn't go through the books.

'So when the police called you wondered if it was about that?' he said when he thought he had a little of her confidence.

The woman nodded.

'I didn't know there was a little girl missing. Not until I saw the news yesterday.'

'And?'

'I'd taken out most of the rubbish already. It was in the bin down the street. No one ever asked me about that.' She shrugged her narrow shoulders. 'You should have.'

'We should,' he agreed.

'When I heard I went back and got some of the stuff I put in there.'

'When was that?' he asked.

She stared at him.

'This morning.' She looked round the waiting room. 'Mr Smits doesn't like the police. I thought you people might find her.'

Koeman folded his arms and told himself to keep calm.

'And?' he asked.

She reached into the bag and started to take things out.

A crushed orange juice carton.

Several screwed up tissues in a plastic bag.

'OK,' he said. 'Those I'll take.'

'No need to sound grateful,' she muttered. 'And this.'

A kid's colouring book. Again in a clear plastic bag. She'd been thinking about this.

'Thanks,' Koeman said without much feeling.

'I went through it,' the woman told him. 'I got to . . .'

She showed him the inside back cover. He looked at it and said another thank you, meant it this time.

There was a sound at reception. Hanna Bublik was there, asking for Vos.

'Is that her?' the cleaner asked. 'The mother? The woman who . . .'

'Thank you,' he repeated, smiled, got up, shook her hand. Extracted a name, a phone number and an address.

'Mr Smits won't know it came from me, will he?' she asked again.

'I'll see to it,' he said and went to the desk.


Twenty minutes to go before the call. Hanna Bublik sat in a side room with a woman uniform officer. Vos was with Bakker and Van der Berg in the morgue inventory office watching Aisha and her phone geek remove Ferdi Pijpers's belongings from a storage box.

A small pile of bloody clothes built up on the desk. She was sifting through them with gloved hands. Thijs watched, wide-eyed, looking a little green at the gills.

The young forensic officer had requisitioned the on-board CCTV from the ambulance that had taken the dying Pijpers to the hospital. It was running on a PC at the end of the desk. Two medics had fought for Pijpers's life in the race to the emergency department. Mirjam Fransen had watched them from a seat by the back all the way.

'You'd think she'd be looking after her own man,' Bakker wondered.

'Thom Geerts was dead already,' Aisha Refai suggested. 'Pijpers . . . not quite. Our friend from AIVD doesn't do anything but sit there. Not that I can see.' She left the clothes for a moment and zoomed in on the video. Fransen leaned against the side of the ambulance glassy-eyed, in shock. 'I'd say she looks in quite a state.'

'All the same . . .'

Bakker grabbed the mouse and scrolled backwards and forwards through the video. Fransen had sat and watched the medics working on the bleeding man on the gurney. She didn't move a muscle until the ambulance came to a halt. Then the team took Pijpers out and she vanished with them.

'We need to get footage from the hospital,' she said.

'Tried that,' Aisha replied. 'Not easy. There aren't cameras in most places.' She smiled at Vos. 'You're going to have to do it the old way I'm afraid. Go and talk to people.'

'In good time,' Vos said. 'How did we get his things?'

She pulled up a log on the computer.

'An AIVD desk officer phoned just before midnight and suggested we pick them up. Along with his body for a routine autopsy here in the morgue. Two hours. It could have been anyone in there.' She hesitated then added, 'Or here.'

'It's got to be AIVD,' Bakker cried. 'They've been jerking us around ever since this began. Before—'

'Laura,' Vos cut in.

'This is all wrong. If I can see it I'm sure you can.'

He didn't answer. Aisha Refai and the phone geek were getting embarrassed.

'Or aren't we supposed to question them? Are they above the law? They seem to think so.'

The sound of heavy feet and a smoker's cough interrupted the argument. Koeman was at the door. He had a book in a plastic evidence bag.

'I'm not interrupting something, am I?'

'No,' Vos said. 'What is it?'

'You remember the cleaner at that boat in Westerdok? She found something.'

Koeman placed the bag with the book in it on the desk. It had a picture of a cow jumping over the moon on the cover. Bright and colourful.

'Aisha,' the detective said. 'You're the one wearing gloves.'

They stood round her as she opened up the bag and started to turn the pages.

Most bore nothing but printed drawings. Cats and dogs. Mothers and fathers. Children playing happily in the sun.

'The back,' Koeman said.

She did as she was told.

The writing was careful and clear. Each letter printed as if it mattered deeply.

> *One of them is called Carleed or something.*
> *I think he's a kind of boss.*
>
> *He's got dark skin, a big beard, all black and shiny,*
> *like a pirate.*

*I think he knows I've seen him.*

'How the hell did we miss this?' Bakker wanted to know.

'It was already in the bin by the time we turned up.' Koeman glanced at the door. 'The woman's downstairs if anyone wants to talk to her. She's scared as hell. Mr Smits isn't the nicest of bosses apparently. I don't think he declares his rent from that little boat. She'd rather we didn't tell him she was here.'

'Carleed,' Bakker said. 'Saif Khaled. The beard . . .'

'It's a really common name,' Aisha pointed out. 'I mean *really* common. Like Smits. And as for beards . . .'

'I know,' Koeman added. 'I checked. But after I talked to her I got a call from the team in Chinatown.'

He checked his notebook.

'They talked to a nosy old bird who lives down the street. She says she saw a little girl at the basement window last night. Long blonde hair. The window's blacked out but the kid pulled back the sheeting apparently. Not long after she met our friend Khaled in the local shop. He was buying fruit juice and sweets. Oh and a colouring book and crayons. Did he mention that?'

Vos checked his watch. Ten minutes. He needed to talk to Hanna Bublik.

'He said the place was empty. The only visitors he had were young Muslim men in trouble.'

Van der Berg took out his phone.

'I'll call De Groot and see if he can get us entry.'

Vos shook his head.

'No time. We need to take this call. Put a team close to Khaled's place and a control van around the corner.'

Van der Berg didn't move.

'Was I being cryptic?' Vos asked.

'It's all there in black and white in the logs, Pieter. Saif Khaled's on an AIVD watch list. We're not supposed to go near him without their say-so.'

'Just fix it, will you?' Vos said, looking at his watch. 'I need to take this call.'

There was a place to hide. A kind of alcove near the bottom of the steps.

The kid from Anatolia was weak and slow. She'd let him walk down the stone stairs, look around, food in his hand. Then come out and surprise him.

She was eight years old. He was maybe twice her age. But she had the sharpest of the utility knives from the box. She'd use it too.

Shivering in the pink jacket she could see it was getting dark through the tiny gap in the sheeting over the window. He'd come back before long, with food, to empty the bucket. She knew the routine for this place now.

A noisy key opened the door at the top of the steps. He never bothered to lock it behind him. Too lazy for that. Because there was only a little girl at the bottom, scared and silent in the cellar.

Natalya shuffled into the shadows at the foot of the steps and waited. Had no idea how long this would take. She didn't have a watch. They'd removed that from her in the first place where she could hear the ducks outside and the water lapping against a timber hull.

Nothing now but black bricks and the sound of footsteps tap-tapping on the cobbles of the street above.

Voices. All kinds. Men and women. Children sometimes. Dutch. Foreign. Chinese maybe. Something else.

Waiting.

Nothing else to do.

She'd stay hidden as long as it took.

———

An interview room. Hot and stuffy. From the canteen below rose the smell of cooking fat and pungent steam.

Vos, Hanna Bublik, Bakker and Van der Berg. One of the specialist team from the snatch squad assembled for the ransom handover. The red suitcase, closed, ready to go. Vos was going to take it, a GPS tracker inside his jacket, another sewn into the lining of the case itself. Three pursuit teams ready to follow wherever the pickup was going to be. A helicopter would be in the air the moment they knew a location and time.

De Groot was in a meeting beyond Marnixstraat, out of contact. That was odd but not unwelcome.

The clock on the wall turned four. Vos stared at the old Samsung on the table, hooked to a charger, volume turned up to full. Four bars of signal. Everything ready.

He'd told Hanna what he could. The truth mostly, if not all of it. She'd listened and not said a word. There was something wrong here. She seemed in pain. Physical as well as mental. Bakker had noticed it too, asked if she was OK. Offered to fetch a doctor.

All she asked for was a glass of water. Vos thought there was a whiff of dope about her and didn't want to think about that.

So they waited.

At five past four she looked at Vos and asked, 'What's happening?'

'They don't always keep to schedule,' he said, making it up on the go as usual.

'You told me he was adamant. It was four o'clock. On the dot.'

'He said that.'

She watched him.

'And what else?'

Decisions. The truth or a well-meant white lie. Vos felt they were beyond that now.

'He said there'd be no phone call if he felt he couldn't trust us.'

'You're the police. Of course they don't trust you.'

'What they mean,' Bakker said, 'is if they think we don't intend to go through with the drop. If we . . .'

Hanna Bublik stood up, got to the suitcase before any of them could stop her. Quickly unzipped it and ran her fingers through the notes there.

One second and she was into the blank paper.

'Shit,' the woman from specialist operations said. 'I wish you hadn't done that. We've got ink on those things.'

'Ink?' Hanna shrieked. 'What ink?'

The officer pulled a detection lamp out of her bag and shone it on the notes. A numeric code appeared on all of them, and the blank pieces of paper underneath.

'We'll get them,' the officer insisted. 'We'll bring these bastards to justice.'

'Justice?' Hanna shrieked. 'I don't give a shit about justice. I want my daughter back. That's what matters. Not . . .'

She shoved the case off the table. Real and fake money scattered everywhere. No one moved until Vos got to his feet. Persuaded her to sit down again. Then the operations woman took a deep breath and started to pick up the notes, trying to tidy them back into the case.

Hanna waved a dismissive hand at the mess.

'So they won't call if they think you're going to screw them around? And this is what you do?'

'Standard practice,' the woman said.

'Standard practice is you fuck up?'

Vos waited a moment then said, with the slightest of shrugs, 'Sometimes.'

He hated lying. So did Laura Bakker. It was one of the few things they had in common.

And waiting. They both loathed that too, though in different ways. Bakker was young. For her it was just plain impatience. Vos, older, not wiser in his own eyes, just more experienced, found the empty hours simply increased his curiosity, his instinctive penchant to be mistrustful, occasionally about matters that were entirely innocent.

They watched the phone.

The phone didn't ring.

'We told you we couldn't pay the full ransom,' Bakker said as gently as she could.

Hanna ignored her, turned her fury on Vos again.

'Did you do something? Something they might have found out about?'

'No,' Vos said then looked at her. 'Did you?'

A straight question. And the way her hurt face flushed made him realize she hated lies just as much as he did. Which must have been difficult given the life she led.

'We should talk.' He gestured to the others. 'Alone.'

Bakker blinked and stared at him.

'Vos! You're waiting on the call!'

'I can take a phone call without you. Come on.' He nodded at the door. 'Outside.'

Shaking her head, the red hair flying everywhere in anger, she got up. Van der Berg and the specialist woman followed.

The two of them then. The suitcase. The silent phone. Frying smells rising from the canteen. The air conditioning whirring as it pumped too much heat into the cramped interview room.

'I can't make these men trust me, Hanna,' he said. 'I can only hope they do.'

'Hope. You keep using that word so much.'

'That's because we need it. Just as I need you to have faith in me.'

Her narrow face was still flushed.

'Well,' he added. 'Do you?'

She kept staring at the Samsung.

'Hanna?'

'What do you want of me?'

'Is there something I need to know? Something . . . relevant.'

He couldn't put his finger on it. But she'd changed. 'You look ill. You look different.'

'My daughter's been missing four days. How am I supposed to look? Like Renata Kuyper? All make-up and smart clothes?'

'I just . . .'

She sat back and closed her eyes.

'You haven't asked me,' he said.

'What?'

'Why it hasn't rung.'

'Do you know?'

'No. But we specialize in unanswerable questions here. It's part of the job.'

'Funny,' she snarled. Then glanced at the clock on the wall. Four fifteen. 'How long will you wait?'

'Until it rings. At least . . . someone will.'

Vos got up and called them back into the room. Told Van der Berg to stand down one of the three snatch teams and tell them to wait for new orders. The helicopter could stay on the ground.

De Groot was still out of the building somewhere.

'I want Koeman in here to sit by this phone. If it rings he answers and says I had to take a meeting because he was late.' He glanced at the woman in the shabby black jacket. 'Get Mrs Bublik something to drink. Something to eat if she wants it.'

She was on her feet.

'What's this now?'

'I have to go,' he said and got his jacket.

'And I'm supposed to stay here?'

'Where else would you want to be?' he asked.

Outside, in the corridor, they could hear her yelling at the support team woman waiting on Koeman to turn up.

'What the hell was that about?' Van der Berg asked.

'I wish I knew,' Vos said. 'Let's pay Saif Khaled another visit. I want to see inside that place.'

———

Mirjam Fransen's office was behind Dam Square. Small room. Heavy security throughout the building. Miserable people that day. Thom Geerts's colleagues may not have liked him much. But they respected him. Now there was a funeral to organize. The awkward business of negotiating pensions and compensation for his family. He and his wife were on the brink of divorce. The bureaucrats in The Hague might think that complicated matters. That it gave them the excuse to make the pay-out smaller.

After the difficult briefing with De Groot she now had to meet one of the insurance people to talk through compensation. A place round the corner. A chance to get out of the building.

It was getting dark. Rain on the way. Christmas shoppers cramming the streets. On Sunday they'd had a couple of Black Petes abseiling down the building. Special ops men in curly black wigs and costumes, grinning all the time as if this were a game.

Perhaps it was, she thought, as she stepped out into the cold street. A distraction gone wrong.

Fransen hadn't walked ten steps when he was on her. She glanced at him, couldn't believe this was happening, then marched straight into an alley by the building.

Henk Kuyper followed, grim-faced in a winter anorak, hood pulled over his head.

'Are you out of your mind?' Fransen asked.

'Maybe.'

'Jesus . . .' She grabbed the lapel of his jacket and pulled him further into the shadows. 'We really shouldn't be seen together.'

He looked bad. Tired and depressed.

'No one tells me anything. I hear more from the police than from you.'

'That's how it is. How it has to be. We're in too deep to start breaking cover now.'

Kuyper didn't seem much impressed by that.

'Will they get her back?'

'Who?' she asked, not thinking. Still astonished, outraged, he should turn up like this.

'Who do you think? That little girl? This wasn't supposed to—'

'No blame games,' she interrupted, and ran her hand down the front of his dark anorak. 'Not now. Plenty of time for that later. And it will happen. Believe me. Those bastards in Marnix-straat will see to it.' A pause. 'How are you?'

He pulled himself away from her. Fransen laughed.

'Aren't we friends any more, Henk? Don't we get to meet again when this is over? I liked it when we did. I thought you did too.'

He leaned back against the cold damp wall and closed his eyes.

'This is just one big mess. I never—'

'Will you listen to me for once?'

Her voice was shrill, commanding. Hard to argue with. Always had been.

'Well?' Kuyper asked.

'You stay low. You stay quiet. You go back to work as if nothing ever happened. Pretty soon things will calm down. They'll see this for what it was. A brief criminal case. One that ended bloodily on both sides.'

'The girl . . .'

'The girl's Vos's problem now. There's nothing either of us can do to change that.'

He didn't move.

'You've no idea where she is?' he asked.

'Have you?'

'I gave Renata some money. As much as I had. She seems to think they can pay a ransom somehow.'

She wanted to hit him.

'For the love of God, Henk. Don't turn stupid on me now. These are dangerous times.'

He looked mad then.

'It's our fault that kid's out there!'

'And so's Barbone. Have you forgotten that?'

She waited.

'Have you really got nothing for me there?'

'Nothing.'

She took a deep breath.

'Sometimes people forget which side they're on. Find themselves lost in the wilderness. No waypoints. No bearings. If I start to think . . .'

'I know who I am. I know who you are too.' A pause. 'I know we owe that girl.'

'All wars have innocent casualties. Only a fool thinks otherwise. And this is a war. One that's never going to end.'

He stared at her.

'So you're doing nothing?'

'I'm still trying to break Barbone's ring. Is that nothing?'

Henk Kuyper turned to go. She grabbed his arm.

'This is dangerous and stupid. Don't do it again. If I want to talk to you I'll initiate contact the way we agreed.'

'And if I want to talk to you?'

'Then you'll have to bide your time. Go home, Henk. Be with your wife and your daughter. Act normal. Don't give me reason to worry.'

A scowl, a curse, and he strode back into the street.

She went to the end of the alley and watched him. Then she called the office and got through to one of the surveillance people.

'Henk Kuyper's walking out of Dam Square. He's headed for the Nieuwe Kerk. I think he's going back to the Herenmarkt.'

'And?'

'I want him watched. Tell me where he goes. Who he sees.'

Silence and then the voice on the other end said, 'Isn't he one of ours?'

'You heard,' she said.

———

On the way out Vos phoned Aisha and told her to keep looking for the missing memory card. Two minutes later he was in a van with a four-man armed entry team, all body armour, helmets, belts full of gadgets, ready for trouble.

'This thing about not telling De Groot,' Van der Berg began.

'He's still in a meeting somewhere.'

'And skipping the paperwork . . .'

'If you don't want to come . . .' Vos said as they parked themselves on the bench seats in the back.

'Wouldn't miss it for anything,' Van der Berg replied watching the officer opposite him slap his body armour then check his weapon.

The van lurched out into the street.

'Are we holding Hanna Bublik?' Bakker asked.

Vos shook his head.

'We can't. We don't know she's done anything wrong.'

Bakker's sharp eyes never left him.

'We don't know.'

'Been here before, Laura. Think like her. There's no call from the kidnapper. Even if there is we plan to give him a suitcase that's mainly pieces of paper.' He met her gaze. 'What would you do?'

No answer.

The van had slowed. They were getting into the red-light district. Neon signs beyond the security glass. Sex shops and dope houses. It was dark now with rain falling on narrow, winding streets. Huddled figures going from window to window idly scanning what was on offer. Then the first signs of Chinatown. Garish neon lights. Exotic smells. Bunches of men gathered together talking by the little shops.

Vos had been going through the files. There was nothing to suggest a connection between the oriental crime syndicates and extremism. They were too busy making money to get involved in politics. It was more likely to be one of the groups from the Middle East or North Africa. Of which there were plenty.

But all that was speculation. When it came to Saif Khaled they had hard fact. The name in Natalya's colouring book. The fact a neighbour had seen a blonde-haired girl at his basement window. The shopping trip.

They had to make this raid. There was no choice. Even if he didn't feel good about it.

The van came to a halt. The senior man up front, full gear, all black, a belt with a Taser and pepper spray, semi-automatic cradled in his right arm, looked over and apologized for interrupting.

Khaled's tidy little house was across the road.

'What do you want us to do? We can take down the door really quickly. Just flood the place.'

'Stay here,' Vos said and climbed out of the van.

Two of the plain-clothes men who'd been quietly observing the address wandered up. They stood in front of the Chinese restaurant where Mirjam Fransen's surveillance plant had gone through the needless argument. AIVD would have people in the area too. They were probably phoning her now.

Bakker and Van der Berg joined him.

'Something's going on in the basement,' one of the observation team said. 'We saw a light go on down there. I don't think we should wait.'

Vos glanced back across the road. One of the officers in the rear of the van was playing with the ram they used to break down doors. The lead man came and asked again what he wanted them to do.

He checked his watch. Quarter to five. Vos called Koeman in Marnixstraat. The phone hadn't rung. Hanna was getting more and more agitated. De Groot was back from the meeting that had detained him. He wanted to know what was going on.

*Don't we all*, Vos thought.

He knew what she craved. Knowledge. Certainty. Doubt was a cruel companion in grim situations like this. It only served to torture her. Torture them all if he was honest.

'You'll wait,' Vos told the man in black. 'All of you. Stay here unless I call.'

He strode across the street, ignoring their muttered curses, pressed the bell, stood on the front step close enough to get his foot inside the door if he needed to. There was a shape in the front room. It looked like Khaled himself. From the step Vos could see down into the well that fronted the basement. Blacked out windows. But the light behind it kept flickering as if someone was moving around down there.

Saif Khaled had lied. And perhaps it was his name on the book the cleaner had found in Smits's boat in Westerdok.

Finally the door opened and the Egyptian stood there furious, glaring at him.

'We need to talk,' Vos said. He nodded at the corridor. 'Inside. Now.'

The man was nervous. That ought to be good.

Without a word he slammed the door hard in Vos's face.

A decision made.

He waved back to the van. It took seconds for the team to get there, bring the weighted ram with them, two men wielding the long steel cylinder.

Vos stood back and watched. In the little street in De Wallen the din they made was loud. Turned louder still when they were inside.


A sharp knife. A sharp mind. Natalya Bublik could get by in three languages. Her own. Dutch. English.

None of the kids at school bullied her. A couple tried to begin with. It never happened again.

She was Georgian. A Bublik. Her mother's daughter. Life had been a battle for as long as she'd known. When trouble came you didn't shrink. You fought back with all the force you could muster.

Maybe she should have done that already. Would have if it

hadn't been for that first man. The one who sounded like a teacher. Who seemed interested in her. Not hard. Kind even given the chance.

But he was gone and she was somewhere new.

Crouching by the cold stone stairs, listening to people outside on the pavement beyond the taped-up windows.

The kid from Anatolia would come back. They had to bring food. Take away the bucket she used for a toilet.

*Waiting.*

*Cold.*

*Scared.*

Night had fallen. She could just make out the flashing of the neon signs from the restaurant across the road.

Then there was a noise at the door upstairs and voices. Angry ones it sounded like.

Still she clutched the little knife. Now was the time. The only time. It had to happen. She wanted home.


In the narrow house in the Herenmarkt, at the table in the dining room, another eight-year-old girl sat facing an unwanted confrontation.

Saskia Kuyper shivered in a T-shirt and jeans. Her mother, coat on, breathless from stomping the chill night outside. Candles on the table. Food, uneaten. Christmas lights alive in the window, red, green and blue.

'Where is he?'

A shake of the head. Excuses.

*I've been doing my homework. Busy in my room.*

'Saskia!'

She reached out and took her daughter's small, cold hands. There'd never been much love between them. It was a horrific pregnancy. Painful, difficult, with Henk working most of the time. From the moment they came back from the hospital there was always a distance between them. Reasons for it too. That happened sometimes.

'Dad went out,' the girl said, snatching away her hands. 'I don't know where.'

'You're eight years old. He shouldn't leave you on your own. It's against the law.'

'The law,' the girl snarled. 'Who cares about that?'

She phoned him. Just voicemail again.

'You don't own us,' the girl said. 'Even if you think you do.'

It had to be said.

'Why do you hate me? What did I do?'

Her eyes were small and shifty. She took after Henk so much. Physically and in other sly ways.

'I asked a question.'

'Why do you hate Dad?'

'Things don't always work out the way you'd like.'

'He said you wanted to leave. To take me away with you.'

'People say things when they're arguing. Things they don't mean.'

A sudden look of childish fury.

'At least Dad cares . . .' Saskia murmured.

'And I don't?'

No answer.

'Who was it took you to see Sinterklaas when he was busy? Who gets your clothes? Fetches you from school? Sees you to all those parties?'

A nasty little scowl.

'Dad could get a servant to do that if he wanted.'

Henk's words. Thrown at her more than once when they were fighting.

'No, he couldn't. We don't have the money.'

'Grandpa can pay.'

Renata had heard that too.

'Why should he? We're grown-ups, aren't we? Lucas helps us enough as it is. Perhaps too much.'

Then, with a savage, childish sneer, 'It's not Dad's fault you're always miserable.'

She was silent for a moment, wondering how they came to make her like this. Bitter, surly. Deeply unhappy. That was the worst thing.

'I know.'

'So why do you blame him?'

'I don't.'

She took the girl's cold hands again, bent down and looked into her pained, embarrassed face.

'How can I make things right with you? How can we be friends again?'

*Again?*

The word just slipped out and they both knew it was a lie.

'I'm not leaving,' Saskia insisted. 'You're not taking me to Grandpa's. I'm staying here with Dad.'

She nodded.

'So am I. We should be together. Like a family.'

*Again.*

The little fingers stayed where they were. Renata squeezed them and smiled.

'We should do things this Christmas. Go places. Wherever you want. You tell me. Let's be happy for a change. No one likes being sad.'

Eight years old. God, she thought, what will she be like when she turns teenager?

''Kay.'

It was a small, conciliatory sound. But there was a little hope in it.

'I guess Dad's gone for a beer. He'll probably come back stinking drunk. And singing.'

She belted out a snatch of one of the rude songs she'd heard in a bar down the Jordaan. Saskia laughed then. Her teeth were so even. Those of a toddler almost.

'Dad doesn't get that drunk!'

'Oh he does. It's just you don't see it. Sometimes . . .' She stroked the girl's blonde hair and Saskia for once didn't recoil. 'Sometimes he's so funny. We need to make him laugh again. We all need that. Don't we?'

The girl picked at her food. She didn't eat enough. Too skinny. Maybe there'd be problems with that before long.

'You know the other night,' Renata added, 'when we came back from all that nonsense in Leidseplein we got drinking together. After you went to bed.'

A shake of the blonde head.

'You don't drink, Mum. Don't tell lies.'

'I did that night. We'd lost you. I couldn't think straight. And Dad was so fed up because that little girl was missing.'

The knife went down. The fork too. Renata kept smiling as if this was all in the past and didn't matter much at all.

'Dad told me what happened,' she added.

'Told you what?' Saskia asked in a quiet, nervous voice.

Head down. A conspiratorial smile between them. The way a mother and daughter were supposed to speak, in secret confidences.

'About the trick you played. You vanishing in the square like that.'

Her eyes shot wide open.

'It was just a game, Mum. He said you wouldn't mind.'

Renata laughed and patted her hand.

'Of course I didn't. I get too serious sometimes. You should take me down a notch or two. There . . .' The smile again. 'I said it.'

'He just said to run away and see the Black Pete. But I picked the wrong one, didn't I? He wasn't Dad's friend. Not nice at all.'

'The wrong one,' she agreed. 'So many Black Petes around that afternoon. Easy mistake.'

The girl looked worried. Ashamed too.

'Wasn't our fault that other kid went missing. Dad said so.'

'No. It wasn't.'

'But. But . . .' Saskia's little hand came out and gripped her arm. 'You mustn't tell, Mum. They'll blame him. The police. They hate him anyway. It wasn't our fault.'

'Of course I won't tell! Why would I do that?'

'To get him into trouble.'

She shook her head.

'And why would I do *that*?'

The girl looked a little guilty.

'I don't hate him, Saskia. I love your father. He loves me. We both love you. But sometimes love goes wrong. It's like a . . . a bike. You pedal it everywhere. You get used to it. You take it for granted. Then one day it breaks down and you think . . . it's the bike's fault. When really it's yours for not looking after it.'

'My bike broke down.'

'And we fixed it, didn't we?'

'Dad did.'

True, she thought. But that's what they were for.

'Well we'll fix this too. You and me and him.' A smile. 'OK?'

The softest, meekest answer.

'OK.'

She bent down and stared intently into her daughter's face one last time.

'And you don't talk about what happened in Leidseplein again. Not with me. Not with Dad. Anyone. It's done with. Forever. If you mention it . . . to him even . . . he'll just get upset again. We don't want trouble, Saskia. We've had too much already.'

Saskia nodded.

'That girl he took? The one who had a jacket like mine? The one on the TV?'

'What about her?'

'Is she dead?'

Renata shook her head.

'No one said that, did they?'

'Dad . . .'

'Dad doesn't know, sweetheart. No one does except the bad men who did it.' She tapped the plate of food with her finger. 'Eat your supper. We'll get a game for your iPad if you like. Or a video.'

'Dad said . . .'

'What happened then's over and done with. Let's think about Christmas. Sinterklaas. Tomorrow we'll buy Dad a present to cheer him up. And you can write a poem to go with it too.'

Saskia giggled.

'When he comes back drunk I can say we saw him!'

It was an odd Dutch custom. With the feast day came verses, cheeky ones sometimes, naughty prods about past misdeeds forgiven.

'You can.'

There was a nice kid somewhere in there, she thought. Not a bright one. She'd never be that. And it didn't matter at all.

Renata looked at her watch, went back to wondering where he was.

'You have to keep that a secret too. Like what happened in the square . . .'

Her finger went to her pursed lips.

Saskia did the same. Then through them whispered, 'Ssshh-hhh . . .'


Vos watched the four entry officers go to work and wondered whether they did anything in their spare time except watch action movies.

It was all noise and fury. Then the door was down. They were in. Pushing back Saif Khaled as he yelled at them balling his fists.

Dirk Van der Berg followed it all from the pavement, shuffling from his big left foot to his big right one. Laura Bakker much the same.

When they had Khaled on his knees, face up against the wall, Vos entered, his two colleagues behind them.

There was a door at the end of the corridor. Probably a set of stairs there leading down to the basement. The Egyptian was yelling all kinds of abuse. None of it obscene. That was new.

One of the specialist men checked the rooms ahead, guns out, as if expecting trouble. Then he tried the door at the end of the corridor. Locked. He called for the weighted ram again.

'Wait, wait, wait,' Vos said and intervened, hand out, stopping them.

He looked down at the angry man on the floor. Western clothes. Western haircut. Good Dutch.

'Khaled. We're going to take a look. Like it or not. We can break the door down if you want.'

There was a curse then. Or something that sounded like one.

'I think there's a little girl down there,' Vos added. 'I don't want to scare her any more than she's been scared already.'

'Fuck you, Vos! Why can't you leave us alone?'

'Because we're looking for a child who got snatched from her mother,' Bakker told him. 'What do you expect?'

Vos held out his hand. Then nodded to the officers holding Khaled to release his arms.

They did. The man leapt for him, screaming, fists flying. The biggest specialist team man was there in an instant. One hard punch to the face that sent him down to the floor. Then a boot to the gut for good measure.

Blood was pouring from his nose. It looked broken.

'Wonderful,' Vos muttered then glanced at the door. 'Take it down.'

It was old. Solid. Harder to defeat than the more flimsy, painted thing on the front of the house.

'I'll go first,' Vos said as it started to shatter on its hinges.

Too late. This was their moment. And the big one seized it.


A shape on the stairs. Natalya Bublik hid in the shadows and watched. Then slid to the side as he came down the steps. Looked up. He was holding out his hand, calling her name. The way her mother did. The way grown-ups did everywhere, wanting to take you away like property, anywhere they liked.

The knife came out, firm in her fingers, slashed sideways, found flesh. A shriek of pain. A figure stumbling on the stairs. Like a lithe cat she stole past him, dodging his falling legs. Raced up the stone steps, into the cold night.

People there. Lights. Noise.

No idea where she was. Which direction to run.

*Away.*

That was all. Flee this place. Find warmth. Find someone living in the light and ready to listen.


Back in Marnixstraat Frank de Groot returned from his meeting with AIVD. One he could have done without. There was nothing there he wanted to hear. Nothing he could change. And these people had sway over him. The ears of politicians and shadowy security figures south in The Hague.

In the end they won. One way or another.

He went straight to Vos's office, found it half-empty. Got briefed by one of the juniors on the raid at Saif Khaled's house. Fought to hold on to his temper.

Koeman was in the interview room with Hanna Bublik. The suitcase, the Samsung phone on the table. No one had called. No one had heard back from Khaled's place.

He dragged the detective out of the room then down the corridor, out of earshot of the woman.

'I'd be really grateful if someone filled me in on what the hell's going on around here,' he said then put his face so close to Koeman's he could smell the man's cheap aftershave.

'We didn't hear from anyone,' the detective told him. 'Some stuff came in about the Egyptian. They thought it better to be there than here.'

De Groot had the gift of being able to turn an intimidating nature off and on at will.

It was on full now.

'Did anyone point out to Vos that Khaled's on AIVD's watch list? And that we're not supposed to go near him without their say-so.'

Koeman nodded down the corridor.

'Someone ought to stay with her. She doesn't much like me but Vos said—'

'Mirjam Fransen told me about that raid,' De Groot cut in. 'I was in the AIVD offices when she got a call to say it was happening.' He slapped Koeman on the back. 'When Vos gets back here it had better not be empty-handed.'

Koeman said something that didn't mean a lot. Then went back to the office. Hanna Bublik was gone. A woman police officer was picking up the empty coffee cups.

'Where the hell is she?'

The question seemed to offend her.

'She took a call and said she had to leave.'

The Samsung still sat on the table. Silent.

'On that?' he asked.

'Do I look stupid, Koeman? On her own phone. She wasn't in custody, was she?'

'Get her back,' he ordered. 'Where is she?'

'Do I look psychic?' the woman asked.

No answer.

'Well?' she persisted. 'Do I?'

———

'What is this?' Vos asked when he forced his way through.

Saif Khaled's basement wasn't the grim cellar he'd expected. The place was well furnished, with bright walls, lamps, a sofa, a double bed. A TV set and a computer. Everything shut off from the street by the black plastic taped to the front windows.

'Fetch him,' he ordered and listened as Khaled was dragged down the stairs.

A woman in a long black dress sat in the corner, terrified, defiant, her arm round a child. A girl. No blonde hair. Just a yellow headscarf. They both looked foreign. Middle Eastern. The kid's eyes were on the floor. She seemed even more scared than the woman.

Vos walked up, Bakker followed. Van der Berg came with the Egyptian.

'We're police,' Vos said, taking out a card, approaching the woman slowly, carefully. 'Making inquiries. And you are?'

'Guests,' Khaled interrupted, dabbing at his bloody nose with a tissue as he pushed his way to the front. 'Guests who've no need to be intimidated by the likes of you.'

Bakker smiled, crouched down in front of them, looked at the little girl. Held out a hand.

'Can I see your hair?' she asked gently. 'Just that and we can go.'

The girl looked up at her mother. She glared at Bakker but nodded anyway. Then gently unwound the yellow scarf from the child's head.

Laura Bakker must have guessed. There was no hair. The girl, her face pale and skeletal, was completely bald.

'I'm sorry,' Bakker said and squeezed her hand anyway.

'Upstairs,' Vos ordered, and followed Saif Khaled all the way.

The Egyptian was at full rant by the time they got into the front room.

No more secrets now. It all came out. The mother was Syrian, the daughter born in Amsterdam. The girl was being treated for a brain tumour. Chemotherapy had led to hair loss. They'd been kicked out by the father, a Dutch national, who'd lost patience with the cost of private treatment. Khaled had taken them in, found someone to keep paying the medical bills.

Probably from his own funds, Vos thought. Not that he was saying.

'Why in God's name didn't you tell us?' Vos demanded.

The question didn't infuriate him at all.

'The husband's a pig. A violent bastard. She's terrified of him. It's the last thing she needs right now.'

'She should have come to us,' Bakker complained. 'That's why we're here.'

Khaled closed his eyes for a second, shook his head.

'She did come to you. Five times. When he was threatening to hit her. You said there was nothing you could do. Not until he did.'

Van der Berg took a call and went into the corridor.

'Look . . .' Khaled was struggling to be reasonable. 'We really don't need this.'

Vos told the specialist team to get the front door fixed.

'They're going to stay here for a couple of days,' the Egyptian added. 'Then I think we can get them out to a safe house in Leiden. Two more sessions at the hospital. After that Lisa can take a break.'

'Is she going to be OK?' Bakker asked.

He nodded.

'With a little luck. And a lot of prayers.' He waited. 'I don't suppose you do prayers, do you?'

Van der Berg came in and took them to one side.

'We need to get back to Marnixstraat. De Groot's going berserk. Hanna Bublik walked out of the building. They can't find her. AIVD are mad we came here.'

Vos walked into the street and called her number. The rain

was steady and determined. Across the road the Chinese restaurants were getting busy.

Three rings and then she answered. Firm voice. Determined
as always.

'Don't you want to know?' he asked.

'Know what?'

She was outside somewhere. He could hear voices. Traffic.
Even the sound of a bike bell.

'What we found?'

'Tell me.'

'A little girl. A sick girl. Someone was hiding her. There were
family problems. They didn't want us to know.'

Silence.

'Why did you leave, Hanna?'

'Because I can't sit around doing nothing. That suitcase, Vos.
Did you really think it would fool anyone?'

A good question.

'It might have fooled them long enough for us to find her.'

'And did they call?'

'Not me,' he said. 'How about you?'

It was out in the open now. And he was glad of that.

'I don't know what you're talking about,' she answered and
finished the call.

He hadn't noticed Bakker slide out of the house and stand
next to him, leaning against the wall, arms folded.

'We need to follow her,' she said. 'I'll fix surveillance.'

'No.'

'Pieter!'

Vos rarely lost his temper. It was close now. The fact they'd
chased Khaled for no good reason. The sick girl in the basement.
Hanna Bublik loose, on her own again.

He jabbed a finger in her face.

'I said no, Laura. And tell no one I had that conversation.
Understood? Otherwise . . .'

He paused.

'Otherwise what?' she asked.

The specialist team were looking at the broken door. Surly and embarrassed. As if this was all Vos's fault.

'I've seen enough here,' he said and wondered where he'd find a cab.

Up the stairs. Into the street. Cold rain spat on her young face. It felt like freedom.

Cobblestones shining with the mirrored reflections of restaurant neon, red and green, blue and yellow. Foreign faces looking at her, saying things in foreign tongues.

Natalya Bublik ached for her mother, craved a way to find her.

*Run.*

But which way?

The alley had an exotic smell, of food and spices. Lacquered ducks hung from hooks in windows like strangled ornaments. Next to them pieces of meat she couldn't begin to identify. Guts and fat, livid on cruel and shiny spikes.

*Run.*

She turned right, started. A big shape blocked the way.

Looked up. Saw a face smiling at her. A hand extending down.

'Come, little girl,' the man said, beaming. 'Let's find your mummy, shall we?'

His hand was the colour of the dead, mangled ducks across the road. But she took it anyway and when she did his fist closed on her tiny fingers and his free hand closed round the collar of her filthy pink jacket.

The smile grew broader.

She knew then she was lost.

'Come,' he said, no warmth in his voice now.

Dragged her back to the steps, Natalya screaming all the way.

The men across the street turned and stared at the windows. The strung-up carcasses. Their reflections in the glass.

Back down the cold stone steps. The door slammed behind them.

The boy from Anadolu was at the bottom holding his leg, whimpering.

More afraid of the man than the wound she'd slashed into his flesh.

Outside a tune struck up from somewhere. Loud pop music streaming out of a cafe maybe. She wondered why. If whoever did that knew something. Had got a message from the big man, understood what was required.

'Sit, Natalya,' he said and shoved her onto the low, small bed. 'Sit and watch.'

Then turned to the dumb teenager who was supposed to keep her trapped here, lost and hidden underneath the city's blind, chill streets.

It took a moment for her to understand about the music. Then it came.

He needed something to hide the screams.


Bakker followed him to the cab and pushed her way in before he could close the door. They went to Marnixstraat in silence, his choice not hers, through streets crowded with holiday shoppers.

When they got to the station he strode to the interview room where they were supposed to be keeping Hanna Bublik. Told Koeman to deal with the suitcase, the real money, the counterfeit notes, the pointless technology they'd sewn into the seams.

Then pocketed the Samsung for no good reason and went round to the morgue to see if Aisha and her phone geek Thijs had got anywhere with the search for the memory card from Ferdi Pijpers's phone.

'De Groot really wants to see you,' Koeman said on the way.

'He's very pissed off. I think that Fransen woman's been giving him hell.'

'Frank can wait.'

Aisha and the phone geek had been through all Pijpers's belongings. Found nothing at all.

'Let me look,' Bakker said and started to sift through the bloody clothes they'd taken from the dead man in the hospital.

'Vos . . .' Koeman began.

'AIVD wiped his phone,' Bakker cut in, as she went through Pijpers's jacket. 'God knows what else they've been playing at while we try to find that girl.'

'They'd say they were doing their job,' the detective snapped back.

'I'm sure they would,' Vos agreed.

Aisha again. 'You're sure there was a memory card?'

Thijs nodded.

'Unless he took it out just before he got shot. If there was something incriminating he'd hide it, wouldn't he?'

Bakker had found a tobacco tin.

'Oh, Christ,' Koeman grumbled. 'He wanted to smoke that stinking thing in reception when he came in yesterday. Got all uppity when I said he couldn't.'

'Pipes,' Bakker said. 'My uncle Kees used to smoke a meer-schaum.' She sniffed the tin. 'I liked it when I was little.'

'That's because you were a kid,' Koeman said. 'You didn't know any better.'

She gave him a caustic look, opened the tin, smelled the tobacco. It was strong. The earthy aroma drifted over the hot, busy room.

Bakker took out a packet of cigarette papers and held it up.

'Why does a man who smokes a pipe need these?'

'Maybe he does roll-ups?' Aisha suggested, making a gesture with her fingers. 'You know . . .'

'Not with pipe tobacco,' Vos said.

Bakker opened up the little slit through which the slim papers emerged. Then she retrieved a tiny plastic sleeve from inside.

'Hallelujah,' Thijs said and took it deftly from her, removed his glasses, looked at it close up. 'Two gigs. Old. But this is a micro SD card.' He pulled an adapter from his jacket pocket. 'Anyone want to take a look.'

They walked over to the nearest PC. Frank de Groot marched in and told Vos he wanted a word.

'In a minute,' Vos replied.

'Did I say I wanted a word in a minute?' the commissaris growled.

Thijs popped the card into the computer and started to work the keyboard.

'Now,' De Groot repeated.

Vos didn't move. He joined the rest of them crowded round the monitor. De Groot's voice went up a couple of tones. Got louder too.

'These are the pictures,' Aisha said. 'The ones we got on thumbnail.'

'Dead right,' Thijs agreed. 'Taken on Saturday. Some of them at two in the afternoon. Some of them at four. Look. You can see the light's dying.'

Vos stared at the images coming up on the screen.

'To hell with the light,' Bakker said. 'Who's on it?'

The commissaris barged into them and told Aisha and her friend to get out of the room.

Her dark eyes lit up with anger.

'But. But—'

'Leave now,' he ordered. 'You're done for today. Shift over. Be gone.'

Koeman was shuffling on his shoes looking scared and uncomfortable.

'You too,' De Groot added and the man left in an instant.

Bakker went to the keyboard.

'Leave that,' he ordered. 'I want to know what happened at this Khaled's place. What the hell you were doing there.'

Vos told him.

'We didn't have anything else to chase, Frank. That call wasn't coming in. We knew . . . or at least we thought we knew . . . there was something suspicious going on there.'

'Am I just here to sign off your time sheets? Didn't I deserve to be told?'

'You weren't around. There was a decision to be made. I made it.'

'And we've nothing left now? No clue why this bastard didn't call? What he's up to?'

Vos patted the keyboard and said, 'We've got this, haven't we?'

Without waiting to hear more Laura Bakker pulled up the pictures, went through them one by one.

The newest, from four o'clock came up first. Martin Bowers, Mujahied Bouali, no Black Pete costume this time. Just a pale-faced young man with a scrappy ginger beard standing in the shadows somewhere. Talking to . . . no being talked at . . . by a big, intimidating individual in a long grey coat.

Thom Geerts. Unmistakable.

'Christ,' Laura Bakker murmured. 'He's showing him something. Look. There's a bag.'

A big bag. The kind people used for camping equipment. Even from this distance the young Englishman looked scared as he peeked inside.

Then the next frame. Geerts holding something that looked much like a canister grenade.

De Groot didn't say anything as she skipped through the shots.

'Who the hell's that?' Bakker asked when she came across the other figure. 'I don't know him. Shall I put this through to intelligence?'

'You don't need to,' the commissaris said.

269

'But . . .'

Vos put his hand on hers to stop it on the keys.

'That's Lucas Kuyper,' he said. 'Henk's father.'

'The soldier?' she asked. 'The one who got into all that trouble in Bosnia?'

De Groot walked to the computer and pulled out the memory card then, while the machine was bleating, stuffed it into his pocket.

'You need to leave us now,' he said. 'I want a word with Vos.'

'Fine, fine.' She was thinking. 'Do you want me to put together a team and pick him up? We should pull in Mirjam Fransen too. Geerts worked for her. She must have—'

'Officer,' De Groot barked. 'The door. Now. You tell no one what you saw here. No one. Do I make myself clear?'

Laura Bakker was almost as tall as him. She shook her head, hands on hips, and glared at him.

'Not exactly. This is all we've got. You want me to forget about it?'

He was getting red in the face. The walrus moustache was twitching.

'What I want . . .'

Vos intervened, put a gentle hand to her back, pushed her towards the door.

'Pieter,' she whispered. 'What the hell is going on here?'

'Just . . .'

He tried to usher her out.

'You never wanted me on this case, did you? Not you. Not . . .' Her eyes flashed towards the big man in the dark suit by the PC. 'Him either. What they . . .'

Vos closed the door, waving his fingers as he did so.

Not long after the argument began, so loud it echoed all the way down the corridor.

———

Hanna Bublik walked into the house in Oude Nieuwstraat, shook the rain from her black jacket, stood in the narrow hall.

The shoulder was hurting again. She went upstairs into the tiny room she'd shared with Natalya. Didn't bother to close the door as she stripped off her clothes and looked at herself in the mirror. Turned. Saw the dressing Renata Kuyper had put there.

'It'll heal,' said a voice from the landing.

Chantal was there. Young. Stupid. Regretful. Sympathetic for once maybe.

'You hear anything about Natty?' she asked.

'No.'

The girl nodded.

'It'll heal. It's just a tattoo.'

'It's not a tattoo,' she said. 'Not this.'

A look of fear in her dark, dim eyes.

'Oh. I heard he did something different sometimes. When he thought you were special.'

'Special?'

This kid was so dumb. Sometimes Hanna Bublik wanted to shake her to see if just a little sense would spill out of that stupid, pretty mouth.

She closed the door. Changed the dressing. Wondered if Vos would pester her again. How she'd react if he did.

Half-dressed, her phone rang. Cem Yilmaz. He sounded cheery, assured as usual.

'Have you heard something?'

'He called me. When I was in Marnixstraat.'

A worried pause.

'Did you tell the police?'

'No. They don't know anything.'

'It's important it stays that way. What interests them is not what interests us. So long as Natalya gets free . . .'

'Don't tell me what I know already,' she interrupted.

A pause in the conversation. He didn't like it when she answered back.

'And the money?' Yilmaz asked. 'What did he say about that?'

'I can get hold of sixty myself. If you come up with a hundred . . .'

Silence.

'I told him I could make a hundred and sixty.'

'I offered you seventy. That's what you're worth.'

She'd understood this argument was coming.

'He won't take any less. I'm thirty short. If you come up with it I'll do . . .'

*Anything.*

'I'll do whatever you want.'

'Your daughter . . .'

'Yes. Natalya.'

He thought for a moment.

'Then it's settled, you'll have a hundred from me. I won't ask anything of the child until she's older. I'm not an animal.'

The room shrank in on her when she realized what he was saying.

'No, no, no. Please God no. She's my little girl—'

'You want her alive, don't you?'

'Of course but—'

'I fail to understand you, woman. If this profession is acceptable to you why should it be objectionable to your daughter. Besides . . . these things tend to run in the family.' He laughed. 'Unless you think she's going to be a lawyer?'

No words. The enormity of what she'd just accepted unwittingly silenced her completely.

'That's my offer. There's no going back,' Yilmaz added. 'Don't think that, please. A bargain's a bargain.'

Silence. She wasn't sure how she could say it.

'I'm a busy man,' Yilmaz added briskly. 'I require an answer now. Yes or no.'

'Yes,' a frail voice said and it was her.

'Good. Then we have an understanding. What else did he say?'

'He's going to call me in the morning and arrange the pickup. After that they'll let Natalya go.'

'So I'll add one hundred to your sixty on this basis. Bring along your contribution so I can see it. Do what the man asks. Cem Yilmaz will get your daughter back. You keep my name out of this. Understand?'

She couldn't think of anything to say.

'Are you still there?' he demanded. 'Do you understand?'

'Yes.'

'The police must suspect nothing. I require you to act normally.' He was thinking. 'They're not stupid. Perhaps they'll be watching you.'

Hanna Bublik leaned over on the bed, wanted to cry.

'Normally?'

'Don't do anything to make them suspicious. Go to work tonight. Find a window. Be visible. I know I said I wanted no more of this. But it would be best for appearances. I stake my claim when your daughter's back home. Then we speak of future arrangements.'

Her mind was racing. There was nothing she wanted less than work at that moment and he surely knew it.

'Not tonight . . .'

'I risk much here too. For no immediate return. You'll do what I say or I can't help you.'

She whispered something. Wasn't sure what it was.

'Call me tomorrow when you hear something,' he said. 'Goodnight.'

Natalya's bed was in the corner of the tiny room, close to the gable window. All made up. She walked over and tidied the sheets. It felt as if she'd been gone for weeks, not days. The room seemed empty without that smart, questioning voice, the sudden laughter that came from a book or a cartoon on the little TV they owned.

She called Renata Kuyper's mobile and told her they'd need the money in the morning.

'Fine,' she said and didn't sound that way.

'Can you do it?'

'I've got our thirty. Henk's father's matched that. I'll bring it round when you tell me.'

'Thanks.' It was hard to say that word. 'When I get the chance I'll repay you . . .'

'That's hardly likely, is it?'

'No,' she agreed. 'It isn't.'

Renata Kuyper hesitated then said, 'I have to ask. Have you seen him?'

'Who?'

'Henk.'

'Why would I see your husband?'

'He went out this afternoon. I haven't heard from him since. He doesn't answer his phone.' There was something curious in her voice. Puzzlement more than trepidation. 'It's not like him.'

'I've not seen your husband. I'll call tomorrow.'

That was it. No more prevarication. Yilmaz had told her what he wanted and asked a price she couldn't refuse. Doubtless he'd have his men check the street to make sure she did as she was told.

She went to the wardrobe and got the things for work. The cheap satin underwear. The condoms. The gels. The wipes and two clean towels.

And an old shawl that had followed all the way from Georgia. She'd put it round her shoulders to hide the wound on her back.

Then she went out into Oude Nieuwstraat. There was only one empty cabin. The red neon light flickered manically and would, she knew, make her headache worse. But a few minutes later she was sitting on a stool in the window, half-naked, staring out at the passing faces, praying no one would ring the bell.


Twenty minutes Vos and De Groot talked alone in the side room of forensic. The rain had turned heavy, the sky black. The down-pour made a constant drone beyond the barred windows. Even that didn't cover the angry voices from forensic. Louder and louder they rose until everyone in the adjoining office could hear.

Laura Bakker and Dirk Van der Berg did their best to work. Koeman checked the logs to see if there were fresh leads. Nothing came in. Hanna Bublik remained on voicemail.

The case, such as it was, had slipped into the debilitating rhythm of failure. It needed Vos to take it somewhere new. And Bakker thought she understood exactly how that ought to be done.

They had to bring in Lucas Kuyper, his son, Henk's wife, and the girl Saskia. Go through everything that happened that previous Sunday in Leidseplein. Try to sort truth from myth. Then work out where to go.

She watched Van der Berg's face as she went through all this again. He was mid-forties, a few years older than Vos. A detective who'd never go further up the ranks. Too lacking in ambition for that. Happy with his lot at the foot of the scale. She'd be his boss in a few years if things went right. And at some point probably have to give him hell.

'We can't ignore those photos,' she added. 'Can we?'

He blinked and asked, 'What photos?'

'Kuyper. Thom Geerts. What do you mean . . . what photos?'

He shook his head.

'The commissaris took that memory card, Laura. It's up to him and Vos now. We just do as we're told. It's how things work.'

'That's the oldest excuse of all, isn't it?'

'One of them,' he agreed. 'Stay here long enough and you'll come across plenty of others.'

'There's a little girl missing out there . . .'

'Do you think De Groot doesn't know that? Or Pieter?'

'Then . . .'

His face fell. She saw something rare: a sign of temper. A considerable one.

'You fight one battle at a time, Laura. The one that matters. Whatever those bastards in AIVD have been up to they don't know where Natalya Bublik is. Not now.'

'You seem very sure of that.'

'We'll find out what went on there. When we do . . .'

He stopped. There was a sound coming from along the corridor. Loud voices. Angry shouts.

It took a moment for Bakker to realize who one party was. She'd heard De Groot roaring with anger dozens of times. Vos never raised his voice with anyone. Now she realized he could shout down the commissaris any day of the week, with a vocabulary to match.

Red-faced, fist clenched, De Groot followed him into the office.

'Clear your desk now, Vos,' the commissaris roared. 'And I want your card. I was a fool ever to think you deserved it back.'

Bakker and Van der Berg watched in shock. Vos had a look about him Bakker hadn't seen in a long time. Defeat, despair. He'd been this way when De Groot first sent her to lure him back into the police from his lost days spent staring at the Oortman doll's house in the Rijksmuseum.

'I always think this kind of conversation is best settled at leisure, over a beer or three,' Van der Berg suggested. 'Can we calm things down a little?'

'That's it!' De Groot bellowed, jabbing a finger as Vos went to his desk and picked up a few things. 'Go boozing with these losers you surround yourself with. Lock yourself in that damned boat of yours and smoke your life away. You're done here . . .'

He followed, grabbed Vos by the shoulder, clicked his fingers. A big man with a powerful physical presence. Vos looked slight by comparison.

'The card,' De Groot ordered. 'Your weapon.'

Vos reached inside his jacket and took out his police ID. Then fetched a key from his drawer.

'The gun's still in the locker, Frank. You know I don't like those things.'

'Think you're too damned clever for us, don't you?' De Groot said. 'Didn't work out so well for this girl.'

A crowd was slowly assembling on the edges of the argument. Hanging on every bitter word.

Vos looked into De Groot's florid face. Thought of saying something. Changed his mind.

'No,' he agreed eventually. 'It didn't.'

Then he picked up his donkey jacket and headed for the stairs.

'This sideshow's over,' De Groot shouted at the group of men and women who'd come to watch. 'Back to what you were doing.'

He was still furious, breathing hard.

'Speaking of which,' Bakker said icily, 'I assume you want us to bring in Lucas Kuyper and the Fransen woman?'

De Groot glanced at his watch.

'You two are both over shift now. Go home. Be in my office at eight tomorrow. I'll be handling this case personally from now on.'

She stayed where she was.

'You can't bury this,' Bakker told him. 'Don't think that. I won't allow it.'

Next to her Van der Berg sighed and covered his eyes for a moment. The commissaris came up to them.

'Won't you?' he asked.

'No. The law's the law. And those people have broken it.'

'Jesus,' De Groot muttered. 'It's bad enough taking lectures from Pieter Vos. Without listening to his little girl.'

'I'm not little, Commissaris,' Bakker replied. 'Or a girl.'

'No. You're a pain in the arse like him.' He pointed to the door. 'Eight o'clock tomorrow in my office. Now goodnight.'


The monster was real. In that little basement room. A big man, foreign. With a cruel laugh and something wicked in his eyes.

He kicked the stupid kid from Anadolu. Punched him. Banged his bleeding head against the wall. Then when the boy was nothing more than a bag of broken bones, still by the stone stairs, the monster came and sat next to the trembling Natalya Bublik on the bed.

His strong arm went round her slender, shaking shoulders.

'See, child,' the monster said. 'This is what happens when a little girl doesn't do as she's told.'

The big arm squeezed her wrist. She thought she might pee herself.

'You don't want to be bad, Natalya. I'd have to tell your mother then.'

She steeled herself to stare at him.

'Yes,' he said. His arm let go. He placed his giant's hands on his lap, nodded. 'I know her. This . . .'

His hand swept the room.

'This is the grown-up world. The real world. My world. Not a place for children and their dreams. There are matters that do not concern you. Important ones. Life and death.'

Natalya glanced at the stairs and wished she had the strength to run from this place.

'Your mother and I have agreed,' he added. 'You'll stay here until the time's right to leave. It's safest that way.'

His head came down. Two calm, dark eyes bore into hers.

'Safer for both of you. You want that, don't you?'

She nodded. He expected that.

'So you'll do as your mother wants. Be good. No more trouble, please.' He nodded at the prone shape across the room. 'You did this, Natalya. You're a bright girl. You know what you're responsible for.'

The eyes were back on her. She wanted to cry but wouldn't.

'Who did this?' he asked.

In a faint, firm voice she said, 'Me.'

His big hand slapped her leg. Then he got up. Said as he walked towards the body across the room, 'I'll send someone else to look after you. Tomorrow, if you're good, you'll see your mother.'

The monster lugged the kid from Anadolu up the stairs. The boy didn't move, didn't make a noise, didn't even breathe as far as she could see.

After that the creature was gone, leaving in his wake the sharp and caustic smell of blood.


Van der Berg followed Laura Bakker through the front doors into the constant rain. She knew where Vos would go. Straight down Elandsgracht into the warm, familiar interior of the Drie Vaten. There he'd sit at one of the battered tables and stare into his beer, Sam the terrier curled at his feet.

She got her bike. Van der Berg caught up with her before she could ride away.

'Where are you going?' he asked.

'Where do you think?'

'Laura. Just for once will you listen to me?'

He looked so desperate she agreed. And so the two of them went to a place she didn't know a couple of streets from Elandsgracht. A gay bar from the look of it. Lesbian. A charming woman with a crew cut served up a couple of beers she'd never seen before.

Van der Berg thanked her by name then found them a table in the corner.

'Do you know every beer joint in Amsterdam?' Bakker asked.

'Big city. I have to keep looking.'

He raised his glass. The beer was the colour of honey. Then the woman came over with two freshly boiled eggs, a little saucer of salt and some napkins.

'God we know how to live, don't we?' she whispered.

He laughed, raised his glass.

'It's nice to hear you cracking jokes. Means you're getting settled.'

'That was a joke?'

He tore the egg in half, dipped a chunk in salt and popped it into his mouth.

'What's going on?' Bakker wondered.

'We fouled up big time. Someone's kicking down on Frank de Groot. So he's doing what management do best. Kicking down on the first person he finds beneath him.'

He pushed the remaining egg over the table. She declined.

'If Pieter was the usual brigadier he'd be kicking down on us right now. But he's not.'

'We can't sit back and watch him take the blame. We all screwed up. Besides . . . those bastards in AIVD . . .'

The studious way he held up the glass of beer and admired it silenced her.

'True,' he said.

'So?'

'So we do what the commissaris asks. We turn up in his office tomorrow. We listen to what he wants. We try to find the Bublik girl. Maybe in a week or so De Groot will change his mind. This isn't the first time we've had a few explosions.'

'And we just leave Pieter on his own? Not a word of support? No—'

'He was an aspirant under me when he joined up,' Van der

Berg broke in. 'I was the one supposed to hit the heights. Pieter was just this smart, soft kid everyone liked. Felt sorry for really.'

'What happened?'

Van der Berg smiled at her.

'He was just the same then. You couldn't really talk to him. Tell him anything. He went his own sweet way. Got the job done. Then in a couple of years he got promoted. I got . . . nowhere.'

The beer was finished. The barmaid came over with another without him asking.

'What happens with him happens inside. When he's on his own. I learned long ago. You have to leave him to it. With his little dog and that nagging conscience. There's nothing we can do. You or me. Except wait.'

He poured some of the bottle into her glass then chinked it.

'Are you willing?'

'What's the alternative?' she asked.

'We barge in there doe-eyed and full of sympathy and he shrinks back into his shell. Where you found him all those months ago. Remember?'

She knocked back some beer and loved it.

'I hate feeling there's nothing you can do.'

Van der Berg's heavy eyebrows rose.

'I said we'd wait. That's not the same now, is it?'

No answer.

'I'll walk you home,' he added. 'It's on my way.'


Two streets away Vos was sitting where Bakker said: at his usual table, dog at his feet, a beer and a glass of old jenever in front of him. Sofia Albers eyeing him from the bar.

Close to eleven. He was the Drie Vaten's last customer and didn't look ready to leave.

'How's your mother?' Vos asked, knowing she was planning to throw him out.

'A lot better thanks. How are you?'

He raised the glass, toasted her, then emptied it.

'That's enough,' she said.

The dog, recognizing the words, stirred at his feet, got up, shook his wiry coat.

'That's for me to decide, isn't it?' Vos wondered.

'Stop doing this, Pieter. You're starting to worry me.'

'Doing what?'

'Looking like you used to.'

'I could drink all night if I wanted.'

'You could. Just not here.'

Vos glimpsed a shape outside by the boat. Slim, familiar. Furtive. Everything had a risk.

He got up and took Sam to the bar then held out his lead.

'Things to do.' He wrapped the loop of the leash around the nearest beer pump. 'Sam'll think he lives here pretty soon.'

'That's ridiculous! I just look after him. He's yours.'

As always the dog knew when they were talking about him. He had his paws against the counter, tail wagging, hoping for some last scrap of food.

'He can hear you walking down the street,' she added. 'Long before I can. You should see—'

'I don't have time for this,' Vos said. 'Not now.' He pointed to the lead. 'Please.'

She took Sam behind the bar. The dog seemed more puzzled than dejected.

'This is about that girl, isn't it? I know you can't talk about work . . .'

'Work. Yes.'

She was an attractive woman. Divorced. Alone a lot of the time. About his own age. Looking for someone, but not desperately. When his world fell apart and he retreated to the solitary cabin of the houseboat across the road she saved him after a fashion. Vos never said thanks. It seemed presumptuous somehow.

And unnecessary. She was from the Jordaan. People like her helped others without a second thought, and with no expectation whatsoever of reward.

'What about your daughter, Pieter?' Sofia Albers asked. 'Have you heard from her lately?'

He pulled a postcard out of his jacket pocket and handed it over. A beach in Aruba, where Anneliese now lived with her mother.

It was posted six weeks before. For some reason he kept it with him. There was one sentence on the reverse: a simple message, 'Miss you, Dad. When are you coming to enjoy the sun?'

'When are you?'

'I don't like . . .' Vos hesitated, searching for an excuse. 'I don't like hot places so much. She'll come back. When she's ready.'

'And in the meantime you beat yourself up trying to save others? All on your own?'

He pocketed the postcard.

'I'm back in the police, aren't I? It's what I'm supposed to do.'

'You won't find that kid if you go down that old black road again, will you?' Sofia Albers said.

Vos was taken aback by that. They were the most severe and damning words she'd ever uttered to him.

He looked around the dishevelled little bar, at the woman who ran it.

'I'm not entirely on my own, am I?' he said then smiled sheepishly, tipped an imaginary hat and wandered out into the night.

The lone figure who'd risked so much was waiting by the bridge. He took the thing she brought and said goodbye.

Cold winter rain was coming down steadily. It made pinpricks on the canal glittering under the street lights. A tourist boat went past, cleaving through the black water. Figures inside, men in evening suits, women in colourful party dresses. Glasses of champagne in their hands. Laughter and music around them. The city went about its business regardless. No time to worry about injured creatures like Hanna and Natalya Bublik. It wasn't cruelty or want of sympathy. Just a simple practicality born of experience. When there was nothing to be done why worry? Let others do that if they could.

At the Berenstraat bridge the coloured street lights in the Nine Streets became visible, reflecting on the feathered, rippling waves left by the wake of the vanishing cruiser. The city had a strange and solitary beauty at that moment. One that wouldn't last.

He pulled out his fisherman's hat, wool, not much use against the wet. Then wandered the way he'd planned all along.

There were plenty of bars still busy if he wanted them. Though he couldn't tell Sofia Albers drink wasn't what he required, or the black road she suspected.

Ten minutes and he was in the narrow confines of Oude Nieuwstraat, searching out the address he had for Hanna Bublik. A young woman answered the door. She looked Malaysian or Filipina with the kind of fragile innocence the imported whores possessed, for a while anyway. Until time and the city took it away.

'Hanna's not here,' the girl said. 'Besides she don't do business from home.'

He didn't have an ID card to flash any more. It was an understandable mistake.

'Where?' Vos asked.

'I don't know. I'm here. I do,' she said with a coy smile.

Something in his disappointed expression made her close the door in his face.

Down the street an argument was starting. A customer and a woman. A pimp involved maybe. Fights, drunks, shouting, screaming. It all kicked off long before midnight in these parts. Then, by the morning, was gone. Parents walked their children to school down the same street, not watching as the cleaner dealt with the sick and the rubbish, the syringes and spent condoms.

Vos wandered towards the racket, thinking perhaps he'd intervene. Try to calm things down. Persuade people to behave with the common sense he sometimes found so hard himself. His own life had retreated from the edge when an offer of redemption from Frank de Groot and Laura Bakker's muscular persuasiveness drew him back into the police. But the precipice was always there. They knew it too.

His eyes strayed to the window on his left. Red light. Bright neon tube. A figure in the window, head down, eyes closed, face full of pain. An old scarf round her naked shoulders. Shiny satin bra and knickers, legs crossed, arms folded. The kind of pose that said, 'Go away. Not now.'

Something you never saw around these parts.

Vos forgot about the argument down the street. Walked up to the glass. She still didn't open her eyes. He pressed the bell. Hanna Bublik did look then and he struggled to interpret what he was seeing. A curious mix of hatred and despair. And perhaps a fearful touch of hope.

Her eyes flitted down the street, checking anxiously for someone.

Then she went to the intercom and said, 'No, Vos. Go away. I beg you.'

In the persistent rain he opened his jacket, took out his wallet, removed all the notes there, maybe three hundred euros in all, and pressed them to the glass.

She didn't move from the phone tethered to the wall. Hanna was glancing down the street. Someone was watching and he realized, to his dismay, he'd forced her into accepting him. To refuse would somehow cause her more pain.

'Please . . .' he begged.

'Will you never leave me be?'

'Not right now.'

'Go home.'

'I can't . . .'

A curse. One in her own tongue he guessed.

He watched her walk across the narrow cabin. The scarf fell from her shoulders. A dressing was stuck to the top of her back, red flesh around it.

The long scarlet curtains at the window closed. The narrow glass door buzzed and fell open to the pressure of his fingers.

Vos entered, grateful to be out of the rain.

# 5

Henk Kuyper checked out of the hotel in Zeedijk at seven, shaved, got dressed, went for breakfast in one of the cafes on the edge of Chinatown.

Thursday. Bright cold morning. Hard winter knocking on the door.

The place was empty. He ordered coffee and two croissants. The previous night he'd kept the drinking at bay. Just a couple of beers in a sleazy bar near the Oude Kerk. Felt better for that. It had taken two hours to shake off the tail that had followed him from the house in the Herenmarkt. One man, one woman, working together in sequence.

He'd learned the technique himself. They weren't that good. Mirjam Fransen ordered the cover he guessed. Pissed off he'd had the temerity to try to talk to her near the office.

As if any of it mattered any more. The operation to trap Barbone was in tatters. It would take a miracle to get that back on the rails. Natalya Bublik was different. His responsibility. An innocent put in harm's way for no good reason. And Fransen didn't care. She made sure she only saw the bigger picture, never the individual. That was the way they were taught. There was a little mantra he'd learned on training.

*Ordinary people are the ones we're trying to protect. They just need to stay out of our way.*

He'd half believed it once.

Five hundred euros in his pocket, taken from the stash he'd withdrawn for Renata the previous day. Just a pittance left in the account to keep it open. Before falling into the flophouse he'd made his way into one of the cheap foreign shops in the red-light district, the kind that did anything for you.

There, for a hundred euros, he'd picked up a cheap mobile with a pay as you go SIM and some credit. He didn't dare use his own phone. Didn't even feel confident he could look at his emails. AIVD would be watching the way they always did.

Mirjam Fransen was good at all that. They'd fallen into bed together on one of those training courses. He'd never summoned the courage to tell Renata. It wasn't an affair. It was an event. A way to ease the boredom, to scratch a curious itch. For him at least. For her it was a considered career move. One that made things so easy when she decided to pull him from AIVD and edge some bait out into the world, a renegade, an activist, looking to tug in interest from the people they wanted to penetrate.

No point arguing about the cost to him, to his family. It was a plea doomed to fall on deaf ears. And just to rub it in she fetched his father into the equation. Lucas Kuyper, the shamed coward of Srebrenica, pilloried by the press for no good reason. Now a reclusive, paid adviser to AIVD for a new, more secret war.

How did he say no to both of them?

Henk Kuyper got the waiter to turn on the TV. The news headlines were coming up. The lead item: economic news. Some fresh figures claiming the country was turning the corner. The slump was coming to an end. Good times on the way. For some, the reporter said, they were already here.

The report switched to footage of the Nine Streets. Moneyed people window-shopping, eyeing expensive clothes and novelties. Pointless glitzy luxuries they didn't really need.

The missing Georgian girl was item three on the news behind trouble at a football match. Natalya Bublik was fading out of the public consciousness. The world had a short attention span. Life was easier that way.

He finished his breakfast then went outside, pulled his hood around his face, walked to the Nieuwmarkt and found a bench in the shadow of the castle-like building called the Waag.

Kuyper scanned the square. No one had followed him that he could see. He was alone. The way it was meant to be. Mirjam and his father told him from the start: he was a free agent. Allowed to make whatever arrangements he thought necessary. Answerable to the department for nothing except eventual results. And they might take years to come, if ever.

A week ago success seemed within reach. Sinterklaas and his Black Petes were supposed to herald a rare victory. Bring down the network that had haunted them for years.

Then Marnixstraat got overzealous and spoiled the party.

He took out the new handset, got data, pulled up Skype. Prayed she'd have her iPad with her.

A long pause as the call went through then Renata asked, voice booming as she spoke to the tablet, 'Where the hell are you, Henk? Where've you been?'

'Thinking.'

'You can think at home, can't you?'

She sounded tired and mad at him.

'Not always. How's Saskia?'

Another silence.

'Puzzled. As am I.' He could hear the deep breath she was taking. 'She told me. About the game. In Leidseplein.'

'Oh.'

'And all that crap about orang-utans. The lies you tell so easily . . .'

A tramp was drifting aimlessly across the square, stopping passers-by, begging for money. Kuyper watched him, wondered.

'Who are you?' she asked. 'Do you know?'

Five years he'd been living this lie. Trying to break through. To convince the contacts he'd slowly built up he was what he said: a former spook turned angel. Theirs.

'Sometimes. When I get to step away.'

'Is that what you're doing now?' she asked with a sudden sharpness.

The tramp lurched on, a can of Heineken in his grubby fist. This wasn't one of Mirjam's.

'Jesus, Henk! How can you play with a child's life? Saskia's? That girl's?'

'I wasn't playing with Saskia. I made sure they wouldn't get her.'

'You got me to take her there!'

'I had no choice. They were watching. If I'd just . . .'

So many operations in training. Real life was different. He'd thought this through as much as he could. It was important Saskia was in the square. Important that Bouali picked her up at first. And then, on his instructions – kept strictly between them – let her go and call the others. Tell them to look out for a girl in pink.

'You lose sight of things,' he murmured. It sounded so pathetic. 'It was never meant to be like this.'

'Well it is,' she barked. 'We're paying the ransom. Hanna Bublik's got some money from somewhere too.'

'The police?'

'She doesn't trust them. She called me last night. Vos got suspended and he's the only one she had some time for. She doesn't even know who's running the case now.'

He thought about that then asked her for Vos's number. Tapped it into his phone when she came back.

'Why did you do it?'

Such a short sentence. Such a big question.

'Because I was supposed to. I wasn't going to let them take Saskia. That was never . . .'

The grey day closed on him. His mind went blank.

'Are you still there? Henk? I tried your father three times this morning. He's not even answering his phone. What the hell's going on?'

Life, he thought. The kind he'd chosen. Or had chosen for him.

'Later. I'll tell you everything. I promise.'

'Promises . . .'

That sour, disappointed tone had never been in her voice when they first met. It came from him. Another unwanted gift.

'You're going to give them the money?' he said.

'That's the idea. What else can we do?'

He didn't know.

'When are you coming home?' she asked.

'Soon.'

He said goodbye. The wind was getting lively. White clouds dotted the bright horizon. Change on the way.

'Stay safe,' she said and cut the call.

Henk Kuyper looked at Vos's number.

There was one name he had to deal with first. The only link to Barbone he had.


Vos had watched the slow winter sunrise from a wobbly chair on the front deck of the boat. Pale rays chased around the tatty tinsel on the silver dancer as if amused. He found a stray cigarette from somewhere. Lit it. Tried to think. But all that came was the realization he didn't much like smoking any more.

Not long after he heard a familiar pitter-patter across the gangplank. Sam trotted over, his lead trailing behind him, sat on his haunches on the deck, nose in the air, sniffing, staring intently.

He kept looking at the cigarette until Vos responded.

'I can do this. OK?'

The terrier's long nose stayed where it was.

'Wonderful,' Vos moaned. 'Now I'm being nagged by a dog.'

He threw the cigarette into the canal. Sam listened to its dying hisses then wagged his tail.

'We don't want you starting that again, Pieter,' Sofia Albers called from the pavement.

'I threw it away, didn't I?'

'And don't take your hangover out on me and Sam either.'

'Don't have a hangover,' he grumbled.

There was a sound from inside the boat. The door was thrown open. Hanna Bublik stuck out her head. A towel round it. She was wearing Vos's black bathrobe.

'Sorry,' Sofia muttered. She looked shocked, embarrassed. 'I didn't mean . . .'

Vos got up and led Sam back to the pavement. The dog grumbled with every step.

'One more day.' He held out the lead. 'Then it's back to normal.'

'Do you know what normal is?'

Hanna Bublik was watching them as she towelled her blonde hair in the morning sun.

'I can't explain,' he told Sofia.

'You don't have to. Not to me.'

She took the lead and tried to coax Sam to the Drie Vaten. The dog dug in his toes until she mentioned the word 'treat'.

When he got back to the boat Hanna nodded across the street. 'She likes you.'

He'd spent the night on the sofa in the bows, leaving her to the bedroom. Vos was determined he wouldn't let her out of his sight. Not until the ransom was paid. By him if he could manage it.

'Everyone likes me. I'm a popular kind of person.'

She didn't laugh.

'I want to hear Natalya's voice when he calls,' she said. 'I want some . . . proof.'

Vos gestured to the cabin. It was time to go inside.

'What's wrong with that?' she asked when he kept quiet.

'Nothing.'

'Then why don't you want me to do it?'

He started up the coffee machine. Pointed out a couple of pastries he'd bought earlier that morning as the little bakery in Elandsgracht was opening.

'Why . . . ?'

'Let's be careful,' he said. 'We might not get any more chances after this. Just give them what they want. Get her back. Forget the rest. I have.'

'And all those others? In Marnixstraat?'

They'd been through this the night before while she got dressed in the cabin in Oude Nieuwstraat. A surveillance team would probably turn up in the morning to try to track her movements. That was one more reason he got her to scuttle off with him to the boat.

'Don't complicate anything. Don't press them. Don't argue. We'll hand over the money. Find Natalya. After that De Groot can go hunting. AIVD too for all I care.'

She scowled, started to take off the bathrobe then grabbed her clothes. Vos sighed and shielded his eyes.

'Christ,' Hanna muttered. 'I forgot there are still prudes in the world.'

'Never been called that before,' he complained then got his phone, walked to the cabin door and checked his messages.

Nothing new except a short, awkward text from Laura Bakker.

> **This is wrong and we all know it. If u want
> 2 talk just txt. Me an Dirkll come.**

Kids. Living in a world devoid of punctuation, syntax and grammar. Just the thought made him feel old. He deleted the message, checked the phone had charged overnight then put the handset in his jacket pocket.

She was dressed by the time he went back inside. Finishing her coffee and pastry.

He wondered what to say. Hanna Bublik didn't do small talk.

Didn't want to discuss where she came from. What brought her here. The life before.

Her hair was wet. He found a dryer from somewhere, one he never used. She plugged it in. Nothing happened.

He apologized and found her a fresh towel.

Tried conversation again. Got nowhere.

Then she asked, 'Why do you do this?'

'This being . . .?'

'Helping. Me of all people.'

'Can't think of anything else to do. It passes the time.'

'That's a reason?'

'Seems to be. I thought you might understand. The bit about not thinking of anything else to do.'

The briefest wry smile in return.

'Ah. I see what you mean.'

He had to ask even though he knew she didn't want to hear.

'After this . . . if there was a job. An ordinary job. Would you take it?'

She closed her eyes and looked ready to scream.

'I'm sorry,' he added quickly. 'I suppose you hear that kind of thing a lot.'

'Helps ease the guilt, I suppose. I mean . . . you can't feel that bad if you're acting nice afterwards, can you?'

He didn't say anything.

'OK,' she admitted. 'This isn't an afterwards.'

'I just wondered . . .'

The towel went down. Her blonde hair curled round her neck.

'Natalya and me have been on the road for the best part of seven years. All her little life pretty much. Scraping a living here and there. I went begging when I needed to. Not her. Never her. Been homeless a few times. This is all I know, Vos. What else am I good for?'

'Maybe lots of thing if you try—'

'Don't say that!' she yelled. 'Don't you think I'm trying now?

We've got a home. Some money. Some security or so I thought. Maybe one day if I save I can break out of all that crap. But not yet. Not now. Maybe not ever.'

Her voice had faded almost to silence.

'Hanna . . .'

Then the phone rang.

'This is how it stands,' Mirjam Fransen said. 'I've got absolute authority from the ministry. It's important you all understand that. This is our operation. It has been all along if only you'd realized.'

Eight o'clock in De Groot's office. Bakker, Van der Berg, Fransen and Lucas Kuyper in a grey suit and heavy grey overcoat. He'd given them a business card when he turned up, making a point. Consultant to AIVD. Might have read 'untouchable' the way he presented it.

'The law . . .' Bakker began and got a sour look from the commissaris.

'The law's for ordinary people,' Lucas Kuyper cut in. 'None of this is ordinary. It wasn't from the start. If you people had acknowledged that we'd all be in a better place.'

Even Van der Berg bristled then. The photos from Ferdi Pijpers's phone were on the table. Kuyper and the late Thom Geerts talking to Bouali, showing him what looked like a grenade.

'We should arrest both of you,' he said.

Fransen swore.

'You can't. We're in the middle of a very delicate situation. Lives at risk. Years of work in jeopardy.'

'And a little girl missing,' Bakker added.

'She's probably dead by now,' the AIVD woman said with a shake of her head. 'You made sure of that the moment Vos barged into Westerdok.' She looked at De Groot. 'Where is he?'

'Suspended,' the commissaris told her. 'I'll deal with Vos later. That farce with Khaled yesterday—'

'They knew!' Bakker cried, jabbing a finger at Fransen. 'They knew we were wasting our time.'

'But not ours for once,' Kuyper muttered.

De Groot glowered at the AIVD pair.

'I don't like this. Any of it.'

Mirjam Fransen leaned forward.

'It's not yours to like. Henk Kuyper belongs to me.' She glanced at his father. 'This investigation too.' A pause. 'And you now.'

He stayed silent.

'I want you to keep your team downstairs pretending there's something to chase with the Bublik girl,' she went on. Then she nodded at Bakker and Van der Berg. 'These two can liaise with me. Anything I share doesn't go any further. Ever.'

Still Frank de Groot kept quiet.

'Good,' she added. 'Now that's understood. Lucas?'

Kuyper folded his arms, leaned back, closed his eyes and for the first time since that Sunday in Leidseplein Laura Bakker thought she just might be about to hear the truth.


Hanna Bublik answered the call. Voice hard and determined again.

She asked all the things Vos had told her to avoid. Demanded to talk to her daughter. Got nothing but angry when they said no.

He waved a hand. Mouthed, 'Calm down.'

A furious stare came back at him.

'Let me talk to her, you bastard, or I don't give you a cent,' Hanna barked.

Vos put his head in his hands.

When he looked again she was somewhere else. Eyes bright, fixed on a sight in her imagination.

*Listening.*

Then she spoke a few words in a language he couldn't understand.

A handful of short sentences and the phone went down.

She looked at him and said, 'Centraal station midday. They want all the money in a bag. From me. No one else.'

His heart sank. The station was massive. Always busy. The best place from their point of view. They could take the ransom and vanish into the crowds.

'Whereabouts?'

'Don't know. He said he'd call me when I got there.' She went for her coat and her bag. 'I need to get the money. You're not coming.'

'Hanna . . .'

'Forget it, Vos. This part's mine.'

He knew some of the cash was coming from the Kuypers. But there was another source and he was in the dark about that. Where she wanted him.

'I don't think it's safe. A lot of money. You on your own.'

'I'm used to being on my own. Besides, we agreed last night. There are things I have to do you shouldn't know about.'

'Did Natalya tell you anything?'

'They made her speak in English. All she could say was what they let her.'

Then nothing.

'Which was?' he asked.

'She's fine. She loves me. Can't wait to be home.'

'And you?'

He watched the way she picked up the green plastic and canvas holdall she'd brought. He hadn't looked inside. That was a stupid omission.

'I told her the same. What do you think?'

On the gangplank she checked her watch.

'When I get the money I'll phone. Don't come looking. Where's the nearest cheap hairdresser? I want to look different.'

'Why?'

The sullen stare.

'To make it harder for your people to see me.'

He took her two streets from Elandsgracht to the first one he could think of. She went in and he heard her argue for the cheapest trainee they had.

Vos went to the cafe opposite, a place where they didn't know him. Watched through the window. Checked his phone again.

Something was happening in Marnixstraat. Maybe they had a lead.

That thought nagged at him.

Twenty-five minutes later Hanna Bublik came out. He barely recognized her. The long blonde hair was gone. Short now, dyed brunette. When he walked over she pulled a pair of old-fashioned spectacles out of her pocket and put them on. In her right hand was the green holdall, cheap and battered.

Hooker to schoolteacher in a few brief minutes. She was good at this. A practised skill.

'You like it?' she asked.

'You look as if you're getting ready to run.'

'I don't run any more,' she told him. 'Those days are over.'

Her hand went to her hair.

'This is what it looks like really. I'm not blonde. I did it for business. That's all.'

'It would help if I knew where you were going.'

'No,' she said. 'It wouldn't.'

In the cold basement Natalya's fingers clutched the phone. He had to prise them away to get it off her.

Another man. Just as big. Black this time. Gruff English voice. Dreadlocks and a coloured band in them.

'Good girl,' he said. 'You did like I said.'

His vast hand patted her head as if she were a pet. Dirty hair now. There was nowhere in this new prison to shower.

All thought of escape had gone. She still saw in her head the bloody kid from Anatolia slumped on the floor by the stairs. Getting kicked and stamped and punched.

Dead, she thought.

That was what it looked like. With that last lunge of the monster's boot something left the dark and freezing cellar. Flitted away like a bird released from a cage.

*Dead.*

'What did your mum say?' the new man asked.

Her words were in Georgian, so strange now. Old-fashioned. Belonging to another place, one she didn't really remember.

*You're the light of my life, child. If they have hurt one small part of you they'll pay. I'll make them. But first I'll set you free.*

'Well?' He was persistent. 'What?'

'She wants me home.'

The big hand went to her head again.

'We all do, sugar.'

'When?'

He laughed. The sound came from deep inside his stomach.

'When we get some money. What do you think?'

There was a knock on the door at the top of the stairs. He went to answer it. Voices. Another of them there. He had something.

The new man came back carrying another bag. The kind she and her mother had used when they flitted from place to place. Even theirs wasn't as old and grubby as this one. Nor did it have such a strong zip and a padlock attached to each end.

Natalya looked at the thing. The size, the shape of it.

Looked at herself.

Then at him.

He wouldn't meet her eye at that moment.

'You be a good kid,' he said.


Lucas Kuyper told them AIVD had spent five years trying to plant his son inside Barbone's network. He was his son's only direct contact with the organization. Since they were family that was deemed safe. The cover was his sacking after leaking a bunch of papers that were either unimportant or deliberately inaccurate.

Set loose on his own as bait.

A month before he'd reported back that someone was finally circling the hook.

'Work it out,' Fransen added. 'We're talking big players here.' She frowned. 'Barbone met Henk once. It was out of the blue. He caught Henk on the way from taking Saskia to school. In that little park opposite his house.'

'Barbone knew where he lived?' Bakker wondered.

'That and a lot more maybe,' Lucas Kuyper told her. 'This is a game of chess. Of poker. That's why you people should stay clear. Barbone wanted proof. Evidence Henk was on their side. The Alamy case was coming up. They wanted him to get the preacher freed. I think they understood Alamy might give them all up to save his own skin otherwise.'

De Groot sat motionless, no expression on his face. Then drank his coffee, said not a word.

'They asked him to offer up Saskia,' Kuyper went on. 'They knew about me. About my past. They thought they could ransom her for Ismail Alamy. She'd be safe, they said.'

Van der Berg's eyes never left the commissaris.

'So your son went along with that and set up a sex worker's daughter to take her place?'

Fransen shrugged.

'Henk's a free agent. Left to his own devices. We gave him the support he asked for. No footprints to them. None back to us if things went wrong.'

Bakker picked up the photos: Bouali with Thom Geerts and the man next to them.

'These are footprints.'

'If we'd let them find their own weapons do you think he'd have thrown smoke bombs?' Lucas Kuyper asked. 'No one was going to get hurt . . .'

'Except a stupid British kid you conned.'

Fransen scowled.

'Bouali was the drone they gave Henk to work with. The idiot pulled a gun on us. If he hadn't I'd have got him out of there . . .' She hesitated. 'Somewhere safe.'

'Away from us?' Van der Berg asked.

'Why do we have to keep repeating ourselves? This was not your business,' Kuyper said archly. 'Besides if you live by the sword you die by the sword. My family have served the Dutch military for a century and a half. We know that even if you don't. And Henk—'

'If Vos hadn't barged into Westerdok we'd have stayed in control,' Fransen intervened. 'Either Barbone would have showed and we could have grabbed him there. Or we'd have implicated Alamy and persuaded him to talk to get himself free.' She stared at De Groot. 'The girl would have been released. The screw-up's at your door.'

'And then they'd know your son was jerking them around,' Van der Berg said.

She threw back her head, shook her dark hair.

'Jesus. It's like talking to children. We knew Henk wasn't going to get inside whatever he thought. He's white. He's Dutch. They're never going to trust him completely. That wasn't a serious option.' She looked at Kuyper. 'Maybe they thought this was a play on our part all along. Which frankly I find worrying.'

They waited.

'One more day and we'd have been there. Either Barbone in our hands or Alamy tied to the kidnapping and desperate to cut a deal.' Her face hardened. 'If he knew he was never getting free he'd have served us the whole network on a plate.'

Her fingers went to the table and scattered the evidence photos there.

'That was the prize. Years of work. Thrown out of the window because Vos wanted to play hero.'

'We were looking for a missing girl,' Van der Berg repeated. 'We still are.' He stared at De Groot. 'Aren't we?'

Fransen did the patronizing stare again and said, 'They didn't come up with a ransom demand, remember? The kid's gone. And so's Henk. Somewhere.'

She glanced at Lucas Kuyper. He nodded, took over.

'AIVD tried to track my son yesterday. He's been acting . . . out of character.'

'Free agent,' Fransen repeated. 'He's trying to recover something out of the mess you people dumped on him. Alone. The idiot.'

'And we're supposed to find him for you?' Bakker asked.

'AIVD are looking too,' Kuyper said. 'This is important. Henk's on our side. He's risked a lot. He could maybe still deliver. And . . .' That shrug again. 'He's a soldier. Like I was. If they think he was playing them all along . . .'

'He's dead too,' Fransen intervened. 'Should that happen . . .' Her finger pointed at each of them in turn. 'You will all pay.'

She picked up her phone, checked the messages.

'There may still be something for us to recover here. For your sake I hope so. Lucas?'

Kuyper got up. Put his trilby hat on his head. Looked like a genial old man again.

'These two . . .' She pointed at Bakker and Van der Berg.

'They'll keep us informed on anything and everything you hear and do. About Henk. The Bublik kid. A full log. As it happens. You know where to find me.'

They left then. Bakker, Van der Berg and De Groot didn't move.

The commissaris's desk phone rang. He took the call. It was a long one. De Groot made careful notes on a pad.

'News?' Bakker asked the moment he was finished.

'We've found the second boat where they were keeping the girl,' De Groot told them.

He pushed across an address. Then pulled up a map on his monitor and turned it round. Showed them the spot.

'Jesus Christ,' Van der Berg muttered. 'She was right under our noses.'

A red houseboat, no windows visible, moored on Bloemgracht just a few streets away.

'On it,' Bakker said getting to her feet.

De Groot sighed and stopped her.

'No, you're not. Give me a chance, will you?'

Van der Berg hadn't moved an inch. He knew this man.

'I'm going to give this to AIVD,' De Groot said. 'We can send some people along to accompany them. Let's keep this Fransen woman busy. Maybe she'll be grateful in the end.'

Bakker shook her head.

'We want her gratitude? What about . . . ?'

Van der Berg did get up then and said, 'What do you want us to do, boss?'

De Groot scribbled out a name and an address then passed it over.

'This boat was rented too. From the same owner as the one in Westerdok.' He pointed to the map. 'Smits, the man Vos talked to. His office is behind Damrak. Go and ask him if he happens to know Henk Kuyper.'

'And AIVD?' Van der Berg asked. 'That nice woman seemed to think we were her go-betweens.'

'I'll deal with that,' De Groot said.


Vos went back to the Drie Vaten, did his best to make pleasant small talk with Sofia Albers while she made him a coffee. It wasn't easy. She looked both mad and embarrassed.

Then she decided he could spend some time with his dog and fetched Sam from the flat upstairs. She'd bought him a new toy. A rope shaped like a bone.

'Tugging,' Sofia said. 'You're good at that. So's he.'

He went to the bar's narrow, timber-planked upper floor with his coffee and a *speculaas* biscuit in the shape of a Christmas tree, holding the rope in one hand while Sam growled and grabbed at it with his sharp white teeth.

What he'd told Hanna Bublik was right. The dog would never give up. There was only one way out of this and that was to trick him.

'Oh, Sam,' he said, looking at the door. 'There's Laura!'

The terrier gave up straight away and turned to check, tail wagging madly.

Vos chuckled. When Sam's furious, cheated gaze came back on him he launched the rope bone the length of the bar.

The dog loved this game. He scampered through the rickety chairs and tables, raced down the steps to the main bar, careered through the furniture chasing the toy.

It had fetched up by the door. By the time he got there three chairs were on their sides and a glass had shattered on the floor.

Sofia looked at it.

Vos looked at it.

'Oops,' he said.

She marched out with a dustpan and brush and reached the shattered glass before Sam could get there. Then went to the dog who happily let her take the rope from his mouth, something he'd never allow of Vos.

The two of them came back.

'How do you do that?' he asked. 'I mean . . . get him to give it up?'

'I don't know!' She handed him the toy. Sam sat down, performed a passable impersonation of obedience, wagged his tail until Vos let him tug at it once more.

'Are you really OK, Pieter? I know it's none of my business.'

'I'm fine,' he insisted. 'Hanna Bublik was there because I'm working on her daughter's case. And I didn't want her left on her own down Oude Nieuwstraat. OK?'

She said nothing. Looked half-convinced.

'I can't tell you any more,' he added. 'I'll be gone in a little while. Don't worry.'

'Gone working?' she asked hopefully.

He saluted and said in a very serious tone, 'The Amsterdam police never rest, do we?'

She muttered something that sounded like 'sarcastic bastard' then fetched him another *speculaas*.

There was a shadow at the door. The part-time barman had turned up.

'Come on, Sam,' she said. 'Bert can look after this place. I'll walk you. Where's your lead?'

*Where's your lead?*

She'd taught him that little incantation. It worked immediately. The dog dropped the toy and trotted off to the door.

Bert came over and said hello. He was a tall man with elegant silver hair and a permanently cheery smile. When he wasn't working in the Drie Vaten he doubled as a bit-part actor and appeared in adverts.

'Anything you want, Vos,' he said. 'You just ask.'

He winked and sipped at an imaginary glass.

'I will.'

When he'd gone back to the bar Vos took out his phone. He hadn't peeked inside Hanna Bublik's green holdall but he had placed the bug in a little side pocket. One that looked as if it never got used.

The app for his smartphone he'd got from Aisha with a little help from her geek friend.

It seemed simple enough. A map of the city came up. A red blip moved along Spui. Then, as he watched, stopped.

Smits. No first name. No details. Just a mobile number and an address for the agency. It was a tiny office on the ground floor of a block in an alley off Damrak. In the main street there were hordes of tourists heading for the dope cafes and dodgy attractions. The racket of a construction site in the busy road. Touts and baffled visitors, struggling with maps in the steady breeze.

Henk Kuyper left them all, dodged into the narrow alley, checked the numbers.

He'd never been here before. Had dealt with Smits by phone alone. The two of them had met briefly on the boat in Westerdok when the Georgian girl was first snatched. Kuyper insisted on that. He wanted to make sure she was well treated. To have them understand the cover story: this was a mistake on their part. He had offered his daughter as ransom for Ismail Alamy as Barbone demanded. But Bouali had screwed up somehow and the others in the team – men he didn't know and couldn't control – had snatched another young girl, in a similar jacket, instead.

Did they believe him? He wasn't sure. Smits still wouldn't let him meet anyone else. Too soon, he said. The moment Alamy was free . . .

The idea was AIVD would pounce and free the girl if Barbone showed up. If not they'd raid the place after two days and link the plot to Alamy. Then offer him a grim choice: a life in jail or another identity, in another country, in return for giving up the network.

After that Henk Kuyper would go back to being what he was: an AIVD agent. The games, the pretence, the lies would come to an end. Finally he'd get his life back, try to mend his marriage. Mirjam Fransen had wanted him to go all the way from the very beginning. To see if he could infiltrate himself directly into one of the cells as a participating member.

A nice idea when they first floated it in a genteel office in The Hague five years before. His father was there, smiling proudly. This was what Kuypers did. Gave themselves for their country.

*Duty.*

A sly, all-encompassing word. But Lucas Kuyper had worn a uniform. Taken orders. Given them. Paid the public price when things went wrong and thousands died for no good reason. Then privately surfaced inside AIVD as an adviser in a new world where the line between good and bad, friend and enemy was so much harder to define.

His son had taken on the job without a second thought. He was a Kuyper. One of the warrior class as his father reminded him. There was a service to be rendered. It was in his blood, after all.

None of them had known a dogged Amsterdam police officer would track down the houseboat in Westerdok within a day. Nor that Barbone's men would spirit the girl out of there, without Kuyper's knowledge, to an unknown location before she could be rescued.

Kuyper found the place. A narrow house, no sign, opaque windows, red door. Just a bell and an intercom. He pressed it, said his name when a voice that sounded like Smits answered.

Long pause. A bunch of tourists wandered past the end of the alley wearing jester hats. Someone on the construction site shouted out a warning. The bell of a passing tram rang through the racket.

'Have you lost your fucking mind?' Smits asked through the fragile speaker.

'I'm standing here until you let me in.'

Nothing.

'Smits. I'm not a fool. No one's followed me. I'm on my own. We need to talk.'

'I don't even know what you are, man,' the gruff Amsterdammer moaned.

'There are things you need to be told,' Kuyper said, improvising. 'Face to face. Right now.'

The door buzzed. He walked in. One office on the right behind the opaque window.

Smits was a beefy man with a heavy moustache on a face so flabby it seemed beyond expression.

'Where is she?' he asked.

'Who?'

'The kid.'

Smits wore a tatty black jacket over a shiny white shirt. No tie.

'You just do this for the money, don't you?' Kuyper said when he got no answer.

'And your reasons exactly?' the man remarked, clearly angered by the accusation.

'The deal was the child went free. All along.'

'The deal was she was your kid,' Smits responded. 'The fact she wasn't . . .' He sighed, put his hands behind his head. 'What are we supposed to think, Henk? Really?'

'I want to talk to Barbone. There are things he needs to hear.'

'You've seen him once. I guess you don't understand this but he wasn't impressed.'

Kuyper could feel the heat rising in his cheeks. Smits laughed.

'He asked you to put your own daughter on the line to prove yourself? *Your own kid?* You didn't even hesitate.' A wry smile. 'Do you think he was . . . convinced?'

'I need to talk . . .'

'Tell me. I'll pass it on.'

Voices. Someone walked past outside. The alley was narrow. People used it to cut through to the shopping street behind.

'I want the girl. I was promised she'd come to no harm.'

Smits looked at his fingers, shook his head.

'The girl's gone. We're packing up here. Earlier than planned now. Thanks to you . . .'

'If they don't let her go I'm talking to the police. To AIVD. To anyone who'll listen. If . . .'

Smits broke into a broad grin and pointed at him across the desk.

'Please, Henk!' He laughed. 'Do you think we're fools? Do you imagine we'd even speak to you once we had that girl to ourselves?'

'What I did . . .'

All humour vanished.

'It was for them. Not us. For the people who ran you.' He leaned forward, serious in an instant. 'That's the trouble with strings. You can pull them two ways. And here you are . . .'

'On my own,' Kuyper explained.

'On your own,' Smits repeated and seemed interested in that.

'This is really simple. Just let me know what I can do to get her back. Once that happens I'm gone. You, Khaled, Barbone, you're safe. Nothing to worry about.'

'Is that so?' Smits asked.

'I guarantee it.'

'You think you're in a position to guarantee anything?'

'I do,' Kuyper insisted. 'This is an offer. A bargain. If it were anything else I'd be here with men to arrest you? Wouldn't I?'

A moment's silence. Then Smits picked up the phone and made a call.

It was protracted. In Arabic, a language Kuyper couldn't understand.

Something in the conversation made Smits curse under his breath then stare hard at him.

'Understood,' he said in Dutch then came off the phone.

He picked up a notepad on the desk, scribbled something with a pen and pushed it over.

An address. Rapenburg, close to the IJ tunnel.

Smits got up and started going through the drawers, pulling out folders, papers. Stuff Kuyper couldn't see. Then he walked to a grey metal filing cabinet, opened the bottom drawer and retrieved a plastic petrol can.

'That's what you wanted, isn't it?' he said, nodding at the paper. 'Take it and get the hell out of here. I've got things to do.'

He screwed the lid off the can then started to walk round the room, shaking petrol everywhere.

'Your man's going to be there for the next two hours. After that he's gone and so am I.'

Kuyper picked up the paper and got to his feet.

Smits kept walking round, sprinkling the petrol everywhere. The smell was rising in the air.

'If—'

'Just go, will you!' Smits bellowed.

Henk Kuyper went out of the red door, walked head down along the alley, back into Damrak. Started on the long walk across the city.


Hanna chose the cafe. Vinyl records on the walls. A few lowlifes on the narrow seats. Not the kind of place the middle class frequented.

It was colder. Renata was wearing a fake fur coat when she came through the door. Carrying what looked like an expensive scarlet bag that matched her lipstick. Hanna put her cheap holdall on the floor to release the seat she'd been saving.

'This is busy,' Renata said.

Hanna asked what she wanted and gave the order to the man behind the counter.

'I like busy.'

The red bag went on the table.

'There's everything I could get in there,' Renata told her. 'Sixty. Half from us. Half from Henk's father.'

'You're very generous.'

'His dad can afford it. We can't.' She scowled at an old man struggling to get out of his chair two tables away. 'You could have picked somewhere else.'

Hanna looked round to make sure she wasn't being watched. Then unzipped the red bag. There was a shoebox inside. DKNY. Renata nodded. She took the box and put it in her holdall.

'Will it work?' Renata asked.

'I don't know. How can I?'

'And the police . . .?'

'The police know nothing. I told you.'

Renata kept quiet.

Hanna turned her head to one side.

'What is it?'

'You look so different. The hair. The glasses. Why?'

'I don't want to make it easy for Vos's people if they try to follow me.'

Renata Kuyper's face hardened.

'Vos isn't on the case any more. You said last night.'

'I don't want them interfering. I got a call about the ransom. Noon. Today.'

'Where?'

The question seemed odd.

'It's best you don't know. I'm doing this on my own.'

That awkward silence again.

'I'm not going to run away with your money if that's what you think. I want my daughter. I'm not a thief.'

Renata Kuyper looked as if she'd rather be anywhere else in the world.

'These things shouldn't happen here,' she muttered. 'It's not right.'

'Where should they happen? Far away? In foreign countries? To lesser people?'

That didn't go down well.

'You're starting to sound like my husband. You're sure you haven't seen him?'

She shook her head.

'You're the only one who's given me money today.'

'I could ask for it back.'

Hanna Bublik placed her hands on the holdall.

'But that would be rude. A gift's a gift.'

'Why do you hate me?' Her voice was getting louder. People in the cafe were starting to stare. She realized this and said more softly, 'I'm trying to help.'

'I know. I'm sorry. I've never been very good at gratitude.' She checked her watch. 'I have to go.'

'I hope it works.'

A brief moment of regret then. She'd been harsh on this woman.

'Your husband will come home. He's bound to. Where else has he got to go?'

'That's a reason?'

'Seems a good one to me.'

Renata Kuyper got to her feet, tried to pay for the coffee.

'I'll do that,' Hanna said and watched her leave without another word.

Ten thirty. Time to get to Spooksteeg and Cem Yilmaz's contribution.

Then she'd call Vos and meet him at the station. She wanted him there. But not in control.

When she paid she looked at the holdall again. It already held more money than she'd ever known. Soon, if Yilmaz kept his word, there'd be a hundred and sixty thousand euros in there. She'd be rich for a moment. Rich and alone. She'd give every penny to get Natalya free. All this and more.

'Here,' the waiter said when he came back with her change.

'Keep it,' she told him.

It was cents anyway.

She'd bought the holdall in the Noordermarkt one Saturday. Lots of little zip pockets on the side. So small she couldn't imagine how or why anyone could use them.

One of the zips wasn't quite closed. She was a precise woman and would have noticed if it was like this before.

Hanna opened the tiny pocket and took out a round shiny black plastic disk. Looked at it in the bright fluorescent lights of the cafe.

Smoke was drifting in from the dope place round the corner. The smell of it reminded her of how she'd fallen into a place like that after Yilmaz had branded her. Neither was an experience to be repeated.

The thing was electronic. That was obvious. Only one way it could have got there. On the base was an on-off switch and she so nearly used it. But then Vos would become even more suspicious than usual.

Cold outside. The holdall weighed heavily on the end of her right arm. The gun and the ammunition she'd stolen from the Turk took up most of her small shoulder bag.

Both were vulnerable. But one was more precious than the other. So she hooked both handles of the holdall through her arm and held it close to her chest. Walked on into the red-light district, wondering how much she'd have to explain to Cem Yilmaz about the hair and the glasses.

She was his now. He might not approve.

———

Twenty-five minutes separated Henk Kuyper's exit from Damrak and the arrival of Bakker and Van der Berg on their bikes.

'Where the hell is this place?' she asked, checking her phone.

He nodded at the alley.

A heavily built bearded man with dark skin and a friendly face was marching out, hands deep in the pockets of his black business coat.

'Morning,' he said for no reason then went on his way.

Intelligence had sent some information about Smits as they cycled to his office. His agency in Amsterdam was just three years old. Before that he'd worked in property maintenance in Saudi Arabia and the Yemen. Nothing on file to link him to any terrorist cell. But the company accounts showed meagre turnover while Smits lived in a fancy apartment near the Rijksmuseum, one he owned.

Van der Berg flicked through the details.

'This guy's a mercenary. Doesn't matter who pays.'

'Nice,' she said and they went down the alley.

A smell.

She stopped, looked at him.

'What's that?'

'Smoke,' he said and started to run.

Halfway down the alley they got there. The red door was open. Flames behind it. There was a woman outside, in what looked like the uniform for a hairdresser. She was on the phone already looking shocked and tearful.

Bakker started to walk for the office.

'You don't want to go in there,' the woman said, holding out a hand. 'I've called an ambulance. Jesus . . . I just heard a scream.'

There was a salon three doors down.

Van der Berg flashed his police ID.

'An ambulance?'

Laura Bakker was through already. He followed her.

The smoke was from a small bonfire of papers next to a grey filing cabinet. On the floor in front was the body of a corpulent man in middle age. Mouth open, arms out, legs akimbo.

Dead eyes staring at the ceiling. The red mass of a bullet wound off-centre in his forehead.

'Shit,' Bakker gasped, checking him for signs of life, finding nothing. 'Shit.'

Van der Berg was stomping on the flames, managing to put them out.

'We missed this by minutes, Dirk.'

'Yeah.' His big feet kept pummelling at the paper. 'Look above the door.'

'What?'

'He's got CCTV. Probably on the computer.'

There was a small lens in the corner of the room, pointed back towards the desk. She went to the PC, pulled out a pair of latex gloves, started on the keyboard.

Van der Berg came over. The flames were out. Sirens were sounding outside somewhere.

Then the crowd started to turn up.

Ten minutes later the place was packed. Fire officers. Uniform police. Mirjam Fransen and some fresh goons from AIVD.

Bakker didn't take any notice of them. She'd been working her way back through the video on the computer.

'What have you got?' Mirjam Fransen asked.

'Maybe,' she said, 'Barbone.'

She wound back to a few minutes before they arrived. A hefty man with a full black beard and a cheerful face coming through the door. Smits stops walking round the room sprinkling petrol everywhere, looks up. Says something they can't make out. Seems surprised. Worried too.

The man with the beard smiles, marches up, pulls out a gun and shoots him in the head. Looks at the flames. Piles a few more papers on them. Leaves.

'We passed that bastard in the street,' Bakker added. 'He's big. Unusual. I'd know him again.'

'You passed him?' Fransen asked.

'Yeah,' said Van der Berg. 'And lots of other people too. Do you want—?'

'Shut up, Dirk,' Bakker told him.

The detective stood there on his flat feet, lost for words.

'This . . .' Bakker said, finger jabbing at the screen. 'Barbone wasn't the only visitor.'

She'd gone right back to Henk Kuyper's arrival. They watched him turn up. What looked like a difficult conversation.

'What the hell was Kuyper doing here?' Bakker wondered.

Then Smits's phone call.

'Get this emailed to my office,' Fransen ordered. 'Technical can take a look. Maybe we can work out what they were saying . . .'

'He wrote something down!' She found the sequence. Smits taking out a pen and a notepad. Scribbling a few words. Handing over a single sheet. 'That's what Kuyper wanted. That's where he's going.'

The image was so indistinct. She took a photo with her phone then sent it back to Aisha in Marnixstraat. Thought again and ran through the sequence, snapping it as a video. Sent her that too. Perhaps they could recreate something from the movement of Smits's pen or arm or . . .

Three scene of crime officers had turned up alongside the AIVD crew and were looking at the body on the floor.

'I'm running this operation,' Fransen insisted. 'You wait on my say-so.'

'This is a murder,' Van der Berg cut in. 'And you've got our best homicide detective suspended. Back off.'

She took a step towards him.

'I said back off!' he yelled.

'Dirk,' cut in the lead scene of crime man.

'What?'

'We don't work when people are shouting. Can you shut up or what?'

Bakker went out into the street and called Aisha.

'I need you to look at those photos I sent you straight away . . .'

'I am looking at them,' the forensic officer came back.

'And?'

'And what? You didn't tell me what you were looking for.'

'He scribbled something on a pad. I want to know what it was.'

A long moment then Aisha said, 'Sorry. You can't even see the words from this angle.'

'You can see the pen. Can't you work out what he was writing from that?'

Aisha sighed and said, 'I perform science, Laura. Not magic.'

Bakker swore.

'Find the pad he used,' Aisha suggested. 'See if he pressed hard enough to make a mark on the page beneath. Bring it in anyway . . .'

Back inside and she started sifting through the burned papers by the filing cabinet. There was only one notepad there. It was a charred mass of burned paper and metal spiral ring. Nothing easily recoverable.

She sent Aisha a photo of that.

'Sorry,' came the reply. 'This will take time. If we get there at all.'

'I don't—'

'Enough,' Aisha snapped. 'I've got Vos on the other line bleating on about his problems.'

Fransen was still arguing with Van der Berg. Within earshot.

Bakker moved to the door.

'Vos is suspended,' she said.

'Got to run,' Aisha told her. 'Bye.'

———

'Get in there,' the man with the dreadlocks told her.

The bag was open on the floor. Big enough for her twice over. She saw they'd put pillows in there and a blanket and didn't know whether that was good or bad.

'Come on,' he said and shook his head, the long dark locks swinging from side to side. 'They told me you could be a little bitch. Not now, kid. Just get in. We're not going far. After all your games . . .'

He bent down and peered into her face.

'The boss man told me. You don't get the chance to run away again. In the bag. Or else.'

Then he pulled something out of his pocket. She saw it was a long, clean bandage, the kind they had in the medicine chest at school. Before she could speak he'd wound it round both his hands, pulled it over her open mouth, gagged her with the thing tight between the teeth. The dry fabric made her choke for a moment.

He pushed her towards the open holdall.

Natalya got down on her knees on the blanket inside. Twisted round. Sat for a moment. Then lay down.

'Good girl,' he said. 'Won't be long.'

Then she saw the zip closing and her little world turned dark. *Monster.*

No room for it here. No space at all.


His second cup of coffee was going cold. The dog was getting bored playing with the bone. Bert had put music on the sound system in the Drie Vaten. Vos hated when he did that. He liked to pick what he heard. Not have it chosen for him. And Golden Earring really didn't match the mood.

The red dot hadn't shifted for twenty-five minutes. He'd nagged Aisha to check the system was working. She insisted the bug was where it said. And that wasn't right. He'd already zoomed in on the map and worked out the cafe where she must have gone. Not somewhere he knew.

But there was a name and when he looked it up there was a phone number too. Getting desperate he called, described Hanna, short brown hair, glasses, asked if she was still there.

'What is this?' the man on the end of the line asked. 'An answering service?'

Then put the phone down.

Vos led Sam back to the bar where Bert started clucking over him. The dog barely noticed when he slipped out of the door and hailed a cab passing slowly beneath the bare lime trees in Prinsengracht.

Ten minutes along the canals and he was there.

He checked the phone again. The dot still hadn't moved. Talked to Aisha once more. Something was happening with the Kuyper case and AIVD.

'Smits, the booking agency man, got shot, Vos. They think this terrorist did it. Henk Kuyper had been there too.'

He tried to think that through.

'Also we're not supposed to be talking, are we?' she added. 'You're sure you set it up right like I showed you last night?'

She'd slipped him the satnav tracker outside the Drie Vaten after De Groot briefed her. Taking care to make sure no one saw her leave Marnixstraat and head out into the dark. It was vital AIVD, more than anyone, didn't understand he was still inside the case.

'I did just what you said. I'm here. Right where the dot's showing. I can't see her anywhere.'

She did something on the system. He looked at the phone again. It had zoomed right in to the cafe.

'That's as near as it gets,' she said. 'If you can't see her now I can't help.'

Vos looked at the screen and how it corresponded to the layout of the place then went in.

There was a pathetic, dried-up geranium in a dusty pot on the window ledge by a table. Two cups of coffee still on it. One of them with lipstick round the rim. One just marked with a brown stain.

He reached over and rummaged beneath the dying leaves.

The black plastic bug sat there among the roots.

'Found her?' Aisha asked.

'Not exactly,' Vos said then went back into the busy street, looked around, saw nothing.

Hanna stood outside the block in Spooksteeg then drew back the jumper from her wrist and looked at the numbers there, scrawled in ballpoint. A code for the door. A second set of numbers for the lift. Three floors up, straight into his living room.

She'd watched him key in those numbers. Written them down in his bathroom after he branded her. But now she didn't need them so she pressed the bell, felt the wound on her back sting and waited. That mark would never go away. She'd wear this man's initials for the rest of her life.

Soon she was upstairs. Foreign music playing gently from somewhere. He was alone on the sofa. In a suit for once. The place didn't smell of sweat or cologne. Cem Yilmaz looked . . . businesslike. Another side to him. One she hadn't seen before.

'You've got the money?' he asked as she walked in.

She nodded.

'I need to see it,' he said.

'Why?'

He shook his head and squinted at her for a moment.

'Because of what you are. I get cheated from time to time. This doesn't sit lightly on me. Or those responsible.'

She opened the green holdall and took out Renata Kuyper's DKNY shoebox. The sign on the label on the side said it was for a pair of girl's trainers. Almost two hundred euros.

Yilmaz opened the lid and looked at the carefully stacked bundles of notes. Then flicked through them, checking they were all real.

'This is good. We need trust between ourselves. For the years to come.'

He didn't need to go to the drawer. The money was stacked neatly on the desk. Green one hundred euro notes. She'd never touched one before.

'You take this,' he ordered. 'You find your girl. Tomorrow, when things are back to normal, we talk about how matters stand between us. What work you'll do.'

She blinked.

'I thought we'd agreed what work that was.'

'We did.' Cem Yilmaz smiled. 'It's whatever I ask.'

He gestured at the money. She put it into the bag, carefully stacking it inside.

'Why do you look different?' he asked. 'Those glasses.'

'I don't want the police to follow me.'

'What if he knows what you look like?'

She took out her phone and showed it to him.

'This is how he knows me.'

Yilmaz grunted something. Then added, 'In future you don't change your appearance unless I say so. This . . .' He came over and his vast hand went to her head. Roughly. Then he fingered her hair as if he was buying it. 'Blonde's better. Men desire it more. When you go back to work you'll dye it again. And let it grow.'

Hanna hesitated for a moment then said OK.

'We're finished here now,' Yilmaz told her.

She bounced the heavy bag on the end of her arm.

'Don't you want to know where?' she asked. 'Or when?'

'I want to know nothing,' he snapped. 'Why would I? I'm the banker here. Nothing more. You understand?'

He gripped her hard by the right shoulder. Squeezing on the wound, the signature he'd left in her flesh.

She winced. Not as much as he liked. So he squeezed harder. She felt blood start in the healing scab. Finally couldn't stop herself whimpering with the pain.

'Good,' he grunted. 'You understand. Go now. Be here tomorrow morning. Ten o'clock. Then we discuss what comes next.'

Bakker took Van der Berg to one side in the doorway of Smits's office. The place was starting to smell, of smoke and blood and the chemicals forensic used. Mirjam Fransen and her people were getting frustrated. The technicians were settling in for the duration.

'Is there something you'd like to tell me?' she asked.

He shuffled on his big black shoes.

'About anything in particular?'

'About Vos.'

He glanced at Fransen, talking quietly down her phone.

'Not really.'

'Dirk . . .'

He sighed. A long, deep, familiar sound.

'Later. OK? We've enough on our plate.'

She'd phoned back to Marnixstraat again and got nothing but evasion.

'So he's put himself out on a limb? To try to get this ransom paid separately?'

Van der Berg nodded at the AIVD crew. His finger went to his lips.

'Why am I the last to know about everything?' she wondered.

'Shall we kind of . . . slide out of here? I could really use a . . .'

'Coffee,' she interrupted.

'Coffee,' he agreed.

They walked down the alley without a word. Found one of the chain cafes on Damrak. Two cups of cappuccino and Van der Berg got stuck into a cinnamon bun too.

Bakker had been working on her clumsiness of late. It had become something of a Marnixstraat legend. That didn't stop her upending her coffee as she gestured with her hand. Hot liquid spilled everywhere.

'Damn!' she yelled.

Van der Berg was there in an instant, mopping up with napkins.

'This is very hard,' she complained.

'Carrying a cup of coffee? Just a case of practice.'

'I meant being kept in the dark.'

He dumped the napkins then waved the sticky bun around.

'Yes,' he agreed. 'I suppose it is.'

They could see down the alley. The AIVD crew had come outside. Two or three were smoking. Mirjam Fransen was on the phone again. Looking madder than ever.

'Whatever Vos is up to I hope he's having more luck than us,' Bakker moaned.


Centraal station. Ten minutes to twelve. Vos walked there, hands in pockets, head down, trying to think.

She'd called him twenty minutes before. Said nothing except that she'd be outside where the trams stopped. He wasn't to come near. They communicated by phone. That was all.

The thought of dealing with a ransom drop here filled him with despair. A quarter of a million people passed through Centraal every day headed for the train and metro lines, the trams and buses. The sprawling red-brick building, a hundred and twenty years old, was a Flemish leviathan of towers and crow-stepped gable roofs, a warren of halls and tunnels, platforms, shops, offices. Almost a small city in itself.

Hanna Bublik was where she said, out in the cold bright day. The green holdall on her right arm. A smaller bag on her left. She'd changed too. The black jacket was gone like the long blonde hair. In its place a plain brown coat. She looked even more like a teacher or office worker.

He walked past her and went to stand by the ticket machines. Then he phoned.

'Let's keep this brief,' she said. 'He's supposed to call any minute. You didn't bring anyone, did you?'

He groaned.

'Just me. Like I said. Is that so hard to believe?'

She was watching him from the tram stop. Glancing round everywhere too.

'You're so desperate to be trusted, Vos. Someone must have really let you down once upon a time.' A pause then she added, 'Or you did that to them.'

'Probably both,' he remarked.

'I'm sorry about that little toy you planted on me. I hope it wasn't expensive.'

He muttered something under his breath then said, 'Have you got everything?'

She raised the green holdall.

'Is there any point in asking where you found the rest?'

'None at all.' She stood back as a bus lurched towards her. Then checked her watch. 'I'll call you when I hear something.'

Vos bought himself a coffee from a stall. Thought about how he'd handle this from the other side. They had to assume she was being watched even if she didn't know. A simple hand-off – go to the man in black, give him the bag – wouldn't work.

Stations were good for crowds. Good for other things too.

For ease of mind he went to the nearest ticket machine and bought two singles to Schiphol. An obvious destination. One of the most popular short routes there was from here. And the tickets would save them any hassle on the train.

There were two towers on the station. Hanna was looking from one to the other. Puzzled. Most people were. One was a clock. The other looked like one but with a single hand that baffled newcomers since all it indicated was the direction of the wind.

Northerly, Vos thought. He knew that steady bitter chill of old.

Then she stopped, raised the phone to her ear. Eyes fixed on the cobbles and the steel tramlines through them, listening intently.

It couldn't have lasted more than a few seconds. After that she was marching into the station, phone locked to her ear.

He watched her go past, not a glimpse in his direction. Then she called.

'He says I have to catch the train to somewhere called Vlissingen. Platform five. Carriage three. The upstairs compartment. It goes in four minutes. Where the hell's Vlissingen?'

A three-hour ride south.

'A long way,' he said. 'There are lots of stops before that.'

Schiphol. The Hague. Delft. Rotterdam. Middelburg. They could be headed anywhere.

'Hanna. I've got a ticket you can use.'

She was walking so quickly it was hard to keep up.

'I've got a ticket already,' she told him.

Platform five. The double-decker train was pulling in as they got there.

It was one of the long-distance services. Lots of space. Not too busy.

She went upstairs in the third carriage and sat in the last part of the forward section. He went to the opposite end.

Quick turnaround. Station staff yelling at tourists to get on the train.

Then they pulled out. Vos picked up a spare paper someone had left. Pretended to read it. Looked around.

Eleven people. Four women. Six men. One kid no more than twelve. A boy.

Hanna was staring out of the window. Phone in hand.

Natalya might be anywhere on the train. He could put in a call, halt it at an early stop. Haul everyone off. Question them until they narrowed things down.

Vos put down the paper and wondered how he could be so slow.

They wouldn't have the girl here. Too obvious. Too easily detected. It had to be more complicated than that. And when things were complex you approached them slowly. Let a picture emerge. Analysed it. Worked out where to go next.

Maybe seven minutes to the next station, Sloterdijk. After that Lelylaan.

Then the airport station at Schiphol.

He couldn't believe they were going far.


Rapenburg was a quiet narrow street. Old houses. Some offices. Neat cobblestones. Like Zeedijk without people, neon and sleaze. Residential, Kuyper guessed. He didn't know this part of the city well. But it was obvious most people were out to work.

A good place to hide.

Another red door. Much like Smits's office. No name on the bell. He rang it anyway. Waited a long minute. The sound of bolts being drawn back, a key in the lock. Then a curious, not unfriendly face. Clean-shaven, recently by the looks of it. There was the rough, red shadow of a vanished beard on his cheeks.

Perhaps fifty. A bulky man he wore a capacious knitted brown cardigan, the sleeves too long, and pale cream trousers. The size of him seemed odd. And gross.

'Henk Kuyper,' he said. 'Come in. Please . . .'

He followed the waddling figure down a narrow corridor into a small room at the back. There was one window onto a tiny courtyard. Nothing else except a desk with a computer on it and two chairs.

The man took one, fell into it heavily. Kuyper sat opposite him at the desk. The sound of a radio newscast was coming out of the PC. More about the economy. And the football riot. Nothing else.

'I am Khaled,' the man said and held out a flabby hand.

Kuyper took it. Warm, soft and dry. Five years he'd been waiting to get close to these people. Now it felt unreal.

'Here.'

He poured two glasses of water from a bottle next to the PC. San Pellegrino. Warm. Flat.

'What a mess,' Khaled said with a shake of his head. 'So many high hopes at the beginning. That we might free our brother Alamy. Right a few wrongs.'

'The girl . . .'

'And this offer of yours. A daughter. Granddaughter of a monster. It seemed so . . . generous.'

'I thought I'd meet Barbone.'

Khaled's eyes narrowed.

'Who's Barbone?'

'Please . . .' Kuyper sighed. 'Smits said—'

'Smits is an employee. A minor one. A fool. He shouldn't speak out of turn.'

'The girl—'

'—was not your daughter. The weapons Bouali possessed . . . they were not what we expected. You toyed with us, Kuyper. This was all a game, wasn't it? A dangerous one. From everyone's point of view.'

The man's attitude annoyed him.

'If you thought I wasn't genuine why did you go along with it?'

Khaled frowned, puzzled.

'Curiosity. And because we believed there might be some advantage. Why else?'

'I did my best to help you,' Kuyper insisted. 'If I wanted you in jail why am I here alone?'

The man in front of him puffed out his cheeks then looked around the room.

'What was it that play of yours says? Conscience just makes cowards of us all.'

'A coward wouldn't be here,' Kuyper said.

'True. But you have a conscience, don't you? It's cost us all dear. Now Barbone is mad. With you. With me. With everyone. He tells me I must leave Amsterdam. A city I enjoy. He's not a man to upset. Life isn't safe here any more. Why?'

'You took the wrong girl. Not my fault.'

Khaled opened a drawer and retrieved a sheet of paper.

'Pink jacket. Blonde hair.' He pushed the printout across the table. 'This is the picture you sent us. This is the girl we took. Please, Kuyper. Abandon this pretence. Barbone's no fool. He saw through you that first day in the park.'

Kuyper looked at the sheet. The photo was Natalya Bublik. He'd taken it in the street surreptitiously when she was coming home from school with her mother. Cropped Hanna Bublik out of the picture. If things had gone the way they should none of this would have mattered.

'I must have made a mistake,' he murmured.

'A big one,' Khaled agreed. 'Not to know what your own child looks like.'

The way he sat was wrong somehow.

'This girl you took has no value,' Kuyper said. 'If you let her go . . .'

The bemused look again.

'You assume she's still ours. You assume so much. Why?'

'Because I don't believe an eight-year-old child's your enemy.'

A shrug. Then Khaled took a packet of cigarettes from the right hand pocket of the bulky cardigan, shook one free, lit it. His hand was trembling.

'What can I give you?' Kuyper asked.

'Freedom. Tell your people I want out. Safe passage from Holland. Let me be honest. I'm like Smits. An employee. Not a fanatic. I do this because I must. My family's in their custody in Iraq. You think I choose to cause this trouble?'

Kuyper stayed silent.

'I sense we're both at the mercy of others, Henk. If we can find a solution that's to our mutual advantage . . .'

A glimmer of hope.

'I'll take you in myself. See what we can do.'

'No, no, no,' Khaled said firmly. 'After all this nonsense how can I deal with the likes of you? Get me someone whose word means something.'

'My word . . .'

He stopped. The fat man opposite had leaned back in his chair and was gazing at him, amused.

'What do you want?' Kuyper repeated.

'Bring me your handler. Your boss. Someone who's what they seem. Not a fool who can't see his own shadow. If I hear it from him then we've something to talk about. Otherwise be gone. The arrangements are made. We're fleeing, man. You understand why?'

He thought about how Mirjam Fransen would relish this opportunity. As always she'd want to raise the stakes.

'If I bring in someone they'll want Barbone. The network.'

The shrug again.

'If it's in my interest I'll give you what you want . . .' A brief smile. 'That's a lot. Believe me. He's still here. Others of his men too.'

'You said they had your family.'

Khaled's big head went to one side, amused.

'What's that proverb of yours? Out of sight, out of mind. Sometimes a man has to look after himself. No one else. There's nothing I can do to help them now.'

Henk Kuyper pulled out his phone. He hadn't called Mirjam Fransen directly in years. So he had to look up the number. Then, in a couple of seconds, he was through.

Just a minute out of Centraal Hanna's phone rang. He could hear the tinny trill all the way down the carriage. Set to maximum volume. What else?

Brief conversation. She was staring out of the window, watching the grey city go past.

Two big men marched down the carriage. Black leather jackets. Grim faces. Could have been anyone. But they were looking. Vos's eyes stayed on the newspaper. They strode past Hanna, went down the stairs at the far end.

*You*, Vos thought and wondered how much use that information might be.

It was another five or six minutes to Sloterdijk. Then four more to Lelylaan. After that another seven minutes or so to Schiphol. Then the train set off on the longer sections of the journey, through Leiden on to the south.

He knew how he'd approach this problem. And when he knew that he'd a pretty good idea how they would too.

Hanna came off the phone, seemed lost in herself for a moment, then called him.

'They want me to leave the money under the seat and get off at the next stop. There's a train like this back into the city in ten minutes. Fifth carriage. They say I need to go upstairs and they'll call me there if they're happy with the money.'

Sloterdijk. Three minutes away now.

'Vos?'

'Do it,' he said.

'Is this for real?'

'Let's find out.'

The pickup pair could be off the train the moment it called

at the next stop and there wasn't a damn thing he could do about it.

'If they screw me around . . .'

'Hanna. This is their game right now. We have to play it.'

They'd worked this perfectly. Whoever was running the operation would have people on the ground at Lelylaan checking to see if there was a police presence at the station. They could pull out before the girl was free.

Except . . .

Trains.

Too public. They'd surely want to keep her hidden until they knew they could release her without getting caught.

If any of this was serious in the first place.

'Do you know what you're doing?' she asked.

'As much as ever. Leave them the money. Cross the platform and wait for the train. I'll be a little way along from you.'

'If they . . .'

'I know,' he said. 'I heard you the first time.'


Van der Berg was on his second sticky bun. Crumbs were piling up all over the table.

'Maybe we should stick with the murder case here,' she thought.

'The commissaris wants us to hang around with our friends from AIVD. What the commissaris wants—'

'He doesn't get,' Bakker broke in. 'Didn't you notice? Mirjam Fransen's running things now.'

He beamed and wiped away some crumbs.

'She certainly thinks so, doesn't she?'

'And Vos?'

Van der Berg wasn't listening. He was looking down the alley. Fransen was off the phone, summoning her team. They were leaving Smits's office.

'Something's happening,' Bakker said.

'Something's always happening.' Van der Berg finished the pastry then swigged the dregs of his coffee. 'Just a question of whether it matters.'

He got up quickly from the table and glanced at her.

'Are we going?'

Bakker snatched at her bag.

'Where?'

The AIVD people had called for their vehicles. Two black Mercedes saloons and a grey van.

'Where they take us,' he said.


The train lumbered into Sloterdijk station. Hanna got up and left by the front staircase. All she had now was the small shoulder bag. With her brown coat, new hair, new glasses she might have been going to the office.

Vos took his paper and left by the back steps.

No sign of the men in black leather jackets. He walked forward, past Hanna, up the platform. Watched as the train pulled out.

They were there, retracing their steps to the upstairs carriage.

Money delivered.

Now, if this was for real, the prize.

Ten minutes to kill.

On another day, in different circumstances, he would have been running this as a full operation. Teams of officers quietly watching, in plain clothes, rail uniforms, from carriages, platforms and bridges. Waiting outside in cars.

All that was beyond him. He could blame AIVD. Bad luck. Circumstance. But Vos wasn't that kind of man. Mainly he blamed himself.

Hanna Bublik found a bench seat and sat outside in the cold bright day. He leaned against a lamp post and waited.

Bang on time the massive intercity train pulled into the

station, brakes squealing, coughing smoke from beneath its slowing wheels.

Barely a handful of people ready to get on. Only three came off.

Fifth carriage.

She went upstairs. He took the seat at the end. The train seemed almost empty.

Hanna's phone rang.

'Mrs Bublik,' a voice said.

She blinked. It wasn't Cem Yilmaz. Just the same words.

'I left the money,' she murmured.

'I know.'

There was amusement in his voice.

'I've done everything you asked,' she pleaded.

'I know that too.'

He was toying with her. Enjoying it.

'Where's my daughter?' she asked.

No answer.

'Where?'


Gagged and trapped it wasn't easy to breathe inside the holdall. The thing was old and smelled of dust and mould. Natalya clutched her chest, lying on the thin blanket, still in the pink jacket that was getting filthier by the hour.

*Sounds.*

She tried to analyse them.

A car engine. No, bigger than that. A van perhaps. Muffled voices. A radio playing pop music. Roads. Bumpy. Slow to begin with, as if they were locked in city traffic. Then faster as they escaped the jams.

There was such a distance between her and the world now. She'd no longer any idea how many days had passed since those strange events when they went to see a man with a long white beard surrounded by strange, funny creatures with black faces who kept handing you spicy sweets from nets with long handles.

It might have been a dream. Or an odd nightmare, like the one with the monster. That seemed gone too. It was as if her life was winding down, shrinking into itself, intent on becoming nothing at all.

*How long now?*

Fifteen minutes. More. Then they came to a halt.

Metal doors clanked open. She heard a brisk breeze. The whine of a distant plane. Voices. Two men talking, low tones in a language she couldn't follow.

It was about her. Of that she was sure. Not that she knew how.

When they dragged out the bag she banged her head on something. A wheel arch maybe. It was hard. Hurt.

She whimpered.

'Quiet!' a man yelled in Dutch.

Natalya Bublik, eight years old, not afraid, just concerned, curious too, curled up more tightly inside the stinking holdall.

They were carrying her. Two men. The bag in their arms.

She wondered where.


Shaking and rattling back towards Centraal station. Other trains joining them as the lines converged.

'Where?' Hanna asked again.

'Look around you,' he said.

She did. An elderly woman. A teenager with a pair of earphones clamped round his skull. Vos in the corner, pretending not to see her.

'For the love of God I gave you the money. Where?'

'Little girls play games. Why shouldn't we? Hide and seek. Good day, Mrs Bublik.'

She slammed her fist hard against the window. Vos was staring at her now.

Hanna marched over, told him what she'd heard.

'Is he saying she's on the train?' she asked.

Head turning, one way, the other. People starting to look.

'Where do I start?'

'Hanna . . .'

He had his own phone out now. Pressing a button.

'Not here,' she muttered. 'How big's the train?'

'Hanna . . .' His hand was on her arm. She barely noticed. 'I'll have officers waiting in the station. We'll go through every carriage. If Natalya's here . . .'

'If . . . ?' Her bright eyes glared at him. '*If* . . . ?'

Such a short journey. They were slowing down already. The vast canopy of Centraal started to enfold them. Vos made a rapid call to control, got straight through to the station office. Told them to have a team waiting on the platform.

'You never thought they'd let her go, did you?' she snapped. 'You think she's dead.'

She was ready to storm off, one way or the other.

'We'll search the train,' he said. 'We'll search the train. If we're lucky—'

'People like me don't get lucky, Vos! Haven't you noticed?'

The few passengers in the carriage shuffled down the stairs. Uniform officers milling around the grey platform as it appeared.

All the mundane activities of Centraal. Announcements. Farewells on the concourse. People lost and bored, some with the dead-eyed look of the reluctant traveller, others excited at the journey ahead.

'We'll find her,' Vos said.


Bakker got into the van without asking and Van der Berg followed. She smiled at two stony-faced AIVD officers in the back.

Then they headed across the city, past Centraal station where blue lights were flashing on a line of patrol cars parked outside, on to a quiet cobbled street. She saw the name: Rapenburg. Looked at Van der Berg. He shrugged. This was new to him too, and the two AIVD men weren't about to enlighten them.

They came to a halt outside a plain, pale brick terrace house. Still just the two black Mercedes and the van. Seven AIVD officers checking their weapons, earpieces in. Bakker and Van der Berg shuffling their feet trying to look inconspicuous.

Fransen pulled the team together behind the van, glared at the two police officers as if they didn't matter, then briefed the group.

Short and to the point. Khaled was inside. The real one this time. He was with Henk Kuyper and ready to offer a deal. Negotiate safe passage for him from the incident in Leidseplein and the Bublik kidnapping. Then he'd give them the Barbone network on a plate.

'Do you believe him?' Bakker asked.

'Doesn't matter if I believe him or not,' Fransen said. 'He thinks we're about to sit down for a nice polite conversation.' She tapped the weapon of the tall, hatchet-faced AIVD officer next to her, failed to notice he didn't like that. 'He's wrong.'

She glanced at each of her men in turn.

'Ready?'

Van der Berg walked to the door. His finger hovered over the bell.

'No,' Fransen said. 'We do this our way. I want an entrance.'

She looked at the tall officer, the one whose gun she'd stroked. Still missed the fact he clearly wasn't impressed.

'Take it down,' she said.

And then the ram was smashing the door to pieces.


Ten minutes after the train had pulled into Centraal every carriage had been cleared. No young girls looking for their mother. No one who looked in the least suspicious.

Hanna Bublik had the air of defeat about her. Angry and final.

Vos stood with her by the platform. He'd checked with De Groot finally. Heard the news about Smits's murder. Mirjam Fransen thought she had a lead. But it was to Barbone, not the kidnap. Nor was she offering any details, though Bakker and Van der Berg were along for the ride.

'At least they've got something,' the commissaris grumbled. 'I'm sorry. It was worth a try.'

'We haven't finished . . .'

'We've lost the girl, haven't we?' De Groot said in a soft and mournful tone. 'I hate saying it. God knows—'

'No,' Vos interrupted. 'You don't know that. Neither do I . . .'

'Pieter. I appreciate your concerns.'

'This is about money, Frank. It has been ever since they handed Natalya over.'

Silence. De Groot was listening. Then he asked, 'So?'

'So you don't destroy something of value. You realize . . .'

Bought and sold. Mother and daughter. Laura Bakker had said that and it was true.

'You realize the value of your asset,' Vos added.

De Groot made sympathetic noises, nothing more.

'I've got to go,' Vos told him and went back to Hanna Bublik.

She was crying. The way hard, brave women did. The tears stood in her eyes. She wiped them away with the sleeve of her new brown coat. Acted as if she should have been ashamed. Wouldn't let them roll down her cheek.

'You have to tell me, Hanna.'

'Tell you what?'

'The money. Where did the rest of it come from?'

She thought for a second then said, 'A pimp. I said I'd work for him.'

'Name?'

One moment's hesitation then she said, 'Cem Yilmaz. He's—'

'Turkish,' Vos broke in. 'Lives in Spooksteeg. Likes to pretend he's legitimate.'

'Isn't he?'

This woman could spot a lie a mile off.

'As far as I know,' he replied.

'I think he had someone break into my apartment and steal some of my things. He's been trying to force me to work for him. I wondered . . .'

She closed her eyes, was in pain for a moment.

'I wondered if it was him. If he maybe had her . . .'

'Why? You have to be specific. If I'm to get a warrant . . .'

'I don't know! No good reason. I said no to him. Lots of times. He doesn't like that. He . . .'

She unbuttoned the coat, dragged up her jumper, lifted the dressing and showed him the raw scar on her shoulder.

The initials in an odd script: CY.

Then pulled the sweater down again.

Marnixstraat had a small team that specialized in human trafficking. A bright, brave woman called Lotte de Jonge ran it. Vos called her, cut through the small talk, and asked if Yilmaz had any contact with people-smuggling organizations.

For a few seconds he heard nothing but the sound of a keyboard.

'Just checking. To make sure. We've never even heard a whisper he's got a trafficked girl on his books. He's too smart to get involved directly.'

'How about kidnapping?'

It was out of her area but she was on the system anyway. Nothing there she said.

He put Lotte de Jonge on hold and went back to Hanna. Ran through what had happened between her and Yilmaz again. It was too flimsy to get any kind of warrant, even if there was time.

'OK,' he said. 'What about his people? Who've you met?'

A shrug.

'There's an old creep who collects the rent. Jerry. I think he works for him.'

'What's his—'

'I don't know his name! He's about a hundred years old.'

She was close to giving up. He couldn't allow this.

'A man like Yilmaz distances himself from anything dangerous. He'd use intermediaries. If you met him with someone.
Anyone . . .'

'He had a friend,' she said and wiped her face with her sleeve.
'More than a friend. They were wrestling.' She thought for a
moment. 'Dmitri.'

'I need more than Dmitri,' Vos pleaded. 'A last name.'

'I don't have a last name. He was Russian. I'm sure of it. He
had these horrible tattoos.'

She fought to remember.

'There was a pair of eyes on his stomach. A skull in a basket
on his chest . . . A bleeding heart inside a triangle. That was across
his back.'

He relayed that to the woman on the other end of the line.

'Jesus,' De Jonge said. 'That sounds bad.'

'Why?'

'It's Russian jail code. The skull means he's killed someone.
The eyes . . . he's gay. The heart . . .'

The keyboard sounded as if it was working overtime.

'The heart?' he prompted.

'Just checking. It means he's a paedophile. I think I've got a
match. Someone on the European system with those tattoos. Let
me send you a photo.'

The picture was on the handset almost instantly. An obvious
prison mugshot. Cyrillic writing underneath. Vos showed it to
Hanna. She looked at it, nodded.

'Who is he, Lotte?' he asked.

'As bad as they come. Dmitri Volkov. Thirty-seven. Male
prostitute. We've intel he moves kids around for a few cells. Never
been able to prove it, of course.'

Hanna was watching him. Aware something was happening.

'Don't suppose you know where Dmitri lives?' Vos asked.

'I can try to find out,' she said.

A beep on Vos's line. He looked at the incoming call. Switched to it.

'Frank,' he said before De Groot could speak. 'I thought we were keeping this quiet.'

'Not any more,' the commissaris told him. 'They think they've found Khaled. I want you there. Get yourself a car.'


Bakker and Van der Berg came in behind the AIVD team. Down a long corridor into a room turning violent and noisy. Henk Kuyper stood up and got out of their way the moment they arrived.

There was a man opposite them. Big. Misshapen somehow. Fat but all the bulk was around his waist. He sat at a desk, arms folded, waiting for them, cigarette in his heavy right hand.

Looked up, furious, when he saw the force he faced.

Got to his feet, arms flying, scattering some papers from the desk.

'What is this?' he yapped. 'I told Kuyper. I'll talk to you people. I can be your friend.'

Fransen stopped in front of him, told the lead officer with her, the tall one with the craggy face and the black suit, to cuff him.

The briefest of struggles, one Khaled wasn't going to win. The cigarette fell to the floor. He was shouting a lot, in foul-mouthed Dutch.

Hands behind his back, held by the AIVD man, still yelling.

'You can let him go now,' Fransen ordered.

'He's offering to cooperate,' Kuyper said, arms folded, back against the wall. 'I think he's a middleman. A fixer. That's all.'

'That's *all*?' Khaled laughed.

The rest of the AIVD team started to hunt around the office, opening filing cabinets, poking at things.

Fransen walked up to him and said, 'Give me Barbone and I'll put you on a plane anywhere you like. Money in your pocket. A new passport.'

'Natalya Bublik too,' Bakker added, getting a filthy look from Fransen for her pains.

Khaled shrugged off the man behind him. Gave a good impression of outrage.

'Who is this woman? I told you, Kuyper. I deal with your boss. Not some bitch with a mouth on her . . .'

She didn't like that. Marched straight up. Face in his. The two of them between the chair and the desk he'd used.

Bakker watched intently. Trying to understand this. Something wasn't right.

'I am his boss, you moron,' Fransen barked at him. 'Head of AIVD in Amsterdam. I report straight to The Hague. If you want a deal I can cut it. There's no one else.'

A pause to let him understand this.

'Then take these stupid handcuffs off me,' Khaled said.

'They stay on until you give me something.' She got even closer. Almost touched him and he didn't like that. 'An address. Some names. A reason to believe.'

Something in his face. Doubt. Fear even.

'Do that,' she added, 'and I'll be grateful. Do that . . .'

His hands shook behind his back. Bakker thought she spotted something odd beneath the heavy cardigan.

Khaled cast his eyes around the room as if calculating something. How many people there.

'This is wrong . . .' Bakker started to say.

But by then Khaled was moving. He bent forward, pushed his big frame into Mirjam Fransen. Launched himself at her, taking the two of them down onto the desk. Pumping with his chest, banging Fransen against the stained wooden surface, pressing her down constantly.

Looking for a button, Bakker thought straight away.

'He's got something on!' Bakker yelled. 'Dirk . . .'

The detective was moving too. So were most of the AIVD officers, racing out of the little office, down the corridor. Henk Kuyper among them.

Khaled fought to press himself down once more to force the explosive vest hard into the woman beneath him.

The best target he had.

The force of his movement ripped the cardigan back. The trap was obvious then, set and loaded. Wires. Canisters. And somewhere, Bakker knew, a trigger.

The house was in a narrow residential street called Joop IJisbergstraat not far from Sloterdijk station where her mother had sat, anxious and depressed, an hour earlier. They carried the girl inside still in the bag. Then unzipped the thing. Told her to get out and stand.

The man with the dreadlocks left. So did another she didn't recognize. Now there was a burly, thuggish-looking individual with a tattoo just peering out from a T-shirt over his bicep. And two men. Odd men. They might have been brothers. Even identical twins.

They wore dark pinstriped suits and reminded her of a couple of characters from a comic book she'd read at school. *Tintin*.

It was in English. They were English too. Thomson and Thompson. These two didn't have heavy moustaches. But they were bald. Almost identical. Old. Podgy. Now they sat on a sofa staring at her, one of them tut-tutting, the other smiling, making noises that sounded as if they were supposed to be nice.

They held delicate teacups and dipped little biscuits in them as they scrutinized her.

'Take that thing off her mouth, Dmitri,' the one on the left – Thomson she decided – said.

Dmitri did and told her to keep quiet or else.

'Name,' said the other one.

'What does a name matter?' the man with the tattoo asked. Natalya recognized that accent from back in Georgia. Russian, she thought. Her mother always recoiled when she heard it.

'Matters if we're caught taking her back to Belgium,' Thompson pointed out. 'You've some papers I presume?'

The Russian threw three things on the table.

'Take your pick,' he said. 'We got them run up last night. Dutch ID. Luxembourg. Georgian.'

'Pretty girl,' Thomson said.

He leaned forward and looked at her. Held out one of his biscuits. Hungry, Natalya reached out for it. He snatched the thing back and laughed.

'Greedy too. There's extra cost. What's your name?' he asked again.

'Mary,' she said.

The Russian grumbled something then glared at her.

'It's Natalya. Fucking Georgians. They couldn't tell the truth if you paid them.'

Thompson tut-tutted once more. Then the other one joined in.

'Little girls who lie,' Thompson said.

'What can you do with them?' the second asked.

'Be firm,' the first added. 'Always. Be wise and careful and never let the little minxes out of your sight.'

The second looked at the Russian and asked, 'How much?'

'Forty thousand.'

The two of them got up in concert and brushed imaginary crumbs from their suit trousers.

'No wonder you never mentioned the price on the phone. To think we drove all the way from Ghent. For this?'

He cast an eye over her again.

'She's pretty. But not so much. Looks like trouble too. It's no fun dealing with that.'

He went to the window and pulled back the long, thick curtains. They seemed to be in the front room of a house. The place
was bare and had an odd smell about it. Something medicinal. Or
like a gym.

'That damned thing eats diesel too,' Thompson said.

She stretched up and could just see outside. In the narrow
road stood a long, shiny black car.

It took a moment for Natalya to realize what it was. A hearse.
In the back, as shiny as the paintwork, a plain coffin.

'You're going to drive all the way home with that thing
empty?' the Russian asked. 'Let me get you some more tea.'

The curtain closed. The pair looked at each other and said
nothing.

'We can talk about this,' Dmitri added, a little desperately.

There was one door to the living room. It was ajar. She could
see the front door through it. Just an ordinary lock. The kind you
could undo from the inside. One quick dash. A bit of luck. Out
into a street she didn't know in a part of the city she couldn't even
guess at.

'The spunky little cow's thinking of running,' Thomson said,
amused. 'I don't believe it.'

Dmitri mumbled something under his breath and stared at
her.

'Best hobble the child,' Thompson added. 'Saves so much
trouble down the line.'

'Hobble?' the Russian asked. 'You mean . . .'

He swung an imaginary hammer through the air.

'Good God,' Thompson remarked with a sigh. 'Do you think
we could sell her like that?'

He came over and told her to sit on one of the chairs at the
dining table.

It was so high her legs dangled off the floor. The other one
opened the curtains for a moment and looked up and down the
deserted street. She could see the hearse clearly.

Something like a scarlet silk sash came out of his pocket. He bound it round her ankles.

'There,' he said and slapped her lightly on the calf. 'That's better.'

He fingered the pink jacket. Stained with earth and mould.

'God this thing stinks,' he said, wincing. 'That's more expense. We'd have to clean this one up good and proper.'

'Tea,' Dmitri said. He'd been in the kitchen and got some more. 'I've got some nice smoked salmon. Some eel too. If you're hungry. Wine . . .'

'Oh we're always hungry!' Thomson announced with a grin. 'When there's something worth eating. No wine, though. Driving.'

'Snacks then,' the Russian said and went out again.

Thomson and Thompson went back to the sofa. The one on the left put his hand to his chin. Then the other did the same.

'Germany,' the first said. 'Hamburg. They'd like her there.'

The other shook his head.

'We'd get more if we moved her further afield. Out of Europe altogether. The Gulf. Africa.' He smiled. 'Little blonde girls. Everyone loves them, don't they?'

The smile left him.

'Except they don't stay that way. Not unless you dye them. You don't think . . .' He came over and fingered her hair. 'No. That's real enough.'

They were quiet for a moment. A radio was playing in the kitchen. There was the sound of cutlery on plates.

'Always the same,' Thomson said with a sigh. 'How does one balance the risk against the reward?'

His finger slipped up his cheek. Their beady eyes never left her.

'We start at three,' he said in a low, firm voice. 'We go to eight. Ten no more.'

'Too generous as always,' Thompson said. 'You leave this to me.'

Dmitri came back carrying food like a waiter. There was the smell of smoked fish.

Natalya looked at him and said, 'They say you're a fool, Russian. They'll pay you nothing. If . . .'

He banged the plates on a table, stormed across the room, fist raised.

Thomson and Thompson were laughing. So hard there were tears in their eyes.

The tattooed man stood over her, ready to strike. She held her head up. Looked him in the face.

'Friend,' Thomson said, coming over, taking his arm. 'Dmitri. No.'

The Russian calmed down a little, said something in his odd and guttural tongue.

'Damaged goods are no use to us,' the man in the pinstriped suit told him.

Natalya glared at all three of them. Unbowed. Defiant.

'Unless it's ours to damage,' the second noted then reached for some delicate eel on brown bread.


Van der Berg was burly, scarcely fit, but he wasn't slow. He got there first. Dragging Khaled back by the collar, tearing at the brown cardigan.

The one remaining AIVD man, the big officer who'd argued with Fransen, joined him.

Bakker saw the obvious. His hands were cuffed so he couldn't reach whatever mechanism was set on the vest. Forcing himself against Fransen was his only way to trigger that.

If they could keep hold of him . . .

Khaled kept screeching obscene abuse, Dutch, English. Anything he could think of. Then Van der Berg got his neck in the crook of his arm, jerked hard, choked his windpipe. Fransen slid out from underneath.

Bakker kept a multi-tool knife inside her jacket, next to the gun. She opened up the sharp blade, slashed at the grey wool. Ripped open the front.

Line upon line of small round tubes. More wires. The AIVD man couldn't take his eyes off it and she knew what his expression meant: enough here to take out the building.

'Just hold him,' Bakker said and they did.

Ignoring his kicking, desperate feet, she got in, cut through the strap on each shoulder, then the one around his waist. Lifted the vest away from him. Stood back with it in her hands.

Mirjam Fransen had fled to the corner of the room. She was crouched in a heap, terrified, gasping for breath.

The AIVD man wrestled Khaled to the floor, pulled out a gun, held it in his face. Said something about wanting an excuse. Any.

Then, when things calmed a little, introduced himself: Blok.

'Why didn't it go off?' Bakker asked, turning the vest in her fingers, curious as always.

Blok pointed to a small square by the waist.

'Pressure pad. You have to depress it for a couple of seconds before it cuts in. If it didn't have a delay you could set it off accidentally.'

'Makes sense I suppose . . .'

She held it up, peered at the little square. Looked ready to start investigating it.

'Careful,' Van der Berg warned.

The thing slipped from her grip, started to fall to the floor.

Blok swore, caught it. Glared at the two of them then barked at one of his men to come and take the vest away.

'That was clumsy,' Bakker said with a quick smile. 'We are still looking for the girl by the way. You owe us now.'

He shook his head.

'You think there's much here? These people are clearing out of town. That's why they killed Smits.' He nodded at Khaled, surly, despondent at his feet. 'Why they left this idiot as a present. So he could take as many of us with him as he could. I'm sorry—'

'We're not giving up yet,' Bakker cut in.

'No,' he said. 'I rather gathered that.'

More figures at the door. De Groot in a long winter overcoat. Vos in his donkey jacket, asking questions straight away.

Then Hanna Bublik. New coat. New haircut. Same old anger.

One look at her face and Laura Bakker knew how well her day had gone. Vos's too.

A short exchange and Vos established what had happened.

He pointed at Mirjam Fransen.

'Take her into custody.'

Blok's mouth opened. But he didn't speak.

'Kuyper too,' Van der Berg said. 'We want him as well.'

Fransen was on her feet. Back to her old self. All bluster and threats.

'You can't arrest anyone! We were on an operation.'

'Not now,' Vos said.

'Christ!' She grabbed hold of De Groot's coat, dragged him round to face her. 'You don't honestly think you can do this to serving AIVD officers, do you? One phone call . . .'

De Groot rolled his eyes.

'You can't throw me in a cell,' Fransen yelled. 'I won't have it.'

The commissaris scowled, turned to the uniforms.

'Make it a comfy one if you can. If not . . . what the hell? Pieter?'

He was kneeling down, trying to talk to the man on the floor. About someone called Dmitri Volkov. Getting nowhere.

'Pieter,' De Groot repeated. 'Where do we go now?'

'I'm one soldier among many,' the Arab bellowed then spat full in Vos's face.

'Boss,' Van der Berg said.

Vos got up. Wiped the mess from his face with the back of his hand. The detective was standing by the desk. In his hand was a Saudi Arabian passport. A photo of the man in front of them and a name: Hakim Fakhoury.

'He probably isn't even Khaled, is he?' Van der Berg threw the passport on the desk. 'We're nowhere.'


'Two thousand,' Thompson said. 'Cash. It's sitting in an envelope in the hearse. You can have it now.'

Dmitri Volkov raised his eyes to the ceiling, put his hands together as if in prayer.

'Please, Lord. I asked you to send me serious men. Not comedians.'

The Belgians didn't look amused.

'We're taking a liability off your hands,' Thomson told him.

'A big liability,' Thompson observed, staring at Natalya Bublik silent on the chair, a scarlet tie around her ankles. 'She looks trouble. You don't want her here.'

Dmitri gestured at the plates, eyes wide, pleading.

'Two thousand and you get free fish?'

'The eel was good,' Thomson agreed. 'The salmon not so much. Let's say two and a half.'

'Oh for God's sake.' Dmitri gestured at the door. 'Be gone from here. You think you're the only ones I've got for this merchandise?'

They didn't move.

Thompson said, 'If you had a local buyer you wouldn't be calling us.'

'We're friends, aren't we?' the Russian objected.

Thomson pulled a big phone out of his jacket and turned it on. Natalya could just about see. There was a story there. A headline about her. A kidnap. A photo of her in the pink jacket, back on one of the boats.

'We have news in Belgium too, Dmitri. A friend would have mentioned these . . . complications. The police know this child. They'll be looking for her.'

'They know nothing!' Dmitri cried. 'They think she's with some crazy terrorists . . .'

Thomson and Thompson folded their pinstriped arms and stayed silent.

'Fifteen thousand,' Dmitri begged. 'I give you a thousand discount off the next one.'

'Three,' Thompson told him.

'I've got a bottom line from my boss. I can't go below it.'

'Make it up from your own pocket then,' the Belgian suggested. He smiled. 'You've got your sidelines. Let's not pretend otherwise.'

'Eight.'

'Three and a half.'

Dmitri picked up a piece of eel, dangled it over his mouth, let it fall.

'Four and a half,' Thompson said. 'Paid here and now. That's as far as we go.'

'Fine,' the Russian agreed. 'But you take her with you. I don't want the little bitch sitting round here staring at me like that.'

Natalya cocked her head to one side, was about to say something then thought better of it.

Thompson laughed.

'Why do you think we brought a hearse?'

He looked at the man next to him. They really were brothers, Natalya thought. Perhaps twins.

'Get the syringe, Jean. Your touch is so much better than mine.'

'Where did you put it?' Thomson asked.

The other sighed.

'In the coffin. As usual.'

Then he glanced at her.

'We'll get you some nice new clothes, poppet. But first you have to go to sleep. No fuss please.'


Vos called Lotte de Jonge again and put her on speakerphone. The room had cleared. Just a couple of detectives, Bakker, Van der Berg and Hanna Bublik. De Groot had gone back to Marnixstraat with the prisoners. AIVD were milling around outside waiting on an intelligence team to come and scan the office for documents and traces of the missing Barbone.

'We don't have an address,' Lotte de Jonge insisted. 'Nor do we have anything to connect Volkov to Cem Yilmaz. Or any terrorist group. I'm sorry but—'

'I saw him there!' Hanna insisted. 'The same man in your photo.'

'He's a bit-part player,' De Jonge insisted. 'An ageing rent boy. Really . . .'

Bakker started messing round with her own smartphone.

'If you give me time,' the woman in Marnixstraat said, with little enthusiasm.

No one spoke. Bakker was getting frantic keying in text into her phone. They all watched and then she looked at Hanna Bublik and said, 'You speak Russian?'

'Why?'

'Volkov is Russian for wolf. Is that right?'

Hanna frowned.

'Kind of.'

'And he's a male prostitute. So he's got to be on the networks. This is the closest I can find . . .'

Her thumbs flew on the screen. Then she held something up.

So small they had to crowd round to look. It was a Twitter feed in the name @dimka_volkova. The profile was a cartoon of a grinning wolf and the words, 'You got money? I got fun'.

'Dimka's short for Dmitri,' Hanna said. 'Volkova means she-wolf.'

Bakker scrolled through some earlier tweets until she found one with a photo. She clicked it, filled the screen with the image.

A grinning man with a crew cut. He was holding a can of beer and showing his biceps. In a club somewhere.

'That's him,' Hanna said.

'Who's on Twitter?' Bakker asked. 'Because I'm surely not.'

Silence then Van der Berg took a deep breath and pulled out his phone.

'It's for the beer, you understand,' he said. 'Me and the lads. We like to know when new stuff turns up.'

The profile photo was a bottle of Chimay Cinq Cents. His username @bier_stofzuiger.

*Beer Hoover.*

Van der Berg took a deep breath and typed . . .

> @dimka_volkova I got money and ket. Lots.
> Want some fun. Where you?

They watched Laura Bakker's phone.

They waited.

Thomson didn't go straight for the syringe and the drugs in the coffin. Instead he sat up front in the long black hearse making a phone call. More than one. At least three Dmitri guessed.

'You might at least pay for her before you sell her on,' the Russian moaned.

'Business always works forward,' Thompson replied. 'What do you expect?'

'Not much,' he grumbled. Then his phone made a chirping sound.

He looked at the tweet. Thought for a moment. A good night's work might bring in some extra. He wasn't joking about

Yilmaz having a base price. It was five thousand. The balance had to come from his own pocket.

A hit of ketamine wouldn't go amiss either.

His big thumbs stumbled over the screen.

> @bier_stofzuiger not now man. Busy. I get back
> to you in an hour.

Thomson was still in the front of the hearse looking at his handset, about to start another call.

'Now you're taking the piss,' Dmitri moaned.

Van der Berg showed them the answer. Vos kicked the desk. Hanna Bublik swore.

Bakker retrieved the phone from Van der Berg's fingers.

There was a little symbol at the foot of the message. A circle with a pointer at the bottom.

She started walking for the door. They followed, not knowing why.

'He's left the location on,' Bakker called back as she marched outside.

Pulling up the map from the tweet she climbed into the back of the first car. Van der Berg and Hanna Bublik squeezed in next to her. Vos took the front passenger seat next to the driver.

The map filled the screen. Bakker zoomed in.

'How accurate . . .?' Van der Berg began to ask.

She showed them. A street. A pin that ran over just three houses on it.

'He's there,' she said. 'Joop IJisbergstraat.'

The driver put on the lights and the siren.

'I want them off when we're close,' Vos told him as they lurched out into the road.

———

Marnixstraat.

De Groot called in the specialist team they used for terrorist work and handed them the man they'd seized in Rapenburg. AIVD would liaise alongside that.

Kuyper and Mirjam Fransen were in adjoining cells for all of twenty-five minutes before the call came through.

He sat in his office, watching the control room log. Aware that Vos was now headed for the address they'd got near Sloterdijk. Might be the last chance they had for all they knew.

From his window he could see Elandsgracht. There was what looked like a school party, kids no older than ten, giggling as they wandered down the street carrying brightly coloured parcels.

He listened to the firm voice on the line and knew there was no point in arguing. A spot of negotiation though . . .

'There are crimes committed here,' De Groot said when the man from The Hague was done. 'Conspiracy. Kidnap. We've probably got a dead child on our hands . . .'

'All the more reason to bury this,' the voice on the end of the line said. 'Don't be naive, De Groot. This isn't a battle you can win.'

'There's a condition.'

The man grunted.

'Please. Don't play these games with me.'

'It's no game. Agree to it or this will blow up in your face.'

A pause then, 'Which is what?'

Just a small thing to them. And that was it.

He checked with the control room. Vos and the team would be there any minute.

Somehow De Groot didn't want to know any more. He had a bad feeling in his gut about this case. It had been there ever since AIVD warned him to stay out of their way the previous Sunday, especially around Leidseplein. He wasn't a man to rely much on instinct. That was a fallible, deceptive route to take. But ever since that first day, aware the security services were making their shadowy rounds of Amsterdam, he'd suspected this would end the way such matters usually did. In the grey mist of uncertainty, with victims, innocent ones, waiting to be counted.

He told control to call him the moment there was news from Vos. Then he took the lift down to the holding cells. Mirjam Fransen was still shaken but couldn't wipe the look of victory from her face when he ordered her release. Henk Kuyper, to his credit, appeared a little shame-faced. Both asked about Barbone. They didn't seem surprised when De Groot said it seemed clear that bloody bird had flown.

Fransen smoothed down her business suit and said, 'Now that nonsense's over I want a full brief on what you've got. Those officers you had working for me. Bring them back. Vos too—'

'No.'

She looked at him and laughed.

'You really don't learn, do you?'

Kuyper hung his head.

'I do actually,' De Groot said. 'You need to call The Hague. They've news for you.'

She blinked and said, 'News?'

'You're on their payroll. Not mine. They can tell you.'

Her skinny finger jabbed at him.

'I'm the head of AIVD in Amsterdam. When I ask for something—'

'Not any more you're not.' He glared at her, then Kuyper. 'If I see your faces in my station one more time I swear I won't be responsible for the consequences.'

He turned to the custody officers, checked his phone.

'See these two out,' he said.


The street was short and deserted. Suburbia. Everyone was at work. The location from the tweet fell between two terraced houses. Vos's car switched off the siren and the light the moment it entered the road. Then they cruised slowly down, checking the windows, the drives.

There was a long black car parked awkwardly outside one of the targets. It took Bakker a moment to realize it was a hearse.

They drew up and saw a man at the back door. He was beside a pale polished coffin, lid up, clearly empty. There was a black doctor's bag by the casket. His gloved hand held a hypodermic. As they watched liquid spurted from the top.

'Don't see that every day,' Van der Berg said opening his door before they even came to a halt.

The man turned and looked round. Froze when he realized what was happening. Then raced for the front of the vehicle. Bakker got there first, folded her arms. Smiled.

He started to babble in French.

A second car followed full of uniform. She handed the curious undertaker over to them.

They were all out now. Hanna Bublik and the driver too. Marching down the path to the half-open door of the nearest house.

She caught up with them.

'Best show them your gun,' Vos said. 'I don't have mine.'

Van der Berg got to the door first, weapon out too. Yelled, 'Police.'

Vos told Hanna Bublik she had to stay outside.

Dog poop on the grass of the tiny lawn. Curtains closed even though it was the middle of the day. Bakker was sure she'd remember this moment.

Then they were in. Van der Berg in full rant. The first time she'd seen this and she realized: this man can be scary too.

As could Vos when he wanted.

Two men cowering back, shocked, scared. One much like the undertaker outside. He had a shaking teacup in one hand. A sandwich in the other.

A couple of strides and Van der Berg was on the other, the

Russian, pushing his face into the wall. Cuffing him so quickly and easily Bakker felt envious. She often stumbled awkwardly over that particular exercise.

A small slight figure on a chair.

Grubby pink jacket. Dirty blonde hair.

She walked over, bent down, smiled.

'Hi, Natalya,' Bakker said. 'Your mum's outside. We've been looking everywhere for you.'

Nothing in return except for a wriggle of her legs. Bakker looked down, saw the scarlet sash tied around her ankles. Found the knife she'd used in Khaled's office, slashed through the fabric.

The girl stood up. Bakker held out her hand.

Natalya took no notice. Straight-backed and serious she walked out of the room, out of the house, onto the little lawn.

Hanna Bublik was there, choking up, but only a little.

Bakker watched, fascinated.

In her mind she'd played this scene so many times. The emotion of the reunion. The joy that the kid was still alive.

But that wasn't their way. Something had changed these two already. Perhaps forever.

The mother bent down, held out her arms. The girl walked inside them and they held one another, silent for a moment, then whispering words Bakker could only just hear. And even then they were in another tongue.

A long moment she left them. When she came close they stood side by side, Hanna holding her daughter's hand. Tears in her eyes. Ones she wiped quickly away.

'We need to have her checked by a doctor,' Bakker said. 'To see she's all right.'

'She's all right. She told me.'

'All the same . . .'

Vos and Van der Berg were taking the two men out of the house. More police vehicles were arriving. This was going to be a big and busy scene soon.

Hanna Bublik forgot about her daughter at that moment. She watched the Russian and the undertaker get marched past her, heads down, hands cuffed behind their backs. Bakker understood for the first time that saying . . . if looks could kill.

If it were possible these two would be dead on the spot.

The tears were brief. Now almost gone.

Vos came back and looked as he always did at these moments: a touch embarrassed.

He crouched in front of the girl, held out his hand for her to shake it. Puzzled, she did.

'Is there anything I can get you, Natalya Bublik?'

She looked at the filthy pink jacket and said, 'Clothes. Real clothes. My clothes.'

Hanna Bublik was watching him. Anxious. Needy for once.

'Vos . . . can't we just go?'

'Soon,' he promised.

# 6

Four hours later. Hanna Bublik stood at a first-floor window in Marnixstraat watching the last of the day disappear. Statements made, statements signed. A stream of doctors. Specialists. Social workers. Well-meant but unwanted attention. She was insistent throughout: all the two of them needed was time. Space. An escape from this drab grey building and the prying attention of well-meaning strangers.

But Vos's superiors wouldn't allow that and she owed him. Debts were there to be paid. Money to be earned. Nothing came for free.

A paediatrician had looked at Natalya and declared her physically unharmed. She was hungry and ate a police canteen meal of fish cakes and chips with gratitude. But that was it and when it came to her mental condition the puzzled psychiatrist they brought in found, to her chagrin it seemed, little to report.

A robust, strong-minded girl the woman said when she'd put Natalya through a series of tests and questions her daughter had found tedious if not downright demeaning.

Hanna would have laughed if she was in the mood. Told a little of their story and asked . . .

*What else do you expect?*

Then Laura Bakker turned up with Van der Berg, the big cheery detective. Two more to whom she owed a debt.

Vos wanted a private word. Bakker and Van der Berg would take Natalya outside for ice cream. They would meet up soon after. And finally go on their way.

It felt odd to watch Natalya leave with the two police officers, reluctantly allowing Bakker to hold her hand.

Vos brought coffee. Took her to a private office. They sat at a table by the window. She saw Natalya and the cops cross the busy road then walk down Elandsgracht. Hanna had a good idea where they were headed.

She turned to him and said, 'Thanks.'

He nodded.

'No need. It's what we do. And we were lucky. Finally.'

'It's what your dog taught you, isn't it? Never give up.'

Vos smiled. A pleasant-looking man, though there was always a shadow of melancholy about him and she wondered why.

'Never look back. Never think yourself too small to matter,' he replied. 'Don't forget that either.'

'Have you found the money?' she asked, a little desperately.

He shook his head. She closed her eyes. Laughed for a second.

'Why did I ask?' she wondered. 'They never meant to let Natalya go, did they? She wasn't even near those men on the train.'

'There were two separate transactions happening here, I guess,' he agreed. 'We're still looking.'

'So why do you look so sheepish? What more do you want of me, Vos?'

He hesitated. She realized there was something to be bartered here.

'Your understanding.'

'I'm a cheap little whore trying to bring up my daughter. On my own. I don't want to understand anything. I just want to be left alone and get on with what I do.'

Silence then.

'On my own,' she repeated. 'When you charge Cem Yilmaz I'm free again, aren't I? Even if I've got that bastard's mark on my back for the rest of my life.'

Vos lost his smile.

'It's not as simple as that.'

She felt a sudden chill, made worse because she half-knew this was coming.

'Why?'

'We need to establish proof he was involved. Dmitri Volkov won't provide that. He's silent as a mouse. Those two Belgians only dealt with him. There's nothing to link them with the Turk. Nothing at all.'

Hanna stared across the table.

'If I hadn't seen that Russian bastard with Yilmaz you would never have found him.'

Vos nodded.

'That's enough to raise suspicion. It's a long way short of proof. We can't raise a warrant without more evidence. He doubtless knows that. Yilmaz has made a career of staying out of our way. He's good at it.'

'That man took her! He bought her. Put that money of his into the pot to lure me into getting something out of the Kuypers. And make me his slave for life. What more—?'

'I'm not giving up, Hanna,' Vos cut in, 'we'll work on it. He's no fool. He's made a career of letting others take the fall. They get rewarded. But one day . . .'

'One day when?'

'Maybe a week. Months.' He met her gaze. 'Possibly never. I've no guarantees which is why—'

'What about your people? Kuyper stole my girl. That woman put him up to it.'

The same silence again.

'Don't tell me they'll walk away from this too. I came here to escape that kind of shit. Not get more of it dumped on me.'

'They're not our people. We don't have . . . complete freedom there.'

She felt for him and wished she didn't.

'What they did was cruel and deliberate. Heartless . . .'

He closed his eyes for a moment.

'You hate cruelty,' she added. 'I saw that in your face. Right from the start. So why . . .?'

'Give me time,' he pleaded. 'There'll be an inquiry. Recriminations if I've anything to do with it—'

'They kidnapped my daughter!'

'I know. But they've got friends. They say they never meant to harm her. I was the one who got in the way. If I hadn't tried to find her in Westerdok—'

'This is what we're supposed to do? Sit back and trust people like that know what's best for us?'

'There are places I can't go right now,' Vos told her. 'I wish I could.'

Hanna sensed his outrage. That didn't help.

'So I'm nowhere different, am I? I thought I traded what I was in Georgia . . . an honest woman with no money, no future . . . for something better here. In return for sitting in those damned windows we got security. Safety. A promise Natalya wouldn't have to go through the same as me.'

Vos kept quiet.

'I was wrong, wasn't I?' she murmured. 'An idiot.'

'We'll provide protection. Counselling for Natalya. For you if you want it.'

She stared at him.

'You don't have to work for Cem Yilmaz,' he said.

'He thinks he owns us. Me. And my daughter. Can you save us forever?'

Vos started to say something. Then stopped.

'You really can't lie, can you?' She looked round the room. 'What the hell are you doing here?'

'My best,' he answered. 'The commissaris would like a word before you go. Then we'll meet up with Natalya. Have a coffee. A drink. I've got a suggestion . . .'

She folded her arms. The brown coat was nice. Better than her old black jacket.

'Where have I heard that before? Oh yes. Everywhere.'

There was a knock on the door. De Groot walked in. Made nice, apologetic noises.

She didn't have the energy to argue or fight any more. So she listened, nodded, shook his hand when he wanted to go.

Then went downstairs with Vos.


When they set him free Henk Kuyper walked out of Marnix-straat, didn't even try to talk to Mirjam Fransen. She was too busy on furious calls to The Hague. To the new acting head of AIVD in the city. To his father.

Kuyper just wandered back into the centre and headed for a bar near Spui.

Sat in front of a big glass of Chianti staring at his reflection in the window.

He couldn't put it off any longer. So he phoned her. Renata was home, waiting, angry in one sense, relieved in another.

'You might have told me,' she said.

'What? That I was a fraud? A liar?'

She sighed.

'I meant you might have told me you'd gone looking for the girl. I would have understood. I was trying to help too, remember?'

'But you were acting out of goodness. And I was doing it out of guilt.'

She groaned.

'The self-pity doesn't help, Henk. Where are you?'

He gave her the name of the bar. She told him to stay where he was and not drink any more. Ten minutes later the orange cargo trike he'd bought them parked up on the pavement outside. The compartment up front was empty. She walked in, got a mineral water, came and sat at his table.

'Where's Saskia?' he asked.

'Staying with one of her friends tonight. Lucy. The English girl. I thought it might be best.'

Renata reached over and pulled the Chianti from him.

'Enough of that. You're coming home.'

'You don't have more questions?'

'Not really,' she said with a shrug.

'Why I . . .'

'Why doesn't matter,' she interrupted. 'Whatever you did to begin with . . . you went looking for her. Maybe I made you get that money out of guilt too. And Lucas paid it. We all screwed up. You can't just blame yourself.'

Silence. She took his hand and said, 'We're going.'

Cold outside. Christmas shoppers tramping idly down the street, looking in the bright shop windows, thinking about the holiday to come.

'You pedal,' she said, and pointed at the saddle. 'I ride for free.'

Then, when he was seated, she climbed into the front bucket, tidied her arms and legs into the tiny cramped space meant for a child, looked back and smiled at him.

Henk Kuyper found he felt better then, for no good reason at all. He lugged the trike round on the cobbles and turned for the Herenmarkt, for home.


'Beer Hoover?' Bakker said, watching Van der Berg raise a glass of obscure Belgian tripel to his nose and sniff at it.

'Don't start,' he told her. 'Came in useful, didn't it?'

'But I don't get why . . .'

He growled something, took a dish of ice cream from Sofia Albers at the bar then wandered to the upper section where Natalya was playing with the dog.

'Strawberry, chocolate and vanilla,' he said and put the dish on the table.

Bakker followed and watched the cautious, interested way she responded. The kid was remarkable. It wasn't that the ordeal hadn't marked her. It had. There'd be counselling. The authorities would insist on it. But there was such resilience in her small, skinny frame. She had the look of someone who bounced back, however hard the blow. Much like her mother.

That stony resilience was supposed to be a good thing. But not in a child of eight.

'Thank you,' Natalya said and handed him the rope bone for Sam to tug.

She spooned the ice cream delicately into her mouth, as if each portion was precious. Vos had stopped in the Nine Streets on the way back from the house in Sloterdijk and taken her and her mother into one of the fancier clothes shops. There the grubby pink jacket was placed in an evidence bag. Natalya had chosen the cheapest clothes they had, ignoring his protests. Not that they were cheap at all. They let the two of them use the showers in Marnixstraat. Now she wore a blue denim jacket, matching jeans and a red jumper, hair clean and tidy, held back behind her head with a band.

The striped woollen hat Vos had picked out in the shop sat in her pocket. Bakker felt sure Natalya thought it a touch too girly. She was with her on that.

'I heard you're getting a dog one day,' Van der Berg told her, sitting down as Sam tugged and growled at the rope.

'Mum said,' Natalya agreed.

'And if she promises something . . .'

The girl stared at him. He was talking down to her and she didn't like that.

Bakker pulled up a second chair. Like all the ones in the bar it was old bare wood, wobbly, close to falling to pieces.

'Your mum's going to need some help for a while,' she said. 'Our help. Yours.'

Natalya Bublik had large, watchful eyes. And a gaze that was quite uncomfortable in one so young.

'OK,' she said and went back to the ice cream.


Vos turned up with Hanna Bublik. Sofia Albers was smiling at them both from behind the bar.

'I'm glad you got your little girl back,' she said, glancing at the small gathering at the table in the upper room. 'She's quite something.'

'She is,' Hanna agreed then ordered a coffee, took it, went to sit with Natalya. The others left the two alone for a while. They were talking in Georgian anyway.

'Beer Hoover?' Vos asked.

Van der Berg rolled his eyes.

'Don't want to talk about it.' He glanced at Bakker. 'I've had enough from her.'

Vos raised his beer and grinned.

'I just like the idea there are still things I don't know about you. After all this time.'

That seemed to dismay him.

'We've all got secrets, Pieter. Even you. Even Laura.'

'I have?' she asked.

A plate of cheese, liver sausage and some freshly boiled eggs appeared on the bar. Sofia told them to help themselves. It was on the house. Even the sausage and the cheese.

'Yours,' Van der Berg declared, grabbing an egg and crushing the shell in his fist, 'is you like hanging round with older men. Must be the food.'

She didn't laugh. Just looked at Vos and said, 'We need to talk.'

'Now?' Vos asked, and sounded pathetic.

'Now . . .'

'I mean . . . right now?'

'Pieter . . .'

She stopped. Hanna Bublik was there. She looked as if she needed something.

'What is it?' Vos asked.

'Can we have a word outside?'

The night was close to freezing. Vos looked at his boat and realized he'd left a light on. It was linked to the line of coloured bulbs he'd wound around the neck of the ballerina statue on the front bows. The old klipper barge looked festive.

'Can you look after Natalya for half an hour?'

'Why? I thought you wanted to go home.'

She had gloves on. Black leather. He hadn't noticed them before.

'I've been thinking. Renata Kuyper. She went out of her way for me. I was pretty horrible to her too. I just want to go and say thanks. And sorry. In person.'

'You could do that tomorrow.'

She smiled then and there was something unexpected and genuine in it. He realized he'd never seen her without the possibility of tragedy hanging round her. There was a different woman here, one who'd stayed hidden.

'I could. But then I'd be awake all night wondering what to say. I need to do this now.'

On the way down from the station he'd talked her through some of the options the social services people could offer to get her out of prostitution. Charitable financial support. Courses to give her a career. She'd listened, hadn't said much at all.

'Are you going to turn up for that appointment? With the people I fixed?'

'Of course I am. And I want somewhere else to stay. I don't want to be around that place, not if Cem Yilmaz still thinks I'm his.'

'I said I can help . . .'

She looked at him frankly.

'I know you can. And I thought I told you before. In this business . . . where I come from . . . you're always wary of a man who
wants to help. It rarely works out well in the end. For both parties.'

He nodded and said he understood.

'Good.'

'What do you think you'll do?' he asked.

She reached up and touched his long, unruly black hair.

'I might be a hairdresser. I could start with you.'

She took her hand away and he said, 'You'd be good at that.'

'I know. There are always going to be hairdressers. Just like
there are always going to be whores. Thanks again. Thirty minutes. Forty at the most.'

Then she walked off over the Berenstraat bridge, into the
bright lights of the Nine Streets where she was soon lost amid
the glitter and the tinsel.


He'd changed his appearance in a backstreet barber's in Chinatown. Black hair dyed grey. Then the beard went. It was twenty
years since the man called Khaled had been clean-shaven. That
meant the stubble hurt and left his pale-brown cheeks pink and
sore. Though not as irritated as his ego. And the beard he'd grow
again when he was somewhere safe. Like Barbone himself now
on board a plane to Cairo, fleeing under a stolen name.

Khaled had left De Wallen behind for good. He was walking
around a different, more elegant part of town, thinking of history
and how little the world changed. A bag by his side. Clothes.
Documents. Four thousand in euros. Five thousand in that
universal currency the US dollar. Three passports, all authentic-
looking, none in the least genuine.

A couple of hours to kill then a car out through the long night
down into Belgium. France. Marseilles. There were friends there.
A boat to North Africa. After that he was free.

The weapon he'd have to leave behind and that hurt too.

Tucked inside a wheeled ski bag it was a Remington Modular Sniper Rifle, stolen from the hands of a dead US scout caught behind what passed for enemy lines during the 2010 assault on Marja in Helmand province. Smuggled out of Afghanistan to Yemen. Then to Barbone who'd passed it on that afternoon.

Never used except for practice when the two of them lived in Milan and would drive into the Valle d'Aosta to find a lone spot and take down chamois and deer.

Time to flee now. To regroup. To face the consequences when they reported back to command.

The weapon was state-of-the-art, deadly accurate, almost silent. It hurt that he had to leave the thing. When he left Amsterdam he'd change identity altogether. Become briefly a doctor. An anaesthetist who'd worked for one of the more famous hospitals in London.

His life, like the world, was built on lies. So many after a while they became inseparable from the truth, even for him.

All that was certain was history. It stood around him in Amsterdam. Reminded the man called Khaled – not his real name either – how little he could alter it by himself.

Finding the place he wanted he looked around, lit a cigarette in the dark.

The ski bag and the precious Remington he'd leave here. Then walk to the small hotel near the station, pick up a car as arranged.

An assignment finished. A job half-done. He loathed failure, in himself as much as others.

He was smoking in a small playground near a pissoir. The grand building next to him was still open. A restaurant busy with Christmas diners. A courtyard, a statue in it. One he knew. Another Dutchman who'd crossed the world hoping to own it. To rob those who preceded him of their identity and dignity. To rule like a master, given that role by God.

A name. He struggled for it.

*Stuyvesant.*

A grim, unforgiving man, no friend to the Jews either.

There was an irony, he thought then threw his half-smoked Marlboro into the child's sandpit by his side.

Hanna Bublik didn't go to see Renata Kuyper. She strode quickly through the city, into the red-light district, on to Spooksteeg.

One code for the door. One for the lift.

The ballpoint scribbles on her wrist had barely faded. Why should they? The last few days seemed like an age. But taken out of grim context they were nothing. To the world around her, to the ordinary people of the city, it was just Sunday to Thursday. A brief interval before the holidays, soon to be forgotten.

In Spooksteeg she looked up. A light at the window. No shapes moving there.

And if there were? If he wasn't on his own as she prayed?

She stopped at the glass door and thought about that. It wouldn't make any difference. The journey had started. Begun by someone else. Continued by Cem Yilmaz. No stopping it now.

A confident, arrogant man, he hadn't changed the code and probably rarely did.

She pushed open the door and stepped inside. The place was hot on this chilly night, even in the lobby. She wondered what there was on the floors beneath his.

Hanna Bublik walked to the lift, checked the second code on her skin, tried that.

Listened to the gears and chains begin to whirr above her.

Would he hear too? And if he did would he think this was for him? Or whoever lived in the rooms below?

Pointless questions. Ones that could never be answered.

The lift came.

The door opened.

She stepped inside, keyed the code, pressed the button for

the top floor. Pictured in her head the room into which the lift opened directly, straight into his home like something from a movie.

Gloves on. She took the weapon from her bag, checked it was loaded. Tried to remember the YouTube video on the web. The only pointers she had on how to use it.

The lift started up. She unbuttoned the brown coat then pushed the gun beneath the front.

And waited, breath short, mind fixed, intent, determined.


Renata bought in supper from Marqt. Seafood linguini. A bottle of white. Italian too though light on the alcohol. She couldn't wean him off that straight away. But she could make a start.

With Saskia away they sat opposite one another at the dining table by the first-floor window. Christmas lights sparkling against the panes. Faces reflected in the glass. The tiny bulbs sent dots, red, green and blue twinkling over their features.

'Early night,' he said with a sigh.

She reached out and felt for his fingers.

'Yes.'

For two months now she'd been sleeping in the spare room. Going in there after she thought Saskia was asleep, hoping the girl wouldn't notice.

A stupid illusion. Of course she knew.

'I'll stay tonight,' she said.

He put down his fork and the glass of wine.

'Only if you want to.'

'If I didn't I wouldn't do it.'

'True,' he agreed with a wry smile.

There were practical questions they had to face. To do with money. The future. On the walk back Henk had started to unburden himself a little. He'd been on a secret AIVD salary ever since he supposedly left his job. Most of the money she thought came from his father was actually paid by the state.

Thinking about it she realized she'd suspected there was something wrong all along. In his furtive manner. All the half-answered questions. Now he was out of the security service for good they'd have to make ends meet. And without any prospect of support from his father too. Lucas didn't like the idea his son might quit the service. He'd already made that clear in a brief and chilly phone call.

'What are we going to do?' she asked.

'Go to bed,' he said, raising the glass again with a hopeful wink.

'And after that?'

He turned serious again.

'Me? Try to be a husband again. A better dad.'

'Saskia thinks you're the best already.'

'Only because I cut you out. Divide and rule. It's what we do. And the Kuypers have always . . .'

His eyes strayed towards the grand building opposite and the statue of the stern, old aristocrat in the courtyard. The man who lost New Amsterdam and now lay buried in a crumbling stone tomb not far from Wall Street, in the city that followed, New York.

'Henk,' she said and took his hand, squeezed the fingers.

He couldn't stop staring out of the window. The West-Indisch Huis. The little park. The trees. The kids' playground. This was home and he'd forgotten about it, completely.

There was a shape across the way, just visible in the weak street lights. A man resting against the metal playground fence, something in his hand.

The lights played on the glass. Red, blue and green, a pretty pattern against the window.

'Henk!'

Her voice was harder, full of angry trepidation. The way it used to be.

Kuyper stared at himself . . . at them . . . reflected in the panes.

Red, green and blue.

One of the red lights was bigger than the others. It was dodging around rapidly, which seemed curious.

Moving on him. Up towards his temple.


Hanna walked straight into the room. A figure on the leather sofa turned to look.

Cem Yilmaz, naked from the waist up. A glass of something in his hand. No one else there. No smell of sweat. Just something like a fragrant tea.

The old green holdall she'd bought in the Noordermarkt an age before was beside him on the floor. Top open. Money ruffled around inside as if he was counting every note.

The big Turk got up, furious as hell, big fist waving, yelling some kind of abuse.

He stopped in front of her, face twisted with rage.

'Who asked you here?'

She retreated a step, out of his reach.

'You promised me my daughter back,' she told him. 'Instead you took her.'

The anger abated for a moment. Amusement there instead.

'And?'

'Why?'

He laughed.

'Why not?'

So much determination before she came in here. Now, faced with the decision, the will began to desert her.

She couldn't find the words.

'You make a poor whore. Maybe you think it's beneath you.'

Hand in coat, shaking, struggling to keep hold of the gun.

He leaned forward.

'Trust me. It's not. But . . .' He shrugged. 'I got sixty thousand profit. Dmitri won't dare say a word. Nor you either.'

Another step closer.

'No recriminations. Nothing owed on either side.' He held out his hand, fat fingers stretched wide. 'Deal?'

Hanna said nothing.

The big hand turned into a fist. The smile vanished from his face.

One more step and his forearm was out, trying to trap her neck. Moving with a speed that seemed unreal.

Gun slipping in her grip as she retreated to the lift.

She tore off the glove. Got her sweaty fingers round the butt, the trigger.

Tried to lift it, to aim.


*One shot.*

It rang out over the Herenmarkt, echoed round the courtyard of the old mansion where the burghers of Amsterdam once gathered to carve the new world into convenient and profitable pieces.

Renata Kuyper watched unable to comprehend what she saw.

Like a dream. A nightmare contained in seconds.

There was a crack at the window. The sound of breaking glass.

He flew back from his chair with a single, offended sigh.

Fell on the plush dining-room carpet. Head a mess, blood everywhere, much else besides.

No sound from him. No time for her to scream, to think.

She stood up, hand to mouth. Went towards him.

Whispered, 'Henk . . . ?'


*One shot.*

Missed.

Cem Yilmaz roared. Kept staggering towards her. Arm up. Furious. Beast not man.

A single thought.

*This was Natalya's monster. He came for me not her.*

The elbow took her in the throat. Fingers round her neck. The grip of a fighter, a wrestler, looking to snap the life from her while his foul breath pumped with anxious pleasure.

The gun faltered in Hanna's grip again, pushed to one side by his force.

She gasped for air. Saw the darkness start to close in from the edges of the too-bright room.

'You fuck up everything, woman,' he spat. 'Everything . . .'


Renata Kuyper stood at the head of the table, looking at her husband's broken bloody frame on the floor.

No movement. No breath. Whatever had entered the room at that moment took him completely.

The night breeze gusted through the shattered window. Christmas lights tinkling against the broken pane.

Wondering what to do. What to touch. Who to call.

Outside, across the street, by a grubby playground sandpit, a figure held a long and complex rifle against the metal fence.

His scrubbed cheeks hurt. A red fire burned in his head.

Soon to be extinguished. Dampened by the needs of flight and the catharsis of a sudden vengeance.

The man once called Khaled peered through the sights of the Remington MSR.

Saw someone there, stiff and shocked in the room across the street. Thought for a moment about justice and decency. Those who deserved to die. Those who didn't.

Didn't think long.

*Second shot.*

A woman in an expensive dress jerked like a marionette tugged by invisible strings.

He pulled the sight from his face. Threw the weapon into the sandpit.

Set off for Haarlemmerstraat on the long straight walk to Centraal. And a deliverance from this place.

*Second shot.*

The gun went off as her shaking index finger struggled with the trigger. Could have gone anywhere.

But Yilmaz was staggering back holding his gut. Mouth open. Eyes in shock.

No one hurt the king. He lived forever.

Not any more.

*Third shot.*

It went into his big broad chest and blood came back, spitting out of a fresh livid wound that opened like a blinded eye.

Cem Yilmaz fell to his knees, mouth flapping, no words, just a grunt of shock and anger. And pain.

*Fourth shot.*

The chest again. That wall of muscle bounced but still he knelt, swaying back, gazing at her in disbelief.

*Monsters do not die easily.*

She lifted the gun, watched his bloody lips try to form a word, a plea.

Hanna stood over him, jerked on the trigger until nothing happened any more.

Van der Berg was with Natalya and Sam now. Throwing the rope bone between them in a game the little dog loved.

He scampered through the rickety chairs and tables. Yapping. Squealing. Not minding what he hit, how many things he knocked over.

Back and forth the rope bone went. Vos and Laura Bakker watched from the bar.

Finally, as Sam lost his footing, fell sideways scuttling across the polished timber before retrieving the toy just as it was about to reach her hands, Natalya Bublik laughed.

'Thank God for that,' Bakker said. 'I can't believe they didn't keep her in hospital.'

'Her mother insisted.'

She looked at him.

'And no one dare say no to her.'

He raised his glass and said all the things he'd planned. Thanks. And praise. And an apology.

'Will you ever trust me?' she asked.

'I do already.'

'So why wasn't I in on the secret? Why did you let me think Frank had really kicked you out?'

It was a question he'd expected. She knew the good ones to ask now.

'Because if it had gone wrong the consequences—'

'To hell with consequences, Pieter! Do you think they bother me?'

'No. Which is one more reason to do what we did.'

Her red hair was tied neatly back. She still kept knocking things over all the time, but that was a trait that would stay with her. Mostly Laura Bakker had mellowed and matured these last few months.

Her long index finger jabbed his shoulder.

'Don't protect me. I can look after myself, thank you.'

'So I gather,' Vos added and chinked her glass.


One last breath. It sounded like an angry beast giving up on itself. Then the Turk's sweaty, bloody chest was still and he tumbled sideways onto the bloodied carpet.

She dropped the gun. Forgot about the glove. If they wanted her they'd find her anyway. She lacked the talent for this.

Not a speck of his blood on the green holdall she'd lugged on the train and left beneath the seat. Hanna tucked the stray notes back inside. From what she saw it was all still there. A hundred and sixty thousand euros.

Then she went to the drawer she'd seen before. The one where he'd kept the weapon among the money and jewellery.

It was closed now but still unlocked. With trembling fingers she pulled it open. Looked at the piles of notes. Euros. Dollars. Currencies she couldn't name.

In all the years of struggle, on the long journey from Georgia to the Netherlands, she'd never stolen, not until she met this man. And even those few notes she took two days before with the weapon that killed him still left her with a sense of shame and hurt.

*No more.*

She grabbed the money, placed it on top of the stacks in the holdall.

Looked at the rest of the things. The jewellery. The watches.

Picked up the necklace her husband had given her a lifetime ago in the little cottage on the edge of Gori they called home. Back when the world was whole and Natalya a little baby, their precious child, dependent on them, looking to a future full of love and hope.

No tears now. No time for them.

Hanna Bublik lifted the silver chain and stared into the amber pendant.

It was real, he'd said the night he surprised her with the gift. A piece of history. Resin from a prehistoric tree turned into a precious gem by all the long centuries. Sometimes there were insects trapped beneath its shining surface. But those pieces were expensive. Hers was plain. Yet beautiful all the same.

*No more*, she thought and placed the thing back in the drawer.

That life was gone.

Hanna went to the bathroom and looked at herself in the mirror. Washed the blood off her hands. Dabbed at the few spots on her brown coat.

Then, green plastic and canvas holdall tight beneath her arm, she left the weapon, the bloody glove, the corpse of the Turk behind. Went into the lift. Out into the street. Found the Prinsengracht. Marched steadily back to the Jordaan.

'The thing is . . .' Laura Bakker began, finger still jabbing away at Vos's jacket.

A tall familiar shape appeared at the door. She fell silent.

Frank de Groot walked in beaming. Hung his big overcoat on the stand. Grabbed the beer Vos offered with glee.

Then he looked around and asked, 'Where's Mrs Bublik?'

'I want my mum,' Natalya said, breaking into the conversation.

'Of course you do,' Laura told her. 'She's—'

'She's there!' the girl cried.

A shape across the road, visible through the long window, threading through the light traffic by Vos's boat.

Brown coat. The spectacles were gone. She looked worn out and pensive.

Vos watched her dodge a passing taxi. Thought to himself.

De Groot was at his most charming. He opened the door, beckoned her in.

'A drink,' he said. 'I know you must want to rest. You and . . .' He beamed at Natalya. 'Your little girl. All the same . . .'

Just a quick smile for Natalya who slid to her side, held her hand, and then Hanna Bublik asked, 'Have you arrested anyone?'

De Groot's cheerful demeanour stayed fixed.

'That Russian crook. Those two Belgian creatures.' He nodded, looked important. 'Those three won't see the light of day for a while.'

'And the others?'

'I told you, Hanna,' Vos cut in gently. 'It takes time. Tomorrow . . .'

'Tomorrow,' she repeated. 'Natalya?'

Hand in hand they went outside. Then the girl stopped on the pavement. Sam had come to the door, whining pitifully, wagging his tail, disappointed the games had come to an end.

It was an embarrassing moment and De Groot never enjoyed those. He told Vos to deal with it then went back to chatting with Bakker and Van der Berg at the bar.

Outside Hanna Bublik caught how entranced her daughter was by the little terrier.

'One day,' she said as Vos came near. 'We'll get one.'

'I'm sure you will.'

She looked at him. Puzzled. Perhaps worried.

'I'm sorry, Vos. I didn't mean to be rude. I'm tired. We both are.'

'I'm sure.' He nodded at the holdall. 'That looks like the bag you left on the train.'

Natalya, sensing an awkward moment, went back to the door and knelt down to talk to the dog.

'What?' Hanna asked too quickly.

'It can't be,' Vos added quickly. 'I know—'

'Do you suspect everyone? Every minute of the day?'

He couldn't take his eyes off the bag.

'Sorry. Stupid of me.'

She sighed, closed her eyes for an instant.

'Renata Kuyper gave me some things for Natalya. Toys and clothes her daughter didn't need.' She shrugged. 'It's her bag.'

A pause.

'Ever the policeman. Would you like to check?'

Her eyes were on him. Begging.

'Should I?' he asked.

'I just . . .' The words were a struggle. She gripped the green

380

holdall more tightly. 'For God's sake let us go, Vos. I never asked you for anything except my girl back. Now one thing more.'

She looked away and called to Natalya. The girl came straight away, held her hand, and the two of them gazed at him. They were a pair. What was left of their family.

'Goodnight,' Hanna said in a voice so soft he scarcely recognized it. 'I know what's best for us. Honestly.'

Silence. He didn't move and nor did they.

Then she reached out and for a moment touched the lapel of his crumpled jacket.

'Please . . .'

'Goodnight,' he said, as brightly as he could manage. Then tugged at his long dark locks. 'When you learn to cut hair . . .'

Tears in her eyes. He felt guilty he'd put them there.

'You're my first victim. For free,' she murmured and turned to go.


He watched the two of them cross the Berenstraat bridge then went back into the Drie Vaten and joined the others.

'What was that about?' Bakker asked. 'Or am I being nosy?'

'You're always nosy. It was about tomorrow. She's going to talk to the social people about getting somewhere new to live. Training for a job. Hairdressing.'

'Good on her,' Van der Berg said, raising his glass. 'Too bright and decent a woman for that kind of life. Especially with that bastard Yilmaz on her back.'

De Groot was staring directly at Vos.

'Is there anything I should know?' the commissaris asked.

'Such as what, Frank?'

Sam was seated at De Groot's feet holding up the rope bone and whining for attention.

'If I understood that I wouldn't be asking, would I?' the commissaris replied, still pulling at the toy.

'It's your round,' Van der Berg told him. 'I know that. Can't remember the last time . . .'

De Groot grunted something and pulled out some cash. Vos took a small one. Bakker said no. Van der Berg was running through the bottles behind the counter, finally picking out something expensive from a Belgium monastery.

'We should focus on that Russian and those two Belgians for now,' Vos insisted as De Groot paid up. 'Let's charge them. Get them in court. See if they'll implicate Yilmaz. Kuyper and Mirjam Fransen can wait a while. So can Hanna Bublik and her girl. They need some peace and quiet.'

'No argument there,' De Groot agreed.

Then he patted each of them on the shoulder and raised his glass.

'Here's to Sinterklaas. We got there in the end. *Proost.*'

On the other side of the canal a taxi had slowed. Two figures. One tall, one small had climbed in carrying a single big bag.

'*Proost,*' Vos answered and watched the car move slowly off, almost tracing the outstretched arm of the silver ballerina on his boat.


In the back of the cab, out of earshot of the driver, Natalya clutched her mother's hand and asked, 'Where are we going?'

'Somewhere nice,' Hanna said.

She called one of the all-night travel agencies and checked what flights they had still free.

Then she booked two tickets to be paid for at the airport, one under the name of Natalya Bublik, the other on Hanna's second passport, the old one with her maiden name, carried with her all the way from Gori. It was Georgian: Tsiklauri. And felt as if it belonged to someone else.

'Somewhere warm,' she added when the call was finished.

Cyprus. A country she couldn't even find on the map. But one that wasn't picky about visas. The other East European women working the street had told her that.

She'd had to read out some details from the old passport to make the booking. Ever inquisitive, Natalya bent over to look. They both stared at the woman there. Short brown hair, like it was now. A face much younger. Fuller. Less careworn.

'You were pretty,' Natalya said.

'Were?' Hanna said with a sob.

She rubbed her cheeks with the backs of her hands and pretended to cry.

A joke between them. The way it was before.

'You *are* pretty, Mummy,' the girl insisted and hugged her.

Hard. Both arms around her waist, head against the brown coat. The two of them close and warm.

At Schiphol, clutching the precious holdall, they picked up the tickets then got through passport control. Close to panic, Hanna took Natalya into the toilets and padded out their pockets with money. It seemed a futile, desperate gesture. If the bag was spotted at security they'd surely be stopped and searched anyway.

But all this was new. She did what came into her head. Had to think it all through later.

When she did she changed her mind. Back into the toilets. All the money came out of their clothes.

They went into the fancy airport stores. Bought clothes and toiletries. Then a large suitcase. Too big to be hand baggage.

The store opened up the case and let her store the new clothes there. The woman assistant was friendly and offered to arrange for it all to go in the hold.

Hanna took the bag with all the money off her shoulder and said they might as well save some trouble and place that in the case too.

Then the three of them went off to see the airline desk. The case was quickly despatched to wait for them at the other end.

Thirty minutes to departure. A quick meal. Through security. Onto the half-empty plane.

Two seats by the window. No one in the aisle.

As they taxied down the runway Natalya's head fell on her arm. Hanna held her, forced herself not to cry.

Amsterdam had been an illusion. She'd fooled herself into believing she could cope with that life. But it was all a lie. Perhaps that was why the monster came for them. As a reminder of the eternal truth: you burned the world or the world burned you.

She might have burned Pieter Vos as well. That would have been so easy. But cruel. He burned himself. And cruelty wasn't in her nature any more than his.

They had the money. Maybe she could be a hairdresser. Or a teacher. Something . . . anything but the dead, drab nightmare they'd suffered before.

The plane charged down the runway, rose into the black sky, turned over Amsterdam.

Somewhere below lay the bloody corpse of a Turkish crook, a grim discovery that would wait two days to be found by an unsuspecting cleaner.

In another part of the city, unknown to Hanna Bublik, the bodies of Henk and Renata Kuyper stiffened in the cold of their first-floor dining room as the winter breeze stole past twinkling Christmas lights through a shattered window. Unseen until a curious Lucas Kuyper comes round the following morning, puzzled that his calls go unanswered.

The fugitive the security services knew as Khaled slumbered in a car driving at a sedate pace on the motorway into Belgium.

In his dilapidated houseboat Pieter Vos lay wide awake in bed, staring at the ceiling, Sam snoring at his feet.

Curious as ever, Natalya peered out of the window at the lights beneath them. The Canal Ring, Herengracht, Keizersgracht and Prinsengracht, stood out like an illuminated girdle round the city.

Hanna thought of the man with his little dog and a solitary life on the water.

Vos knew she was fleeing. And still he let her go.

There was a kindness to be had in the city. But you had to discover it before the monster found you. And there she'd failed.

'Where are we going?' asked a sleepy young voice next to her.

'South,' she said.

The girl gave up on the window and snuggled beneath her arm.

*South.*

Anywhere but here.

# The Killing

*by*

## DAVID HEWSON

*Based on the original screenplay by Søren Sveistrup*

*Through the dark wood where the dead trees give no shelter Nanna Birk Larsen runs . . . There is a bright monocular eye that follows, like a hunter after a wounded deer. It moves in a slow approaching zigzag, marching through the Pineseskoven wasteland, through the Pentecost Forest.*

*The chill water, the fear, his presence not so far away . . .*

*There is one torchlight on her now, the single blazing eye. And it is here . . .*

Sarah Lund is looking forward to her last day as a detective with the Copenhagen police department before moving to Sweden. But everything changes when a nineteen-year-old student, Nanna Birk Larsen, is found raped and brutally murdered in the woods outside the city. Lund's plans to relocate are put on hold as she leads the investigation along with fellow detective Jan Meyer.

While Nanna's family struggles to cope with their loss, local politician, Troels Hartmann, is in the middle of an election campaign to become the new mayor of Copenhagen. When links between City Hall and the murder suddenly come to light, the case takes an entirely different turn.

Over the course of twenty days, suspect upon suspect emerges as violence and political intrigue cast their shadows over the hunt for the killer.

### Praise for The Killing

'As gripping as the TV series. It will keep you pinned to the very last page'
                                                              Jens Lapidus

'David Hewson should be commended for writing such a page-turner of a book . . . *The Killing* has enough twists and turns to satisfy not only any avid follower of the series but also readers that are coming to it first time around'
                                                              shotsmag.co.uk

# The Killing II
*by*
## DAVID HEWSON
*Based on the original screenplay by Søren Sveistrup*

*Thirty-nine steps rose from the busy road of Tuborgvej into Mindelunden, with its quiet graves and abiding bitter memories. Lennart Brix, head of the Copenhagen homicide team, felt he'd been walking them most of his life.*

*Beneath the entrance arch, sheltering from the icy rain, he couldn't help but recall that first visit almost fifty years before. A five-year-old boy, clutching the hand of his father, barely able to imagine what he was about to see . . .*

*The bark of a dog broke his reverie. Brix looked at the forensic officers, white bunny suits, mob hats, marching grim-faced down the rows of graves, towards the space in the little wood where the rest of the team was gathering . . .*

It is two years since the notorious Nanna Birk Larsen case. Two years since Detective Sarah Lund left Copenhagen in disgrace for a remote outpost in northern Denmark.

When the body of a female lawyer is found in macabre circumstances in a military graveyard, there are elements of the crime scene that remind Head of Homicide, Lennart Brix, of an occupied wartime Denmark – a time its countrymen would rather forget.

Brix knows that Lund is the one person he can rely on to discover the truth. Though reluctant to return to Copenhagen, Lund becomes intrigued with the facts surrounding the case. As more bodies are found, Lund comes to see a pattern. She realizes that the identity of the killer will be known once the truth behind a more recent wartime mission is finally revealed . . .

# The Killing III
*by*
### DAVID HEWSON
*Based on the original screenplay by Søren Sveistrup*

*Autumn was giving up on Copenhagen, getting nudged out of the way by winter. Grey sky. Grey land. Grey water ahead with a grey ship motionless a few hundred metres off shore.*

*Lund hated this place . . . She looked across the bleak water at the dead ship listing at its final anchor. Ghosts still hung around her, murmuring sometimes. She could hear them now.*

When a body is discovered down at the docks in Copenhagen, Detective Inspector for homicide, Sarah Lund, is contacted by old flame Mathias Borch from National Intelligence. Borch fears that what at first appears to be a random killing may in fact mark the beginning of an assassination attempt on Prime Minister Troels Hartmann.

The murder case draws attention towards the shipping giant, Zeeland, and its billionaire CEO Robert Zeuthen. But when Zeuthen's nine-year-old daughter Emilie is kidnapped, the investigation takes on a different dimension. It soon becomes clear that her disappearance is linked to the murder of a young girl in Jutland some years earlier.

Hartmann is in the middle of an election campaign, which is all the more turbulent due to the mounting financial crisis, and he needs Zeeland's backing.

Lund must make sense of the clues left by Emilie's abductor before it's too late.

But can she finally face the demons that have long haunted her?

# Carnival for the Dead
*by*
## DAVID HEWSON

*In Venice the past was more reticent. Beyond the tourist sights, San Marco and the Rialto, it lurked in the shadows, seeping out of the cracked stones like blood from ancient wounds, as if death itself was one more sly perform-ance captured beneath the bright all-seeing light of the lagoon.*

It's February, and Carnival time in Venice. Forensic pathologist Teresa Lupo visits the city to investigate the mysterious disappearance of her beloved bohemian aunt, Sofia. But from the moment she is greeted off the vaporetto by a masked man dressed in the costume of The Plague Doctor, Teresa starts to suspect that all is not well.

The puzzle deepens when a letter reveals a piece of fiction in which both Sofia and Teresa appear. Even more strange are the links to the past which gradually begin to surface. Are the messages being sent by Sofia herself? Her abductor? Or a third party seeking to help her unravel the mystery? The revelation is as surprising and shocking as Sofia's fate. And Teresa herself comes to depend upon the unravelling of a mystery wrapped deep inside the art and culture of Venice itself.

### Praise for Carnival for the Dead

'Atmospheric and engaging . . . the central mystery is every bit as intriguing as ever and the unravelling of the solution has the satisfying precision that we know the author delivers so adroitly'    *Daily Express*

'Complex and cunning'    *Sunday Telegraph*

'The Byzantine complexity of *Carnival for the Dead* is a measure of Hewson's inventiveness'    *Sunday Herald*

# The House of Dolls
*by*
## DAVID HEWSON

*Where dark secrets lurk behind every door . . .*

Anneliese Vos, sixteen-year-old daughter of Amsterdam detective, Pieter Vos, disappeared three years ago in mysterious circumstances. Her distraught father's desperate search reveals nothing and results in his departure from the police force.

Pieter now lives in a broken-down houseboat in the colourful Amsterdam neighbourhood of the Jordaan. One day, while Vos is wasting time at the Rijksmuseum staring at a doll's house that seems to be connected in some way to the case, Laura Bakker, a misfit trainee detective from the provinces, visits him. She's come to tell him that Katja Prins, daughter of an important local politician, has gone missing in circumstances similar to Anneliese's.

In the company of the intriguing and awkward Bakker, Vos finds himself drawn back into the life of a detective. A life which he thought he had left behind. Hoping against hope that somewhere will lay a clue to the fate of Anneliese, the daughter he blames himself for losing . . .